THE EXECUTIVE GRAVEYARD

Shaye Mann

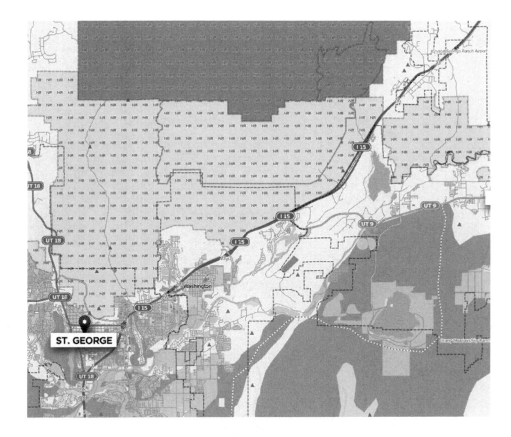

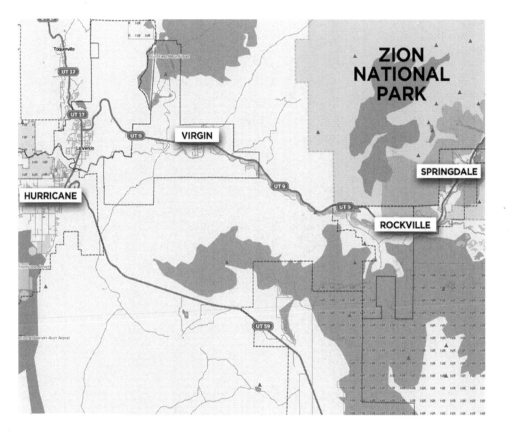

CHAPTER ONE

THE VERDICT WAS IN, but Judge Fulton Donovan Carney wasn't ready to read it. He was too hung over, and the excessive chatter from the gallery wasn't helping the pounding in his head. Judge Carney knew that, any minute now, he'd have to slam the gavel down several times to hush the standing-room-only crowd, and proceed with reading the verdict.

But he didn't want to.

Yes, it would be painful for his temporal lobes. But more importantly, it would signal the end of Washington County's most famous trial, which would also mean the end of his few precious moments in the spotlight. Tomorrow, life would return to normal. No more journalists sitting in the back composing daily reports, no more television cameras focused on his balding head, and no more reporters memorializing every word of what he believed to be brilliant rulings. No longer would the country's top legal analysts contemplate those rulings and analyze what they meant to both the prosecution and the defense. Judge Carney had been drinking nightly since the jury began their arduous deliberations. The *State of Utah v. Donald Leigh Richardson,* a man accused of murdering his wife, was a small town judge's dream come true. Unfortunately for him, the dream was about to end.

The defendant was a fifty-three-year-old entrepreneur from New Mexico who made millions off a string of strategically placed truck stops across the country. Now he was using a significant amount of that money to pay for his defense. He and his wife, Megan, had visited

Southern Utah on a hiking trip but neither had returned. Megan ended up dead, while Donald landed in the county jail accused of her murder.

The prosecution argued that Donald planned the killing to perfection. He took his wife on a hike up several thousand feet, they claimed, and when no one was around, pushed her off the cliff. The defense maintained that, as is often the case, Donald hiked faster than his wife and found himself alone farther along the trail. She never caught up and the next thing he knew, she'd disappeared. Donald's defense: she must have lost her footing and accidentally plunged to the canyon floor. His high-priced defense team had chosen to walk the 'burden of proof' tightrope and argue that there was insufficient evidence to prove his guilt beyond a reasonable doubt. It was a dicey proposition. While technically true—if the prosecution cannot satisfy their burden, the defendant must be acquitted—most defense lawyers know that juries want answers, and if you're going to claim that the prosecution is wrong, you need to show the jury what's right.

Risky? Yes.

But did they have a choice? Not without witnesses.

As the trial progressed, the prosecution delved into Donald's past and when they opened his closet, a plethora of skeletons fell out. The result was a formidable portrait of chronic infidelity. Donald didn't deny his missteps, but insisted he loved his wife. He took the stand and denied any involvement in her death. Looking the jury in the eye, Donald testified that the trip to Utah had been their reconciliation, as he had recently come clean. The trip was supposed to be the beginning of the rest of their lives together.

Donald's lawyers deliberately left out the fact that Megan had also been unfaithful. They feared it would provide the jury with a motive, or that the jury might see it as an attack on Megan's character. It was a decision they would undoubtedly second-guess for a long time if the jury went south on them. And while Donald's story was convincing, the prosecution's portrayal of him was equally, if not more, persuasive.

Seven men and five women took their places in the jury box while Donald sat stone-faced at the defense table. Judge Carney bent to his right and out of view of the cameras, slid open the bottom drawer, and shoved a few Advils in his mouth. Then he came back into focus, forced a slight grin, and summoned the energy to settle the courtroom.

"Quiet please," he said into the microphone after two chops with his legal hammer, and the conversations quickly faded into a chilling silence. Judge Carney cleared his throat. "Has the jury reached a verdict?"

The foreman, a short, elderly man with bold glasses and an outfit last in style in the fifties, stood up holding their ruling. "We have, Your Honor."

The clacking of the Bailiff's boots filled the courtroom, as he made his way to the jury box to retrieve the paper that bore Donald Richardson's future. Without looking at it, the Bailiff handed it to the Judge who thanked him and all but motioned for him to clear out of the picture. Millions were watching and this was Carney's show.

"Would the defendant please rise?

Donald and his legal team rose in unison, and the attorneys buttoned their overpriced suit jackets. The Judge paused a moment for effect and then began reading. "We the jury, duly empanelled in the *State of Utah v. Donald Leigh Richardson*, do hereby find the defendant Donald Leigh Richardson guilty of Murder in the First Degree, for the murder of Megan Richardson."

The Judge immediately smacked the gavel as the courtroom broke out in cheers, jeers, and various expressions of incredulity. As soon as the crowd quieted, the Judge asked each member of the jury if that was indeed their verdict.

Each confirmed that it was.

WHILE THE JUDGE POLLED the jury, a man sitting on the aisle in the back row tried to suppress a smile. The jury had bought it, a unanimous verdict. For the man with the grease-stained hands was the only one in the courtroom who really knew what happened to Megan Richardson. The jury wasn't completely wrong. Megan *had* been murdered and yes, her killer *was* in the Courtroom.

Just not at the defense table.

CHAPTER TWO

One Month Later

"WHAT BRINGS YOU BACK after such a long time?"

That was the question Phoenix Detective Wyatt Orr had been trying to avoid since the moment he walked in. More than two years had passed since his last visit, a self-imposed respite, much like putting off the dentist until a tooth finally cracks. Deep down, Wyatt had known all along that he needed help; he just hadn't been ready to return.

Until today.

Nausea splashed through his stomach like a tidal wave bouncing recklessly against its inner walls. He shifted in the familiar leather sofa and looked around. Not much had changed in the place he had previously revealed some of his darkest secrets and innermost fears. And the same could be said for Wyatt himself, except that he had finally summoned the courage to return. But still, he wasn't quite ready to forge ahead, so for the past half hour, they'd done nothing but engage in small talk. It was mostly Wyatt postponing the inevitable; he was quickly learning that showing up was only half the battle.

"So are you going to tell me what's going on?"

Wyatt's sonorous exhale acknowledged his defeat.

"I've been having the dream again," he confessed.

Joan Tavares was the psychiatrist on retainer with the Phoenix Police Department. She'd been treating the city's finest for most of her thirty-year career. Tavares could easily attest that police officers weren't the "rocks" that people expected. They were, in many instances, more vulnerable than others, given what they did for a living. Getting shot at, viewing dead bodies, and solving incomprehensible crimes was enough to drive anyone crazy.

Wyatt watched the aging physician flip through her file and felt some relief. During his treatment, including the current session, he had often caught her staring at him. Was she interested in him? He had always suspected so, but he wasn't interested in her. Yes she was attractive, but the apex of her appearance was clearly in the rearview.

From day one, Tavares' gaze made Wyatt uncomfortable; it was one of the reasons he'd ceased psychotherapy. That and her repeated insistence on discussing his father's murder. Wyatt knew she was trying to help him get past it, but he had reached the point where he just couldn't discuss it anymore. So much so that he abandoned psychotherapy in favor of a more conventional remedy: alcohol. And that was how he'd been addressing his problems, until the nightmares became unbearable.

Wyatt waited until Tavares looked up and gestured for him to continue. "I've been seeing the whole thing again, beginning to end, starting with when I first heard the intruder."

"I remember the dream. We've discussed it many times."

"Good. Then I guess I don't need to repeat everything."

"Not unless there's something new."

"There is." Wyatt looked away, shifting again in his seat. "And it's really freakin' me out." He caught Tavares looking at her watch, and couldn't help but take a glance at his own. Time was almost up.

"Everything's the same until the gun is fired and my father goes down. It's when I run over to see if he's OK …"

After Wyatt's voice trailed off, Tavares said, "Tell me what you see."

"I see my dad, but he's just a headless torso." He paused to compose himself. "I can't see his face anymore. It's completely gone."

TAVARES LOOKED AT HER watch and breathed a sigh of relief, as the longest session of her career was just about over. When Wyatt abandoned treatment several years ago, she thought it was the last she would hear from him. She had always believed she'd done her best to treat this man who was untreatable. They had spent time together every week for almost a year and then just like that, he disappeared. And that suited her just fine. Wyatt wasn't a bad guy; she had just never met a man who'd been handed a more challenging fate. So when he walked into her office today, she quickly realized that she wasn't prepared. Seeing him again stirred up powerful feelings she had mistakenly thought she had overcome. Of course, Tavares never shared those feelings with her patient and she wasn't about to. The best she could do was to get through the session and then immediately re-evaluate.

To do so, she made a point of examining her notes even though she hadn't forgotten anything about Wyatt's troubled past. The initial consultation had occurred during Wyatt's first year on the force. While apprehending a perp, Wyatt had been too slow to produce his gun and ended up taking a bullet in the shoulder. The experience would've been difficult for any first year officer, much less someone who'd helplessly witnessed his own father's murder. Shortly after the incident, Wyatt scheduled his first appointment to address the trauma and insomnia he was experiencing. They immediately commenced intense psycho-therapy and quickly reached what Tavares believed was at the core of Wyatt's problems.

That fateful night when he lost his father.

Wyatt was regularly experiencing flashbacks of his father's death and, after Wyatt himself was shot, his life went into a tailspin. Rebecca, his wife at the time, filed for divorce not long after the shooting. She had always struggled being married to a policeman, constantly worrying that on any given night her husband may not come home. When Wyatt was shot, her worst fear had nearly been realized and she decided she couldn't handle it going forward. Tavares remembered every detail about Wyatt's past, but she'd made sure today to hide that from him.

And so most of the session consisted of idle conversation. Tavares listened while Wyatt described his last two years as little more than an alcoholic stupor, to which she wrinkled her face with disapproval. Wyatt insisted that he was not a barfly, that he often found himself partaking of a drink or two after work as a way to ease the pain. That's not what she had heard from her contacts on the force, but it didn't matter because she wasn't about to argue with him about the true definition of an alcoholic.

When they finally got down to business, Tavares did her best to hide her discomfort. He was talking about his father's murder again and it was a topic of which she'd already heard enough. So, after forty minutes, Tavares interrupted him and announced that another patient was waiting, even though she knew her lobby was empty. She told Wyatt to call for another session when she had no intention of treating him again. It was all she could think of to get him out of her office.

Tavares watched impatiently as Wyatt left and as soon as the door clicked shut, she held her face in her hands. She sniffled, wiped a tear from her eye and picked up the phone. And when the man on the other end answered, she said, "It's me. Remember the patient we discussed awhile back? He just came in again, and I really need your help." Then she paused.

"I've got a conflict."

CHAPTER THREE

BENNIE ANDERSON NEVER CONSIDERED himself as hardened a criminal as the others. Yes, he consistently broke the law, but in his mind, he wasn't anything like his partners. And while he often despised what they did, there were times he found himself fascinated with their preparation. Today was one of those days. After all, how many killers could practically write the autopsy report before actually committing the crime?

"What's the cause of death?" Bennie asked.

"A blow to the head," said Ethan Briscoe. "Or maybe a broken spine. Whatever he falls on and breaks. Officially, it's called *blunt force trauma*."

"You think the coroner will buy it?"

"Sure," Ethan fired back, as they continued along the sandy trail. "There are lots of steep drop-offs out here, and hikers need to be careful." He flashed a sardonic smile. "How many have lost their lives here over the years?"

Serial killers are usually methodical machines of murder, but Ethan and his cohorts were largely successful by changing things up. For them, variety was the spice of death, and no two crimes were precisely the same. They preferred not to leave any evidence, including a body, but that wasn't always practical. Reality dictated that something was almost always left behind, so they strove to control the evidence in a way that would invariably rule out homicide. And that was how they had managed to escape apprehension, by masterfully controlling their crime scenes. Given their flawless execution, who could ever suspect foul play?

Ethan pointed ahead. "There it is." He turned around and waved his hands in and out. "Hurry up! The clouds are coming in."

Trailing them was Clay Mallis, a man whose name, although spelled differently, was befitting of a hardened criminal. They had started out on the trail together, but Clay had been forced to drop back because the man they had just kidnapped couldn't keep up. So, Ethan and Bennie jumped ahead while Clay swept the rear with their hostage.

The victim's name was Henderson Taylor. His life was about to end, and his sun burnt face portrayed defeat. His brown hair was sweaty and disheveled, and he carried his medium-sized frame with little stability, having already spent the day hiking in the region's intense heat. Taylor had no choice but to follow his captors; the men with the guns were clearly in charge. They had forced him to traverse a deep, sandy trail without water and with his hands tied in front of him.

Clay and Taylor caught up with Ethan and Bennie near the canyon rim, just a few steps away from a death plunge. The emerald waters of the Virgin River cascaded through the narrow canyon thousands of feet below, its waters swollen by a string of recent monsoons.

"Can I have some water?" Taylor pleaded, panting like a dog in the summer heat.

"Sit tight," Ethan responded. "Soon you'll have all the water you'll need." Ethan shared a smile with Clay, who set his backpack against a boulder on which Bennie had just taken a seat.

The sky began to grumble.

"What are you guys gonna do?"

Ethan pulled out a switchblade and seconds later the rope binding Taylor's wrists fell to the floor, along with a dirty mechanic's rag they had placed underneath it. The rag wasn't there to prevent pain, it was there to prevent a rope burn which, when the body was eventually found, would be an easy indication of foul play. Ethan motioned to Bennie and Bennie tossed him Taylor's backpack. Ethan wrapped the pack around their victim making sure to clip the waist and shoulder belts tightly. It was a key component of their plan and they needed to make sure the pack stayed on. No matter what.

"We're not doing anything," Ethan said. "*You're* gonna jump."

Taylor shook his head and looked around. "I'm not jumping off *that*."

Ethan replaced the switchblade with a gun. "Of course you will."

"Or what, you'll put a bullet in my head? It looks like I've got two options: suicide or homicide. Sorry, but if you want me dead, you're going to have to shoot me."

"Come on guys," Bennie cut in. "Let's finish and get outta here. We're exposed on this plateau."

A clear bolt of sky-to-ground lightning struck what seemed like just a few miles away, followed immediately by a stunning boom that shook the area.

"Bennie's right, look over there." Ethan pointed to the east where a dark cloud draped from the sky like a magic carpet. He turned to Taylor. "You better jump. Right now!"

But Taylor refused to move so Clay reached into his pack and grabbed the handle of a Louisville Slugger. He took two steps and swung at Taylor's midsection, as if trying to send a fastball over the centerfield wall. Taylor's scream reverberated through the canyon as he curled in a defensive posture, and Clay smacked him again. Another bolt of lightning struck nearby.

"That's enough," Ethan said. "We're wrapping this up *now*. It's two damn miles back to the car." Ethan pulled the trigger and fired at Taylor's feet. "Jump, or the next one goes through your freakin' skull!"

When Taylor refused, Ethan met eyes with Clay and then tossed the gun to Bennie just as Clay dropped the bat. In an instant, they converged on their prisoner and, despite the resistance, pushed him over the rim. Both stood near the edge until Taylor's final scream was replaced by the thud of his body sticking the landing.

"Did anyone get him a permit?" Ethan joked. "I don't think he's allowed in the Narrows without one." Then he turned to Bennie. "The cause of death? A long fucking fall into the river. Does that answer your question?"

Ethan, Clay, and Bennie scuttled back the way they came, hoping to reach the car before the storm reached them. Their next destination: back to Utah's Zion National Park.

One of the most beautiful places in the world.

And a fertile ground for their deadly enterprise.

HERE'S HOW IT WENT down. After identifying Taylor as their target, the three criminals followed their quarry through the park. In the year 2000, The National Park Service implemented a shuttle system and restricted the use of private vehicles within park boundaries. During peak summer season, tourists were required to park at any one of a number of designated areas and take the shuttle into the canyon. The guys spied Taylor parking at one of those locations, Canyon Junction, and Clay followed him onto the shuttle, while Ethan and Bennie parked their car next to Taylor's. With no idea he was being followed, Taylor spent the day hiking while Clay waited at the trailhead. When Taylor returned, Clay called ahead to notify Ethan that they were on their way back. As the shuttle returned to Canyon Junction, Bennie fired up the engine. Taylor got off the bus and crossed the street, with Clay trailing several steps behind. Taylor disarmed his alarm, popped the trunk, and tossed his backpack inside. But as he reached for the driver side door, Ethan stepped out and pointed a gun at him. Then, Clay came up behind Ethan in a well-choreographed move to keep Ethan's firearm out of plain view. In a placid yet forceful manner, Ethan demanded the keys and ordered Taylor into the backseat of their car. Taylor had no choice but to obey, and that was the beginning of his end.

Ethan swiftly popped the trunk and retrieved Taylor's backpack before jumping back into their car. Clay joined Taylor in the backseat, and tied his wrists together as they zipped out of the park. An hour later, Taylor was dead, and the guys were heading back to retrieve what they had worked for.

Taylor's car.

It was an Acura MDX in excellent condition.

It would surely fetch them a fortune.

CHAPTER FOUR

THE BLUE CROWN VICTORIA squeaked to a stop, as its passenger-side tires interrupted the flow of soapy water hugging the curb. Wyatt cut the engine, stepped out, and lowered his tie, finally freeing his neck from the oppressive hold of a fully buttoned shirt collar. He hated his work attire, but there was little he could do about it. Lawyers wore suits in court to show respect for the judicial system; worshippers, in a church or synagogue, dressed up when praying before their Almighty; even businessmen wore suits to important meetings to show clients respect and earn their business. But why did detectives wear suits to apprehend criminals? And how was the custom established? Was there a wife somewhere who told her husband: "You can't arrest someone wearing that!"

Thankfully, Wyatt's workday was over and the only thing missing was a vodka on the rocks, an urge he'd been working diligently to suppress. He slammed the car door and walked up the driveway, making sure to avoid stepping in the sudsy stream.

"What do you charge for an old piece of shit that everyone knows is an undercover police car?" Wyatt said to his old friend.

Nicholas Perrone was crouched alongside his Silver Dodge Durango holding a large sponge. "A lot more than you can afford."

"You're probably right, but I must say, you do good work."

Nick stood and walked towards the back of the car, a line of soap droplets trailed behind him.

"Just getting this baby ready. I've never been to Zion."

"Me neither, but I don't care where we go. I'm just looking forward to gettin' out there again. Like old times."

Nick began working on the rear bumper.

"What the hell is this?" Nick said, now sprawled on the ground under the car. Wyatt stepped over to take a look. "Right here on the underside. That's quite a scratch. See it?"

Wyatt crouched for a look. "I don't see anything."

Nick waved him closer and Wyatt delicately got on his knees. Those damn suit pants. He leaned all the way in, his head now almost touched the ground. "Oh, I see." Wyatt rubbed it with his fingers. "It looks like the paint's a little chipped. No big deal."

Nick ran his hand across the scratch and scrubbed it with the sponge. Then he pulled a hand towel from inside his waist belt and wiped it dry. Nothing changed. Wyatt stood back up and wiped dirt off his pants.

"Sure it's a big deal," Nick said, as he came out from under the vehicle and threw the towel to the ground. "The car is brand new and this thing is more than an inch in size."

"Oh, come on, you can't even see it. You probably drove over a curb and scraped the underside."

"Never happened," Nick said. "Must've been like that when I bought it. Damn it. I'm gonna take it back for a new one."

Wyatt rolled his eyes. "It's not that big a deal. If it really bothers you, get one of those little paint bottles from the dealer and patch it up. Silver's not a difficult color to find."

"I've tried that before and it sucks. The tone of the paint is always slightly off from the rest of the car, and all it does is accentuate the scratch. I'll take the car to the dealer when we get back; I don't want this to ruin our vacation. I really need the time off."

Wyatt took a few steps back as Nick began hosing down the rear. "I can imagine. When's Ina due?"

"Oh God," Nick said, his voice laced with dread. "In about two months."

19

"And you're not excited?"

"You know how I always felt." He shook his head. "This wasn't planned."

"I remember talking about it when we were in college but that was a long time ago. I thought by now maybe things had changed."

Nick stole a glance at the house, then moved closer to Wyatt and lowered his voice anyway. "I don't want a kid. I don't even want to be married anymore. Women are like cars, you know? They're great and all, but after a while, it's time for a newer model."

"That's kinda harsh, don't you think?"

"Maybe, but I'm in a bad place right now. Nothing against Ina, but I don't think I'm ready for this. I feel trapped."

"You should be thankful for your wife," Wyatt said. "I couldn't hold onto mine, but you better not let go of yours. Ina's a great gal. She really cares about you."

"You're right. But you know what they say: the grass is always greener …"

Nick tossed the sponge towards the bucket like he was taking a free throw. It splotched against the back and droplets of water settled on the surrounding pavement. Then he picked up a towel, wiped his hands, and headed for the front door.

"Come on inside, let's see if dinner's ready."

THEY ENTERED THROUGH A large door fronted by a pair of freshly painted white columns. The house was located in the Biltmore, an exclusive community not far from downtown Phoenix. Nick tossed his keys on a cherry oak table in the foyer. Wyatt followed him down a long hallway, taking a quick peak into the sunken living room with a vaulted ceiling. Wyatt remembered the house, but hadn't been there for several years and he quickly realized that nothing had changed. The room was immaculate and clearly unused. Rich people, Wyatt thought, fairly certain that if he asked Nick when they had last used the room, he'd answer with a number. A year that had passed long ago.

Wyatt stopped to glance at a framed article, and then headed to the kitchen.

"Is Wyatt with you?" Ina called out.

"Yes," Nick said, and excused himself to get cleaned up.

Ina was washing her hands at the kitchen island and turned to grab a towel when she saw Wyatt standing awkwardly at the entrance.

"Wow, look at *you*," Wyatt said, as he entered the kitchen.

He watched Ina brush aside some of her wavy, auburn hair, and tuck it behind her ears. "I know." She patted the lower half of her bulging tummy.

"What is this now, your fifth trimester?" he asked.

"Hey! I'm not *that* big."

"Just teasing. You look fantastic." Wyatt stepped forward and hugged her.

When they separated, Wyatt couldn't help noticing that, aside from the orb projecting from her stomach, pregnancy had not interfered with Ina's physical perfection. *How could the grass get any greener*?

"That article on your wall, what's that about?"

"Nick won an award for closing the most commercial real estate deals last year. And he just started teaching a negotiations class at ASU West. So they did a write up on him."

"Sounds like things are going well."

Ina nodded. "Nick's really excited for your camping trip."

"I can't wait," Wyatt said. "What are *you* gonna do while we're gone?"

"Work." She made a face. "We're hosting a huge corporate retreat down in Tucson."

"The life of an event planner. I thought you're not supposed to travel when you're this close to giving birth?"

She chuckled. "I *cannot* miss this event. Besides, I've still got two months."

They spent a few more minutes catching up before Nick returned and took a seat at the table.

"I hope you're hungry. Dinner will be ready in a couple of minutes, but you guys can start on the salad." She handed Wyatt a colorful bowl with large tongs, which he set on the table next to Nick. Then she joined them.

"So, Wyatt, got your gear ready?" Nick asked.

"Pulled it out of storage yesterday and it really brought back some memories."

"We definitely had some good times."

Wyatt couldn't contain a smile. "Did you ever tell Ina about the tent incident?"

Ina turned to Nick. "I don't think you have."

"I was just thinking about that yesterday," Wyatt said. "We were somewhere up north and after we set up camp, we put everything in our tents and hit the trails. But Nick forgot to close his tent."

Ina smirked. "Did someone take your stuff?"

"Worse," Wyatt continued. "We get back and do our thing, make a campfire, cook our food, hang out. Later on, we decide to call it a night and head for our respective tents. Not two minutes later, Nick screams at the top of his lungs, 'There's a snake in my bag!'"

"Are you serious?"

"It's true." Nick grinned. "But it turned out to be a chipmunk."

"At least you didn't have to sleep alone," Ina quipped.

"I've never seen him move so fast." Wyatt turned to Nick. "That was the last time you ever put your stuff in the tent before bedtime, wasn't it?"

"Yes, it made me a little anal, so what?"

"A *little* anal?" Wyatt countered. "You wouldn't even keep the stuff sacks in your tent after that."

"Hey, what if it *was* a snake?"

They shared a laugh and Ina excused herself, promising to replace the salad with a casserole upon her return.

"So, are you in shape for this?" Nick asked. "We haven't really spoken much in the last couple of years."

"I know, I'll take the blame for it. I—"

"No," Nick cut him off. "We both got busy; it's called life. I'm glad you reached out. Is there anything I can do to help?"

"No, just struggling with the same Achilles Heel."

"Still blaming yourself?"

Wyatt nodded. "Wouldn't you?"

"I love you like a brother but no, I wouldn't. It's been like fifteen years, and you were just a teenager. There comes a time when you have to accept the past for what it is and move on. Everyone faces adversity; the ones who deal with it succeed."

"I was almost eighteen. And not everyone let his father die in front of him. You know what I mean?"

"That your shit stinks more than everyone else's? Come on, don't you think it's time you moved on?"

Wyatt threw his napkin on the table and stood. "You think I should just accept that I basically killed my dad?"

Nick put his hands out in defense. "I'm only trying to help you get past it."

"Your father's alive. Mine's in the ground, and I may have been the one who put him there. This is bullshit." Wyatt headed for the hallway just as Ina returned.

Nick stood to stop him. "Wait, that's not what I'm saying."

Wyatt turned to face Nick. "Oh, I got you, *friend*. Loud and clear."

"What's going on?" Ina caught up with Wyatt in the hallway.

"I'm leaving," Wyatt said, as he made his way to the door. "Thanks for the salad."

Ina followed as quickly as she could. "Why?"

"Ask your husband." Wyatt opened the door, stepped outside, and then turned to her. "Tell him to enjoy his vacation, 'cause I certainly won't be joining him."

And with that, Wyatt headed for his car, not knowing that the decision he had just made would change all of their lives.

Irreversibly.

CHAPTER FIVE

CRIME SCENES IN AMERICA are a lot like Times Square on a Saturday night, crammed with people and bustling with energy. The first responders establish a perimeter, spreading the infamous yellow tape before hordes of onlookers descend on the place. Visitors to the site include firefighters, crime scene technicians, photographers, detectives, medical examiners, and uniformed police officers to interview witnesses and control the scene. And they need to, because there are always members of the media, and even bystanders, who want in on the action. Sometimes lieutenants, captains, and even the Chief of Police make an appearance, especially in high profile cases. Can't pass up an opportunity for some face time on the evening news.

They turn the place upside down, ripping up carpets, tearing apart walls, removing headboards, baseboards, rifling through closets, drawers, and cabinets. They'll take anything that may provide a clue to solve the crime. A normal crime scene is busy, lots of noise, talking, action, lights flashing. Everything is centered on the life of the party: the body lying before them.

But there was no such "party" for Henderson Taylor, because that's not how things are done at Zion.

The National Park Service, an arm of the federal government, runs the park. However, the land itself is owned by the State of Utah. The state allows the Park Service to enforce the law, but maintains the basic rights of a landowner. Rangers can hand out speeding tickets or arrest visitors for disorderly conduct. They even have a jail cell on-site. But when it comes to an unattended death—where the deceased expires outside the presence of a physician—the state has jurisdiction over the case, and, since the park is located in Washington County, its sheriff takes charge of the investigation.

MARTIN RUGIE, WHO HAD been with the park more than thirty years, took a seat at his desk. He'd just returned from the Big Bend, where the Virgin River had taken an unusual turn carving its way through Zion Canyon. Someone had reported scores of bugs and birds of prey furiously circling the base of Angel's Landing, Zion's most famous monolith. And it hadn't taken long to discover why.

A corpse.

Rugie picked up the phone and dialed.

"Amado here."

"We got another Doe," Rugie said to the sheriff.

He could hear Amado sigh. It was already late in the evening and Amado lived, and worked, in a town called Hurricane, approximately an hour outside the park. "Who found it?"

"Tourists."

"Where's it located?"

"Out by Angel's Landing."

"Why am I not surprised?"

Climbing Angel's Landing was not for the faint of heart. A vertical climb of more than a thousand feet, it requires, in many places, the use of chains. One misstep and it's all over.

"Who's preserving the scene?" Amado asked.

"No one yet, we just found it. But the body's on the far side of the river, which is not easily accessible."

"Then I guess you can leave it until we get there, unless you think someone may contaminate—"

"After we hang up, I'll go out there myself," Rugie interrupted. "But I don't have all night."

Rugie smiled; he couldn't help but push the sheriff's buttons. He despised authority and hated the bureaucratic bullshit of deferring to the County for "an investigation." What did they do that he or the other rangers couldn't? *They'll come out, do a dance, and tell us what we already know: some dipshit lost his footing and fell thousands of feet on his ass. Why can't we go out there, toss the body in a bag, and move on?* The park had its perils. He'd seen it before.

"Thanks," Amado said, ignoring Rugie's derision. "I'll make a few calls and we'll be on our way."

"WHAT DID YOU SAY to him?" Ina sat in a cushioned chair in the corner of the bedroom, her slightly swollen feet plastered to an ottoman.

"He started talking about his dad again and how it's been holding him back. So I told him to take responsibility like a man and move on."

Ina sighed, and covered her face with her hands.

"I was only trying to help."

"No wonder he stormed out."

"What are you talking about?" Nick went into the bathroom to brush his teeth. "Do you know how many times I've been there for him? You have no idea how many hours we've spent discussing it."

"You should call and apologize. There's no reason you guys shouldn't go together."

Nick strolled out wiping his mouth with a hand towel. "Forget it, I don't want to go with him anymore. I was looking forward to being guys again, not playing psychologist for a weekend."

"It wouldn't hurt you to help him, Nick. Some people aren't as fortunate as we are. Besides, what are you going to do, stay here alone for a week?"

"Of course not, I'm going camping."

"By yourself?"

"Best company in the world."

"Can't you find someone else to go with?"

"To leave the day after tomorrow? No way."

Ina couldn't hide the concern from her face. It was hard enough dealing with pregnancy and the daily changes to her figure. And she had an important weekend ahead of her. She didn't need more to worry about.

"I know you used to camp a lot but have you ever been to this park?"

"No, but I hear it's amazing. Our company used to do executive retreats there. A lot still do, but we stopped several years ago."

Ina grimaced and wrapped her arms around her belly. "Whoa. Contraction."

"You're not having the baby now, are you?"

"It'll go away in a minute," she said. "And try not to sound too thrilled."

She watched as Nick tossed the towel into the bathroom and headed for bed. "I'm really uncomfortable with all this, and I don't need any more stress right now. If you're not going to call him, then can't you at least stay here?"

Nick shook his head as he slipped under the covers. "Look, I haven't had a vacation in a long time and *you* made a point of saying that this will be my last for a while. So I'm going."

"You're really going to do this to me?"

"No need to worry." Nick positioned his pillows. "It's a National Park with tons of people. What could possibly happen?"

CHAPTER SIX

Thursday

ZION NATIONAL PARK IS a geologic wonderland, a unique array of multi-colored canyons and tree-lined mountains with a river slicing all the way through. Nestled in a grass-filled valley below several vistas, Zion's campgrounds are no less alluring. In fact, there isn't a single campsite that doesn't have an exquisite view.

Nick arrived late Thursday afternoon. He paid the entrance fee, located his assigned campsite, and took a few moments to find the right spot for his tent. He was almost finished setting up when he was interrupted.

"Just get in?"

What gave it away? Nick finished chiseling off some rope with a Swiss army knife. He was using the rope to tie the last stake to a tree. He folded the knife, slid it into the front pocket of his chinos, and decided that, despite his weariness, he ought to be nice to the staff. You never know when you might need them. He made his way over to the man in the golf cart.

"About an hour ago." Nick squinted in the late afternoon sun.

"Just checkin' is all. It's my job," said the large-framed man with the craggy complexion. Baldness had long ago split the sea of gray that had once graced his head, and there was still some left on the sides screaming to be combed.

Nick was a serious golfer, as were most Phoenicians, and he couldn't help but admire the man's ride. Leather seats, large front dash, and a huge oval-shaped windshield, made it look like the man was sitting inside a big, comfortable bubble.

"Nice wheels." Nick made a mental note to look into the Daihatsu cart when he returned to the Valley.

"Thanks, I guess. It belongs to the park. But I get to spend just about every day in it."

"Doesn't sound bad to me."

Nick saw a Bible on the passenger seat, half expecting it to have the words 'Holiday Inn' stamped on the inside cover. How ironic is it that the Bible, of all things, is the one item people steal most from hotel rooms?

"My name's Stan, by the way. I'm the host of this place."

"I got that from the sign." Nick smiled. The words 'CAMP HOST' were painted on the side of the cart in large green letters over a white background.

Stan chuckled. "Dead giveaway, huh?" He reached across the seat and grabbed a clipboard from the passenger side dash. "OK, let's see here, got you down for five nights, party of two."

"It's now a party of one, but yes, I'll be here five nights."

Stan made a notation and placed the clipboard back on the dash. "I'm sure you'll see me patrolling the grounds, but if you need something just holler. I live right there." He pointed to a trailer parked at the entrance to the campground.

Stan pulled away and Nick returned to his tent. Smoke rose from most of the campsites, and Nick planned to build his fire once he finished setting up. He had pitched the tent in the northern portion of the campsite, under a couple of large oaks. The more shade during the day, the cooler it would be at night. Nick went around each side and pulled at the strings, making sure they were firm. Then he checked the rain fly and straightened the plastic tarp he had placed under the tent, before zipping it open and smoothing out the interior. Satisfied all was in order, Nick made the fifty-foot walk to the Durango and popped the trunk. As he reached for his sleeping bag, he remembered the chipmunk and the story Wyatt had recounted just a few nights ago. It made him think twice before putting his stuff inside.

"Damn Wyatt," Nick muttered, as he pulled his sleeping bag and pad out of the trunk. He brought them to the tent, separated them from their stuff sacks, and tossed them in. "I don't need him."

Nick didn't think there were snakes in the area but he still made a mental note to zip the tent when he was done unpacking. He was headed back to the car to grab his pillow and blanket when he saw something that made him stop in his tracks.

His neighbor.

She had long blond hair, skin tanned to perfection, and a strong yet elegant stride. Nick sized her up quickly, deciding that he loved a woman wearing a rugged pair of boots. But the best part wasn't what she was wearing, it was what she was doing.

She was on her way over to his campsite.

CHAPTER SEVEN

Friday

NICK AROSE TO THE soothing vocals of the park's songbirds. He stepped out of his tent as a breeze pushed the faint streaks of smoke still emanating from the orange embers that had narrowly escaped his late-night dousing. It was just before seven and while the sun had already been up for a few hours, the campground was still bathing in complete shade. It would be a few more hours before the sun propelled itself above the towering cliffs that stood guard over the Watchman Campground. After a short visit to the restroom, Nick boiled some coffee, fixed himself a bowl of oatmeal, and prepared his backpack for the day's hike. After breakfast, Nick made sure his tent was zipped shut, as he did not want uninvited company later that night.

The Visitor Center was a short walk from his campsite. Nick underestimated the large, double-paned glass doors, as he clumsily entered the marble-floored building. But then he jumped back immediately upon meeting the dark bulging eyes of the impressive feline predator.

A mountain lion.

It took his brain a moment to register the fact that the life-sized animal was stuffed and encased in a large fish tank. Nick inched closer to get a better look. Something caught in his throat when he saw the sign next to the animal soliciting anyone with the knowledge and skill to volunteer as a tracker. *If they want to keep people off the trails, this is the perfect way to do it.*

Nick glanced around the room. Behind the embalmed Cougar was the park's gift shop, which he'd have plenty of time for later. Instead, Nick went the other direction, towards a wooden sign that read "PARK INFORMATION." There were two desks: the one on the left was for hikers, while the one on the right was for the Zion Lodge, which was located deep in the heart of Zion Canyon. Nick chose the left and waited behind a visitor who was talking to a park ranger. There was no one on the right side, probably due to the "NO VACANCY" sign. While waiting, Nick admired the large posters of unique park features hanging on the wall behind the desk, and scanned a board that contained hand-written park information. The forecast looked good and both campgrounds were full. There was, however, a flash flood warning for tomorrow evening.

To the right of the board, Nick gazed at five white, letter-sized posters thumb-tacked to the wall in two rows, three on top and two on bottom. The top of each poster had the word 'MISSING.' Each contained a picture, a name, some personal data, and whom to contact if you had any information. Nick moved closer, read some of the names, and examined their faces. The dates of their disappearances varied but each had been missing long enough for anyone to realize the obvious.

They would never be found.

The ranger finished and smiled at Nick as he approached the desk.

"What's all this about lion tracking?" he asked, staring at a handout taped to the desk. The flyer had a picture of a lion standing on a rock ledge surveying the landscape, presumably for its next meal.

"Are you here to apply?" She displayed a bright set of perfectly aligned teeth, guarded by shapely lips colored a light shade of pink.

Nick enjoyed her olive eyes and angular face. But her uniform—a gray button-down shirt and khaki pants—didn't do it for him. Too masculine. Still, Nick suspected somewhere underneath was a very appealing figure, and he decided that he wouldn't mind seeing what she looked like when she donned a more appealing wardrobe.

"No way, Velvet." He read her name off the tag displayed above her ample chest. "Are there really that many lions out here?"

"Sightings are rare. But if you see one, let us know."

Nick chuckled. "If I see one, I'll be running for my life so you don't have to add me to those posters. Is that why those people are missing?"

Velvet glanced at the wall. "We don't know what happened to them. I guess it could be, but the lions don't usually bother people."

"That's reassuring."

"Those posters cover more than five years and virtually every National Park has had people disappear. Most of the time it's just people using the park as a diversion, a way to leave their lives and start fresh somewhere else."

Nick's philosophy was never to show weakness in front of an attractive woman, and he wasn't about to abandon that now. But mountain lions, posters of missing hikers, and being alone were starting to weigh on his mind. For the first time since Wyatt walked out on him, Nick felt the slightest bit of hesitation.

"So what are some good places for me to explore?" Nick said, setting aside his uncertainty.

Velvet pulled out a glossy map from under the desk, unraveled it, and highlighted various trails. "There are some nice and challenging hikes in the park. The one to Observation Point is pretty neat. And the one to Angel's Landing is spectacular, although steep and strenuous."

"Which do you recommend I start with? One with, say, the least amount of mountain lions?"

Velvet smiled. "Give me a second. Here comes Kevin, my boss."

Kevin Simpson, the Canyon District Ranger, approached. "Is everything all right out here?" he asked. "Where's Kimberly?"

"Everything's fine. Kim's having car trouble. She's taking it in for service."

"I wish she would've told me because I could've helped out. My son's a mechanic. He's got a shop near Hurricane."

"If she calls in again, I'll tell her to call you."

"OK, tell her to try me on the cell. I'm heading out to the campground to deliver a message, and then I'm going to run into town. Need anything?"

Velvet shook her head and Simpson left. She turned back to Nick. "Sorry about that, someone else usually works this desk. We're a little shorthanded right now so they called me out of the bullpen."

She handed Nick the map and he slid it into his pocket.

"All right then, mountain lions, trackers, snakes, steep cliffs with chains, this is going to be one hell of an adventure."

Velvet laughed. "Have fun. I don't want to see your face up on this wall."

CHAPTER EIGHT

THE BULLET NARROWLY MISSED the target, ricocheted off the canyon wall, and landed somewhere off in the wilderness. Ethan looked around to see if it actually hit something. When he realized it hadn't, he placed the gun on the boulder they used as a shield and grabbed another beer from the cooler.

"You hear the news?" He popped the cap off a longneck. "They found Taylor's body."

"I didn't hear anything," Clay responded, coming out of his crouch. "How'd they find it?"

"You'll love *this*. A couple of foreigners spotted his mangled carcass at the backside of Angel's Landing."

"No shit. The river carried him that far? That's not what we planned."

Dumbass. Ethan took a swig. "That's right, it's way better! We thought he'd get stuck in the Narrows and it would be days or weeks until he dislodged. But the fucker coasted all the way through and somehow came to rest at the base of the Landing. And now, they think he fell off Scout's."

Scout's Lookout was a promontory a thousand feet above the Virgin River, but well below Angel's Landing.

Clay lit a cigarette. "Nice."

"The county sheriff is taking the body to Salt Lake for the autopsy. Nothing's been officially reported, but they're already calling it an accident."

Washington County, including the St. George area, was a growing metropolis, but far from being considered a major city. They didn't have the normal infrastructure and so the closest coroner was several hours north, in Salt Lake.

"And get this," Ethan continued. "They interviewed some witnesses who saw Taylor up at Scouts, and that's the last spot they can place him. I love being in the know."

"Sounds like it couldn't have worked out any better," Clay said. "Are we done shootin'?"

Ethan grabbed the gun and they took up position behind the boulder. He pulled the trigger but nothing happened to the beer cans they had placed on a rock ledge a hundred yards away.

"You suck, dude," Clay said, as they stood. "Worst shot I've ever seen."

Ethan checked to see how many bullets he had left. "I wanna finish my rounds." He pointed the gun at Clay's head.

Clay dropped his cigarette, slightly raised his hands and stepped back. "What the hell?"

Ethan tightened his grip on the gun. "I guarantee you the next shot won't be the worst you've seen."

"You're not really going to shoot your best friend."

"I've done it before," Ethan said.

"Yeah, but I'm not Lyle. I would never do the shit he was planning. Put the gun away, dude, you're scaring me."

Ethan gave Clay a long stare as he lowered the gun. "Fine. But just remember, best friend or not, cross me and it won't take a second. I'll put one right between your eyes."

NICK CHOSE THE HIKE to Observation Point, a popular spot several thousand feet up overlooking the majestic Zion Valley. He climbed the steep, asphalt-paved switchbacks to a junction marked by a small wooden sign, and a neat little rock-bench expertly carved out of Navajo Sandstone. An elderly couple occupied the bench so Nick lowered his pack and took a seat on a large boulder next to it, before retrieving a granola bar.

"Nice day for a climb, huh?" The old man on the bench took sips from a bottle of water.

"Sure is." Nick devoured a chunk of his snack. "I love this shade; hope it stays like this."

"It won't." The old man turned and looked at the wall behind him. "Probably another half hour, forty five minutes till the sun makes its way over the canyon. You headin' to the point?"

"Yup." Nick stretched his legs, flexed, and rubbed both sides with his hands.

"Good choice," the old man said, and his wife nodded.

"Are you locals?" Nick asked.

"Just visiting."

"Where from?"

"Bend, Oregon. We're longtime Duck fans," he said. "I see your USC cap. You gonna watch the game tomorrow?"

"Right. Tomorrow's the first game of the season. I can't remember who they're playing."

"I think Boise State. The Ducks are playing Northern Illinois. By the way, I'm Morty and this is my wife Kayleen."

Nick introduced himself. "I'm glad you reminded me. There's gotta be a place where I can catch the game around here, right?"

"You stayin' in the campground? You can watch the Ducks with us on the dish."

Nick pulled at the blue plastic tube jutting out of his pack and slid the lever on the end, allowing water to rush through. He took a modest sip. "Thanks, but I'm planning to do Angel's Landing tomorrow."

Morty's eyes lit up. "Best hike in the park. You know, it's only four miles round trip? If you start out early enough, you could still catch the game."

"Are there any sports bars closer than St. George?"

"We don't get out here that much and things have changed quite a bit since we were here last. But I do remember some dive of a place between Rockville and Virgin; I think it was called 'The Shack.' It's a hole in the wall just off Route 9, but it's only fifteen minutes or so outside the park."

As he had always done, Nick kept some paper and a pen in the side compartment of his pack, in case he needed to note which direction he had gone at a trail junction. He wrote down the bar's information, placed the note in his pocket, and strapped on his pack. "I better get moving if I'm going to take advantage of that shade."

"Absolutely," Morty said with a faint smile. "Enjoy the game."

"AUTO CHOP," BENNIE SAID cheerlessly into the phone from his dark, dust-filled office.

"It's me." A deep throaty voice. "You got a minute?"

Bennie let out a tension-clearing sigh. "Yeah, where you calling from?"

"A pay phone in Springdale. I just came from the campground."

Springdale was the town immediately adjacent to the park. Also known as the "Gateway to Zion," Springdale housed approximately three hundred and fifty people, the lives of whom centered, in some fashion, around the park and its visitors. Downtown Springdale boasted markets, gas stations, hotels, restaurants, gift shops, a bank, and a fire station. Springdale had its own police department and even patrolled some of the neighboring towns. No one would ever mistake it for a sprawling metropolis, but the town more than adequately serviced the park and its visitors.

Bennie adjusted the phone to his left ear so he could grab a pad and pen. "Hang on a sec." He stepped outside his office and looked around. No one was there. Then, he looked out the back into the yard and saw his co-worker, Tony, walking around and examining their inventory. Bennie returned to the office, closed the door, and sat back down on his torn leather chair. "Shoot."

The caller sighed and Bennie could hear him flipping through pages of his notepad. "There are some unique ones this time, but I'm going to go in the order I took them down." A pause. "Blue Ford Taurus, between 2000 and 2004."

"OK," Bennie said, as he wrote it down. "I could probably find us a Taurus but I need a more specific year. I think they changed styles during that period so let's put that one aside for now. What else?"

"White Subaru Outback, late 90's."

"I don't remember seeing any of those available so I'm going to say forget that one."

"Here's a new one I didn't expect, Maroon Nissan Murano, 2004."

"I love that car, but I don't think it'll work. We could get lucky like we did with Taylor's Acura, but I doubt it. Anything else?"

The caller paused for a moment as a few tourists walked by. "Silver Durango, looks fairly new."

"That's a possibility. I need to double check but I think there was something similar out there last week. I don't remember if the color is the same, but Durango's are so common that I should be able to find something. That it?"

"No. Red Chevy Trailblazer. I think 2003 - 2005."

"I could probably do that one with ease."

"White Dodge Neon, sometime after 2000 is my guess."

"That's also a good bet." Bennie scribbled it down. "That it?"

"Yes, and I need to get back to the park."

"Hang with me for a second." Bennie looked over his list, dotting and crossing some letters darker than he needed to. Then he grabbed a pile of car titles from the corner of his desk and flipped through the two-inch stack. "I thought I might already have something for the Neon but I can't find it. Let me make some calls and see what I can locate."

The caller hung up.

CHAPTER NINE

Saturday

NICK MANAGED AN EARLY start and enjoyed the challenging trek up Angel's Landing. Portions of the trail had taken him along thin edges of the monolith, with the constant stare down at a daunting death-plunge. Thankfully, there were numerous places in which the park had drilled chains into the rock, giving the conscientious hiker something to hold onto. And Nick used them. Angel's Landing had been the source of several of the park's more recent mishaps and, after completing the hike, he could easily see why.

Nick returned to the campground shortly after noon with achy legs and frayed nerves. As he had done the day before, he changed into a bathing suit and slippers, and laid out his hiking clothes on a boulder near his tent. With toiletry bag in hand and a towel slung over his shoulder, Nick walked the quarter mile or so to the river, set his stuff on a jumble of tree roots along the shore, and stepped out of his slippers. Since it was the weekend, the river was full of water enthusiasts. Seeking serenity, Nick walked barefoot along the shore and away from a throng of children frolicking boisterously in the gleaming waters. He stared at several kids floating by in tubes and wondered why he hadn't thought to do that. Further downstream, where it was more tranquil, Nick entered the water and gently exhaled the moment his feet made contact with the placid river. The soreness in his legs departed and it wasn't long before the soothing effect coursed through the rest of his body. Nick slogged through the water until he found a spot that was deep enough to lie down. A smile of satisfaction engrossed his salty face, as he finally gave his legs the respite for which they had been pleading since early that morning.

After a slothful half hour, Nick toweled off and returned to camp, where he changed into the pants he had worn when he first arrived, and fished a USC shirt out of his bag. Nick checked his watch; the day had been perfectly executed with plenty of time to catch some afternoon football. He grabbed his wallet, keys, and cell phone, and checked the pockets of the shorts he had worn while hiking yesterday. But the note with the name of the bar wasn't there. He scanned the area, but the note was nowhere to be found. No reason to waste more time, Nick thought, since he remembered the name anyway. *How hard could it be to find?*

He left the campsite and drove to the end of the loop, heading for the exit. As he passed Stan's trailer, Nick saw the host sitting in a lawn chair outside his RV and when Stan waved, Nick waved back. As he reached the campground entrance booth, Nick saw two rangers walking together. He pulled up next to them and lowered the passenger side window.

"Good afternoon, gentlemen," he said, raising his voice while leaning to his right. "I was wondering if you could help me. Someone told me about a bar called 'The Shack,' but I can't seem to find the note I made with its information. Are either of you familiar with it?"

The two rangers, whose nametags identified them as Martin Rugie and Kevin Simpson, approached the car and leaned into the window. "Yes, it's just outside of Rockville, about fifteen minutes up Route 9. It'll be on your left hand side," Simpson said.

"Anything I should look out for in the way of landmarks?"

"After Springdale, you won't see anything for about ten minutes and then all of a sudden, you'll see a string of abandoned stores on the left side," Rugie explained. "It's right in there."

"Got a big red Utes banner hanging out front," Simpson added. "For the University of Utah."

"Do they have cable or a dish? I want to catch the USC game."

The rangers looked at each other and smiled.

FIFTEEN MINUTES LATER, NICK slammed on his brakes as he came flying around a bend. His tires squealed when he made a sharp left turn across the two-lane highway and onto a dirt-filled service road. The rangers had been right; the barren landscape had practically lulled Nick to sleep until a strip of deserted buildings appeared out of nowhere. If he hadn't seen the Utes banner at the last second, he would've missed the place altogether. He slowed as he drove alongside the rusted storefronts, which made for the perfect ghost town straight out of an old western film. There was no activity along the strip except for the building at the very end.

The Shack.

Nick parked, got out, and looked around. A hot afternoon breeze danced around him, occasionally whipped into a frenzy by cars whizzing by. He squinted as he glanced at the plateau across the highway. It was filled with loose, charred boulders, remnants of volcanic activity from long ago. Then he glanced at the bar, which looked like it had recently undergone some exterior remodeling. Its clean aluminum siding made it stand out from the decrepit storefronts along the rest of the strip. Regardless, the place still looked like a dump. It had several windows that looked like they hadn't been washed since the Cold War. Each contained neon lighting, advertising brands of beer. Between the windows was a wooden door with chipped paint, filled by a large rectangular pane of plate glass. A dusty paper sign hung in one of the windows, beckoning patrons to enter the establishment.

But the eeriness of the setting made Nick think twice. He paused while considering his options and actually turned towards his truck, but after a split second of indecision, the seeds of doubt faded when he caught a glimpse of the large satellite dish on the roof.

The door squeaked and its horizontal blinds swung back and forth, as Nick entered the bar. He paused at the entrance to gain his bearings in the barely lit saloon. To his left, a television clung to a corner shelf, displaying nothing that would ever interest him. Below it was a slightly dented boom box that wasn't on, if it even worked. There were adjoining rooms on each side of the bar; the one on the left was barely large enough to house its pool table and vending machine, while the one on the right was filled with a bunch of broken and dusty furniture. Why, Nick wondered, had the owner chosen exterior work when the inside was so outdated?

Nick took a seat on a wooden stool at the bar. "Bud," he mouthed when the bartender acknowledged his arrival. With the television behind him, Nick turned in his chair and leaned his back against the torn leather bar top. Prominently displayed on the twenty-inch screen was an older woman in her garden holding a hose. What a waste of a dish, Nick thought, and he turned back to the bar at the thud of his beer hitting the countertop.

"That'll be two bucks even." The bartender pushed dirty blond hair out of his face. Nick rustled three singles out of his wallet, placed them on the bar, and the bartender nodded as the bills found the pocket of his torn jeans.

"Will you by any chance be showing the football game?"

"Is there a game on?" The man scratched at a chin that was begging for a few minutes with a razor.

"USC. I was hoping to watch, but I can go somewhere else."

"No, no," the bartender said. "That's what the dish is for. So long as they don't mind." He motioned to patrons on the opposite end.

Nick looked over at three older women facing the bar. They were all dressed the same and, according to their nametags, worked for the park. Each appeared close to social security, which they would undoubtedly squander in a dump like this. Only one responded to the inquiry and she didn't care so the bartender, whom Nick thought resembled a young Axl Rose, grabbed a remote control from next to a prehistoric cash register and changed the channel.

Nick thanked him, took his beer, and dug in for an afternoon that would change his life.

Forever.

CHAPTER TEN

"WHAT ARE *YOU* DOING here on a Saturday?" an assistant deputy asked, as Amado walked through the hallway with a cup of coffee.

"As long as criminals are working weekends, so am I," Amado answered in stride. "What about you?"

Deputy Chad Torkner was young and short, with a freckled face and cropped red hair. The man they used to call 'Dorkner' in grade school certainly didn't look like a lawman and probably never would. It took him twenty-seven years to earn respect from his peers, and it started virtually the moment his name graced a Utah state policeman's badge.

"Work's piling up." He followed Amado. "If our population keeps growing like this, there'll be enough crime to keep us busy round the clock."

Isn't that right, Amado thought, as they entered a large room filled with ten metallic desks, one of which belonged to Torkner. A door in the far left-hand corner led into Amado's closet-sized office. Sure he didn't have much space, but at least he didn't have to share it with nine other deputies. Amado shoved aside piles of paper and set his coffee on the L-shaped desk. He settled into a leather chair, slid over to the fax machine in the corner, and grabbed a stack of papers off the tray.

"This is what I *really* came in for," he said to Torkner, who was standing in the doorway.

Amado separated a few sheets, placing them on top of a pile he probably wouldn't get to for another few weeks. "It's the coroner's report on Henderson Taylor. Dr. Stevens called me this morning, said she was faxing it over."

"What's it say?"

"I haven't read it yet, but no surprises." Amado glanced at the document. "She already told me as much. Accidental BFT."

Blunt Force Trauma.

"Sounds as if she pegged it like we did," Torkner said.

"Pretty much."

"You came in just for that?"

Amado looked up and paused to consider the inquiry; the kid had a point.

"I guess I wanted one last look at the file before I close it. I usually do that."

"Don't you trust yourself?" Torkner shifted his weight against the door's frame.

"I feel like I owe it to the victim. I know Taylor's deceased but it's my responsibility to find out why. I guess I never really think of the vic as dead until I close the file."

"Is there something about this case that's troubling you?"

It took Amado a moment before he popped his head out of the report again. "Nothing major, I just wanted a look at the lividity analysis. That's the process through which the body's blood supply stops circulating after the heart has stopped beating. When that happens, the blood settles directly in accordance with gravity. So, for example, if the body is lying face down, the blood will settle in the stomach area."

Torkner nodded, and took a seat on a folding chair tightly stashed in the corner. "What then is troubling you?"

"It has to do with the direction the body was facing. His head was facing downriver as if he may have traveled with the flow of the water. I guess it looked a little too perfect to have been a random fall. Plus, the body was partially submerged, which could also support a theory that it had been dragged downriver. And if that was the case, maybe this wasn't an accident."

"Sounds farfetched."

"Perhaps, but ever since Donald Richardson pushed his wife off the canyon, I don't think we can treat any fall lightly. It seems a little too convenient to just say someone fell."

Torkner pursed his lips. "But we've got witnesses that saw Taylor up there and it's the last location we can place him. And then his body is found at the base, on the side of the Landing that he was viewing? It totally fits. And we know the water has swelled because of the monsoons, so that could explain the submersion. I mean, if a body falls a thousand feet, it could technically land in any number of positions, depending on where he was facing and how he fell, right?"

"I suppose."

"And we found his car. Were there any appearances of foul play?"

"Nothing suspicious with the car."

"So what else do we have?" Torkner asked.

"That's why the lividity seems odd. We found him on his back, so that's where the blood should have settled. And most of it did, but there was some discoloration on his side. Dr. Stevens thinks it was just bruising."

"Could she tell if it was pre or post-mortem?"

"I think it's almost always before death unless something happens immediately afterward while the blood is still flowing."

"And you think all of this might indicate that he was murdered?"

"It's something to think about."

NICK REFLECTED ON JUST how perfect the day had played out. Angel's Landing was phenomenal, the river soothing, beer refreshing, and USC was winning. For the first time in a while, Nick felt at ease.

The game was approaching halftime and Nick noticed that the bar had become silent. The play-by-play announcers weren't loud enough to drown out the constant moaning of the ancient air conditioner in the poolroom. Nick wondered what kind of toxic air the rusty unit was still producing, and given the looks of the place, he wouldn't have been surprised if the unit had been there longer than some of the area's rock formations.

A sharp sound pierced the silence and Nick jumped until he realized that it was just the phone behind the bar. The bartender reached under the counter and pulled out a cordless.

"Shack," he said. He listened for a moment as he ambled towards the other end of the bar, and then said, "Yeah, game's on … not yet … right here … OK, bye."

Nick finished his second beer as the announcers sent viewers to the studio for the halftime report. He turned to face the bar, contemplating whether to stay for the second half. His Trojans were up by a scant nine points; the game was close enough to warrant continued viewing. Halftime would be at least fifteen or twenty minutes, so Nick raised his arm for the bartender's attention. He would make his decision over another beer. Almost instantly, the bartender removed the empty bottle and replaced it with one that was sweating profusely. Nick took a sip, while glancing at a sign behind the bar: "WARNING: CAN GO FROM ZERO TO HORNY IN 2.5 BEERS."

Tires crunched against gravel and several moments later, the front door opened. A tall, muscular man, with day-old growth on his face, entered the bar wearing a greasy mechanic's uniform. The mechanic met eyes with the bartender and before he took a seat, a beer was waiting for him at end of the bar. Nick peered over his shoulder to see if halftime was over, but the studio commentators were still talking.

As the mechanic settled in, a muted silence descended again. The AC's compressor was working hard and each time it kicked on, Nick wondered if it would be its last revolution. He inhaled a sizable swig and stole a glance down the other end, where the bartender and the mechanic were drinking and laughing and looking his way. Nick began to feel uneasy. Yeah, they were looking at him, but what should he expect? They were regulars and he clearly wasn't. Nick checked out some of the other signs behind the bar, his favorite being: "WARNING: THE CONSUMPTION OF ALCOHOL MAY CAUSE YOU TO BECOME A PARENT."

Nick's legs began shaking while he waited for the second half to begin. Then, the door popped open and in walked a clean-cut guy wearing a white t-shirt, blue jeans, and a Utah Jazz hat. The man marched up to the bar, took a seat next to the mechanic and within seconds, his beer of choice was loitering before him. Nick's stomach began to churn; something didn't feel right. But he told himself to remain calm. After all, he was in some ancient dive bar not twenty minutes from the park. What kind of people did he expect to see? He took a deep breath and, beer in hand, did an about face. The second half was starting. As if waiting for halftime to end, the female park employees gathered their belongings, making more noise than they had the entire afternoon.

Several quiet minutes passed before the two remaining patrons looked at each other, then at the bartender, and nodded in unison. The mechanic stood and lit a cigarette, sauntered over to the window and gazed out in both directions, and then turned back and nodded. He locked the front door, closed the window blinds, and flipped the sign on the door to "CLOSED."

Then he went to the television and hit the power button.

CHAPTER ELEVEN

A PIT PUSHED ITS way through Nick's stomach.

"What's going on? You closing?"

As the mechanic turned towards Nick, the bartender reached under the counter and pulled out a piece of heavy rope. He wrapped both ends around each of his hands to shorten it, and tighten his grip. Nick was about to stand when his entire body was jolted backward as he felt a tight constriction of his neck, like a boa squeezing the life out of its prey. The bartender pulled the rope as tight as he could and Nick's face started turning blue. His arms flailed helplessly and he fell back against the bar, knocking over his stool. The bartender applied more force and Nick's eyes bulged, as he tried to get his hands between the rope and his neck. Nick was pinned back against the torn leather trim of the bar top and it felt like his throat was on fire. He was seconds away from suffocating when the mechanic landed a crushing right to his face. Nick absorbed the blow, and his squawks quickly turned to wheezy gasps for the air of life. Red-faced, he desperately dug for the rope when the mechanic landed the knockout punch.

"Let go, Clay." The mechanic examined his hand and rubbed his knuckles.

Clay loosened his grip and Nick freed himself, grabbed his throat with both hands, and fell to the floor. He was gasping incessantly and grimacing in pain, his body practically curled into a ball. Clay placed the rope on the bar top next to the handgun he'd taken out from under the counter.

"Hey Ethan, should I pull the car around?" the man in the t-shirt asked the mechanic.

"Do it Bennie, and wait for us out back," Ethan responded and tossed the keys.

"We'll just be a minute."

Bennie left through the back as Clay jumped over the bar like a hockey player scaling the boards for a quick line change.

"Give me the rope."

Clay handed Ethan the nylon cord, and Ethan stood with an evil grin while Nick winced in pain. Ethan waited several moments until Nick seemed to let up before stomping on his stomach. Nick took the hit but almost threw up, and as he rolled to his side in agony, Ethan kicked him back onto his stomach. Then, Ethan pulled both of Nick's arms behind his back.

"Help me secure him."

Clay grabbed one of Nick's arms while Ethan took the other, and they quickly tied his wrists together. Nick coughed several times and spit a mixture of phlegm and blood onto the floor. That's when Clay grabbed the gun off the counter and pointed it at Nick's head.

"Don't you spit your shit on my floor." Clay kicked Nick in the side.

"Please stop," Nick pleaded. "What do you want from me?"

Ethan pulled a mini recorder from his pocket and placed it on a table next to where Nick was lying. He pushed record.

"What's your name?" Ethan asked.

When Nick didn't answer, Ethan asked again, this time practically yelling at him. Nick refused to answer. Cars whizzed by on the highway, the drivers oblivious to the pain currently being inflicted inside.

"He just asked you what your name is." Clay kicked him again.

"My name is Nicholas Perrone."

"Where were you stayin'?"

When Nick didn't answer, Ethan said to Clay, "Looks like he doesn't want to cooperate. Maybe we should put him in the other room with your mountain lion?"

"Oh shit! A mountain lion?" Nick tried to pull free, but he was tied too tight. "OK, OK. I was camping in the park. I'll cooperate."

"You can start by speaking only when we tell you," Ethan instructed. He asked Nick a series of questions about his trip and Nick answered. Then, he bent on one knee and swiped Nick's wallet from his back pocket.

"Who's going to clean this mess?" Clay asked.

"You will," Ethan responded. He pulled the cash out of Nick's wallet, stuffed half in his own pocket and gave the rest to Clay. "It's very important to tip your bartender."

Ethan flipped through the rest of the wallet and stopped at a picture of Nick with a woman.

"She your wife?" Ethan asked. When Nick didn't answer, Ethan kicked him in the legs. Nick grunted in the affirmative and spit more blood onto the floor.

"Shit boy!" Clay grumbled. "Keep that damn slop to yourself." He leaned over the bar, grabbed a towel, and wiped Nick's fluids off the floor.

"Don't worry about that now," Ethan said.

"No, I got to. Otherwise, I might forget. Can't have blood on the floor when I re-open." Clay checked his watch, rushed to the window, lifted the blinds ever so slightly and glanced outside. "Let's wrap this up and get him to the house. Some of them cops usually stop by for a drink around now."

But Ethan was still focused on the picture. Then he tossed the wallet to Clay who was walking back from the window.

Clay studied the picture with a pouty smile on his face. "Nice piece," he said, with an accompanying groan. "She ain't with you on this trip, is she?"

An obscenity was on the tip of Nick's tongue, but he smartly held it back.

The beginning of "My Sharona" began blasting in the bar and Clay scrambled to see if a radio had accidentally turned on. But Ethan caught the source immediately.

Nick's pocket.

As the song began its second round, Ethan grabbed the cell.

The ring tone was Ina's favorite song and she had programmed Nick's phone to play it when she called. At first, Nick had objected; he hated the tune. But eventually, he gave in, figuring it would be easy to know when not to answer. But now, Nick regretted his attitude. What he wouldn't give to talk to her right then and there.

"I'll bet that's your bitch calling right now." Ethan held the phone up and read her name from the display before it went to voicemail. Then he tossed the phone onto the bar and flipped through Nick's wallet, pulling out his driver's license. "Her name is Ina and you both live in Phoenix."

"That ain't too far a drive," Clay chimed in. "Maybe when we done with him, we ought to pay her a visit. Looks like she's worth it."

"A woman like that deserves a real man."

"Fuck you!"

The guys just laughed as Bennie came running in from out back. "Car's running, what's taking so long?"

"Yeah," Clay said. "Let's get him outta here so I can re-open."

"Come on," Ethan said. "He never gets any business in this shithole. Besides, see the sign in the window? Says the bar's closed."

"But what if the sheriff ..." Bennie stopped mid-sentence.

Ethan winked at Clay. "The bar will re-open just as soon as Clay returns from church. Now go back to the car and wait."

"Come on Ethan, he's right," Clay said. "There's no point in dragging this out."

Ethan reached into Nick's pocket and grabbed his keys. Clay and Bennie lifted Nick off the floor and onto his feet, and led him out the back and into Ethan's truck. Clay helped Bennie load their wounded prisoner into the backseat, and affixed the seat belt. When they were done, Bennie drove off, and Clay walked around the side of the building to the storefront.

Ethan grabbed the mini recorder and pressed stop.

Then he left the bar.

TWO DEPUTIES EMERGED FROM the vehicle. But they stopped short when they saw the "CLOSED" sign on the window. With curious looks on their faces, they headed back to their car just as Clay turned the corner.

"Afternoon officers."

"You closed in the middle of a Saturday?" the driver asked.

"I was afraid you may have closed down. Is business that bad?"

"Course not." Clay smiled and grabbed his belt buckle, as he walked towards the front door. "Just needed a potty break. Why don't you guys come on in? First one's on me."

Clay held the door open for the law, and, as the officers took seats at the bar, he opened the blinds and flipped the sign back around. He peered out the window and looked both ways.

"Yeah, business is great."

INA WAS BEGINNING TO worry. She had tried Nick's cell throughout the day but each call had gone straight to voicemail. A wave of emotions flooded her brain; fear that something bad may have happened, anger that Wyatt had deserted Nick, and hope that there was a reasonable explanation for Nick's repeated failure to answer her calls. Nevertheless, she tried to keep herself calm, taking deep breaths and telling herself that Nick was hiking in the wilderness where he wouldn't have good coverage. And while there *was* some truth to it, she couldn't suppress her concern because she hadn't spoken with Nick for almost two days.

She decided to call the park.

She booted up her laptop, found the phone number and got a ranger on the line who identified himself as Martin Rugie. After explaining her concerns, Rugie told her rangers don't normally deliver messages for campers but, lucky for her, he was heading out to the campground anyway. He would make an exception just for her.

CHAPTER TWELVE

THERE'S NOTHING LIKE A short commute. Studies have shown the happiest people are those who drive fifteen minutes or less to work. Why waste time driving when there are so many better things to do with your life?

Ethan drove the Durango around the corner behind the bar and through an open dirt field that housed several abandoned backhoes. He maneuvered downhill and over a rusted pulley bridge spanning the Virgin River. Once across, the dirt-packed road curved to the left through a small community of houses, and Ethan followed it to the westernmost residence, a comfortable looking wood-framed home, tastefully painted in aqua blue. Behind it was a virtual postcard of glittering trees and red rock, and like the ocean, the land extended well beyond what the eye could see. But the real beauty of Ethan's house was that it faced the rest of the community so that when he pulled into the back, no one could see what he was doing.

Ethan parked Nick's Durango behind his own truck. Not bad, he thought; they'd transported Nick to the place he would spend the rest of his short life in less than three minutes. He looked back up the hill toward the bar.

Now there's a commute you can't beat.

Ethan flinched at another onset of "My Sharona," as Nick's cell danced inside a cup holder between the seats. *How could he choose such a horrible song? And why was it so damn loud?* Ethan would have tried to adjust the volume but he didn't want to risk inadvertently answering the call. Instead, he stared at the mobile until it stopped ringing. Then he hopped out and opened Bennie's door. Bennie was sitting in the front seat of Ethan's truck but was facing the back, watching Nick.

"Come on, let's take him inside," Ethan said.

Bennie slid out the front seat and they walked around to the other side. Bennie opened the back door and reached in to pull Nick out, instructing him to slide his feet to the ground while he held him by the arm. They marched Nick into the house through a backdoor that opened into the kitchen, quickly filed through the dining room, down a short hallway, and into a small bedroom where they threw Nick onto a wooden chair. Ethan held a gun at his head while Bennie undid the cord. Bennie methodically tied Nick's hands and legs to the chair, and then he and Ethan left the room without a sound.

ETHAN AND BENNIE ENTERED the kitchen and Ethan placed his gun on the counter. "Where's the Durango *you* were supposed to bring?"

Bennie pressed hard on his temples and rubbed his forehead. He'd been dreading this moment. "It broke down." He paused. "All the arrangements were, you know, done. I got the car and everything, but it just didn't make it."

"Why didn't you tell me before we kidnapped this asshole?"

"Because ... when? I thought it would still work out but the car died on me just as I fired it up. It stalled out and I couldn't get it running again."

Bennie pushed out a long deep breath. Talking to Ethan was like being cross-examined by a ruthless shark, when your own attorney hasn't prepared you. *Isn't it true Bennie that you fucked up and I should just pop one of these bullets in your freakin' skull?* That the gun was within Ethan's reach made Bennie all the more uneasy. A hot tickle of sweat launched its way down his chest and then, much like a shooting star, it just faded.

"Why didn't you call me on the way over here, or even mention it when you got to the bar?"

Why *didn't* he call or say something to Ethan before they went ahead with it? Bennie decided not to argue with his hotheaded co-conspirator and as he'd been doing quite often lately, he threw himself at the mercy of the Court. "I'm sorry, man, OK? I didn't call because I didn't think it mattered. I figured we'd still go through with it, because the opportunity to take him had already presented itself."

Ethan said nothing, and the silence became so unbearable that Bennie continued talking. "You're right. I should have said something when I got to the bar. But I was frazzled, nervous. And when I sat down with the beer before we went for it, I kind of forgot to mention it. The thing just stalled on me. Can't you take a look at it?"

"I don't have time for this."

"If it's totaled, I can find another one."

"No, it'll take too long. Once they realize this guy's missing, the first thing they'll look for is his car and if they don't find it, they'll have questions, not answers. And we *want* them to have answers."

Ethan walked past Bennie and out of the kitchen, while Bennie stood there, his eyes peeled to the gun on the counter. A voice in his head told him to do it: take the gun and shoot the bastard once and for all. Then he could free himself. Nick too. In a computer-like blur, his mind rushed through all the possibilities. If he did it, he'd live the rest of his life fearing that they'd find him, and while he hated Ethan and the things they were doing, the truth was that the authorities had no idea what was going on. Their execution was so perfect that Bennie never worried about the cops.

He worried about Ethan.

Ethan came back into the kitchen, blazed past Bennie and said, "Did you at least bring the plates?"

"They're in the car."

"Paperwork? In case I get pulled over on my way back?"

Bennie nodded in the affirmative.

Ethan slammed his toolbox on the kitchen table "Fine, tow it to the shop and I'll do the swap. I'll also see if we can get the other one running again." He exhaled loudly, then grabbed the gun and slid it inside his waist. "I hate having to explain this shit."

Ethan picked up the phone and dialed, and when the familiar voice answered, he said, "We got him, but we've got a problem."

CHAPTER THIRTEEN

THE HOUSE FELT DESERTED, like the streets in Amish country late in the evening. Darkness had descended long ago, and it felt to Nick like it was well past midnight. But he couldn't be sure because his abductors had taken his watch and left him with only his imagination to tell time, or at least pass it.

The room was small, basic, and bare. A holding cell. The walls were white, although it was clear they hadn't been painted in a long time. And there was nothing on them to look at. No paintings of James Dean in a restaurant, famous photos of mountains and canyons, or even a poster of an athlete humiliating another. The room's only window faced the front of the house and was covered by thick wooden horizontal blinds that were closed. There were twin beds against the east and western walls, and between them, against the northernmost wall, was a wooden nightstand that looked like it could have been swiped from any hotel room in America. And it smelled like a bad hotel room. The carpet was in desperate need of a thorough cleaning, but there was no way they would ever bring someone in to clean their house of crime.

Nick wouldn't be using either of the beds as he was securely fastened to a chair between them, facing the door and with his back to the nightstand. The door was closed but he couldn't remember if they had locked it.

What do they want? They had taken his wallet, but he only had a couple hundred bucks and some credit cards. *Would there be a ransom demand*? So far, they hadn't said anything. For what seemed like hours,

Nick had indulged the body's natural hostage impulse, repeatedly pulling his arms and legs to try and free himself. But it didn't work because the rope was too tight and after a while, he decided to stop, to avoid expending the energy. Could he figure a way out? *What would MacGyver have done?* All those times he had imagined himself in peril —nights in his bedroom when he thought he heard a noise—he could always, in his mind, construct a way out. A simple plan that could be formed in seconds: lock the door, grab his machete, and stand next to the door waiting to pounce on the intruder, while also dialing for help. Sometimes he thought of grabbing his car's remote and pressing the panic button so that the intruder would be scared away by his piercing car alarm. On so many occasions, these and other ideas would rush through his mind like opening a soda bottle after shaking it up. But now that Nick actually found himself in a life and death situation, he couldn't think of anything constructive.

Of course, he didn't have his machete, phone, car keys, or even a door to lock. He didn't have the use of his hands or feet. All Nick had was his mind, the same faculty with which he'd made an excellent living outwitting others.

But it was now drawing a blank.

Nick shook himself in an effort to free his hands. But he didn't give it all his might, worried that if he made too much noise, he might invite another painful visit from his captors. There was no give, and when he tried pulling his legs, he achieved the same result. Rope burn. That's when he decided to try contorting his torso and while it got him no closer to freedom, it did provide a glimmer of hope. Because he felt something move around in his left pocket.

His knife.

The one he had used to cut the rope and secure his tent.

Nick recalled slipping the knife into his pocket when the campground host had stopped to introduce himself. He closed his eyes and drew a deep, optimistic breath. Maybe he could escape and survive this ordeal after all.

But hope returned to despair when Nick realized the virtual impossibility of retrieving the knife. With his arms and legs tightly bound, how could he get to it? His mind raced through every possibility but each required a free hand, leg, or both. That's when Nick realized the only way he could do this. He would have to flip himself over, such that the knife would slip out of his pocket and into his waiting hand. Yes it was a long shot, but it was all he could think of.

Nick struggled to turn and assess the amount of space he had behind him. It wasn't easy but he determined that if he tipped the chair directly backwards, he would hit the nightstand. His only option was to drag the chair forward and create himself enough space to fall backwards and land on the carpet. After filling his lungs with air, Nick tried to stand and take the chair on his back, and inch himself forward. But it was too heavy. So, after a short breather, Nick used his weight to drag the chair forward along the carpet and shift it closer to the bed on his right. Several attempts drew him closer and he strained his neck looking back to see if he had now created enough space. He hadn't. He needed at least another foot for a clear landing.

For the next half hour, Nick continued the awkward gyrations as he managed to slowly inch himself and the chair forward. Sweat fell from his brow and Nick winced as it entered one of the wounds he had sustained in the bar. He desperately wanted to sooth it and impulsively tried to pull his hands up, but was quickly reminded that he couldn't. He had no choice but to bear the pain. He was agonizingly close to his destination.

Next, he willed himself for energy and pushed off to get the left side of the chair off the ground, with the right side leaning against the bed. He prayed for a silent landing and got it; the friction from the carpet kept noise to a minimum. Once against the bed, Nick braced himself as he forced the chair to begin its slide to the floor. His main concern was ensuring that his right shoulder, and not his head, would absorb the impact once he hit the carpet. And as the right leg slid out farther and farther, the entire chair began moving faster and within seconds, Nick hit the floor with a thud. He froze momentarily, trying to determine if anyone heard him. He had definitely made some noise but probably not enough to wake someone out of a deep sleep. He listened for a minute or two but all he could hear was the constant thud of his heart nearly beating out of his chest. He had to get the knife.

Pain shot through his right shoulder as he lay on his right side. To get the knife, he had to turn himself onto his back. But he was out of energy. So, Nick decided to take a breather as he surveyed the area to see how much room he had to re-position himself. And then he realized something else; he was right up against the nightstand.

Nick pulled himself closer, opened his mouth, locked his teeth around the knob for the top drawer, and pulled. When it opened, he lifted his head to see inside but to his dismay, there was just a phone book, a pad, and what looked like a dirty camping cup. He massaged his teeth with his tongue and quietly shoved the drawer closed with his face.

He pulled open the lower drawer with his teeth, peered in, and became distressed when he saw what was inside. The drawer was filled with wallets, credit cards, driver's licenses, and other forms of identification. Nick strained for a view, and a California license at the top of the pile immediately caught his eye. He stared at the smiling face, read the name. Until that point, Nick held out hope that his captors were probably just after money and that he would eventually regain his freedom through some form of compensation. But as he read the name off the license, a huge lump caught in his throat. A stark realization that they weren't seeking money, it was his life they were after. For he recognized the name of the California resident who had been previously held captive in this very location.

And was never heard from again.

CHAPTER FOURTEEN

THE MINUTES TICKED AWAY as Nick lay helplessly tied to the fallen chair. He had carefully restored the bottom drawer using his face, after accepting the reality that there was no way he could reach inside. Physically beaten and mentally exhausted, Nick pulled at the rope, somehow hoping that perhaps it had loosened when he'd flipped the chair over. But it hadn't, and after seeing what they kept inside the nightstand, Nick knew that he had to do something.

He had to retrieve the knife.

But how?

He was lying on his side, clamped to the chair. Just getting to that position had physically drained him, and the chair on his back was feeling heavier by the moment. The position Nick was in left him no leverage and a pain-filled scowl occupied his wry face. Having absorbed the weight of his entire body, Nick's right arm and shoulder were screaming in agony. He took a few deep breaths with loud exhales, trying to fight his mind's insistence to shut his body down. Then, using his upper body, Nick tried heaving himself to the left. But it didn't work. Without skipping a beat, he tried again, and again, and kept going in an effort to gain momentum and swing himself to the left. And as he picked up speed, the floor began singing along.

Despite the creaky ground, Nick pushed harder, determined to give it every ounce of energy he had left. Finally, he felt the right side of the chair dig into the carpet and catapult him over and onto his back, before the chair crashed to the floor. As it was happening, Nick stilled his head in an effort to avoid a direct hit. He wasn't successful but at least there was carpeting to soften the blow. He grimaced upon impact; sweat poured uncontrollably down his battered face.

Nick had managed to get himself flat on his back, but his plan hadn't worked. The knife was still in his pocket. Disconsolate and drained, Nick tried wriggling free, but the ropes felt stronger than ever. He had fought to position himself for a possible escape but now he had no idea how to coax the knife out. Although, a bigger problem was announcing its presence, as Nick's body was slowly proving no match for the exertion. His eyes flickered shut and he struggled mightily to keep them open. Sleep was working feverishly to overtake him and Nick was quickly losing the battle.

Nick shifted his hips but nothing happened, and he was starting to lose his patience. He gyrated his midsection relentlessly until he realized that he was pushing too hard for it to work. He had to calm himself. Fighting his body's insistence on shutting down, Nick shifted his hips again but this time, he did so slowly and carefully and finally felt some movement in his pocket. He struggled through the next few minutes, trying various movements until he found the right combination: a movement of hips with some shifting of his knees. The knife dove out of his pocket and onto the carpet, just inches from his hand. A sudden calmness enveloped his heart as he inched towards the knife and wrapped his hand around it.

Lying on his back, Nick looked at the knife and realized that a significant obstacle still remained. How would he open the blade? "You can do this," he grumbled. Nick closed his hand around the knife, as a wave of exhaustion poured through his body. He decided to close his eyes momentarily, just enough for a resurgence of energy. But then the unthinkable happened.

He dozed off.

CHAPTER FIFTEEN

Sunday

ANOTHER PLANETARIUM-LIKE EVENING dissipated, and the skyline was now bruised, black and blue. Within the hour, nature would commence its changing of the guard when the crickets give way to the park's warblers. It was shaping up to be a songful morning. After waiting at the windy confines of Canyon Junction for nearly fifteen minutes, Clay hesitantly boarded the morning's first shuttle. Twenty minutes later, he got off at the Weeping Rock trailhead and began the ascent, as he glimpsed a hint of morning light from the east. Clay hiked as fast as his body would allow at such an early hour. His legs felt sore and heavy, and he cussed himself for not stretching while waiting for the shuttle. The air still had a leftover chill from the previous evening, but was pleasant nonetheless. The canyon was quiet, but Clay's edginess didn't allow him to enjoy it.

This was a business trip.

When he reached the spot they had chosen, Clay stopped and put his hands on his knees to catch his breath. He looked like a college co-ed about to vomit at a frat party. A few breaths later, Clay checked his watch and glanced in each direction. Convinced he was alone, Clay set down his pack, pulled out a bottle of water, and took a sip. Then he replaced the water, grabbed his binoculars, and checked out a water hole in a slot more than a thousand feet below. Recent rains had increased the water level, although he couldn't tell how deep it was due to its murky green color. He placed the strap around his neck and let the binoculars rest against his chest. Then, Clay did something rarely seen on hiking trails in America: he lit a cigarette. He wouldn't normally do that, but he had brought them on this particular occasion to ease his flared nerves.

After an anxiety-riddled fifteen minutes, Clay removed a pair of gloves from his pack and put them on, took Nick's USC baseball cap off his head, and placed it on the ground. Next, he pulled a small backpack from inside his own pack, removed a cell phone, and zipped the smaller pack shut. He slipped the phone into his pocket and checked his watch again; it was still too early, so he lit another cigarette. The plan was to wait until seven a.m., unless he saw other hikers starting up the trail earlier. Just then, Clay heard the squeal of the next shuttle stopping below, and he fixed the binoculars on several hikers piling out of the bus.

Showtime.

Clay took the smaller pack—Nick's pack—in his hand, stepped to the edge of the trail, pulled back, and let it go underhanded like a pitcher in a softball game. The pack smacked against the granite wall and slid down about eight hundred feet. It hit the thorny edge of a prickly pear cactus and, just as they had hoped, came to rest a couple hundred feet above the slot. Clay smiled and shook his head, proud of his work. He stole a glance down the trail and caught a few hikers examining a map at the trailhead. He still had a few minutes. Clay took out Nick's cell and the mini-recorder on which Ethan had dubbed the recording. Then he dialed three numbers.

911.

"WHAT THE HELL?" ETHAN said.

Nick jumped at the sight of Ethan standing in the doorway. His eyes blinked rapidly and in addition to pain and soreness, he had that dreaded feeling of being awakened well before he wanted. Hours ago, he had closed his eyes just for a moment, but it wasn't supposed to be for the rest of the night. Panic gripped him as he realized he was holding the knife in his right hand. After all that work to retrieve it, he had fallen asleep before he could even try to cut himself free.

"What the fuck's goin' on?" Ethan kicked one of the chair legs hanging in the air.

Nick braced for an assault. "I couldn't sleep sitting up." He clenched both hands into fists so as not to draw attention to the hand holding the knife.

"Bullshit! What went on here last night?"

A stern look descended on Nick's face as he locked eyes with Ethan's.

"I just told you." Nick decided to supplement his response. "You beat the crap out of me yesterday and then tied me up to this thing. I was exhausted and, after hours of trying, I just couldn't fall asleep."

It was a good choice, the right choice. Ethan stood over Nick, staring him down. Nick could see Ethan's mind working, trying to poke holes in Nick's story. Ethan was looking around the room. He checked the bindings on Nick's hands and feet, and then yelled down the hallway. "Hey Bennie, get in here and help me lift this asshole."

Ethan went behind Nick and tried to lift the back of the chair, but it was too heavy. He waited a couple of seconds and when Bennie didn't show up, Ethan walked around Nick's left side. Nick followed him closely with his eyes, aware that he couldn't hide the knife much longer. Nick opened his left hand so that Ethan wouldn't see it closed and think that he was holding something.

A rush of fear saturated Nick's body. His captors hadn't disclosed what they had planned, but having seen the cards in the nightstand, Nick now had a pretty good idea. The knife was his only chance for survival and it was clenched firmly in his right hand. But now Ethan was circling him like a vulture, pulling at the knots and making sure nothing was out of order. Nick would have to act fast, his life depended on it. As Ethan made his way to the right side of the chair, a grunt from the hallway indicated that Bennie was on his way. Ethan moved to the door and told him to hurry up.

This was it. Nick knew he had to do something to hide the knife but nothing came to mind. Panic set in. He couldn't slide the knife into his pocket because he couldn't reach. He couldn't continue to hold it because Ethan was checking everything. Soon he'd reach Nick's right hand and if he discovered there was something in it, Nick was done. And if Nick left the knife on the floor, they would surely see it when they lifted him back up.

As Bennie entered the room, Nick carefully slid the knife towards his fingers, all the while fixing his eyes on Ethan. *Don't draw attention to the hand*, he told himself.

"Let me check to make sure his ankle is secure," Ethan said, as he bent and pulled at Nick's right ankle. The rope was airtight; there was no give.

Nick drew in as much oxygen as his depleted body would accept and, just as Ethan stood, heaved and forced a thunderous cough. Ethan jumped back and reached for the pistol resting in his waistband.

"Give me a warning next time," Ethan said. "*Don't* scare the shit out of me like that again or you'll pay."

Nick coughed a few more times for effect. "Sorry, didn't know it was coming."

Ethan motioned for Bennie. "Come help me lift him back up. I don't have all day." Ethan and Bennie stepped behind Nick and began lifting him. Both moaned as, like the tray table on an airplane, they restored Nick to his upright position.

"That's a new one," Bennie remarked. "What'd you do that for?"

"So he could sleep," Ethan interjected. "You believe that?"

"Sure. I don't think I could sleep sitting up."

"Whatever." Ethan turned to Nick. "Nice and smooth, but whatever you were trying obviously didn't work." He locked eyes with Nick. "Not that you'll be alive much longer but try that again, and you'll lose whatever precious moments remain."

They left the room.

Nick rubbed his sweaty right hand against the side of the chair, and glanced at the carpeted floor. It was empty. They had missed it. His cough was the perfect diversion; he'd used it to fling the knife under the bed. Only now, he hoped he didn't throw it too far because after all that work, he was back to square one.

ETHAN PARKED THE DURANGO behind the bar and walked around to the front. The sign raced back and forth as he opened the door in a rush. All three window signs read "CLOSED" but The Shack's front door was unlocked anyway. Clay was standing behind the bar reading the local paper and eating a nutritious breakfast: Twizzlers, a snack-sized bag of potato chips, and a cold beer to wash it down. The bar was stocked with junk food, but as he watched Clay devour some chips, Ethan realized that he had never seen anyone else eat any of it.

"Want some chips or somethin'?" Clay asked, without looking up from the paper.

"Maybe one for the road." Ethan walked to the corner and snatched a bag of barbeque flavor. "So, how'd it go?"

Clay looked up. "Just as we planned. Oh, and here." He pulled Nick's phone out of his pocket and handed it to Ethan.

Ethan frowned. "I thought you were gonna toss this with the rest of his stuff."

"That's not what we said."

"Yes it is."

An empty look filled Clay's face.

"You know what? Forget it. It doesn't matter anymore. The replacement car Bennie got is junk and he says it'll take three to four days to get another one. So, we're gonna have to improvise on this one and maybe having the phone might actually help."

Clay took a drink and held up the bottle. "You want?"

"Too early." Ethan looked at his watch; it was almost eight thirty. "I gotta run. Listen, I'm taking his car in now and I'll be back in a few hours. Make sure you guys are ready to go when I get back."

"I'll check in with Bennie to make sure he knows."

"I already told him. Just make sure you're ready on time. My schedule is tight. Can you prepare the …"

Clay cut him off, smirking. "Don't worry, I'll have the guns in the truck."

Ethan flashed his own devilish smile. "Good. I can't wait."

CHAPTER SIXTEEN

INA LEFT FOR TUCSON early Sunday morning. She stopped off in Tempe, a college town just outside Phoenix, to pick up her assistant, and then hit I-10 for the ninety-mile drive.

"How are we doing on set up?" Ina asked.

Wanda Sorensen removed a pad from a wild green purse she had placed on the floor. The spunky redhead yawned and fixed her eyes on the notes she had made for the big event. An occasional freckle dusted her nose and upper cheeks and blended perfectly with her long, untamed hair. Wanda was a recent graduate of Arizona State, a school known for its parties and attractive women, and from the looks of it, she represented her school well.

"OK," Wanda began. "I've got the pre-con set for this afternoon at 3:30. We'll do the BEO then."

Ina and Wanda were hosting a retreat for a large investment-banking firm from back east. It was planned as a desert-induced morale boost, a five-day weekend to golf, hike, swim, massage, spa, or tour the Southwest. If the bankers were lucky, the only snakes they'd encounter would be Arizona's rattlers, a whole lot better than the ones they dealt with on Wall Street.

The 'pre-con' was a pre-conference meeting in which they would discuss the Banquet Event Order. There, the ladies would submit the itineraries, menus, and planned activities to the hotel, and commit to a final guest count. The first wave of bankers was scheduled to arrive on Wednesday.

"What about the gift bags?" Ina asked.

"I had everything delivered yesterday. I figured you and I could put them together tonight or tomorrow. Maybe we could even get the hotel staff to help."

Ina always enjoyed shopping for gift bags and putting them together. But lately, she routinely fell prey to afternoon exhaustion mixed with a dose of Braxton-Hicks contractions. She wondered how much energy she'd have to run what would likely be her last event before the baby. Ina had decided not to say anything just yet, but if need be, she was prepared to pass the baton to her ambitious protégé.

"What?" Ina looked over and caught Wanda staring.

"Nothing, I just can't believe you are *so* pregnant."

"I know."

"Have you been, like, tired a lot?"

"I didn't sleep much last night. I'm concerned about Nick. Did I tell you he went camping?"

"You may have mentioned it."

"I tried him a bunch of times yesterday but he didn't answer. I was worried so it took me some time before I could finally doze off."

"I'm sure he's fine. When was the last time you spoke to him?"

Ina thought for a moment as they flew by hordes of saguaro cacti, which seemed to be waving at them. "Two days ago?"

"You haven't been speaking every day?" Wanda asked, and Ina shook her head.

"Then I wouldn't worry. I mean, if he's camping, how is he charging his cell? His battery's probably dead."

"Maybe."

"I'm sure that's the explanation," Wanda said. "Did you try him this morning?"

"I was gonna call after we get settled in."

They continued in silence for a few moments until Ina abruptly broke it.

"Oh man!" She grabbed her stomach with her right hand, and drew quick shallow breaths. Wanda reached to steady the wheel.

"Are you OK? Maybe I should drive."

Ina waved her off the wheel and settled into slower and deeper breaths. "Fine, I was just … startled is all." She rubbed her hand along her forehead, exuding a sound of relief. "I didn't see that bump in the road; it came out of nowhere. Here's a rest area. Maybe we'll stop and … rest."

Wanda acquiesced and they exited the freeway. As soon as they stopped, Wanda ran to the ladies room and Ina said she would join her in a moment. She wanted to try Nick first. She calmly dialed and held the phone to her ear. She sighed when, after five rings, Nick's voice instructed her to leave a message. She pushed the red "stop" button and immediately hit the green "send" button twice. Same result. Trying to stay calm, she repeated the steps, this time getting Nick's voicemail before the phone even rang.

She hung up again as a jolt of anxiety shot through her chest.

Ina told herself not to lose it; there was probably a good explanation. The battery, or maybe Nick was hiking in an area with no service. But a feeling in her gut indicated something was wrong. She decided to try again, this time dialing each digit as if she had somehow misdialed the first few times. However superstitious it was, Ina dialed the entire number but after five rings, she reached voicemail again.

Her patience wearing thin, Ina pounded the keys one last time and placed the phone to her ear. She listened to each ring intently.

The first went by without an answer.

The second too.

The third began but was interrupted by a click.

An answer!

But it wasn't Nick.

ETHAN DROVE INTO SPRINGDALE for gas and a cup of coffee, and then set out for his garage in the town of Hurricane. While Clay was a close friend, he wasn't the sharpest of conspirators, so Ethan was relieved that everything had pretty much gone as planned. Their dominos were falling steadily into place, and he was on his way to forge the paperwork and give Nick's car a new identity. A sudden screech startled Ethan just as he was taking a sip of coffee, causing him to swerve. He narrowly missed spilling and burning himself, as the beginning of "My Sharona" began.

He looked at the phone and saw Ina's name on the display, but after a couple of rounds, the phone went quiet. Less than a minute later, it began again. Ethan grabbed the phone, contemplating what to do. But before he could think of anything, it stopped so he put it back down.

Ethan was sipping his coffee when, seconds later, the phone rang for a third time. The noise jolted him and he spilled hot coffee in his lap. "That is one persistent chick."

Ethan grabbed the phone and held it to his mouth, but he didn't press a button. "Hi, you have reached the voicemail of Nicholas whatever," he said, gritting his teeth. "I'm sorry he can't take your call right now, he's about to be shot in the head and left for dead. Stop calling bitch, and don't leave a message. He won't be returning calls. EVER AGAIN!"

It didn't take long for the song to stop but Ethan didn't put the phone down because he knew another call was coming. He wouldn't let her surprise him again. And he was right. Seconds later, the phone started up and this time, Ethan had heard enough. He pulled to the shoulder of the highway and brought the Durango to a stop. Then, he depressed a button on the door and the passenger side window calmly slid out of view. He smiled as he pressed the "send" button on the phone, and with a fierce gale permeating the car, Ethan leaned forward.

He threw Nick's phone into the wilderness.

WANDA RETURNED FROM THE restroom with a jump in her step. Planning events was fun but she would never admit that it wasn't the *job* she looked forward to; it was the chance to meet a rich businessman at one of the events. And she'd brought with her all the necessary accoutrements to reel one in, as she had a feeling this was the weekend it would happen.

She opened the door to Ina's stunned gaze. "Are you OK?"

Ina removed the phone from her ear and held it out. "I called Nick and …" Her voice began to crack. "Listen to this."

Wanda took the phone and held it to her ear. "All I hear is static." She turned to Ina and furrowed her brow. "That's odd." She listened some more. "It almost sounds like a …"

Ina completed her sentence. "Like a highway."

CHAPTER SEVENTEEN

IT WAS TIME.

Clay and Bennie entered the room, and Clay pointed a gun at Nick's head. Without saying a word, Bennie freed Nick's wrists from the chair but immediately tied them together in front of his chest. Next, Bennie untied Nick's ankles, pulled him out of the chair, and led Nick through the house. Clay followed and, when they reached the backyard, Clay and Bennie shoved Nick into the backseat of Ethan's Honda Ridgeline.

"Where are we going?" Nick's eyelids began to flutter.

Clay looked at his watch. "Where's Ethan already?"

"Should be here any minute," Bennie replied. He took an anxious breath. "He called and said he was on his way. Everything needs to be packed and ready because he's pressed for time."

Moments later, Ethan pulled up, shut the engine, and jumped into the driver's seat of the truck. Bennie was waiting in the front passenger seat, Nick was in the back directly behind Ethan, and Clay sat next to Nick watching him like a hawk. Ethan started the truck as Clay tossed a half-smoked cigarette to the ground and closed his door. They quickly made their way through the little housing community and up to Route 9 towards St. George, a steady cloud of dust followed them to the highway. And the car was awfully quiet. Butterflies roamed, nerves frayed, and insides crawled, but the three criminals managed to wear their game faces well. It was like walking through the tunnel before the Super Bowl. No matter how many times they'd done it, the stress of the situation always presented itself. The magnitude of taking a man's life naturally demanded quiet contemplation; no one had anything to say.

Ethan was practically driving on autopilot when a sudden blip jolted him. He shot a glance at the rearview. "Oh *shit!*"

Sirens. Flashing lights. The works.

Bennie nearly shot out of his seat when he turned and saw the policeman behind them, and began a feverish search for his firearm. Clay reached for his handgun and box of bullets on the floor, ejected the magazine and began filling it with fresh ammunition. If all three had a common criminal heartbeat, it was racing wildly.

Ethan put up his hand. "Everybody stay cool, OK? I'm going to slowly pull over and see what he wants."

Bennie couldn't help envisioning the end of this enterprise into which he'd been roped. Or maybe it would be the end of an innocent and unknowing cop who had no idea who and what he was about to approach. They were about to be pulled over with their beaten prisoner sitting right here in the truck; nothing good could possibly come out of this. Simple, flawless, perfectly executed plans, of which Bennie had wanted no part, were about to collapse due to of all things, inattentive driving. Ironically, it was the one thing over which they had complete control. And, they were just minutes away from their destination.

Ethan slowed the truck, maneuvered it onto the shoulder, and came to a complete stop, as the officer cut his siren and stopped his vehicle behind theirs.

Ethan motioned to the front dashboard. "Hand me the what's-it-called from the glove box."

Bennie opened the compartment, pulled out a loaded Sig Sauer 9mm, and handed it to Ethan.

"Not the gun!" Ethan stole another glance through the rearview but the cop had yet to exit his vehicle. "The license and registration."

Clay leaned over the front seat. "What the hell do we do with this guy?"

"What do you mean?" Bennie responded. "We can't just dump him on the side of the road, there's a cop behind us. We're getting a ticket." He paused. "And we'll be lucky if that's all we get."

"He's still sitting in the car," Ethan said. "When he approaches, do you think he'll be able to see that his hands are tied?"

"I don't know, maybe," Clay said. "But if he gets a look at his face he's going to start asking questions and ... I think it's too damn risky to keep him tied like this."

"You're right, undo it." Ethan turned to Nick and said, "One word, and you *and* the cop are dead motherfuckers. You hear?"

"Yeah," Nick said feebly, while Clay struggled to undo the knot.

"Hurry up!" Ethan bellowed, but Clay was still struggling. "He's gettin' out of his car."

"Shit. I can't get the thing loose. We tied it too tight. You got a knife?"

"There's one in the glove box." There was no time to ask Bennie for it, so Ethan leaned over and pulled out a switchblade.

Clay looked behind him. "Give it to me."

Bennie watched as Ethan passed Clay the knife. The cop slammed his door shut. Clay struggled to open the knife. Footsteps were coming up behind the truck. Clay was furiously cutting at the rope. Footsteps were growing closer. Clay was slicing at the rope as hard as he could. The cop walked past Nick's window. Clay was still pulling. Bennie sighed. *Thank God for tinted windows.* Ethan grabbed his gun. There was a poke on Ethan's window.

Bennie watched Ethan decide.

The gun or the window?

That's when Clay announced that he had broken the rope free. He tossed it to the floor next to his feet, and kicked it under the seat. Nick rubbed his wrists as Clay grumbled.

"Better watch yourself."

CHAPTER EIGHTEEN

THE COP LOOKED TOO young to be a policeman. His boyish face was topped off by short blond hair set firmly inside a wide-brimmed patrolman's hat. He walked with both thumbs inside his waistband and his hands grasping his belt, as if trying to hold up his pants. When he reached the truck, he clutched his patrolman's stick in his right hand and tapped on the tinted window.

"Nobody says anything," Ethan instructed. "I'll do the talking."

Ethan placed his handgun in a map holder on the inside of the driver's side door. Then he pressed the button and the window slid down less than halfway.

"Hello officer."

The cop motioned for Ethan to lower the window further. "Good afternoon fellas."

"Is there a problem?"

"Not yet. Know how fast you were going?"

"Not the exact number, but I think it was close to the limit. Why, was I driving too fast?"

"Yup. License and registration please."

The conversation was curt, the tension palpable. Either the cop was in a shitty mood, or he was determined to exercise his authority over a bunch of guys his age. Ethan couldn't help but think that if he had a nice pair of breasts, he would've already been back on the road.

"Sure." Ethan gave Bennie a look of reassurance as Bennie handed him the paperwork. Ethan passed it through the window as his pulse quickened. He was having difficulty suppressing a strong impulse to grab his gun and shoot.

The cop looked at the license, while Ethan stared at the tag on his shirt and made a mental note. The pig's name was William Sloan.

"This your current address?"

"Yes, sir," Ethan lied.

"The limit out *here* is 55, but I clocked you boys at 58 back in town where the limit's only 30. You almost doubled it."

"I must not have realized that we even went through a town. I apologize, Officer."

"Yeah, I get that. There isn't much of a town there, that's for damn sure." With his index finger, he lifted his hat. "Where are you boys off to in the middle of the day?"

"We're on our way back to St. George. Came out to spend some time in the park."

Just then, Nick let out a loud cough that quickly drew Sloan's attention. He peeked into the back. "What the hell happened to your face, boy?"

"Um ... I, uh ... a brawl. In a bar. I was in a barroom brawl," Nick said.

"I imagine that ought to be enough to keep *you* off the whiskey for a bit. You boys sit tight now. I'll be back in a few."

THIS WAS THE BREAK Nick so desperately needed. At least that's what he had thought when he realized they were being pulled over. Elation. And it was clear from his captors' reactions that they had never made such a serious error. Only Ethan, clearly their leader, was able to keep it together. But Nick knew this was his chance and he had to do something to gain the officer's attention.

But what?

As soon as they pulled over, Nick saw that all of them had guns and seemed anxious to use them. Surely, the officer had no idea he could be walking into a massive barrage. *Should I scream for help*? He couldn't. Clay would shoot him and Ethan would ambush the officer; they'd both end up dead. And there was so much he wanted to tell the cop but he couldn't. Because as Nick raced through his options, reality slowly settled in: he and the cop were outnumbered. One misstep and the poor unsuspecting officer would never know what hit him. What if he had a family waiting at home? *I can't ruin two families in one shot.* It was bad enough that Nick's would be wrecked before it started. Nick was already in this mess, but he couldn't be responsible for someone else's death, even someone whose job was to protect and help others.

So, here he was with his best and perhaps last opportunity to make a move, and he couldn't figure out what to do. Every idea led to a dead-end.

Literally.

The cop approached the vehicle and Nick watched Ethan slide the window down. He felt a glimmer of hope when the officer asked Ethan to roll the window further. And as he listened to their conversation, he knew he had to somehow gain the officer's attention. If he just sat there and let the officer write a ticket and leave, it would be like signing his own death certificate. So, Nick decided to wait for the right time. He inched himself slightly to the left to open a better angle of view for the officer, and then forced as loud a cough as he could muster. And it worked. The officer caught sight of his face and immediately asked what happened to him.

This was it. Do or die.

Nick wasn't sure what to say; he hadn't planned it in advance. But that's when he felt something press hard against his side. Nick hadn't noticed but Clay had gotten right up next to him and was pressing his gun into Nick's ribs. The word "help" was on the tip of Nick's tongue, but he stuttered and told the cop that he had been in a bar fight. And as soon as he said it, the pain in his side was replaced by an explosion in his stomach. The stark realization that his life could very well be over.

He was too good an actor to help himself.

It looked like the cop had bought it.

AS SOON AS SLOAN left, Ethan rolled the window back up. Clay turned and watched the officer walk slowly back to his vehicle and when he was comfortable that Sloan wasn't looking, he turned to Nick. "What the hell do you think you're doing?"

Nick was flexing his wrists and pressing his fingers along the door panel. He had once seen a television show in which a victim had wisely left her fingerprints all over the car, making it easy for detectives to later identify her kidnappers. Nick's hands were dirty and clammy, perfect for leaving clean prints. Nick yawned, stretching both hands in the air and in one swift motion, ripped a few strands of hair and dropped them on the floor. If he left some clues, forensic technicians would hopefully do the rest. Whether he survived this ordeal or not, his captors would face justice eventually.

"I'm just working my wrists, OK? They've been tied up for almost a full day."

"I'm not talking about *now* asshole. I mean your little move there to get the pig's attention." Keeping it low, Clay waved the gun at him. "I'm watching you. Closely. Another move like that and I'll shoot one right through your insides. You hear?"

"Easy, Clay." Ethan turned to face him. "Save it for the field."

"I know, but I don't have a good feeling about this."

"Me too," Bennie joined. "What's he doing back there?"

"Probably writin' a ticket."

Bennie looked through the side mirror but couldn't see Sloan, so he turned and looked through the back. "He's on the phone. You think it has anything to do with us?"

"For speeding? I doubt it."

"What if he's calling for backup?" Bennie asked.

"Easy Bennie, cops don't call for backup when they pull you over for speeding. Besides, they've got like five patrolmen on the *entire* force. My dad knows all of them. This guy's probably running a check on the car to see if there are any outstanding tickets or warrants. We'll be fine."

"Maybe he's looking at Ethan and not the car," Clay said.

"Is there anything we ought to worry about?" Bennie asked. "I don't remember discussing your, you know, past."

Ethan smiled. "Don't worry, I don't have a record. At least not like Clay's."

Bennie turned to Clay. "You got a record?"

"Nothing major, a little B and E, and some Grand Theft Auto."

By now, Clay had relaxed and he and Ethan shared a laugh. "What about you, anything we ought to know?"

Bennie sighed. "Nothing other than some petty juvenile shit." He looked at his watch. "I don't like this guys; it's been an awful long time and he's still on the phone. What takes so damn long to write a ticket?"

"He probably ran the license and plates, had a doughnut, jerked off, took a nap, and then wrote us a ticket," Ethan said.

"And what if he asks to inspect the car?" Clay asked.

Bennie chimed in. "I'm worried about that too."

"Can he even do that just because we were speeding?"

"I doubt it," Ethan said. "But that doesn't mean he won't."

"So what do we do?" Bennie said.

"I say we watch the road and when no one else is around, call him back here and take him out," Clay said. "I just hope it's not too late, because if he's called some friends over, it's gonna be a bloodbath."

"Try to stay calm, OK?" Ethan said. "We can screw everything up just by losing our cool. I think we need to—"

"Quiet, quiet, here he comes."

Clay stole a glance and caught sight of Sloan slamming his car door shut. He turned to Nick and pushed the gun back in his side. "Remember, try to be cute and we shoot you and him both. Get it? Dead."

Ethan lowered the window again.

"Here's your license and registration." Sloan gave them back. Then, the officer tore the top sheet of his ticket pad and handed it to Ethan. "I've written you up for speeding. The fine is a hundred bucks, deadline and payment instructions on the bottom. Any questions?"

"Nope." Ethan folded the ticket and put it in his wallet.

"Drive carefully now, and have a good day."

CHAPTER NINETEEN

THE REST OF THE ride felt like driving through a jungle in one of those small jeeps, as Nick's body was jolted every few seconds. As the highway disappeared and they delved further into wilderness, the answer to Nick's question found its way to his gut. The area was completely deserted; the drive felt much like the decisive walk to the electric chair

The dirt road emptied into an expansive field deeply entrenched in rainbow-colored, sandstone cliffs. It was a three hundred and sixty degree view that Nick would have found breathtaking under any other circumstance. And he was pretty certain they were not within the park's boundaries, since there would've been a sign and a gate or fence to pass through.

The perfect killing field.

Ethan pulled the car to a stop and everyone opened their doors. Ethan stepped out first, waved his hand at the dust and coughed. "Tie him up before you get out of the car."

"I can't," Clay responded. "I cut the rope back there and I don't got anymore. Let me see if I can tie the pieces together and re-use them."

Ethan grabbed his gun, opened Nick's door, and ordered him to step out slowly. Nick complied. Turning to Bennie, Ethan said, "Grab the shit from the trunk."

Nick watched as Bennie went to the back, lifted the cover, and removed two shotguns. The sight didn't faze him since he already knew they had guns in the car. But it was the next two items Bennie removed that made Nick's heart pummel like a heavy metal drum solo.

A pair of shovels.

They're not here to make sand castles.

Nick's immediate impulse was to make a break and run as fast as he could regardless of the consequences. Maybe they weren't good shots? In the movies, the good guy runs anywhere he wants with hundreds of bullets miraculously missing him, but this was an enormously large and empty field and Nick was physically decimated. His adversaries were three young, fit gunmen and, even if he managed a good head start, they would certainly catch up.

But wasn't that better than obeying their orders and accepting death without a fight? Nick's conflict was an impossible one, and every thought he had led to his most rational philosophy of survival: stay alive for as long as you possibly can because you never know what might happen. Unfortunately, Nick already felt direfully close to his "as long as possible." That's when he decided that if he wasn't going to run, he'd turn to his best and most valuable resource, perhaps the only one that could save his life.

His mouth.

"So what are we doing here guys, digging for gold?" Nick could barely force himself to mouth the words since he knew exactly what they were there for.

Ethan snickered. "The gold comes *after* the digging."

Clay stepped out of the car holding the ropes he had re-tied. "We can use these."

"I don't understand," Nick shot back.

"Just put your hands out for him."

Clay tied his wrists together.

"That's too damn tight."

Clay tried to loosen it a bit but couldn't, so he left it. "Oh shit!" Clay blurted out. "Did we forget the beer?"

"I didn't pack any," Bennie said. "Did you?"

"I didn't either," he answered. After a pause: "It's probably better anyway. I wouldn't want that cop to have found us with beer in the truck."

"Dude, we had two rifles, three handguns and dirty shovels in the back. A six pack wouldn't have made a damn bit of difference." Ethan looked at his watch. "Forget about it anyway. Let's get this done and get outta here."

Clay and Bennie each grabbed a shovel and walked out into the field. Ethan pointed to a couple of boulders fifteen feet ahead and told Nick to go sit on one. Then, he grabbed one of the rifles, loaded a bullet, and took a seat on a boulder behind Nick.

"Why are you guys doing this?" Nick turned halfway to face Ethan. "Is it money you're after? Because I'm the Vice President of a large real estate firm, one phone call and I can get you guys a pretty nice—"

Ethan cut him off. "Just turn around and stay quiet. I don't want your money."

Nick decided to drop the bombshell. "I know about the others."

Ethan furrowed his brow. "I don't know what you're talking about."

"We both know you're going to kill me, so don't play me like an idiot. You think I don't know that you murdered those hikers posted on the wall at the Visitor Center?"

Suddenly, there was the scraping sound of digging as Clay and Bennie got started. Nick waited a moment and when Ethan didn't say anything, he said. "So this must be where they're buried."

"Those guys are just missing. It's a national park with three million visitors a year."

"And I guess the large mounds of dirt out here are the result of millions of years of miraculous erosion?" Nick paused. "How many people have you buried?"

A pause. "Congratulations," Ethan said in a mocking tone. "You've solved the great mystery of the missing Zion hikers. Too bad you won't be around to collect your prize."

"You guys are such cowards. Do you really believe that no one will catch on?"

"Five years and counting and no one's figured it out."

Nick glanced at Clay and Bennie who were taking a break, standing with their shovels in the ground and chins on their hands.

"Why are you doing this to me?" Nick asked in a low, throaty voice.

Ethan ignored him.

"Tell me goddamnit!" Ethan jumped at the infusion of purpose in Nick's voice. "You're going to kill me in a few minutes and I have a baby on the way. Can't you at least have the decency to tell me why my life is about to end so abruptly?"

The monotonous drone of graveyard digging started again and Nick fought back a well of tears, trapping them inside his eyes. He turned back to Ethan. "Why are you killing innocent people?"

Ethan let out a deep breath, and moved the shotgun to his other hand as he locked eyes with Nick's.

"OK, you're right." Ethan paused. "We're doing it for the money."

CHAPTER TWENTY

INA AND WANDA ARRIVED in Tucson and checked into their hotel, a five-star resort at the base of the Catalina Mountains. Ina settled into her upper floor suite, found the number for the park, and placed the call. Ina introduced herself to the man on the other line, who identified himself as Kevin Simpson, the Canyon District Ranger. She mentioned she had called the previous day and wasn't sure with whom she had spoken. She had asked that they relay a message for her husband to call her, but she hadn't heard from him.

"What's your husband's name?"

"Nicholas Perrone." She couldn't have said it any faster. "Everyone calls him Nick."

The line went silent and Ina sensed something was wrong. She sat on the edge of the bed and massaged her tummy, recalling another reason she needed to stay calm. "You know who he is?"

"I do," the ranger replied. "Your husband called for help this morning from one of our trails."

"Is he OK? Tell me he's OK."

"I wish I could, but I really don't know." Simpson's tone was monotonous. "Our people are out there as we speak. I'm told they found a baseball cap and have retrieved his backpack; it had fallen quite a distance below the trail. The one thing they haven't located, though, is your husband."

"What does that mean? Is he lost? Are you looking for him?" Rational thought was quickly dissipating.

"The best I can tell you is that we've got rangers combing the area. Why don't you give me your number and, if we find him, I'll give you a call."

If they find him?

"Why do you sound as if you don't really give a shit?"

"Mrs. Perrone." His tone didn't change. "I've been here many years and you could say that I've seen it all: murders, suicides, and hikers who have staged their own disappearance. So, when I found out that we'd recovered some of his belongings but not him, I guess it didn't faze me all that much. He could be anywhere."

Ina wanted to lash out, but decided not to fight with the man. Sure, he didn't instill any confidence in her but she still needed his help.

"Listen, I have another call," Simpson said calmly. "It could be my people out at the site. Give me your contact information."

Ina gave him her number and implored him to call as soon as possible, with any news.

"Oh, and one more thing. Can you fax a picture of your husband?"

"Why do you need it?"

"I'm going to make a "MISSING" flier and post it on the wall of the Visitor Center."

He paused, and the next words out of his mouth would send Ina into full-fledged shock.

"With the others."

CHAPTER TWENTY-ONE

"YOU SAID IT *WASN'T* about the money."

"I didn't say that," Ethan replied.

"I thought you said there wasn't going to be a ransom?" Nick shot back.

"I said it wasn't about *your* money. Look over there. They're digging your grave, cowboy." Ethan snickered, as if Nick had some nerve thinking he was worth a large sum. "There's no ransom."

"You wouldn't go to all this trouble if there wasn't a big payday. So where's it coming from?"

Ethan never liked sharing information with a client, but there was a part of him that yearned to see the look on a man's face when reality finally registered. And besides, Nick would be dead in just a few minutes. So why not?

"Think about it," Ethan said. "What's the biggest thing you owned that we now have?"

"Probably my truck," Nick answered almost instantly.

"Bingo."

"You're gonna kill me for my truck?"

Clay and Bennie approached, panting. "All done and ready," Clay said. "Let's do it."

"Good." Ethan looked at his watch, grabbed a shotgun, and turned to Bennie. "You comin' with? Or are you staying here again like a pussy?"

"I'm gonna stay."

"All right. Clay, let's make like a basketball player and take this guy to the hole. I'm gonna grab some bullets from the trunk."

Nick turned to Bennie and pleaded with his eyes but to no avail. Bennie just looked at the ground. That's when Clay grabbed him by the arm and said, "Come with me, little man."

Nick resisted, and pulled his arms from Clay's grasp before turning to Ethan. "You can have my car and anything else I own, but why do you have to kill me?"

Ethan got right up in Nick's face. "I don't have to tell you shit. Now, go get in the *fucking* hole! I've got other things to do today."

Clay pushed Nick towards the ditch. "How many people are buried here?" Nick asked, his voice cracking.

"A dozen?" Clay said. "I don't know, maybe more."

A dozen? There weren't that many fliers posted at the Visitor Center. Who else have they murdered?

"You guys have ruined a perfectly good field."

Clay laughed. "Ruined? I don't think that's a nice thing to say. There's a lot of successful people buried here." Clay began pointing. "In the corner pile is a computer programmer who worked for IBM. And back there, we buried a guy who invented some famous food gadget or something. Pretty sure he made a fortune off it. We looked it up on the Internet after we killed him, and man was there a fight over his will. And let's see, I think we've got a pair of accountants, a lawyer, a doctor, there's even a marketing guy. Or is it advertising? Something like that."

"The net worth of this field is through the roof," Ethan added, trailing behind them.

"Yeah, we've turned this place into an executive graveyard."

"I like that." Ethan laughed.

"You guys are sick, you know that?" Nick said. "You're not going to get away with this. Someone, at some point, is going to discover what you've done and fry you assholes for this sick game you're playing with innocent lives."

"Whatever," Ethan said. "Let's take care of business and get outta here."

Tears of reality slowly slid down Nick's beaten face as they reached the hole Clay and Bennie had dug.

"Time's up asshole."

Clay pushed Nick in the back and he stumbled before falling to the ground. Then, Clay grabbed Nick's arm and yelled at him to get up. But Nick disobeyed, letting his weight hang towards the ground.

"Damn it," Clay yelled. "I need some help."

Bennie made his way over and struggled with Clay to force Nick into the grave. They pulled Nick, inching him closer, but exhaustion was starting to set in. They were still a good couple of feet from the grave.

"You need help?" Ethan asked.

Clay lifted his hand. "I can handle this." He turned to Nick. "I'm losin' it with you, pal. We can do this the easy way for you, or the easy way for me." He pulled out a handgun. "I can shoot you right here and drag your dead carcass into the hole, or you can cooperate with us. What's it going to be?"

Clay waited a few seconds and, when Nick didn't answer, he cocked the gun. "Say good night, asshole."

"Wait!" Bennie yelled. "What are you doing?"

"What does it look like I'm doing? I'm gonna shoot him. We can cover his blood with some dirt."

"I think you should let Ethan shoot him."

"What's the difference who shoots him? Unless *you* want to do it. I'll step aside for *that*."

"I'm not shooting him," Bennie said. "But you should let Ethan do it because your gun's louder than his."

"Actually, Bennie's right," Ethan chimed in. "And, my casings don't go as far."

Clay stuffed the gun behind his waist, and he and Bennie made one more attempt to drag Nick to the hole. And this time, it worked, as they dumped Nick into to the grave, legs first. His hands tied, Nick had no way to brace for the impact and fell face first into the muddy wall. He screamed as he took mud into his mouth and, after spitting a bunch of times, Nick stood erect. His face was slightly above the ground. They had barely dug enough room for his six-foot frame.

"Turn around," Ethan said, asking Nick to face the other way.

Nick turned.

Ethan moved closer, lifted his shotgun, and aimed it at the back of his head. "Any last words?"

"Oh God, please don't do this," Nick said. And even though he wasn't facing the gun, he quenched his eyes tightly shut, as if it would help absorb the impact of a bullet through his skull.

Clay and Bennie backed up over to the side and out of harm's way, as Ethan reached back to pull the trigger.

CHAPTER TWENTY-TWO

BANG! BANG! BANG! THREE shots to the head, each of which easily hit their mark. The asshole never had a chance. No one could survive such an assault at point blank range, and, for an experienced marksman, it was like shooting fish in a barrel.

Practice had made him perfect.

He stood with an empty face, admiring his work. It wasn't like shooting a vicious animal in the wilderness, taking life from a creature that, itself, took lives. Shooting people was different. It required a singular mindset, a different kind of being. Someone with a frosty heart and a callous mind. He had learned over the years that it took more than just sheer talent to kill. Your mind had to be comfortable with the product of your actions; your conscience had to first sign off.

Over the last several years, he could feel his heart grow colder every time he pulled the trigger, and, before he knew it, he had grown accustomed to the idea of shooting those created in God's image. Scary as it may have felt growing up, now he actually looked forward to taking a twelve pack out to the desert and shooting out holes until they pissed their contents to the ground. Perhaps a lucky desert rat would experience the immense pleasure of human intoxication, if only to take the edge off. One night without that constant fear of being hunted. Now *there's* something people take for granted. Our gift is not just life itself, but the quality with which we are able to live it. Animals spend every moment fixated on survival, while people spend their days planning and anticipating a lengthy existence. We lock our doors at night and set our alarms and, in the rare event something happens, we need only dial three numbers for help. On the other hand, if a deer crosses paths with a mountain lion, he must outrun it or dinner is served.

With the day's goals accomplished, he put down his firearm and pulled in a long, lasting breath. A brief air of satisfaction passed through him and he forced a half smile, not sure how long the feeling would last. He hoped it would until the next time. He'd long ago lost count of how many times a week he paid this place a visit. When he'd first started, he would just come out here and stare, reliving the past each time. It took him a while until he could actually pull the trigger but once he did, he starting firing off shot after shot, finally gaining the retribution he'd so desperately sought.

Killing the killer.

He relived the past every day, although the details were getting sketchier with the passage of time. Still, there were certain things he would never forget: The sound of the shot; the blood; the shock; and his father's last gasp of life. Burying his father had actually been the easy part for Wyatt. His real challenge had been closing and burying his own emotional coffin, the hole in his heart from that night was so much larger than his father's grave.

If only he didn't freeze.

If only he could've pulled the trigger.

And now, if he could just get past it and move on.

Wyatt put the gun down, removed his headset, and at the push of a button, a paper criminal with holes in its head came flying at him. He took the paper from the slide and, figuratively, did what he should've done that fateful night, crumpled it with both hands and ceremoniously tossed it in the garbage. Sliding the gun back in his holster, Wyatt turned on his heels but immediately stopped dead in his tracks.

"I had no idea you could shoot like that."

Wyatt took a moment to gather himself. "I guess it's like anything in life, if you do it enough you become good at it." He locked eyes with her and could tell she wasn't right. They moved closer and engaged in a light embrace. "What are you doing here?"

Ina managed a faint smile, which she could only hold for a split second. "Is there someplace we can talk?"

The room sounded like a bunch of kids jumping on bubble wrap. Despite the weekend, several officers were putting in time honing their sniper skills and Wyatt could see her quiver with each shot. "Let's get you out of here. This can't be good for the baby."

Ina followed Wyatt to a conference room that looked more like one of those icy interrogation rooms at Headquarters. He pulled out a chair and watched her drop her purse on the table and settle in. Then, he went around to the other side and sat, explaining that no coffee was available because it was Sunday. But Ina said nothing and when he met her gaze, she slowly turned away and looked down.

"Aren't you supposed to be in Tucson?"

She looked up at him. "Nick's missing."

Wyatt felt a wave of shock course through his body. "What do you mean?

"After you backed out, Nick went by himself. He left Thursday morning and I spoke with him just once since then. I've been trying to call, all day yesterday and again today, but there's been no answer." Her eyes were like a levee fighting back the inevitable rush of water. "So, a couple of hours ago, I called and spoke to a park ranger and he told me that Nick had called for help while hiking this morning. And now they can't find him."

"Are they saying he's actually missing, or that he called for help and when they arrived, he wasn't there anymore?"

She took a deep breath. "They found his backpack and baseball cap on the trail, but there's no sign of him." Tears rained down her face.

Wyatt retrieved a box of tissues. "What about his car? Where did he leave it?"

"I don't know. I was in such a daze that I didn't think to ask. Besides, I don't think they have all the answers yet."

"Then let's not get crazy. I'm sure he'll turn up."

"I'm really worried." She grabbed a tissue and wiped tears from her cheek. "The ranger started telling me about people disappearing and hikers dying, and this is right after he tells me my husband is missing. Am I supposed to feel reassured?"

"He's probably worried that you're going to blame the park if something happened to Nick, which I'm sure nothing has. Trust me, *I* researched the park for this trip and it is *very* safe."

Ina looked around. "You interrogate people in here?"

"No, we usually do that at the station. This is the shooting range and we don't bring suspects here. This is more for phone calls and meetings among officers. Why?"

She glanced around again. "I don't see any cameras, but I don't want anyone recording this."

"No one is, but why?"

"Is Nick cheating on me?"

Wyatt knew from his conversation with Nick the other day that it was a reasonable suspicion. "Of course not, why are you ..."

"I don't know. I guess I'm a little insecure. Scared too. I kept calling him every few minutes and I got really frustrated when it kept going to voicemail. And then, one of my calls was answered but all I could hear was traffic or something. And I'm screaming into the phone, 'Hello? Nick?' But he didn't answer and when I tried again, I got voicemail. Now they tell me that he called 911 earlier that morning and they found his hat and backpack on a trail somewhere? It doesn't add up, and I started worrying that maybe he's just cheating and decided to leave me."

"I'm pretty sure you're wrong. He loves you."

The room was silent as Wyatt waited for her to continue but she had nothing more to say. Finally, she locked her pleading eyes with his and, as always, she had the clear advantage. "I need your help."

Wyatt took her hand and held it momentarily. "Of course, you guys are like family to me."

He waited for her to say it and she never did, but he could see it in her eyes. *Had you gone with Nick, nothing would've happened.*

Not exactly an indictment, but it was enough to fuel his guilt and get him to Utah.

CHAPTER TWENTY-THREE

CLAY AND BENNIE ASSUMED their positions as Ethan pulled the gun back and squinted through the scope. The target: dead center—the back of Nick's head. Ethan pumped the lever back, chambered a round, and took a deep breath to steady himself. His heart pounded as he reached for the trigger with his index finger.

"Wait," Bennie yelled.

Ethan lowered the gun. "What?"

Bennie turned back towards the truck and then said in a low tone. "I think I hear something."

"Come on, man," Clay said. "Let's shoot the bastard already. I don't hear anything."

"Just listen. I don't think we're alone out here. "

The three of them stood still, shushing each other.

"Over there." Bennie pointed towards the winding dirt road leading into the field. "See the dust in the air?" A car was not yet in sight.

"I think he's right." Ethan frowned. "Not again. Come on, quick, let's get behind the truck." Ethan and Clay began sprinting towards their vehicle.

"What about him?" Bennie yelled.

"Leave him," Ethan called back. "There's no time to pull him out."

Bennie ran to the truck and crouched next to Ethan. Clay was inside the truck grabbing another gun.

"But you can see his head above the ground," Bennie said. "We're caught. What are we gonna do?"

Clay slammed the door shut and kneeled with them behind the truck. "Whoever it is, we ambush him and when we're done, we finish off Nick and get the hell out of here."

The gravelly sounds grew louder and Ethan's arms began shaking. "OK, we jump out and shoot as soon as he arrives," Ethan whispered, as if whoever was coming might hear if he spoke in his normal tone.

"It's all right," Clay said, confidently. "The worst thing is that we're going to have to dig another hole."

Bennie moved towards the back of the truck to peek around it. His heart was already racing but when he first caught sight of the vehicle, it practically stopped. The road wasn't level so he couldn't see the entire car, but it was quickly coming into view and he could see something red on the roof.

A light bar.

Police.

"Shit. It's the cops."

Ethan blew out a mouthful as he positioned himself by the front tire. He was sitting on one knee holding the shotgun in his hands. "That pig must've followed us after he pulled us over. When he gets close, I'll start counting, OK? We pop out on three."

Bennie peered out again and watched as the vehicle bounced along the road, quickly getting closer. "It's not the guy who pulled us over. This one's an SUV, not a sedan."

"But it's the cops, right?" Clay asked, his legs shaking in anticipation.

Bennie watched the white SUV come into focus. He could see the green stripe wrapped all the way around the sides. It may not have been a patrol car, but it was definitely the cops. Bennie moved back towards the middle of the truck as the driver approached and slammed on the brakes. Ethan quickly counted to three, yelled, "Now," and popped out. In a flash, Ethan aimed the barrel and was about to pull the trigger when the driver raised his hands in the air.

"Don't shoot!" the driver yelled through the open window.

Ethan shot the man a look and then smiled with raised eyelids. He lowered the gun and jogged over to the vehicle, shaking his head over the enormity of what he had nearly done.

He had almost shot his own father.

WYATT SPED THROUGH THE parking lot of his apartment complex on Central Avenue, just a few minutes north of downtown Phoenix. He parked crookedly and climbed a series of stair-banks two at a time to his third-floor studio. The complex was a maze of contemporary stucco apartments with red-tiled roofs that resembled every home and condominium that had popped up in the desert over the last ten years. Although he inherited the house in which he was raised, after witnessing his father's murder, Wyatt couldn't stomach living there. So he sold the house and left the proceeds untouched.

It was the middle of a steamy afternoon and Wyatt didn't have a lot of time. Grabbing a flight to Vegas would be the easy part. He would then have to rent a car and drive one hundred and fifty miles north just to get to the park. It was a long journey complicated by the fact that it was unplanned. The best he could hope for was a late arrival tonight, a little rest, and then get started first thing tomorrow morning.

Wyatt slammed the door and went to the closet for a suitcase, which he promptly tossed onto the bed. With no time for folding, he scanned the room for as much as he could grab and had a stuffed bag within minutes. He filled a knapsack with some snacks and hiking gear and took that and the suitcase to the car. After tossing them in the trunk, he pressed a button on a box attached to his window visor and walked briskly across the parking lot to his garage. The door moaned as it slowly rose and receded out of view. Wyatt went straight to the back for the big box in the right hand corner. Huddled around it, he used his car key to cut through duct tape and rip the box open. He shuffled a few things inside until he found an extra gun, ammunition, switchblade, flashlight, and a nightstick. Wondering what else he might need in Utah, Wyatt searched the contents one last time to see if there was anything else worth taking. He grabbed a pair of night vision goggles, set them down with everything else he was taking, closed the box and pushed it back along the wall. Not once did he look at or focus on the two words written on the outside of the box.

Dad's Stuff.

AFTER ETHAN FIXED HIS shotgun, Nick closed his eyes and cringed, bracing again for the end. It was hard to comprehend. And just as it was about to happen, Nick opened his eyes when he heard Bennie yell, "Wait." Nick turned to face them but no one was looking his way, they were focused on the road behind them. And from his vantage point, Nick could see the dust-filled air in the distance, a sure sign of a backcountry intruder. Had his prayers been answered?

This was his chance.

After blowing an opportunity during the pullover, he couldn't forego another one. As his captors took cover behind their truck, Nick started trying to extricate himself. He scraped out some mud with his hands and feet, hoping to find a rock for support. It was an opportune time for a mad dash since his killers were focused elsewhere, but Nick couldn't get any leverage.

He was stuck.

His fate would remain in the hands of others.

Nick stood upright and affixed his eyes on the road. The horizon looked like a bunch of baseball players had slid safely into all four bases. His eyes lit up, and his heart did a little boogie when he saw the light bar. And as the car bore down on them, Nick played out the upcoming scene in his mind. The cop would mow down and dispose of all three killers, and rescue Nick for a happy ending. He saw himself walking by their pale, lifeless bodies lying next to Ethan's truck. For poetic justice, Nick even envisioned all three cadavers in the hole they had dug for *him*, and saw himself staring out the back window of the police car, as he was safely returned to society.

The vehicle came into view and Nick's elation dropped a notch when he realized that it wasn't the cops. It looked like a police car, until Nick saw the brown logo with a large green pine tree painted on the door.

A park ranger.

"OK," he told himself, maybe not the *best* but given the circumstances, a close second. Rangers were trained in law enforcement and carried deadly weapons. Nick knew that while they didn't have jurisdiction outside the park, they could easily resort to deadly violence in a life and death situation such as this. He was numb as he watched things unfold. The ranger was bearing down on them and Nick realized that his captors had a decided advantage. It was probably three against one, and the three had the element of surprise. The ranger would never know what hit him.

Nick tried to chisel out a small rock—it was all he could find—so he could throw it and gain the ranger's attention. But it was useless with his hands tied. The best he could do was hold his hands above his head. Weak, but it would have to do. The ranger pulled to a halt. Dust rose from the tires like a balloon set free in an open field. He cringed, as he saw Ethan about to pounce. Everything seemed to happen in slow motion. They were about to shoot the ranger and Nick's intuition was correct, it was three against one. The ranger pleaded for them to hold their fire and they did. And then Nick's heart sank like the Titanic, when he heard Ethan mouth a single word.

Dad.

A park ranger.

Reality set in: Dead campers. Missing hikers. Mountain lions. Dangerous trails. Posters in the Visitor Center.

The rangers were in on it.

CHAPTER TWENTY-FOUR

Monday

IT WAS SHORTLY BEFORE nine and Wyatt was stuck in a line of cars at the park's entrance booth. He took the opportunity to check out his surroundings. The area was almost completely enclosed by multicolored rock walls rising thousands of feet. Seemingly endless trees danced in the early sun, adding color and flavor to an already exceptional portrait. Wyatt marveled at the bright yellow leaves of the Fremont Cottonwood, and the greenish-blue berries dangling from the stems of the Utah Juniper. Along the top of the canyons stood hundreds of white rock figurines called "hoodoos." Together, they looked like a huge crowd of people giving the park a permanent standing ovation.

After ten minutes, Wyatt eased his car forward, paid the entrance fee, and took a map and copy of the park's newsletter. The ranger manning the booth rambled on about the park and Wyatt quickly understood why the line had taken so long. The entrance fee was good for seven days, although he hoped he wouldn't need it for that long.

Wyatt went right to the Visitor Center, parked the car, and was immediately greeted by the embalmed mountain lion when he entered the building. He snickered at the sight and went to the information counter. There were several hikers on line before him but when his turn arrived, he couldn't get any words out. Whatever he'd planned to say quickly left his brain, as it was busy trying to register what his eyes were staring at on the wall.

It was a picture of Nick. The most recent person missing from the Park.

THE RED F-150 RACED around the back of the house and abruptly came to a stop. Bennie stepped out of the truck, coughed, and waved his hand in a useless effort to clear the dust from his face. Ethan was waiting outside for him.

"What do you need?" Bennie asked.

"Guess who's staying with him today?"

"Come on." Bennie frowned. "I did this shit yesterday. What about Clay?"

"He went home last night."

Clay lived in a boxy mobile home that was barely set back off Route 9. It wasn't exactly prime property as it was literally steps from the highway. And it barely had a bed and toilet. But Bennie never heard him complain, probably because he spent most of his time at Ethan's house.

"I can't stick around today."

"No, you *will*. I've got to take care of the cars and get them ready, plus my dad's been having problems with his truck. And Clay needs to run the bar like normal to avoid suspicion."

"I've got work too, Ethan, and the shit I do is important for us."

Ethan lifted his shirt so Bennie could see the butt of his pistol resting inside the waistband. "I recognize your contributions, but you also have someone there to pick up the slack. You're staying here today."

Bennie exhaled a stress breath and put his hand to his forehead. He wished the gun would go off right where it was and cut a hole through Ethan's crotch.

"CAN I HELP YOU?"

Wyatt blinked a few times before he realized someone was talking to him. He met eyes with the young ranger and then glanced at the nametag hovering above her right breast. It identified her as "Velvet" from Athens, Georgia. She wore little makeup, and a few strands of her long black hair managed to escape the captivity of her large-brimmed ranger's hat. Wyatt felt a surge of energy rush through his body.

"I'm sorry," Wyatt said. "I flaked for a moment."

"Happens to all of us." She smiled and grabbed a trail map to answer what she presumed would be a hiking question.

Wyatt averted eye contact and looked instead at the map. "I didn't come here to hike. I'm actually here because my friend is missing."

"What's your friend's name?"

Wyatt pointed to a picture on the wall behind her. "Nick Perrone. That's not a very good picture."

She turned to take a glance and then turned back to him. "His wife faxed that yesterday and it just went up this morning. She's supposed to get us an original."

Wyatt placed an envelope on the counter and slid out a photo. "She asked me to give you this."

Velvet put her hand up. "Normally I would take it, but now is not a good time. You should give it to someone in the law enforcement division. I work there but we're a bit short-staffed this week so I'm filling in here. If I take the picture now, there isn't much I can do with it."

Wyatt shook his head and replaced the photo in the envelope. "Any leads?"

"I was out at the site yesterday, but since I'm working the desk now, I'm not really up on the investigation."

"Fair enough." Wyatt pulled out his badge. "Who would you suggest I speak with? I'd like to offer my assistance."

Velvet touched the badge with one of her fingers. "Phoenix, huh? And what do you do there?"

"Homicide," Wyatt said, as if he'd investigated hundreds in his career.

She smiled in admiration. "Go see Kevin Simpson, my boss. He's the Canyon District Ranger and in charge of the law enforcement division."

"Can you let him know I'm here?"

"Actually I can't. This is the Visitor Center. Our office is just up the road in the Emergency Operations Center. It's a fairly new structure on the left side, about a half a mile up."

Wyatt nodded, and there was an awkward moment of silence.

"You sure made it out here quick. This whole thing just went down yesterday."

"Why wait?"

"Right. I mean, isn't the first twenty-four hours crucial in these kinds of things?"

Wyatt smiled. "More so in kidnappings because the more time that goes by, the farther away the perpetrator gets. But time is always of the essence. I'm here to help so we can get that picture down as soon as possible. I'm sure that's always nice to do."

Velvet furrowed her brow and said nothing.

"You have removed posters before, right?" Wyatt asked. "I'm sure you've found missing hikers."

"Not that I can remember."

CHAPTER TWENTY-FIVE

NICK AWOKE TO A nightmare.

He was back in the chair of death. His wrists and ankles tightly tied, as before, but at least he wasn't standing in a makeshift grave out in the desert where no one would find him. Ethan's father had saved Nick's life.

For now.

After spending the afternoon baking in the sun, Nick was badly dehydrated. And when they brought him back to the house, he pleaded for water. The request prompted an argument amongst his captors, but Bennie came through with a bottle that Nick downed in one shot. The day proved to be more than he could handle and Nick had virtually passed out once they re-secured him to the chair.

Morning arrived with Nick falling in and out of consciousness. When awake, he tried passing time thinking of Ina and the baby they'd conceived. And he was able to do that until the guilt overtook him. Not just for what he'd done in the campground, but also for the attitude he'd displayed since learning Ina was pregnant. A montage of their lives together zipped through his head, and the one thing that stuck out was a health scare several years earlier, just before Nick's thirtieth birthday. He'd been experiencing severe headaches and underwent extensive testing. At first, the doctors thought it was a deadly tumor, but later determined it was nothing more than extraordinary stress. Ina had been by his side throughout, and she even, at times, seemed more concerned than he was.

Sitting there, bound to a chair, Nick realized that Wyatt was right. She really did care.

How could I have ignored her calls?

Maybe, Nick thought, he deserved his captivity as some form of punishment for the way he'd recently behaved. Here he had this beautiful, loving person who wanted nothing more than to have a family with him, and he was gallivanting around Southern Utah acting like a teenager. Regret filled his heart and a wave of panic splashed inside him, as he realized that he was truly in this alone. Nick shifted in the chair feebly trying to wriggle himself free. But they had tied him as tight, if not worse, than before. Still, Nick tried every few minutes, it was impossible to condition his brain to accept the fact that he was helpless.

And that's when he remembered the knife.

Was it still there?

Nick couldn't see under the bed but working through the possibilities led him to conclude that it was. Wouldn't the guys have said something if they'd found it? That asshole Ethan probably would've beaten him over it. Or with it. And besides, *when* would they have found it? The only time they weren't in the house with him was when they took him out to the field. But what about Ethan's father, had he been to the house? Did he find the knife? Nick decided that it was unlikely since the man was a ranger and there was no indication that he'd spent any time here. The knife was probably still under the bed.

And why, Nick wondered, did Ethan's father stop the execution? Did he change their plans? Clay had said that Nick knew too much for them to cut a deal. What were they going to do with him now?

The questions swirled inside Nick's head, as if someone had taken his emotions, thrown them in a blender, and flipped the switch. But Nick fought to put those thoughts aside and focus on something more important.

Survival.

"Hello?" Nick shouted. "Is anyone here?" He felt the familiar tremor from his stomach. The door to his room was slightly open.

Nick shifted in the chair again, this time because his back was sore. The chair was made entirely of steel, except for the seat, which was made from wood. The scary thing was that it was the same chair in which you might unnoticeably sit in a coffee shop, yet the guys had discovered another use. It was ideal for bounding and torturing a would-be murder victim. Indeed, it had all the characteristics of the perfect hostage chair, it was heavy to move and easy to secure rope to.

"Hey, is anyone here?" Nick tried again.

Bennie walked in a moment later. "What's all the screaming about?"

"I'm starving. I haven't eaten in two days."

BENNIE BLEW OUT A deep breath at the strange request. He wasn't sure what to do. They'd never fed a captive. Not that he couldn't, but it had never been an issue. The guys almost always disposed of their victims in less than twenty-four hours. But something unusual had occurred yesterday. Something unprecedented.

No one had ever returned from the Executive Graveyard alive.

CHAPTER TWENTY-SIX

THIS IS A NICE place for an office, Wyatt thought, as he stepped out of his car and took in the magnificent backdrop. He had parked facing a fleet of GMC Suburbans the rangers used to patrol the park, a pair of fire trucks, and an ambulance. The building alone made the park feel like its own little city. Wyatt pulled the door handle but it wouldn't budge, so he rapped on the glass pane and waited for someone to let him in. Seconds later, a plump, white-haired lady unlocked the door and held it open.

"Can I help you?"

Wyatt explained that he was a detective from Phoenix, and asked to see Kevin Simpson to discuss the Perrone investigation. She asked him to wait while she checked if Simpson was available. Wyatt watched as she walked to the end of the carpeted hallway, peeked into an office and a moment later, motioned for him. Wyatt made his way down the hallway and as he entered the office, Simpson stood from behind a cherry wood, L-shaped desk.

"I hope it's not a bad time," Wyatt said as they shook hands.

"There's never a good time, but I think I can find a few minutes. Have a seat." Simpson pointed to a black rubber chair across from his desk. "You're a detective?"

"Yes, in Phoenix. Homicide."

Simpson looked more like law enforcement than a park ranger, as he exuded a strong, intimidating presence. An unusually tight jaw line nicely accentuated his narrow face, and was topped by shiny and neatly cropped black hair, thanks to some wonderfully strong hairspray. In

Wyatt's estimation, Simpson was pushing fifty, but he still looked athletic, if not healthy. Muscular biceps escaped from the short sleeves of his park-issued shirt, undoubtedly meant as a warning not to mess with him. The shirt was neatly tucked into khaki-colored pants, held firmly in place by a belt and holster. Simpson carried a pistol, an extra magazine, radio, flashlight, gloves and pepper spray. Wyatt presumed he also carried handcuffs, but that was because they were wrapped around his office doorknob. His equipment made quite a bit of noise as he sat down.

"So what do you need from me?"

"Nick Perrone is a close friend and no one's heard from him for several days."

"The whole thing just went down yesterday and I've been in touch with his wife. Funny, she never mentioned you." Translation: does she not trust local law enforcement?

"That's probably because she wanted to act fast. I'm sure you know that if a case isn't solved in the first forty eight hours, the odds of clearing it decrease considerably."

Simpson leaned back in his chair with his hands on his head. "OK."

Wyatt removed several pictures from an envelope and slid them across the desk. Simpson leaned forward and took them.

"I did ask her for pictures, but I hope you didn't come all the way here just to deliver them."

Wyatt tried to keep a firm tone. "I'm here to help."

"I appreciate that, but I think we're good." His tone was becoming contentious.

Wyatt shifted in his chair. "Who's working the case?"

Simpson tented his hands on his head and paused a moment, as if deciding whether to be nasty or cooperative. "The Washington county sheriff. Jess Amado. It's standard procedure to call them for anything more than a misdemeanor."

"So they're helping you investigate?"

Simpson locked eyes with Wyatt. "Look Detective, I know where you're coming from, worried about your friend and all. I get that. And I'll tell you what you came here to find out. But just so we're clear, this ain't Phoenix, OK? We don't need help, and you have absolutely no jurisdiction or authority here."

"I understand," Wyatt said.

"Good," Simpson replied, with a slight inflection in his tone. "Yes, we are jointly investigating your friend's disappearance with the county sheriff. But technically, it's their investigation."

"How does that work?"

Simpson drank what was left of a cup of coffee on his desk. "They have resources we don't. We run a national park, not a police precinct. We call them in to process crime scenes and we assist them however we can, usually by interviewing witnesses, setting up road blocks, stuff like that. In your friend's case, we called them to process the scene since we're not equipped for that."

Wyatt raised a brow. "Ina didn't say anything about a crime scene."

"We asked them to process the location where we could last place him. Here's what we know. Mr. Perrone went hiking yesterday. He was headed to a place called Observation Point. It was early morning, and we're not sure but we think he may have encountered a mountain lion and decided to go back down the trail. At least that's what we gleaned from the 911 call."

"Do you have the tape?"

"I don't, but I've been told that's what he said."

"Is there any other evidence?"

"You'll have to check with the sheriff." Simpson leaned forward, resting his elbows on the desk. "Look, I doubt he's alive. We searched the area best we could, but it looks like that boy fell quite a ways into a slot that's just too narrow. And right now, it's filled with grimy water. There's no way anyone could survive that. We couldn't even get someone down there to look."

"I see," Wyatt said. A pause. "Where's his stuff?"

"Still at his campsite, although I think we're going to remove it pretty soon. Better yet, when you get a chance, go see Stan at the campground. Nice old geyser. I'll have him take the tent down and give you whatever's there so you can take it back to the wife."

Wyatt didn't respond. He was pondering Simpson's assessment that Nick was probably dead. "Maybe you're right, but I'd like to look around a bit. You know, for the family."

"It's a free country." Simpson stood.

Wyatt put his hand out and Simpson shook it. But Simpson held it firmly for an extra moment, as he did Wyatt's gaze.

"I can't stop you from being a *curious civilian*, although I can tell you that we've already interviewed many witnesses. But make no mistake. If you in any way hamper or impede this investigation, you'll have me to deal with. And if I catch you playing detective on my turf, I'll have you arrested."

WYATT PULLED UP TO the entrance booth for the Watchman Campground. The ranger slid open the window and Wyatt told her that he wanted to survey the landscape and find a suitable campsite before signing up. The ranger lazily waived him through. Several minutes later, he pulled up next to the small wooden sign marking the site in which Nick had camped just a few days ago. He parked on the gravel at the site's edge and got out of the car. The place had the quiet, eerie calm of a ghost town. There were tents pitched everywhere but, save for a few beer-drinking campers in beach chairs, the campground was practically deserted.

The corner site was nestled under large oak trees that amply shaded about half the area. An ideal place to pitch a tent. But the site was completely empty; Nick's stuff had already been removed. He walked slowly, almost aimlessly, to the farthest corner, bent to one knee, and examined the gravel. Lines in the dirt demarcated the spot in which Nick had pitched his tent. Holes lingered in the ground where,

Wyatt surmised, Nick had inserted his tent poles. Wyatt took a deep breath and blew it out hard as he stood and looked around. The imprint was all that was left from Nick's visit.

Then something caught his eye. There was an object in the dirt a couple of feet away. He ambled over, kneeled to one knee, and lifted a penny off the ground. Wyatt examined both sides of the coin before flinging it into a grass field across the road, the old saying "a day late, a dollar short" entered his mind. He hoped it wasn't true. Wyatt turned back and headed to the front of the campsite towards his car. There was an in-ground barbeque pit and an aluminum picnic table with benches attached on both sides. A bundle of firewood rested under the unsteady table and Wyatt knew it belonged to Nick. Good campers always keep their firewood covered in case it rains, and Nick was a good camper.

How could something have happened to him?

The table creaked and shifted when Wyatt sat. He leaned his back against it, looked around and felt lost. The area was just an empty lot, but Wyatt continued looking, hoping, almost willing *something* to pop up. He decided to walk the perimeter again and check every square inch for clues. But in the site itself, he found nothing. He was about to leave when he spotted several large boulders behind where Nick had pitched his tent. The area wasn't part of the site; it was neutral ground that extended behind every site in the loop. It consisted mostly of tall grass and weeds, and the occasional boulder that must have, lifetimes earlier, fallen from the majestic hills. Wyatt entered the field kicking at the tall grass and weeds. Reflexively, he jumped back at the sight of an animal until he realized that it was just a lizard darting across the boulder. Resetting himself, Wyatt circled the boulders and caught sight of some trash. He nudged away a granola bar wrapper and an empty, snack-sized bag of potato chips with his feet, when his eyes came to rest on a small piece of paper. He picked up the grass-stained post-it and read the handwritten message:

The Shack - Virgin.

Wyatt tried to recall Nick's handwriting, but realized that he had never actually seen it. He couldn't be sure if Nick had authored the note, and the location didn't necessarily mean it was Nick's, since he was standing in an area behind a number of campsites. It could've easily belonged to another camper, especially when winds in the area can be fierce. And Wyatt had no idea what the note meant. With plenty of questions and not a single answer, Wyatt slid the note into his wallet and made his way back to the car. But he couldn't rid himself of the dreadful thought that just days ago, Nick had been camping in this very location, and now there wasn't a sign of him.

Anywhere.

CHAPTER TWENTY-SEVEN

"WHO'S CALLING THE SHOTS?"

Bennie responded like a member of Congress. "I'm not at liberty to discuss that. Just thank your lucky stars you're still alive."

"I don't have lucky stars," Nick replied. "At least not right now."

"Whatever." Bennie had no retort. "Just tell me what you want to eat."

"Tell me who he is, the guy who saved my life yesterday."

"We're not discussing that. You asked for food so I'll give you something. That's more than I'm supposed to do. You got thirty seconds to tell me what you want before I walk out of here without returning."

Nick considered his options and decided on yogurt because it required a utensil. Bennie left for the kitchen, and Nick called for him to also bring him a banana. Several minutes later, Bennie returned carrying a yogurt, spoon, and banana in one hand, and a bowl of Fruity Pebbles with milk in the other. He had already started eating the cereal in the kitchen, so now it looked more like colorful porridge. Bennie placed everything on the dresser to sort it all out.

"Fruity Pebbles?" Nick asked, and Bennie nodded. "That wasn't on the menu. I want some."

"You'll have the yogurt and the banana."

Nick watched as Bennie hesitated before kneeling at the side of Nick's chair. But then he stood again and waited apprehensively.

"What's it going to be?" Nick sensed Bennie's angst. "Are you going to untie me or just feed me like a baby?"

The sarcasm in Nick's voice was deliberate. Nick wanted to be forceful and assertive because he'd been observing Bennie's body language and recognized that Bennie was timid. Bennie didn't carry himself with buoyancy, as did the others. Rather, Bennie vacillated, appeared indecisive, and had trouble making eye contact. Bennie's uneasiness was also evidenced by the way he handled his gun. Ethan and Clay always came to Nick's room with a firearm, which they promptly aimed at his head and made sure Nick was aware of just how close he was to taking a bullet. Bennie, on the other hand, was clumsy and tentative, and sometimes forgot to bring his gun with him. He was, in Nick's estimation, an inexperienced and uncomfortable terrorist.

"Huh?" Bennie came to from his momentary daze.

Nick almost had to laugh. "I wanted to know what you were going to do, but never mind. Please just untie my hands so I can eat like a human being. I promise I won't try anything."

"I can't untie both your hands. Maybe I'll just …"

"You'll what?" Nick asked, not looking for an answer. "Come on man, I'm hungry. Untie my hands so I can eat the damn thing and then you can tie me back up. What can I possibly do with both my knees tied to the chair? And besides, you afraid I'm gonna attack you with a spoon full of yogurt?"

Bennie considered it and then stepped forward and knelt at Nick's side. "Here's what I think we'll do, I'm going to untie one of your hands because that's all you need to eat." Bennie started loosening the knot before realizing that he was well ahead of himself, "I forgot to ask, are you a righty or lefty?"

"I am a lefty in hockey but a righty yogurt eater."

"I'm going to untie your right hand so you can spoon-feed yourself."

Bennie worked on the knotted rope, struggling with it for a moment until he finally managed to loosen it. Immediately, Nick enjoyed a long, deep breath before lifting his hand and flexing his fingers. There were indentations on his wrist but the rope hadn't cut off his circulation. Bennie removed a handgun from his waist and placed it next to the food on the dresser. Then he opened the yogurt and mixed it before extending it out to Nick's hand. Nick grabbed it, and Bennie went back to his cereal.

"What am I supposed to do with this?" Nick said.

"Eat it, and fast," Bennie responded with a mouthful of cereal.

"You need to untie my other hand," Nick said. "I can't hold the yogurt *and* spoon it out with just one hand?"

Exhaling his annoyance, Bennie took the yogurt from him and placed it on the dresser. Then he peeled the banana and handed it to Nick, "Here, eat this first and when you're done, I'll hold the damn yogurt for you."

Not exactly what Nick had hoped for, but he was making progress. At least he would put some food in his system and, maybe then, he would have energy to figure a way out. It took Nick less than thirty seconds to wolf down the banana. He announced ready for the yogurt, and Bennie checked the gun with his eyes, like a cop touching his holster before busting into someone's house. Then, Bennie took a seat on the bed next to Nick and held the yogurt for him.

The room was quiet while Nick ate, and he carefully took his time, relishing his right hand's ephemeral freedom. A palpable awkwardness filled the air and Nick feared that the end of his meal would mean Bennie's exit. If he was right about Bennie, there was a weakness to exploit. He had to do something.

"Why did you guys bring me back here?"

"I don't know."

"Oh, please. All this talk about the Executive Graveyard; why am I the lucky contestant that gets to come back and play again?"

"I know you don't believe me," Bennie said. "But it's true. I don't know."

"You mean to tell me you have no idea what they're going to do to me?" Nick used a friendly tone and emphasized the word "they're," to exclude Bennie.

"I have no idea."

"I just don't believe it. You guys are so … together. Efficient. Methodical."

"You gonna eat the rest of this?"

"Soon. Can't I take a break?"

Without answering, Bennie put the yogurt on the dresser and grabbed the gun. Then he slid across the bed, sat against the wall facing Nick, laid the gun next to him, and made himself comfortable.

"They're going to kill me, aren't they?"

"I'm pretty sure of it," Bennie responded. "No one's ever survived."

"I guess I'll have to buck the trend."

Bennie smirked. "Good luck. They're real killers, in every sense of the word."

"And *you're* not?"

Bennie looked down and scraped an index finger on the gun handle a few times. "I'm not a killer."

"That's not how everyone else will see it."

"Nobody has a clue."

"But they will. We both know that this won't last forever and when you guys are finally made, you'll be considered a murderer just like your buddies."

"I've never killed anyone."

"Sure you have. Everyone you guys have murdered." Nick tried to keep an easy tone, especially because Bennie was fingering the gun. He didn't want to push too hard.

"Not that I have to justify myself to you, but I never shot or harmed anyone. Ethan and Clay are the ones who do that."

"But aren't you a willful participant?"

"No, I'm not."

"I have a hard time believing that. The gun's aimed at *my* head, not yours."

"I wish it were that simple, but it isn't," Bennie said. "If you only knew."

CHAPTER TWENTY-EIGHT

THE PEACH-COLORED BUILDING was situated in a stretch of open land not far from a park with a small, crystal-blue lake. A large white sign supported by wooden posts and surrounded by tumbleweed declared it the "WASHINGTON COUNTY SHERIFF'S OFFICE AND PURGATORY FACILITY." Wyatt drove past the sign and entered the lot. How sad, he thought, cops and robbers sharing the same office space.

A young girl who couldn't have been more than twenty sat behind a glass partition in what wasn't much of a reception area. There were several doors that probably led to offices or holding cells, for authorized personnel only. Now, Wyatt thought, the purgatory part made sense; it felt more like a prison than the sheriff's office. Fortunately, there was no line and Wyatt went right up to window. He hesitated; the setup was more like a doctor's office than law enforcement. He half expected her to slide the glass open and pass him a clipboard with paperwork to fill out. Behind a large set of awkward bifocals, the pimple-faced girl eyed Wyatt before leaning into a microphone and asking what he wanted.

Wyatt asked to see Amado.

After grabbing lunch in Springdale, Wyatt had called Ina to update her, but she wasn't available, so he left a message. He also called ahead to make sure Amado was in the office. He didn't want to make the hour-long drive only to learn that Amado either wasn't there, or wouldn't talk to him.

The girl pointed to an adjoining room where Wyatt could wait. He took a seat in a red cushioned chair with wooden armrests, and grabbed a park magazine off a nicked-up coffee table. He didn't get very far when he began listening to the conversation of two people sitting to his right. Wyatt stole a glimpse of a longhaired, grungy looking guy with body piercings, the locations of which made Wyatt cringe. The guy was wearing torn jeans and beat up converse sneakers, with a green t-shirt on which he proudly proclaimed, in big bold letters, "FREE SEX." Wyatt looked away. *An offer few could refuse.*

But apparently, he was wrong.

Mr. Grunge was seated next to an exact replica, twenty years his elder. Papa Grunge. And it was truly amazing, and scary, to witness firsthand just how far genetics can go. Wyatt faked perusing the magazine as he listened to Baby Grunge lament the fact that he had *no* idea she was underage. "She looked eighteen to me," the kid's scruffy voice and tone suggested the consumption of too many intoxicants. It was loud enough to serve as a confession, if only the deputies had overheard. But Wyatt was practically beside himself as Papa Grunge tried to placate his felonious son by sharing his own stories of drug-induced misdeeds. "Ah hell, nowadays, them twelve and thirteen-year-olds will get all of us in serious trouble. They're blossomin' early and with all that makeup and shit, they look old enough. Hell, I'da made the same mistake myself. Lord knows, I did that plenty of times when I was your age. Just never got caught."

What a father figure.

Then, Wyatt heard his name called. He dropped the magazine and headed towards the glass partition where a young-looking man held the door.

"Detective?" The man put out his hand and Wyatt shook it. "Jess Amado." He motioned with his head. "Come on back."

Wyatt introduced himself and thanked him for taking the time, as he entered the hallway and waited for Amado to lead the way.

Amado stood five eight and rail thin in his khakis, golf shirt, and boat shoes. Wyatt sized him up as no older than thirty-five, even though he looked younger. He had to be in his mid-thirties, at least, as it would take some time to make sergeant, even in small town Utah.

Wyatt followed the sergeant through a hallway maze. He would definitely need help finding his way out. A mouse couldn't find Amado's office, even if they placed a nice big block of cheese outside the door. They entered a large room with ten desks, almost all of which had people working on computers. In the corner of the crowded room was a wooden door with Amado's nameplate on it. They entered the closet-sized office where Amado offered Wyatt a seat in one of two wood-framed guest chairs. Wyatt sat in the corner next to a bookcase filled with reference books on psychology, and police procedure manuals. Behind his head was a large window covered with white horizontal blinds that were closed. Oddly, the window provided nothing more than a prime view of the department's hallway.

Amado settled in behind a large cluttered desk. "So what can I do you for?"

"Nicholas Perrone." Wyatt blew out a breath. He wasn't finished, but took a long enough break that Amado thought otherwise.

"My latest case. If you know where he's at, you could save us a lot of trouble." Amado chuckled.

Wyatt smiled and then his face turned serious. "He's a buddy of mine. I wanna help."

Amado nodded. "OK." The word dragged before he continued. "How?"

The question, and presumably the answer, seemed obvious enough, but Wyatt somehow had trouble explaining it. "With the investigation, I guess."

"I'd appreciate whatever assistance you can provide us."

"Really?" Wyatt couldn't hide his shock, especially after the cold reception he'd received in the park.

"Sure, so long as you keep me informed of your progress. If you interview a witness, I'll expect you to file a report like you would on your own files."

"No problem."

"Truth is, you being close to the family and all adds an element of familiarity with the victim that we don't have. Perrone was alone, no pun intended, and we don't have much on his routine or what kind of person he is, so any assistance would be helpful. The problem is that I just don't think there's much here."

"What do you mean?"

"There's just not a lot of evidence to go on." He reached over his desk and grabbed a small manila folder from a stack near the corner, handed it to Wyatt. "See for yourself."

Pretty thin file, Wyatt thought, as he took it in his hands.

"We did an intensive air and ground search, which came up empty. Out here, that usually means one of three things: either he's trapped or dead in some hidden crack or crevice we can't get to; perhaps the animals got to him before we did, although that's unusual, especially when we received a distress call; or he simply seized an opportunity to disappear and start over somewhere else."

Wyatt cringed.

"We see a lot of that out here," Amado continued "Especially in the last few years, with the economy as bad as it is."

"But you recovered some of Nick's stuff, didn't you? I was told a hat and a backpack, and the pack had his wallet inside, so he probably didn't just run away."

"Yes, we recovered those items. The hat's been sent to the crime lab in Salt Lake for DNA testing of the brim. Unfortunately, that'll be a dead-end until we have a sample to match it with. The wallet? You wouldn't need that if you were going to start over with a new identity, would you?"

"I guess not."

"We had a similar situation last year. Some guy went hiking near Springdale and vanished. But in that case, he left his car at the trailhead. We did an aerial and ground search but there was no sign of him so we brought in the sniffing dog and picked up his scent. But just as soon as the dog picked it up, he lost it."

"It didn't lead you up the trail?"

"No. And so we thought it was a staged disappearance, a 'walkaway.' Fairly common in these parts."

Wyatt nodded; he was familiar with the term.

"We started checking phone records, credit card bills, ATM withdrawals, but found nothing. Finally, we caught a break when we checked prescriptions and learned that he had miraculously filled one a couple of days *after* he went missing. At that point, we knew we had a line on him. The prescription was filled in Southern California, so we checked every airport in the area and got a hit. The guy had obtained a passport and booked a trip to New Zealand. He was trying to get away from his wife and avoid paying child support. Needless to say, he never made it. In fact, you wanna meet him?"

Purgatory.

"I'll pass, thanks," Wyatt said. "So you think Nick did the same thing?"

Amado leaned back. "It's possible. No witnesses, no body, no car. And we've looked everywhere. I've even got the FBI working with us on the car. They put out bulletins in Utah and all neighboring states but nothing's come of it. To me, that's the deciding factor. If this were a kidnapping, or even a hiker's death, we would find the vehicle presumably near one of the shuttle stops. But we haven't. The easiest explanation is that he's still driving it. Remember, he had more than a five hour head start."

Wyatt flipped through the file and examined pictures of the scene. The baseball cap looked familiar, as did Nick's pack. "Simpson at the park told me you might have a copy of the 911 tape."

"I'm working on it. I should have it tomorrow."

"Any thoughts on the scene?" Wyatt asked, as he laid out pictures along the corner of Amado's desk. He fixed his eyes on a photo of Nick's backpack. The picture depicted sheer rock that extended several hundred feet and was sloped at the bottom. It looked like a long and painful slide down a banana-shaped rock face leading into a dark, narrow slot canyon. "You think Nick fell in there?"

Amado shrugged. "I don't know. We lowered a camera but couldn't see very far in. And it's too dangerous to send someone down."

"Any traces of blood on the rock?"

"Whatever you see in the pictures."

Wyatt examined a photo. "Has it rained since Monday?"

"Yes. We're at the tail end of the monsoon season, so if you go up there and don't find blood, it won't mean anything."

Wyatt flipped through the other pictures and pulled one out. He held up the photo, which contained a picture of boot marks in the sandy trail. "What about casting shoe impressions?"

Amado leaned over to look at the picture and Wyatt handed it to him. "Forget it, the sand's too coarse. Just to be sure, I called the FBI and they agreed that there was no way. Nielsen's the name of the agent, Marco Nielsen." He let out a breath. "The sand was too loose and the trail too heavily traveled so even if we *could* get a cast, the print could belong to anyone."

Wyatt looked through the photos again. He was running out of ideas. As if sensing his frustration, Amado cut in, "Like I said, there isn't much evidence."

Wyatt collected the pictures, put them back in the file, and handed it to Amado. "So where do we go from here?"

Amado held up both hands. "We treat it like any other case. We don't stop asking questions until we get our answers."

CHAPTER TWENTY-NINE

"HIS NAME WAS LYLE Prettyman and believe me, the name didn't fit. We used to kid him about it. But he was a good guy, a mechanic in town that I did business with. I run a junkyard near St. George. I buy cars to rip apart and sell off the parts, stuff like that."

"Can you make a living doing that?" Nick was trying to engage Bennie in conversation.

"You won't get rich, but you won't starve either."

"So what about him?" Nick asked.

"To make a little side money, I used to locate cars for people. Lyle and Ethan were mechanics I did that for. They'd call with a make and model and range of years and I would find it for them. I'd have it shipped to the yard and Lyle would come pick it up. We became friends."

"So what happened to him?"

"I'm getting to it. They started asking me to find higher-end cars, and, all of a sudden, they were paying me a lot. So much that I would go the extra mile to make sure I found exactly what they wanted. I figured they had a nice client base and were fetching a hefty sum for the parts. You know, the better the car, the more valuable its parts. It was great money for easy work, and I made it clear I was interested in doing more business."

"I can see where this is going," Nick said, although he really had no idea, but wanted to help push Bennie along.

"Living out here, you hear stories about dead or missing hikers, but that's just Zion and no one thinks much of it. Anyway, Ethan calls me one day, asking if I can deliver one of the cars I've located for them. He says that Lyle can't make it and that if I bring it over, he'll make it worth my while. I could always use extra cash, so I agree, and Ethan gives me directions to some field."

"The Executive Graveyard," Nick said, barely above a whisper. "So what happened next?"

"I went. I get there and they introduce me to Clay. They told me he was one of their associates ..."

Nick would've been on the edge of his seat if he wasn't tied to it.

Bennie took in a breath loud enough to include the semblance of a sniffle. He was looking at the bed. Anywhere but Nick's eyes.

"And that's when I noticed something strange. It was in the backseat of Ethan's truck, or should I say *he* was in the backseat. I pointed at him with my head and said something like, 'What's with the guy in the truck?' Ethan told me he'd let me in on a little secret. He motioned to the car and Clay pulled this poor bastard out. The guy was bruised and bleeding, I'd never seen anyone so scared. They marched the guy over to some dug-up ditch, threw him in, and put two bullets in the back of his head. Point blank. Just like that. Without a word.

"I was beside myself. Not just at what I had witnessed, but also at the efficiency of it. I mean, they made sure that when they fired off the shots, the shells flew into the ditch. And within minutes, they had closed the hole and the ground looked like new. It was as if the guy had never even existed."

"Did you say something?"

"What could I say? Everything happened so fast and they all had guns. Everyone but me. Besides, you've met Ethan and Clay, what would *you* have done?"

"I don't know."

"And they weren't finished. There was a second ditch, which they had dug right next to the first one." Bennie paused. "I'll never forget this. They were laughing about the guy they had just killed, when Ethan and Clay suddenly grew serious and Ethan pointed his gun at

Lyle's head. And Lyle starts screaming 'What are you doing?' But they calmly pushed him into the second ditch, apologized, and told him they loved him but that they had no choice. He begged for his life, but there was no mercy. Ethan said that they had discovered he was planning on leaving them. Lyle had met a woman and decided he wanted out of the enterprise, but the guys couldn't risk it."

"So they shot him?"

"They killed their best friend in cold blood. *My* friend too. And in just the same way. The shells fell into the hole, they closed it up, and just like that, Lyle's existence was erased."

"And so you decided to join them?"

"Ethan came at me next, waiving his gun and all. He said they had decided that I was going to replace Lyle because I was already involved. I said, 'the hell I am. I've got nothing to do with this.' But Ethan put the gun against my forehead and told me that if I went to the police, they wouldn't believe me and that the proof was all that money they had paid me. They'd set me up! He said that if I reported what I had witnessed, they would hunt me down and also kill my sister and her kids. He pulled out a piece of paper and read off their names and address. He said there were other guys working with them and so even if he and Clay were caught, my sister and her children would never be out of harm's way."

Nick was speechless.

"And it was true. They'd paid me a shitload of money for what I did for them. How would it look? If I explained that the money was only to locate cars, would anyone believe me? Of course not. Truth is, though, I didn't have much time to think it through. That afternoon, Ethan gave me a choice: join them and get rich, or take up residence next to Lyle.

"And I'm ashamed to say, I chose the former."

THEY WERE IN THE parking lot when Wyatt told Amado that he wanted to see the scene but that Simpson hadn't taken kindly to his presence.

Amado said he would arrange it, and they agreed to stay in touch as things progressed. As Wyatt reached his car, the skies opened and it began pouring. He jumped into his rental, a Ford Taurus, and as soon as he settled in, took out his notebook and made the following notations:

The car?

Nick's wallet – ask Ina.

Time? Shuttle? Anyone see him?

Cell? On his person?

Come back. 911 tapes.

Medical prescriptions?

Wyatt started the car and was about to pull out when a stocky bald man in a loose fitting, white and black striped jumpsuit with the words "Washington County Purgatory" etched on the back, went running through the parking lot with no one following him. Wyatt watched him run in wonderment. He didn't want to know. Whatever the explanation, it was certainly not a good sign.

He decided to get out of there as fast as he could.

CHAPTER-THIRTY

WYATT PULLED UP TO a two-story structure that looked like one corner of the Pentagon. The building sat near the top of an incline, which overlooked most of the downtown area. Then again, the word "downtown" in St. George was grossly misleading, since it was really no different than the rest of the city: a mix of fast food restaurants, gas stations, the occasional strip mall, and a few car dealers nestled among red rock canyons fronting vast mountain vistas.

Marco Nielsen was well proportioned, with sparse black hair that seemed to be struggling making a decision: turn gray or simply bolt. Right now, it looked to be choosing both. He wore a charcoal suit and a red paisley tie with a white button-down shirt that wrinkled at the base of his small, yet rounded stomach. Wyatt did not see a gun or holster but definitely noticed Nielsen's badge hanging from his belt.

Nielsen gazed at Wyatt through long rimmed glasses. "Are you the detective that's asking for me?"

Good guess. He was the only one in the waiting area. Wyatt introduced himself and showed his badge.

"You can put that away and keep it there," Nielsen said firmly, raising his hand. "If you want to use it, I suggest you drive about ten or fifteen miles south on the 15 across state line by the Virgin River Gorge. There, you can flash your Arizona badge all you want. But this is Utah. Now, if you want to follow me, I'll give you five minutes because I'm extremely busy."

Wyatt followed Nielsen down a nondescript hallway and into a small conference room. Wyatt had worked with the FBI just once in his career, on a bank robbery turned deadly in the Phoenix area. Since the federal government insures banks, robberies fall within the FBI's jurisdiction. They weren't bad to work with on that particular case, although Wyatt had heard of the great ego clashes and jurisdictional conflicts they had with local law enforcement in larger cities like New York and Los Angeles.

They each took a seat.

"So what's the Phoenix Police doing in Southern Utah?"

"My friend's missing; he was hiking in the park. Name's Nick Perrone."

"I'm familiar. So what do you want from me?"

"Sergeant Amado mentioned that you're assisting in the investigation."

"I'll have to remember to thank him," Nielsen said, as Wyatt shifted uncomfortably in his chair.

Wyatt started to talk but Nielsen cut him off. "Let me make this easier for both of us and set the record straight. I have no idea why Amado sent you here. The FBI is *not* investigating your friend's disappearance. We are, however, lending a hand in a *very* limited capacity solely due to the scarcity of the county's resources. So I really don't know why you're here. Truth is? You're just a private citizen to me, and I don't know why I should even talk to you about an active file."

Wyatt felt like an attorney being chastised by the court for filing a frivolous motion.

"I would suggest you direct your inquiries to Sergeant Amado," Nielsen added.

"I've already talked with him, so please indulge me for a few minutes and I'll be on my way. I just want some information."

"I don't have much, but what I've got goes to the county unless they tell me otherwise."

"Let's cut the bureaucratic crap, OK?" Wyatt said. "Yes, I'm an outsider here, but I somehow learned that you're involved. A miracle?

135

Of course not. You want to call Amado? Be my guest. But it'll be a helluva lot quicker if you answer a few questions so I can get out of your hair."

Nielsen engaged Wyatt in a momentary staring contest and Wyatt's game-face never wavered.

"Fine. The sheriff called and asked if we could help pull a print off the sand where your guy was last heard from, but since the sand is coarse and the trail heavily traveled, there was little we could do."

"Amado mentioned you're trying to find his car."

"Durango, right?" Nielsen asked and Wyatt confirmed. "No sign of it. I've had agents check all the shuttle stops and canvass the surrounding area, which is not that difficult. We've tried the Motor Vehicle Bureau, used car dealers, mechanics, chop shops, you name it. I've also got APB's in Idaho, Nevada, and Arizona, but so far, nothing."

"Amado thinks that maybe Nick took the car himself and disappeared."

"And he could very well be right. It's been done many times out in these parts. Either Perrone's alive and has the car, or he's gone and it was taken. Those are the only possibilities since, if he parked anywhere near a shuttle, we would've found it."

"You see a lot of auto theft out here?"

"Not really, but we're following the textbook anyway. We searched through town on the oft chance that someone took it for a joyride and dumped it. We've also checked to see if it was taken and dismantled for parts. Another dead-end. The only other possibility we're considering is identity theft; it's called VIN swapping, but it's a complicated crime that I've never seen or heard of up here. Are you familiar with it?"

Wyatt shook his head. "Vaguely."

"Changing a car's identity isn't easy. You need an old, usually salvaged or wrecked vehicle of a similar make and model with the stolen car. The VINs are then exchanged and the stolen car assumes the identity of the wrecked or salvaged one. Then, clean ownership requires nothing more than a title transfer."

"The problem with that crime, I presume, is catching it."

"Precisely. Once the swap is made, the car looks legit and our only chance of recovery would be if the car has another means to identify it, like a bumper sticker or something. It's that simple. It's also pretty elaborate for this area, since VIN swappers transport the cars elsewhere, usually overseas. That's where the money is."

"What kind of money are we talking about?"

"You can rake it in if you can manage to get the car into a third world country. If you ship a car to a place where there aren't dealers on every corner like we have here in the States, we're talking six figures. High-end vehicles can fetch three, four hundred grand, or more." Nielsen looked at his watch. "I gotta run."

Wyatt shook his head repeatedly while he took notes. Despite Nielsen's boorishness, he felt good about the fact that the FBI was involved. Their jurisdictional capabilities and vast resources certainly gave him hope. "I appreciate it. I'll let you know if I need any more information."

"I don't think so." Nielsen stood. "You've got your answers, *detective.* Now keep your nose out of someone else's investigation. The authorities out here: us, the sheriff, police, park rangers, we're all quite capable and I really don't know what you're doing here. Leave us to do our jobs and you'll get your answers when *we* give them to you. Now if you'll excuse me."

ETHAN WRAPPED HIS GREASY paws around the longneck and felt the stress of the day begin to dissipate, as a wave of ice-cold lager slid easily through his palate. He savored the flavor for an instant, but it didn't last long enough, so he quickly poured more down his chute. The late afternoon crowd consisted of an old barfly at the opposite end, and a middle-aged construction worker sitting in the corner by the television, listening to country music playing on a boom box. The man was fast becoming a regular ever since he broke his arm. He was sporting a hard cast on his right forearm, on which a well-humored friend had colorfully written: "FRAGILE – DO NOT BEND!"

Ethan downed the beer and motioned for another round. He held up the empty bottle, which was still sweating, until Clay made his way over.

"Sorry about the interruption, man." Clay slid a chair over and sat. "You know what they say: the customer is always intoxicated."

"Here, here." Ethan held up his new bottle and took a swig. "Where's yours?" When Clay shrugged, Ethan said, "How many have you had today?"

"I don't know, enough for a minor buzz, but not enough to make me forget that I have a shitty business."

They laughed, and Ethan leaned in against the counter. "We got ourselves a juicy new development. The Phoenix Police is in town."

"What are they doing here?"

"Apparently, Perrone has a friend. He came to the park today and started asking questions."

"Then we should take Perrone right back to the Graveyard and put him down. Don't you think?"

"I don't know. I don't care."

"What does your dad want to do?"

"With Perrone? He's not sure yet. With the cop friend? Nothing. Let him poke around, he's not gonna find anything. Dad said you did a nice job with the evidence."

"Course I did. So, what, we continue with business as usual?"

"That's right. Don't worry about the cop, my dad's on top of it. He's going to try and figure some way of keeping tabs on what he's doing."

"But what if he starts getting close?"

"Easy," Ethan said, putting the bottle to his mouth. "We can always dig another hole."

CHAPTER THIRTY-ONE

TWO OUT OF THREE was bad.

Wyatt had met with all three players and two of them had pretty much told him to stay away. Wyatt's only solace was that the one who didn't, Amado, was in charge of the investigation. Still, attitudes made Wyatt uneasy, especially Simpson's, because Wyatt intended to poke around in the park more than anyplace else. Bureaucratic bullshit. It was something every cop had to deal with, no matter where they were.

Wyatt pulled his car to the side of the road because there was something pressing he had to address. He'd been dreading it all day. The red light flashing on his phone, indicating multiple voicemails, told him he could not put this off any longer. He dialed.

"Wyatt? Where the hell are you? I got a body in a dumpster downtown and I'm short-staffed. You said you would be here."

Not the reception Wyatt had hoped for. But, things had happened so quickly yesterday that Wyatt had left Phoenix without first clearing it with his captain.

"I know, Cappy, and I'm sorry. Remember me and my buddy were going to go camping in Utah?"

"Yeah, but you cancelled. I was counting on you being here."

"Right. But my buddy went without me and now he's missing. His wife came by yesterday hysterical and next thing I knew, I was in Utah trying to find him. Sorry I didn't call sooner, it's just …"

"You know what? It wouldn't have made a damn bit of difference." He paused, and Wyatt could just sense him pacing his office. He lowered his tone. "Your father was a great man, the best. My partner for thirty years, and I couldn't have asked for better. I miss him. I made him a promise and I'm a man of my word, so I'm telling you Wyatt, as your godfather, I will always be there for you. But as your boss, and captain of this department, I'm tired of your shit."

"I can't leave a close friend hanging. His life is at stake."

"I understand. And I hope you find what you're looking for, because we've reached the point where even Frank would've done what I'm about to. Son, you've got talent and can be an excellent detective. But the shooting, divorce, depression, alcohol, performance issues, I put up with all of it because of who your father was. But the statute of limitations has passed, and I'm tired of you struggling to fit the department into your life when it should be the other way around."

"But Cappy—"

"We all make decisions in life and you made yours without checking with me. We've supported you through the rough times but it's clear to me that you do not have the department's best interests in mind." He paused. "Got your badge and piece with you?"

"Yes," Wyatt said quietly as he felt the onset of a massive headache. The fear of what came next was already pounding at his temples.

"I'll expect them on my desk the moment you return."

"CAN I HAVE A drink?" Nick asked. "Some water would be great. I'm really dehydrated." Nick began breathing harder to sell it and Bennie eyed him momentarily, probably to determine if he was up to something. But seconds later, Bennie relented and left the room.

Bennie's story had flowed easily and Nick's contributions were deliberately terse with one goal in mind: keep Bennie talking. Nick felt the unceasing dread of an inevitable confrontation. But then he had finished eating and sensed that Bennie was ready to leave the room. Nick's challenge was to find a way to keep him there and ultimately, break through the barrier. The next few minutes with Bennie would be crucial and Nick started planning it out in his mind. But that didn't last long when Nick realized Bennie's oversight.

His gun. It was on the dresser.

Nick knew he had to move quickly. And this was different than grappling for the knife because Nick now had a free hand to work with. He thought of using it to untie his other hand, but decided there wasn't time. It had taken Bennie several minutes to undo the one knot and he had failed, choosing instead to just cut the rope. If he wanted the gun, he would have to lunge for it. Nick leaned forward and pushed off the bed with his free hand to get some lift and just at that moment, Bennie swiftly returned, scooped up the gun, and held it in the air.

"Almost forgot this," Bennie said. "Don't go anywhere." Then, seeing Nick, Bennie smirked. "You didn't think it would be that easy, did you?"

Bennie left the room and returned a moment later, handed Nick a bottle of water, and went to sit on the dresser.

"I don't know how you do it," Nick said, taking a sip.

"Do what?"

"Live like this. I'm sure the money's great but your very existence must be filled with fear.

"Every time we hit that field I wonder if I'll be coming home. And every time we're there, I can't get Lyle's execution out of my mind. The money is meaningless because of the fear, and the saddest part is that no one would ever believe my story."

"*I'm* having a hard time believing it." And just as he said it, Nick felt the inevitable dread of confrontation. His plan all along had been to bait Bennie into moral conflict and see if he could turn him. But had he pushed too far?

"You think I made that shit up?"

"Whoa, relax. I don't doubt you." But it didn't come out very convincing.

"Hell, I could've told you anything I wanted." Bennie raised his voice. "What I shared with you was the truth. I never wanted *anything* to do with this."

"Then why didn't you help me back there?" Nick raised *his* voice, but only to a level of cautious annoyance. "When we were in the car, or the field, or when the cop pulled us over. You had plenty of opportunities. Why didn't you do something?"

The words hung in the air like a cloud of smoke in a nightclub. Bennie seemed surprised at the obvious question and didn't know how to answer it. He closed his eyes and held them shut. "Because they would kill us. You and me both."

"But you said they'll probably kill you anyway. They shot Lyle, your predecessor, right before your eyes. Why are you any different?"

Bennie was unable to meet Nick's gaze. "I'm not."

There it was, the admission Nick had been waiting for.

"Look, we can go to the authorities and you can tell them what's going on. They'll cut you a deal. You never killed anyone and you can prove it."

"Can't do it. It would be my word against theirs and no one will believe me. If anything, they've got the proof on me. I took the money, a lot of it. There's no way anyone would get that much money just to locate a couple of cars." Bennie clutched the gun. "They set me up good."

"You're wrong," Nick said. "They missed something huge. You've got evidence."

"Forget it. Whatever it is, it won't work. I'm ensconced in this thing and it scares the shit out of me."

"Then that leaves us with one other option."

"What's that?"

"Kill them before they kill us."

CHAPTER THIRTY-TWO

WYATT TOSSED THE PHONE on the passenger seat, rubbed his eyes, and laid his head on the steering wheel. Golf-sized hail pelted the rental, which, much like his life right now, was going nowhere. Wyatt had finally accomplished the inevitable; he'd been fired by the Phoenix Police Department. And who was he kidding? He'd been a problem for them since joining the force. He'd tested their patience until they reached their boiling point. It no longer mattered who his father was. That Frank had been the chief of police helped Wyatt get started, but at the end of the day, he was no different than any other officer.

Absorbing the impact of his termination, Wyatt wondered if perhaps, subconsciously, he had wanted it all along. He was a good detective and well regarded by virtually everyone but himself, but he was often depressed and lacked the swagger and self-confidence you'd expect from the city's finest. Had he suppressed a desire to be fired? Sure, there were times that his heart wasn't into it, but there was something deep and powerful that always motivated him to go to work in the morning.

The memory of his father.

Deep down, Wyatt knew that leaving the force would be the final abandonment of his father, and it was something he couldn't bring himself to. Perhaps, Wyatt wondered, that was the root of his troubles, the desire to be something other than what his father was. If that were the case, he'd finally succeeded.

Wyatt reached for the phone and dialed for some support, but after several rings, Tavares beckoned him to leave a message. He tried thinking of what to say when he slowly realized it didn't matter. He was divorced, unemployed, a not-so-completely-recovered alcoholic, and stuck on the side of a dark road in Utah in the midst of a towering rainstorm, searching for the slightest clue as to the whereabouts of his closest friend, someone he'd barely spoken to in the last five years and whose disappearance he could very well be responsible for.

His shoulders weren't broad enough.

NICK WAS REELING FROM his failed attempts to convert Bennie. And what was he thinking? Did he really believe a twenty-minute conversation would turn a killer into his savior? Still, Nick had been certain of Bennie's vulnerability and had no choice but to try and take advantage of it. And he'd felt so close to a breakthrough, only to see Bennie storm out on him and his plans for their sovereignty. But Nick knew that he couldn't dwell on it because every minute that passed with him in the chair brought him one minute closer to execution.

Now. Do it now!

Nick's mind quickly shifted gears. His still had use of his right hand; Bennie had forgotten to tie him back up. How much longer did he have until Bennie realized his misstep? As he had done yesterday, Nick pushed off the bed and began falling to his side, this time trying to break the fall with his right hand. As he slid off the side, Nick fell forward and absorbed the impact with his right knee. He had to hurry. Landing on the carpet had produced a thud loud enough for Bennie to hear in the other room.

Laying on his side, Nick extended his hand as far under the bed as he could and swept it along the carpet. Nothing. He grunted as he pulled himself closer to the bed and, once again, extended out his hand. In another sweeping motion, he ran his hand along the floor and finally felt the cold edge of the knife. It was barely within reach. Suddenly, there were footsteps coming from the kitchen. Nick tried mightily to get himself closer so he could reach out farther. Now, he was right up against the bed but the footsteps were getting closer. With no time to waste, Nick swept his hand along the carpet and touched the knife again. This time, he laid his finger on it hoping to slide it along. But instead, his finger slid off the knife and hit the carpet. Time was running out. Sweat jumped off his brow as he tried to figure out how to retrieve the knife.

Friction.

Nick licked his finger and then rubbed it dry on the carpet. Then, he stretched as far as his limbs would allow, grimaced, and tried to withhold the kind of grunt you might normally hear from a female tennis player on a powerful forehand. That's when Nick pushed down on the knife and dragged it slowly along the carpet and it came to rest several inches closer. Nick sent his hand back out, this time taking the knife in his palm. And just as he grabbed it, Nick heard Bennie approach the room so he quickly slipped the knife back in his pocket. When he looked up, Bennie was staring at him with suspicious eyes and Nick tried to avoid showing a guilty face. But it was a tough sell; perspiration enveloped Nick's forehead and he was out of breath.

"What the hell are you up to?"

Bennie bent down and looked under the bed.

"Find anything under there?" Bennie asked, laughing as though whatever Nick had tried was futile. He pointed at the chair. "You want to tell me what this is?"

"This chair and this position? It hurts my back and when I tip myself over, it relieves the pain."

WAITING OUT THE STORM had cost Wyatt forty-five minutes of anxiety-filled contemplation and the one thing he took out of it was that he needed some relief.

Immediately.

The Bit and Spur was a Mexican restaurant and saloon in Springdale, at which Wyatt sat at the end of the bar in the place designated for someone about to get plastered. He fancied whiskey, but a beer was his way of "sticking with the program," sort of like drinking a diet Coke with a five course meal. The bartender, a bald and burly fellow named Hank, placed a longneck Budweiser atop a napkin in front of him. Wyatt was about to take his first swig in a while when he heard the word, "detective?"

Wyatt turned and managed a smile when he saw the olive eyes and flowing hair. He put the beer down. "Velvet, right?" She was still in her ranger's uniform, but had removed her nametag, ditched the hat, and let her hair down for the evening.

She flashed a smile. "You remember my name. I'm flattered."

"How could I forget? Besides, it's not like we met several weeks ago, it was just this morning."

She lost some of the grin.

"What brings you here? Are you meeting someone?" he asked.

"No. I come in here pretty often for dinner. There isn't much else out here."

Wyatt patted the stool next to his. "Care to join me then?"

"Maybe a quick beer before I take out." She smiled and sat down. Wyatt lifted his arm but she beat him to the punch. "Hank," she called out, "Bud Light." Then she turned to Wyatt, looked at her watch and said, "Drinking early are we? Didn't think you'd have time for a beer so soon. Everything all right?"

He thought about sharing his termination, but then remembered how impressed she had been with his badge, so he decided to keep it to himself. "Is it that obvious?"

She laughed as Hank set the beer in front of her. Velvet reached for her purse, but Wyatt had already thrown a five on the bar. "No luck, huh?"

Wyatt shook his head.

"Look, I'm no detective but I'm sure these things take time. I just hope you're prepared for what you might find."

"And that is?"

"Nothing, other than the fact that maybe Nick wanted to disappear. Have you considered that possibility?"

Wyatt looked at his bottle. "How could I not? It seems to be the company line out here. That and the fact that I have no business being here."

"This land is their land," she hummed. "I work for the park police and I know the county sheriff, and they're capable. How would you feel if the friend of the victim in a crime *you* were investigating showed up asking questions and insisting that he be involved? Wouldn't you feel like maybe someone doesn't have confidence in you?"

"I hear you. I guess I kind of hoped that when someone's life is at stake, grown men can put aside their egos and work together. A perfect world it isn't."

"Just do your thing. It's not all bad. By the way, my partner, Martin Rugie, asked me to escort you to the scene, at Amado's request. So, let's talk tomorrow and see if we can get up there. I was one of the rangers who processed the scene and there was no sign of him anywhere. And when I later heard that his car was nowhere to be found, I knew exactly what we had."

Their eyes locked and she continued. "I hope I'm wrong, but I think you may leave here disappointed." She took a long pull and Wyatt watched her hair dance back and forth.

"Why so pessimistic?" Wyatt asked.

"It's not pessimism; it's reality. I've been here five years and seen everything that goes on. Look, it's a rugged park with difficult trails and steep canyons. Accidents happen. Just a couple of weeks ago, a hiker fell into the river and died. I mean, the statistics aren't pretty. We have, I'd say, five to ten deaths or disappearances a year. They are accidents, suicides, and sometimes just hikers who are unprepared. But we also have people who use the park as a diversion to start a new life. You saw those posters in the Visitor Center. They've been there so long; we're never going to find those people. Each case is different, but if someone doesn't want to be found, you're not gonna find him."

Velvet finished her beer and motioned for Hank. She pulled out her wallet and paid as he placed her dinner on the bar. Then, she pulled out one of her business cards and wrote something on the back. "If I can help, or if you just want another beer, call me." She handed him the card. "Home number's on the back."

Wyatt examined the card and shook his head. "I may just do that."

"I hope you do."

"If nothing other than to let you know that you were wrong."

CHAPTER THIRTY-THREE

Tuesday

JUST LIKE HER NAME, Kathy Evans was a simple person. The senior from Boise, Idaho, had retired from teaching more than ten years ago, but had since had trouble filling the void in her daily life. In 2000, a friend told her about the new shuttle system being implemented in Zion. The park was looking for volunteer drivers, and Kathy thought it would be a perfect way to spend her golden years. It didn't take long for the park to hire her, and she immediately fell in love with her new surroundings. The job was easy. She drove ten loops a day, five days a week, each loop taking about a half hour. The shuttles ran from May through October, which left Kathy half the year to do other things.

WYATT YAWNED AND RUBBED his forehead as he approached the pink concrete bench outside the Visitor Center. Wyatt had consumed one too many beers the previous evening, and it wasn't much of a consolation to the headache he was now suffering that he'd been able to walk away before inflicting more damage.

Kathy stood to greet him. "Are you the detective?"

"Yes," Wyatt said with hesitation, deciding not to explain yesterday's career-changing event. "I won't take much of your time. That missing hiker from the other day is a friend of mine."

"And you want to know if I saw him on my bus?"

Wyatt shook his head. "I was hoping you might remember."

"I see." She smiled and they shook hands. "We can sit for a minute or two, but that's all the time I've got."

They sat on the bench and Wyatt pulled out pictures.

"This is Nick. He went missing on Monday. He was last heard from in the morning while hiking to Observation Point." He handed Kathy pictures of Nick and his baseball cap, and explained that he was probably wearing it that morning.

"That's the Weeping Rock stop," she said, examining the picture. Then she looked at him. "Do you know about what time he would've taken the shuttle?"

"He called 911 at shortly before seven, and he was already about eight hundred feet up the trail."

"Do we know where he got on?"

"I was hoping you could help me answer that, since we haven't been able to find his car."

"That's odd. I don't know how long it would take to hike that far but if it's more than a few minutes, he couldn't have been on my shuttle. I drove the 6:30, which would have reached Weeping Rock at about ten to seven."

She handed him back the pictures as if there was nothing she could do for him.

"What about the way back? Do you remember if he got on your shuttle for the return trip?"

She looked at him askance. "I thought you said he went missing after he called for help. How could he have been on my return shuttle?"

"We're not really sure what happened to him, but we are looking at everything, including the possibility that the 911 call was a diversion."

"You mean faking his own disappearance? I've heard that happens here quite a bit. I think we had one last year, heard it on the news."

"The fact that we can't find his car may support that theory." Wyatt pulled out Nick's picture again, this time holding back the photo of the baseball cap. "Take another look at him but ignore the hat this time. We found it on the trail, so if he did take your shuttle on the way back, he wouldn't have been wearing it."

"OK. Truth is, that makes it easier for me because that early in the morning isn't very busy. Most people are going out to the sights, not coming back. So I'm trying to picture the shuttle stop. I probably would've noted someone returning from Weeping Rock that early but …" She wrinkled her nose. "I just can't remember, I'm sorry. I'm not getting any younger." She looked at her watch. "And I have to go."

"I appreciate your time."

She smiled as she stood. "My pleasure. Maybe you'll have better luck with the other drivers, the earlier shuttles I presume. There would've been two of them that day. But I have to be honest with you. We see thousands of visitors from all over the world and I think it would be virtually impossible to remember a single one of them."

THE CLICKING SOUND ON the door stirred Simpson out of an early morning reverie. He looked up and smiled as he caught his friend, Martin Rugie, rapping on the door with Simpson's handcuffs. "Got a minute?" Rugie asked.

Simpson motioned with his head to come in. "You look annoyed. What's on your mind?"

Rugie entered with a file in hand and sat in one of the visitor chairs. He placed the file on the edge of Simpson's desk. "Like you, I'm also disturbed that this cop came out here from Phoenix."

"Not just that," Simpson said. "But he's here in my office the very next morning."

"I was reading up on the file, thought I might supplement my reports. Then I read the summary you prepared after you spoke with the wife, and I found something interesting. She told you this never should have happened because Perrone wasn't supposed to be here by himself. He was supposed to be with a friend."

"I remember."

"Did she give you any details?"

Simpson wrapped his hands around his head and leaned back to think. "I recall something about them having a fight and the friend bailed on him."

"Did she tell you who the friend is?"

"I don't think so."

"Take a look at this." Rugie pulled out a document called *Watchman Campsite Reservation Form* from the file. He slid it across the desk. "Have a look at the *friend* who actually reserved Perrone's campsite."

"Wyatt Orr." Simpson read the name off the form.

"The cop," Rugie said. "He was supposed to be here with Perrone, but they had a fight."

Simpson grinned. "I knew something wasn't right when he showed up first thing the next morning."

"Think about it. That means—"

Simpson cut him off. "That he was here on the day his friend went missing.

CHAPTER THIRTY-FOUR

AS SOON AS SHE heard his voice she wished she hadn't answered the phone. Tavares had caller ID but had let her guard down while preparing for an early session with a stressed out, big firm lawyer.

"I really can't talk now. I'm about to start with a patient." Her tone was firm, almost condescending.

"Did you get my message?" Wyatt asked.

"Yes, but—"

He cut her off. "I really need help. I'm having the nightmare just about every night now."

Tavares told Wyatt to hold on, put her hand over the receiver and apologized to the young barrister. Explaining it as a patient crisis, she promptly excused herself to another room.

"I'm back," she said to Wyatt, as she walked down the hall to her kitchen.

"What do you think it means?"

"I'd have to dig deeper before I can give you an analysis, and I can't do that right now."

"When can you?"

She hesitated. "Look, I've been meaning to tell you something and I don't know that this is the best time or way, but we can't see each other anymore."

"What are you talking about?"

Realizing it sounded more like a relationship break-up, Tavares clarified, "I can't treat you anymore." Then she whispered, "I'm sorry."

"I don't understand. How can you do this? I'm your patient."

She switched gears, trying to avoid sharing her feelings. "I've arranged for you to continue with someone else, an excellent therapist. I've already told him about you."

"You discussed my problems with someone else, without asking me?"

Tavares put her hand over her brow and tried to hold back the flow of tears. "I didn't give him specifics, I just told him I was sending you over. Look, I've got an irresolvable conflict and I *must* terminate your treatment. Trust me, it's best for both of us."

"What conflict? None of this makes any sense and I want to know where this came from. It's all so sudden and out of the blue."

"Trust me, it isn't. I've been ..." She wanted to tell him that she had thought it through, but decided she didn't want him to know that she'd been contemplating this as far back as several years ago.

"Your timing is for shit, you know that? I'm having terrible nightmares every night, and I got fired yesterday."

"Fired? What for?"

"I don't even want to get into it. Truth is, that's what I need you for."

"Honestly, this is for the best. Besides, if you're no longer on the force, I'd have to stop seeing you because the department's not going to pay for it."

"I don't care about the money. I can pay you on my own."

She exhaled her stress into the phone. "I really have to get back to my patient. Call me later and I'll give you Dr. Jennings' number."

She hung up.

But before Wyatt could process what had just happened, another call came in and Wyatt switched over. He listened to the voice on the other line and said:

"I'm on my way."

A CONFLICT?

What did *that* mean? Wyatt had just been fired, and given his troubled past, it didn't come as a complete surprise. But being dumped by his shrink, especially when it was unrelated to his termination from the department? *What the hell?*

Wyatt dug deep into his memory bank, but couldn't figure out what could possibly be the problem. Was she attracted to him? Wyatt had always taken notice of her appraisals, especially early in his treatment. But he had convinced himself that a counselor twenty years his elder would be professional enough not to develop feelings for a patient. Or would she?

Maybe she was upset that he had abruptly ended his treatment a while back. But why should she care? Her job was to help those who asked for it, and Wyatt was the one to decide when he needed her. Neither theory clicked in his mind, and Wyatt's frustration was quickly mounting.

And what about Nick? Was he alive? *If I'd only gone on the trip.* The guilt was eating at him.

Could things get any worse?

And then they did.

CHAPTER THIRTY-FIVE

"I'VE GOT SOME INFORMATION on the Perrone case."

Amado stood as Torkner entered his office. "I'm going for a smoke, wanna join me outside?"

Torkner looked at his watch and made a face. "Isn't it a little early for that? It's not even ten o'clock."

Amado grinned as he walked by Torkner and through the doorway, "When you're a cop who smokes, and most of us do, the words 'early' and 'late' don't exist."

Torkner followed Amado to the parking lot where Amado was tearing the strip off a new pack. With the look of a man anxious to feed his urge, Amado smacked the bottom until one of the stingy cigarettes finally fell out.

"So what do you got?" Amado lit up.

Torkner held up a bunch of papers. "Cell phone records. I think you'll find them interesting."

Amado took a puff. "Shoot."

"The 911 call wasn't his last. The wife called him and he answered the phone. But get this, the call was made several hours later."

"I already know about it. That's what got her so worried that she called the park. But she said when he answered, she heard nothing but static. I read it in Simpson's summary." Amado blew out a ring. "Where was he when he answered?"

"Based on the cell tower that picked it up, the Springdale/Rockville area."

"So our theory is looking better by the minute," Amado said. "It was a ruse. He planted his shit on the trail so we would think he was in trouble, but the call from his wife proves he slipped out of the park *after* he called 911."

"That would be my guess." Torkner hesitated and Amado picked up on it.

"Why not?"

"If we're saying he was bolting for Bettersville, what was he doing there in Springdale while we were searching for him in the park?"

Amado thought for a moment. "How do you know he spent any time there?"

"The call was made several hours after the 911 call. If he was moving on, you would think he would want to get as big a head start as he could. Why wait around a few hours?"

"It's a good point, but unconvincing. He ditched his stuff high up on the trail and it's not like he was in a big city where the police would be there in a few minutes. He knew it would take time just to get there, not to mention climbing all the way up that trail. So a couple of hours isn't very long."

"Yeah but why risk being seen?"

"Maybe he didn't. Maybe it was part of his plan. Maybe he hung out to make the call and then dump the phone. Did any other towers pick up a signal?"

"None."

"So that's it. Maybe he dumped the phone out there."

"Yeah, but if you're going to leave your phone behind why not drop it in the canyon with the rest of your stuff? And why answer one last call from the wife? There's something about this that doesn't fit."

Amado blew out some smoke. "He wants us to close our file quickly. The call with the wife was nothing more than static, but he was telling us he's moving on. Do we have anything else? Has he used his credit card since?"

"No."

"What about money, any bank activity?"

"None."

"Prescriptions? Airline tickets?"

"No."

Amado tossed the cigarette to the floor and mashed it with foot. He started back toward the door.

"What if there was foul play?" Torkner said. "Don't we have to consider that possibility?"

Amado turned around. "What would be the motive?"

"Murder? I don't know."

"Murder is an act, not necessarily a motive. *Why* would there be foul play?"

Torkner shrugged, as Amado patted the bottom of his pack and this time a cigarette slid out easily. He stuck it in his mouth. "I'll answer that for you. Money? What about the one thing no one can find? His car."

"I guess so."

Amado was enjoying mentoring his young deputy. "So take it forward now. Why do *you* suspect foul play?"

"Maybe leaving the pack behind was a plant, and the 911 call a misdirection."

"Make it look like an accident? I'm with you. But I keep coming back to the same question you had. Why wouldn't the perps ditch the phone with the pack?"

Torkner shrugged again, his facial expression showing a lack of confidence in his theory. "They needed the phone for the 911 call, the misdirection."

"No they don't. Make the call first and *then* dump the pack and the phone together. But you know why your theory has legs? Because the Springdale call could *be* the misdirection. If someone else is behind this, maybe they dumped the phone in Springdale to make it look like Perrone bolted."

"So it's a draw. How do we break the tie?"

"Simple. Get the 911 tape and call the cop friend back in to listen to it. Here's where he can be helpful. He'll be able to tell us if it's Perrone's voice on the tape."

"I'M MARTIN RUGIE, ONE of the park rangers. Thanks for coming in."

"No problem," Wyatt said, and took a seat in the corner of Simpson's office. Rugie sat next to him in the chair closest to the door.

"Where were you on Monday morning?" Simpson asked, eschewing any pleasantries.

Wyatt furrowed his brow. "What was Monday morning?"

"Just answer the question." Simpson said.

"That's when Perrone went missing," Rugie interceded.

Wyatt's eyes widened. "Wait, are you saying I'm a *suspect*?"

"Why don't *you* tell us, *Detective*? Where were you when your friend disappeared?"

He looked at both rangers. "This is ridiculous. And you guys aren't even running the investigation. I don't have to answer to you."

"Sure you do," Simpson said. "We're working with the sheriff and we have police jurisdiction here in the park. Now, we know you were in Utah on Monday and that's the day Perrone disappeared. We also know that you were the one who reserved Perrone's campsite. But you didn't go camping with him in the end. Why not?"

"Because I changed my mind."

Simpson shot Rugie a look and the two smirked at each other. Simpson was dying to blow this right out of the water. "Why don't you tell us about your fight with Perrone."

"What are you talking—"

Simpson cut him off. "Cut the shit and don't lie to us. His wife told me you had a fight and bailed on your *buddy* at the eleventh hour. What are friends for, right?"

"Were you angry with him?" Rugie asked.

"Don't even try this crap with me," Wyatt said.

"I had trouble with your presence here so early in the investigation, until it hit me: you were here when Perrone went missing."

"You're barking up the wrong tree, Simpson. What you're doing now is the perfect reason for me to be here. Your incompetence."

"Why shouldn't I take you into custody right now?"

"I don't have to deal with this." Wyatt stood. "You wanna arrest me, come find me."

He stormed out.

Simpson and Rugie laughed, and then Simpson picked up the phone. He dialed a three number extension, and, when Velvet answered, asked her to stop in. Seconds later she was standing in the doorway.

"What's going on?" she asked.

"It's the cop from Phoenix; we don't trust him. I know we're short-staffed, but I want to know what he's up to. Can you keep tabs on him and report back?" Simpson stood and felt for the keys in his pocket. "Sorry to cut this short but I'm going to run into Springdale for some breakfast. Can you help with this?"

"Consider it done."

CHAPTER THIRTY-SIX

WYATT POUNDED THE STEERING wheel with his fist as he pulled into a tight parking spot under a large oak in the Visitor Center lot. *What assholes.* So what if Wyatt had reserved the campsite, or even had a fight with Nick? Does that mean that he followed Nick here to kill him? Ridiculous. Would a killer so boldly immerse himself in the investigation of his victim's disappearance? The suggestion was absurd.

Wyatt reached into the glove box to make sure his gun was loaded. If they planned on arresting him, he certainly wouldn't make it easy. He arched his head to the left until he felt his neck muscles snap, and took a deep breath upon the release of tension. Then he dialed Ina's cell and when he got her voicemail, he let it all out.

"You won't believe what just happened here." No hello or identification of who was calling. "They think *I'm* a suspect because you told them that Nick and I had a fight before he came out here, and then I showed up the morning after. I really wish you hadn't spoken to Simpson because the man is a prick. I just stormed out of his office and I don't know if they're going to try to detain me, or bring me in for questioning. Simpson's got two things that scare me most: an ego the size of Texas, and police power in the park. There's actually a jail in his office.

"Anyway, can you do me a favor right away? Please call a guy named Jess Amado. He's the county sheriff and seems like a decent guy. You *must* tell him that you came to see me in Phoenix on the day Nick disappeared. I know it sounds completely ridiculous and I can't believe I even have to ask, but it will at least give me the alibi to get these park assholes off my case." Wyatt paused a moment. "And where are you? I'm building a relationship with your voicemail. Please call me back."

He left Amado's number and hung up.

The day was not progressing as Wyatt had hoped. The meeting with Kathy Evans came up empty, and then he was accused of murdering his best friend. It wasn't even noon.

Wyatt had a little less than an hour before his next appointment. Late morning wasn't the best time to scour the campground for witnesses, since most campers had already left for the day. And, while Nick had disappeared only two days ago, the park and campground had a high rate of daily turnover. Many people stop through the park for just a day or two before moving onto their next destination. The chances of finding witnesses were deteriorating by the minute, but Wyatt was there and had some time to kill. And, he'd been a detective long enough to know that, sometimes, just one witness who could tell you that things weren't as they seem, could change the course of an entire investigation.

MORTY AND KAYLEEN WERE those witnesses.

They were the ones whom Nick had met when he first went hiking, several days before his disappearance. They could easily attest that, yes, Nick had climbed the trail to Observation Point, but he had done it two days *before* he went missing. Chances were, he wouldn't climb the same trail two days later.

Northeast of the Visitor Center was the Watchman Campground's Loop C, exclusively used for RV camping. It looked like a playground for the rich, each site filled with a bus-like vehicle containing endless collections of travel gadgetry. At night, the wives would stare at the stars, while the husbands watched sports on their satellites, or spent time admiring other RVs. The guy in the next site always seemed to have the more advanced toy.

MORTY AND KAYLEEN'S WAS practically the size of a Greyhound bus. It had different shades of brown and green with the camouflage look of the United States Army. Morty stepped out and, as you would when leaving a hotel room, did one last look over to make sure they didn't leave anything. When he was done, he peeked through the screen door. "Come on Kay! Everything's packed and we should hit the road. It's a long way home."

But Kayleen wasn't there.

"Sorry, I was just in the ladies room." She was running back slowly. "Are we ready?"

"Everything but the food. Did you prepare sandwiches?"

"I figured we could stop and grab something in town on the way out."

Morty fished keys out of his pocket. "Then let's get going already so we don't spend too much time driving at night."

And just like that, Morty and Kayleen prepared to leave the campground. They hadn't been back to the Visitor Center or seen the new poster.

They had no idea that Nick was missing.

ETHAN ANSWERED THE PHONE in his closet-sized office. His desk was a mess of papers, most of which had oily fingerprints on the edges. He was a mechanic and a criminal and working on cars all day meant that if the police ever suspected him, it wouldn't be difficult to get his prints. Perfect greasy sets lurked everywhere. Ethan's shop was a modest-sized facility with a tiny office and three bays. He had several locals working for him part-time. It wasn't a lucrative business, but he supplemented it with other ventures. Ethan had also built a separate garage with two additional bays in the back of the property, which he kept locked at all times. That was his private garage in which he stored stolen vehicles and swapped out their VINs. And that's where Nick's Durango was resting at the moment.

"It's me, you busy?"

"I'm free, Dad. Where are you calling from?"

"Springdale."

"Good. What's up?"

"Is my car ready?"

"Today or tomorrow."

"What the hell's taking so long?"

"I'm busy, I don't have a lot of help, and I'm trying to swap out the VINs so we can ship them out. You'll have it soon."

"When's the transport scheduled for?"

Ethan stood and looked through the window from which he could see his employees working. "We were supposed to do it tomorrow, but I won't be ready. These newer models have VINs in unusual places so it's a more difficult swap. I postponed the shipment until Friday. Why?"

"Because we have a change of plans. Finish as soon as you can because I want you and Clay to take a road trip."

"Really? Where?"

"Phoenix."

CHAPTER THIRTY-SEVEN

WYATT LEFT THE PARKING lot on foot, and turned right onto the main road into the campground. He immediately stopped in his tracks as a behemoth bore down on him, and he hopped onto a patch of grass lining the road to let it pass. Wyatt made eye contact with the driver who gave him a "thank you" wave. Wyatt waved back, even though he hadn't stepped aside as a courtesy; he'd done it to avoid becoming road kill.

He walked past the entrance booth and to the fifth wheel trailer at the host's site. There were several vehicles parked there, but Stan's signature golf cart wasn't one of them. *Could he still be doing rounds?* Perhaps, Wyatt thought, but he would check anyway and see if the guy was around. The gravel crunched under his feet as Wyatt approached the trailer's door. As he did yesterday, Wyatt climbed the two steps and knocked several times but received no answer. He stepped back from the staircase, took a seat by the picnic table, and wrote a note for the host to call him. He pinned it under a rock on the second step.

As he left the site, Wyatt realized he still had some time, so he decided to walk the mostly vacant campground. Nick's site was the best place to start; he would fan out from there. As he made his way over, Wyatt noticed two campers, a man and a child. He approached and showed them Nick's picture, but neither recognized Nick. And for good reason; they hadn't arrived until Monday night. It was just the response Wyatt feared he'd receive from most of the campers.

Wyatt thanked them, pardoned the interruption, and pressed forward. He took a quick pit stop in a restroom situated in the middle of the loop, and then made his way towards Nick's site. Diagonally across the way, Wyatt caught sight of a couple of youngsters sitting on opposite sides of their picnic table, a blue and white cooler resting comfortably on the tabletop between them. Wyatt's first impression was that of rebellious teenagers sporting unsightly tattoos and serial-killer facial hair. Did they not have a good salon in town? Despite appearing to be underage, the kids were sitting around drinking cans of beer. Perfect, Wyatt thought. What he wouldn't give to sit in such a beautiful place with a cooler full of beer and not a care in the world.

Wyatt approached the campsite and introduced himself to two empty faces. They were either already plastered, or dumb as shit. Ready for the "Sorry, haven't seen him" response, Wyatt presented Nick's picture to a thin, scruffy-faced teenager. Scruffy turned the bill of his Los Angeles Dodger cap to the back of his head and examined the photo. The hat looked awkward over his shoulder length hair but it didn't matter because, almost immediately, Scruffy said, "Yeah, I seen him." He pointed across the way at Nick's campsite and held up the picture. "Kyle, ain't that the dude who was camping right there on the end?"

Kyle was a bushy-haired youth whose well-rounded gut pressed tightly against a t-shirt from the rock band *The Offspring*. Kyle glanced at the picture as he took a swig of beer, and nodded his agreement.

"What's this all about?" Scruffy asked.

"This man has disappeared and I'm trying to find out what happened to him."

"You ain't some kind of cop, are you?" Kyle asked, a concerned look on his face.

"I'm homicide, in Phoenix," Wyatt said, hoping to scare them just enough to talk. "But don't worry fellas, I won't rat you out, so long as you tell me what you know."

"Cool." They smiled, and said it at virtually the same time.

"Dude, you wanna beer?" Scruffy offered with a big smile, but Wyatt declined.

"So, like, wait a second, something happened to that guy?" Kyle asked.

"He's been missing for a few days now."

"Probably ran off with that chick he was with," Scruffy said.

"He was with somebody?"

The guys looked at each other. "Oh yeah. A hot blonde." Scruffy paused. "I dig blondes."

"Wait a second, when did you see him last?"

"Couple a nights ago, I guess."

"Tell me what you saw."

"OK. See that site next to him?" Scruffy pointed across the road at the site adjacent to Nick's. "She was camping there all by herself. Figuratively speaking of course, 'cause just about the whole damn campground wanted in. Prettiest thing I've seen in the wild."

"We ogled for a while and talked about going over there," Kyle added. "But this guy, your friend, beat us to the punch."

Like you guys had a shot, Wyatt thought.

"Lucky bastard," Scruffy continued. "We watched them for a while, sitting by a fire and shit. Then it started getting hot and heavy and we stopped watching because they seemed to be looking around a lot, you know, in between. We got the feeling that they knew people were watching, so we just left it. Truth is, we knew we had no chance with her anyway because we had a numbers problem. Two of us and only one of her. But man ..." He paused to take a sip of beer, "I would have loved to clone *that*."

Wyatt knew Nick wasn't happy at home, but according to these guys, Nick had hooked up with another woman. "What exactly were they doing when you said they were 'getting heavy'?"

"Just makin' out," Scruffy said. "I don't know what else; we turned in before they did."

"Is the woman still here?"

"Dude, I wish. She's gone. For a few nights already."

"Did you see her leave?"

"I didn't, but I sure as hell miss her."

"Me too," Kyle lamented.

"So you wouldn't have any idea if my buddy left with her, right?"

"I don't know. And I think that was his stuff that Stan just took down."

"Stan?"

"The Camp Host. He's a good dude."

"I was told his stuff was left at the campsite until Tuesday," Wyatt said.

"Yeah, but I'da left my shit behind too if I had the chance to go off with her. Hell, I would have left Scratch here behind. We call him Scratch because he, you know, has a problem down there. He rubs his package more often than a major league ballplayer."

"Shut the fuck up, Ronnie."

"Guys, stay with me for a second," Wyatt said. "I'm going to ask you this again because it's important. Do you know if he actually left here with this woman?"

The beer drinkers looked at one another and shook their heads.

"This is serious guys. He's married and his wife is very pregnant."

"He's married?" Scruffy said. "Wow! He sure as hell wasn't acting like it."

CHAPTER THIRTY-EIGHT

ETHAN FLEW DOWN THE highway, headed for home. It was late in the afternoon and his adrenaline was flowing like a river in a flash flood. He was excited about the trip on which he and Clay would soon embark, and he couldn't wait to see Velvet tonight.

Ethan glanced at his hands on the steering wheel. He had washed them with soap six times before leaving the garage but there was still some stubborn, lingering grease that never seemed to scrub off. No matter what, a mechanic always took some home with him.

When he looked up again, Ethan immediately slammed on the brakes because the car in front of him was moving at a snail's pace.

"Come on, this ain't Florida!"

Ethan felt impulsive, mischievous, the excitement of the day's events still prominent in his mind. Eyeing the gun on the passenger seat, he contemplated what to do next. He pulled dangerously close to the bumper of the Toyota Corolla, the very definition of tailgating, when he realized why the driver was so slow. It was the orange bumper sticker, "STUDENT DRIVER." He snickered. Criminals by nature were impulsive, but ironically, they shared a common characteristic with doctors, lawyers and other professionals. Each had to exercise due care and discretion and avoid legal trouble if they wanted to stay in their respective professions. And this time, prudence got the best of him, as Ethan waited for an opening to pass the neophyte.

AT A FEW MINUTES to twelve, Wyatt made his way back to the Visitor Center and took a seat on the same bench he had shared with Kathy Evans. The bench wasn't far from the curb, where a shuttle sat idle, its doors closed. Wyatt started wondering what he was doing in Utah. Just the other day, Nick had complained about being married, and now Wyatt knew that Nick had been here with another woman. *Had everything been carefully staged? Did Nick purposefully push my buttons so I would back out of our trip and he could come here alone?*

The shuttle doors squeaked open.

"You that detective?" A bald, heavyset man wearing a maroon golf shirt and sand-colored khakis leaned out from the doorway.

Wyatt stood and started walking towards the bus. "Marshall Owens?"

"That's me." The man didn't move an inch, as he waited for Wyatt to reach him. They shook hands when he did.

"Are you coming out? I thought your shift was over."

"It is. But the bus is a lot cooler so let's talk in here. And quickly." He looked at his watch. "I've got things to do."

Wyatt regarded the elderly driver and then pulled out Nick's picture. "Seen him?"

"This guy? No. Thanks, it's been nice meeting you." And he opened the door for Wyatt to leave, as if he had to rush over to his girlfriend's before the Viagra wore off.

But Wyatt didn't flinch, and instead, took out a picture of Nick's hat. "He would've been wearing this."

Marshall touched his glasses before taking the picture. "Tell me again why you ask?"

"Because I think he rode your shuttle early Monday morning, to Observation Point."

"Weeping Rock," Marshall corrected him. He examined the picture, then looked at Wyatt and laughed. "Look at me, Detective. I'm an old man just passing my time driving circles around Southern Utah at twenty miles an hour. It's the same thing every day. Same route, people on, people off. Three million a year. You think I can remember one of them?"

"Just take a gander at the photo and see if you can remember anything," Wyatt prodded, feeling the same despair he had felt when speaking with Kathy Evans. He waited while Marshall quietly examined the two photographs. Then, Wyatt added, "It would have been early, maybe even the first shuttle of the day. That's before six isn't it?"

"First shuttle leaves at 5:45."

"I figure you probably don't—"

Marshall put up a hand. "Shut up will ya? I'm thinkin'. Fellow my age takes a minute or two to get the ole' motor up and running."

Wyatt waited and then a moment later, the man nodded.

"You know what? I think I *did* see him."

Wyatt's pulse picked up.

"I would never recognize this guy if it weren't for the hat. USC. Yeah, he boarded at Canyon Junction and, now that I think about it, I remember it vividly because I went to Notre Dame and I was going to say something. You know, the two schools play each other every year. Anyway, I stopped the bus right where he was standing so all he had to do was get on. But when I pulled up, he walked to the back and got on. I thought it was rude."

Most of Zion's shuttles have an accordion-like extension to another car, to service double the amount of passengers on each ride.

Wyatt pointed at the photo. "You sure it was him?"

"I'm sure about the cap. The face? I didn't get a good enough look."

"Do you remember where he got off?"

"You said Weeping Rock."

"Yeah, but I wanted to know if you had an independent recollection."

Marshall shook his head. "I didn't really focus on it."

"Did you by any chance see him get back on your bus later on? And I mean any time that day. He wouldn't have had the hat on because it was found on the trail."

"Sorry, but there are plenty of other buses and I doubt anyone would remember him, especially without the hat. I'm willing to bet this week's salary that no one's going to recognize him on the way out."

Marshall Owens put his hand on the door opener, hinting to Wyatt that his time was up. Wyatt stepped off the bus and turned at the door.

"I appreciate your help. By the way, what's this week's salary?"

"Nothing." Marshall Owens closed the door.

CHAPTER THIRTY-NINE

COULD NICK HAVE REALLY used the park as a diversion? Wyatt was driving Route 9 towards Hurricane, his mind returning to the thoughts he'd had before speaking with Marshall Owens. Wyatt had met with Amado and Simpson and he could understand how they could have formed such an early opinion, because they'd seen others do it before. And they knew nothing about Nick, so their preliminary hypothesis wasn't completely unreasonable. But now, Wyatt started wondering just how well *he* knew Nick. Sure they had been best friends in college, but that was more than ten years ago.

Had Nick used him?

Wyatt began reviewing the evidence. Nick had been intimate with another woman who was conveniently camping in the site next to his. Coincidence? He recalled the conversation they'd had in Nick's driveway, where Nick had made it clear that he was unhappy with his life. Nick felt "trapped" and joked that it was time to trade in his wife for a "newer model."

Wyatt parked the car, cut the ignition, and sat in silence. The pieces fit. The stick up Nick's ass was the perfect diversion. His overt insults were meant to strike Wyatt at the core, to get him so incensed that he would abandon the trip. Then, Nick could come out here alone and run off with his "newer model." He'd been seen, by Marshall Owens, going out to the trail, but no one had seen him coming back. He'd called 911 early in the morning, and then used his phone several hours later. And the best way out of the park was using his own car, which was nowhere to be found. It was all coming together.

But the real beauty of Nick's plan was what hurt Wyatt the most. Ina would never know what really happened to Nick, but the person she would blame for his disappearance would be Wyatt.

There was just one thing Wyatt couldn't reconcile.

There was something unusual about Marshall Owens' observation.

ETHAN ENTERED THE HOUSE and went straight to Nick's room. Clay was already there.

"Finally, you're back," Nick said to Ethan. "I really need to go to the bathroom and they wouldn't let me until you showed up."

Ethan chuckled.

"What's so funny?" Nick asked. "I understand you're not used to this, but I've been holding it in all day."

"You're right, we aren't used to it. You people are usually dead by now."

"Then why am I here? Just shoot me already. It can't get any worse."

An evil grin filled Ethan's face. "It's about to get worse."

"What are you talking about?"

Ethan looked down and paused for effect. "Clay and I will be taking a road trip to your hometown. Phoenix."

"Are you taking me with you?"

"I said, Clay and I."

"What are you going to do there?"

That's when Ethan pulled Ina's picture from his back pocket. He looked at it and licked his lips, as Nick pulled hard at the rope.

"We're planning a Perrone family reunion."

Ethan turned to Clay and handed him the picture. "We can take turns." Then he turned to Nick. "I've got a girlfriend, but Clay here is like a caged animal. Every once in a while, we try to get him some action to, you know, satisfy his animalistic needs."

"Speaking of girlfriends," Clay turned to Ethan, "I forgot to tell you Velvet cancelled for tonight."

"No biggie. I'll just save myself for the beautiful Mrs. Perrone."

"Don't do this," Nick pleaded. "My wife is seven months pregnant; just leave her alone. Whatever you want, I'll give it to you. If I don't have it, I'll get it. Just please, keep her out of this."

EVERY PART OF NICK'S body pulled at the rope but there was just no give. The panic of his helplessness was as paralyzing as the ropes. What was happening? The escalation made no sense. They had never done this to other victims. It was a bold and daring venture that seemed contrary to everything Nick had learned about his cautious captors.

Nick's mind raced as he tried to answer the burning question, but nothing came to mind. He was stumped. And as he sat there trying to determine what they were hoping to accomplish, one thought came to mind. A solace.

Thank God Ina was in Tucson.

She'd be there the rest of the week.

CHAPTER FORTY

"HAVE A SEAT," AMADO said, and Wyatt took the same chair in which he'd sat the previous day. Amado grabbed a large, bulging yellow envelope off his desk and pulled out a disc.

"I want you to listen to this and tell me if that's Perrone's voice on the recording."

"No problem," Wyatt said. "I'm eager to hear it myself."

Amado pushed a button on his computer and the disc drive opened. "While I get this set, tell me, have you found anything of interest?"

Wyatt contemplated whether to tell Amado that Nick had been messing around with another woman. Yes, he had agreed to share everything, but he wasn't yet convinced Amado's theory was correct. And he didn't want to share crucial information that Amado may just use to justify his suspicion that Nick was a walkaway. He wanted the file to remain open.

"Not much. I did, however, learn that Nick picked up the shuttle at Canyon Junction. I spoke with the driver and he remembered Nick by the baseball cap."

"So that confirms his car is gone because that's the most popular place to park, and it's the first place we looked."

"Right, although we pretty much knew that anyway," Wyatt responded. "What about you guys?"

"We got an interesting tidbit this morning. We found out that a little less than two weeks ago, Perrone took out an insurance policy. Several million dollars on his life with his wife as the beneficiary."

Unhappy in his marriage, fooling around with someone else, and now an insurance policy to take care of Ina?

The screen came up showing the disc as ready, and Wyatt moved his chair and leaned forward on the edge of Amado's desk. Amado clicked the play button and sat back, as he had already heard the recording. There was a slight pause and mild static before they finally heard a voice:

Operator: 911, *what's your emergency?*

After a brief pause, the operator's voice came back again.

Operator: *What is your emergency?*

Caller: *I'm hiking in Zion National Park and … shit, a mountain lion …*

Operator: *Where in the park are you?*

No Answer

Operator: *Sir, where are you?*

Caller: *Observation Point Trail.*

Operator: *Sir, are you injured? Sir? Sir?*

And then the call abruptly ended.

"Is that your boy?"

The voice had been faint and there was a lot of static, but it definitely sounded like Nick. "Can you play it again? I think it's him but I want to hear it again. And this time, jack up the volume."

Amado replayed the recording, and, after it ended, Wyatt shook his head and pursed his lips. "Pretty sure it's him. Do mountain lions attack people here?"

"Rarely, but they can. They're most active at dusk and dawn and Perrone was out there at first light."

"Do you believe he was attacked?" Wyatt asked.

"I don't. If I saw a lion, I wouldn't have time to call for help. And we can't find his car. The call in Springdale. I think the mountain lion was a ruse. And now we know that right before he left, he made sure his wife would be taken care of. You don't agree?"

Wyatt nodded. "I admit your theory is looking more and more viable. But Marshall Owens, the bus driver who remembers the baseball hat, told me something that doesn't make sense. He pulls his empty shuttle up to Canyon Junction and stops the bus right at Nick's feet. That's when, according to him, Nick turns, walks, and enters the bus from the back. Even though it was completely empty and Owens stopped right in front of him. Why would he do that? You would think that if a guy was about to fake his own death, he would probably go out of his way to have someone see him on the way in, so long as no one sees him on the way out."

Amado tented his hands on his chest and appeared to consider this for a moment. "I think it does make sense. He knows he's going to be taking a shuttle back so he doesn't want *anyone* to be able to recognize him. And if he steps on in front, maybe the driver talks to him, or sees enough of his face so that he can later identify him."

"Yes but, think about it, didn't he risk it all by entering the shuttle from the back? That one little move actually made him stand out," Wyatt countered.

"Yeah, and that was OK because he was wearing a hat he knew he'd be leaving on the trail," Amado replied. "If he steps onto the bus and the driver sees his face and they start talking, then he may have a problem if that same driver sees him on the return bus. So I actually think it makes sense. As it is, his plan worked perfectly because the driver remembered the hat, but not the face, right?" He didn't wait for a response. "That's exactly what he wanted."

Wyatt sighed. Amado had a point. Marshall Owens had only remembered the hat; he had no idea what Nick's face looked like.

The phone rang and Amado stole a glance at the caller ID. "Is there anything else?"

"If you can spot me a desk, I'll write up my interviews for the file," Wyatt said.

A secretary buzzed and announced that Raymond Jensen was holding. Amado pointed out the door. "Just grab a free desk out there. I need to take this call. It's the County Attorney. He wants to discuss issuing a warrant for Perrone's arrest."

"You want to arrest Nick? For what?"

Amado locked eyes with Wyatt.

"Insurance fraud."

CHAPTER FORTY-ONE

THE CHALLENGE OF DETECTIVE work can be complex and beyond the average person's comprehension. Each case is its own game of cat and mouse in which the detective must solve a criminal puzzle using pieces left, for the most part, by the adversary. And while every piece of evidence is significant, there's one aspect of detective work that goes largely unnoticed, something that can't be taught.

Instinct.

Wyatt was blessed with keen instincts, which he undoubtedly obtained as a generic passing of the torch. Had his career not been derailed, he was on his way to becoming one of Phoenix's best detectives. But as things stood, when Wyatt eventually returned to Phoenix, he would do so as an ordinary citizen. Wyatt had been in Utah less than two days, in which time he'd lost his job, his therapist, realized he was still attracted to alcohol, and was busy chasing empty leads in a strange place he was clearly unwelcome. And all this was happening while searching for someone he was learning a lot about, things he didn't like.

How much had changed in the last thirty-six hours.

Wyatt was doing everything right, but it was unfortunately leading to a gut-wrenching conclusion. The inevitable, heartbreaking news he would give to a woman who would soon give birth to a baby, by herself. What would he tell her? How much detail would he provide? Before the trip, Nick had told him he wasn't happy in his marriage. And Wyatt learned that Nick had been unfaithful. The mounting evidence was quickly pointing to a smooth and calculated disappearance, but something was holding Wyatt back.

Instinct.

Yes, Amado's explanation as to why Nick would move to the back of Marshall Owen's shuttle was plausible. But after executing a perfect plan, would Nick risk everything by answering a phone call from his wife? Was Nick so sinister as to make her sit and listen to the empty sounds of a highway while he hightailed it out of town? It didn't make sense unless Nick wanted to shove it in her face one last time. But why would he want to do that?

That's when it occurred to Wyatt. A hunch. He was pretty sure there was another piece to this challenging puzzle, and it had nothing to do with anyone in Utah.

He picked up the phone to find out if he was right.

THE CALL RANG THREE times before it went to voicemail. Wyatt muttered a profanity and, with one hand on the steering wheel, hung up before the beep and dialed again. There were several more rings and then finally, Wyatt heard Ina's voice for the first time since he'd been in Utah. Man, it was impossible to reach her, and *she* had complained that she couldn't reach Nick!

"Where have you been?" he asked.

"Wyatt," Ina answered in a soft and conciliatory tone. "I just stepped out of a meeting, some last minute things with the hotel before my clients start arriving."

"I understand, but why is it impossible to reach you?"

"I apologize, but my reception here has been spotty and I've been busying myself to keep my mind off Nick." She paused to catch her breath. "Have you made any progress?"

"Not as much as I hoped. I can tell you that we're pretty sure Nick was on the first shuttle into the park on Monday morning. The bus driver remembers him by the hat he was wearing. Other than that, there's very little to go on."

"Contraction." Ina breathed heavy and then after a few seconds, it sounded as if it receded.

"Do they really think Nick ran away?"

"I'm afraid so. It's called a 'walkaway' and it's not uncommon. And I think I've worn out my welcome here."

"Sounds like you were never welcome to begin with. I don't care what they think. What do *you* think?"

"I admit the runaway theory is persuasive, but I'm still not convinced."

"Are you going to keep digging then?"

"Yes, but first I have a question."

"Sure."

He paused momentarily. There was no easy way to ask what was on his mind.

"Did you and Nick plan this baby?"

Ina began crying and he asked if she was OK.

"Yes," Ina responded to the inquiry.

"I'm going to ask you something as a detective, not a friend, OK? Is the baby Nick's?"

"Of course it is," she answered in a hushed scream. "You think I would cheat on him?"

Wyatt knew immediately by her reaction that he shouldn't have asked.

"Look, I'm trying to find any reason why Nick would up and run, especially with you being so close to having your first child. Why would he do that if you had planned a family together?"

"I need to call you back in a few minutes," she said. "I'm in the hotel lobby and I'm not comfortable here. I want to go to my room."

"Answer the question and do *not* hang up."

"I can't do this here. I have to call you back."

"No! Not with how difficult it's been to reach you. You wanted my help and I'm here for you. But something's going on and now I need yours."

Ina sniffled, sighed, and took her time before responding.

"Did you know that, just a few weeks ago, Nick took out a multi-million dollar insurance policy on his life and made you the beneficiary?"

"I had no idea," she said. And after a second, "What good would it be if he never told me about it?"

"I guess he figured you would've found out somehow. But what I'm more concerned with is why he did that just before this trip. You're telling me the truth, right? You planned this baby together?"

"Yes we did, OK? Are we done here? I have to go."

"No, we're not done. I need your help."

"What more do you need?"

"I need you to check your records for unusual activity. Any large withdrawals from your bank, strange credit card charges, new accounts, stock sales, anything you can find that might give a glimpse into what Nick was up to before the trip."

"You want me to go through his stuff?"

"Yes. I need you to go home."

Phoenix.

CHAPTER FORTY-TWO

NICK GRITTED HIS TEETH so hard his jaw was starting to hurt. He wasn't a violent person but if he had a bat, he'd enjoy smacking these guys in the back of the head.

"If this was all about stealing my car, why are you going after my wife? Are you planning to take her car too?"

"What does she drive?" Ethan joked.

"I don't know how many people you've murdered but was it worth the couple of thousand dollars you got for each car? I mean, why don't you just steal cars, rather than kill innocent people?"

"Believe me, it's worth it. We get a lot more than a few thousand per car. See, we're well connected overseas where people pay a shitload, try two or three *hundred* thousand dollars, sometimes more."

Nick wrinkled his face. "How are you getting so much money for a car worth twenty or thirty grand?"

"We sell them to rich people in third world countries, where there aren't dealers all over the place. They pay hefty premiums for cars from America."

"But why do you have to kill for it? Just take the car."

"That's how we started, in St. George, but it was problematic because every time we stole a car, the police were looking for it. And us. This is a complicated operation that must stay under the radar. That's when we realized that the park was the perfect front. Accidents happen, lots of them. People fall, die in flash floods, commit suicide, or use the park as a diversion to run away and start fresh. The park was a gold mine sitting right under our noses, and when we finally realized it, we decided to take advantage."

"I don't get it."

"It's simple. We locate salvaged vehicles that reasonably match the make and model of our targets, which are cars belonging to park visitors. When we find a match, we stage a crime to fit one of the accident categories I just mentioned. I take the cars and swap the VINs, and we leave the salvaged car, with the new VIN, wherever our victim last parked it. When the police find it, the numbers match and they aren't suspicious of foul play. Case closed. The rest is easy: kill the victim, ship his car, make a load of cash."

"So when they discover the body or, like in my case, that someone is missing, they find what they think is the guy's car and once it's ruled an accident, you're home free?" Nick said. "And your dad works there and makes sure they are always ruled an accident."

Ethan folded his arms. "For our purposes here, yes."

"What the hell does that mean?"

"It means you don't need to know all the specifics about how investigations are done here in Washington County."

"Then why my wife?

"Sorry partner, but this is where today's lesson ends. Rest assured we will deliver mother and baby intact. We wouldn't want to deprive the Perrones of a full family burial."

WYATT LOOKED AT HIS watch and wondered when Stan would finally arrive. He was sitting on a picnic bench outside Stan's trailer, with his notebook and file resting on the table. The sun had been overshadowed by an endless sea of gray clouds, which now held sole dominion over the sky. Leaves rustled, and smoke from early evening campfires danced in every direction. The wind picked up and Wyatt jumped, quickly pouncing on his file before it flew away. He grabbed a couple of rocks off the ground, placed them on the file, and sat back down.

Several minutes later, a motorized cart pulled up behind a beat-up pickup. Stan stepped out and crossed over some wires he had taped to the ground outside his trailer, and approached the table. "You the detective friend of that missing camper?" He was carrying a clipboard and a Bible.

"I left you a note earlier today. I'm Wyatt." He put out his hand.

"Stan." They shook. "I hope you haven't been waiting long."

"Not at all," Wyatt said.

"What can I do for you?"

"I came to pick up his stuff."

"I packed it in a box and I'll grab it for you in a moment. Sorry, I got your note and was going to call you back but they've got me too damn busy for an old man."

Busy? What was there to do other than patrol the campground a few times a day?

"I figured as much," Wyatt said. "But since I happened to be in the area, I thought I'd drop by again and see if you were around."

Stan smiled, the wrinkles on his face parting like the Red Sea. "Most people think this job is easy, but it ain't. There's a lot to do to run this place. That's why I carry this with me." He held up the Bible. "When I took the job, I thought I'd have lots of free time to study. Sort of a relaxing early retirement with just a little responsibility to fill my day. But it hasn't quite worked out that way." A pause. "I shouldn't complain. It's pretty nice out here."

"And it looks like you got a great set-up."

"Sure do. They give me water, sewer, electric, phone, two shirts and a cap. They also pay me a nominal amount that's so small they don't even call it a salary. It's a 'stipend.' I supply everything else."

"They give you enough to pay the bills?"

"What bills? It suffices. I'll never strike it rich here. Even if I won the damn sweepstakes, whoever runs that thing now would never be able to find me."

"But you never need a vacation because, look at this place, it's amazing."

"At first, I thought the same thing. But then I realized that we all need a break. Thankfully, we got a few other hosts here and we alternate weekends. I've got this one off. But you're right, check out the beauty of God's country. He's a hell of a lot closer to us here than in most other places. I can feel it. That's why I came here, you know? To study God's Bible in *His* land. I just wish I had more time to do so."

"It's definitely scenic, but beauty is also defined by what happens in a place."

Stan smiled in concurrence. "Sure does. But unfortunate accidents occur any place this rugged."

A gust sent the edges of Wyatt's file up. He reached over and smoothed it out, adding a few more rocks to hold them in place.

Stan motioned to the papers with his head. "Whatcha got?"

"Just my file. I was going over it before you came. Has anyone talked to you about the case?"

"Simpson, the head ranger, comes around quite a bit. He was here the other day. Asked me when I seen him last and I told him early in the weekend, not long after he arrived. Other than that, I have nothing to add. Simpson asked me to gather his things and clear out the site, which I did." Stan sighed. "The terrain remains the same year after year, but the people who come to see it change daily."

"That's what makes this so difficult, but I appreciate it anyway. If I can just grab his gear, I'll be out of your hair. I'll take it back to his wife."

"Wait here a sec while I go get it."

Stan walked around the side of the trailer and returned carrying an open box. Inside were Nick's tent, sleeping pad, and sleeping bag, all neatly wrapped in their stuff sacks. There was also a pillow and blanket, a flashlight, and a book. Stan set the box on the table.

"Anything else I can help with?" Stan asked. "If not, I'm fixin' to do some Bible study. You're welcome to join me if you'd like."

"No thanks," Wyatt said. "I'm going to take off."

INA SAT ON THE balcony with her bare feet stretched out on a small plastic table. She massaged her belly. Cumulus clouds, shaped like perfect large balls scooped right out of a melon, lined an otherwise perfect sky. The sun was setting behind the hotel so the balcony was full of shade. Ina's third floor room faced the Catalina Mountains, a view she'd easily enjoy any other time. Her emotional state called for alcohol and cigarettes, yet her physical state allowed just tea and gum. She sipped iced tea from a bottle she had purchased at the gift shop and placed it on the floor as she heard a knock.

"Thanks for coming," Ina said when she opened the door.

Wanda strolled in wearing a bikini top and a sarong wrapped tightly around her narrow hips. She immediately caught a glimpse of Ina's bloodshot eyes.

"Are you OK?"

"Come on outside." Wanda followed Ina to the deck. "Where are we on preparations?" Ina asked, as they sat.

"Good. They won't start arriving for a few hours but everything's in place. Room assignments, gift baskets, activity schedules, meals, everything's in order.

"And tomorrow's welcome brunch?"

"Done."

"You're the best. I don't know what I would do without you."

Wanda smiled. "Any word on Nick?"

"I spoke with the sheriff and he thinks Nick faked his own disappearance and ran off."

"What? Like, he left you?"

Ina started crying. "Nick's friend, Wyatt, is a cop in Phoenix and he went out there to see what he can find out."

"And does he also think that Nick ran away?"

"He says the evidence is pretty convincing."

"But why would he do that? You're, like, the best."

The answer was simple and, after lying to Wyatt, Ina wanted to be honest, even if only to Wanda. She needed the support. She blinked back as many tears as she could, but a few escaped and slid down her cheek, taking some of her makeup for the ride.

"This is why." She tapped her belly.

"You think he doesn't want a baby?"

"It's all my fault."

"For getting pregnant? Of course it's not. It takes two."

Ina avoided eye contact while Wanda's eyes widened. "You didn't cheat on him?"

Ina wiped her nose with her sleeve. "Of course not." She shifted in her chair and took a few deep breaths. "He thought I was on the Pill but I wasn't. I had stopped. Deliberately. Nick never wanted kids."

"Oh my," Wanda said, a stunned look crossing her face. "Why did you do that?"

"To save our marriage. Nick and I were drifting apart and ... it's hard to explain, but, you know how sometimes something just feels right? That's how I always felt with Nick, like we were meant to be together. But we started fighting and he was working late and then I thought maybe he was cheating on me. We've been through so much together and I was afraid to lose him. So, I thought that if I could get pregnant, it would keep us together and ... maybe even bring us closer. I'm so ashamed but I felt like I had no choice. When he found out I was pregnant, he confronted me. I denied it, of course, but he's always suspected otherwise."

Ina was riding an impossible roller coaster. If Nick left her, she'd have to raise their baby on her own. But if something happened to Nick, he could be in serious trouble, or even dead. There was a part of her that hoped he'd simply left her because that would mean that at least he was still alive.

Wanda pulled her chair closer and hugged Ina.

"I feel so bad," Ina said after they separated. "Wyatt asked if the baby was planned and I lied to him. Here he dropped everything to go to Utah, and I couldn't tell him the truth."

"*Completely* understandable. All of it," Wanda replied.

"I was afraid that if I told him, he would reach the same conclusion the sheriff had and if he did, he would give up and leave."

"That's a tough one sweetie, and I promise I won't breach your confidence. But you should really think about telling him because he needs to have all the pieces. I think you have to trust that he will do everything he can to help you, no matter the circumstances."

"You're right. And it's actually one of the reasons I called you. Wyatt asked me to return home and go through our records. He wants to see what Nick was up to recently. Think you can run the event?"

Wanda smiled. "Of course. I mean, it will make it harder to find prince dollar bills but that can wait until next time."

"Thanks. I'm going to leave first thing in the morning. And if you need to reach me, I'll be at the house."

CHAPTER FORTY-THREE

"THANKS FOR MEETING ME."

Wyatt looked Velvet over and was amazed. Gone were her hat, park shirt, and trousers. Instead, her long hair flowed just past her shoulders and onto a sexy white blouse that clung to her chest for dear life. Her miniskirt would easily invite sexual harassment if it ever found its way into the workplace. Black pumps completed the ensemble, and Wyatt felt as though he'd won the jackpot. Wyatt knew rangers rarely wore makeup. But tonight, Velvet's gorgeous features were perfectly accentuated by the right mix of colors.

"My pleasure." She smiled.

Wyatt smiled back and waved at the chair next to his, relieved that he had stopped by the hotel for a shower and shave. Velvet waved to Hank, the bartender, and then sat next to Wyatt and removed an envelope from her large pocketbook.

"Before I forget, we had new fliers made up. I brought you a stack." They were the exact same posters Wyatt had seen in the Visitor Center, except in color, and the picture of Nick wasn't blurred by a fax machine. Wyatt thanked her and glanced briefly at the fliers before putting them away.

A waitress gently placed two dinner menus on the table. They ordered beers to start and asked for a few more minutes to decide on dinner.

"Any progress today?" she asked.

"A little. I found out that Nick parked at Canyon Junction and boarded the first shuttle. I got a positive ID on the shuttle out, but none on the way back. I'm interviewing another driver tomorrow morning."

"That's going to be a tough one. It's already pretty busy after seven."

The waitress set down two beers and took their dinner order.

"So what's the next step?"

"I wanna visit the site. I'm waiting to hear from my escort."

Velvet brushed some hair from her face. "That would be me. How does tomorrow morning work for you?"

"Perfect. Can you go dressed like that?"

She blushed. "What else did you learn today?"

"That's about it. He was in Springdale a few hours after he called 911. His wife called and he answered the phone, although she says all she could hear was static."

"That's odd. Then do you really need to go to the site?"

"Yes. Think about it. If he faked his own disappearance like everyone here wants to believe, why would he take a call from, his wife of all people, when he was already headed for freedom?"

"Good question. I don't know."

"That's why I'm not yet sold on that theory. I'm hoping that visiting the scene may shed some light."

"Yeah, but do you really think he could be stuck in the canyons while his phone's answering calls in Springdale?"

"Sure, if he was a victim of foul play. We've checked other sources and there's no post-disappearance conduct. No ATM withdrawals, credit card use, filling prescriptions, or airline ticket purchases."

"Wouldn't that be the case, though, if he opened accounts under a new identity?"

"Yes. But if he was careful enough to do all that, don't you think he would've been more careful with his cell? He probably would've gotten a new one rather than take a call from his wife several hours after staging a disappearance?"

Velvet laughed. "That's why you're the detective and I work for the park."

"I'm not saying you're wrong. Truth is, we also discovered that before he left, Nick took out a multi-million dollar insurance policy and made his wife the beneficiary. So, maybe you have a point."

"Thanks, but that's easily explainable. His wife *is* pregnant isn't she?"

"Yes. But you have to admit, the timing is … coincidental."

"I guess so." She seemed tired of debating the possibilities.

The waitress brought their dinners, and they ordered a second round of drinks.

"Enough about Nick," Wyatt said, as the waitress left. "Let's talk about you. "What made you become a ranger?"

"I was a small town Iowa gal who got involved with the wrong guy. An abusive, possessive, crazed nut. And where I come from, a restraining order means he can't come over unless he's invited. I decided to pack up before my family was forced to bury me young."

"Now I get it. It's easy for you to assume someone like Nick might start a new life because it worked so well for you."

"It's been pretty good. I was a realtor back in Iowa and I stashed away some cash before I became a ranger so, yeah, I'm doing fine. It's probably the reason I'm one of the few rangers who owns a home. Most of them stay in the ranger quarters in the park."

For the next hour or so, they made small talk about her family, hiking in the area, and what it was like living there.

"I'm glad you agreed to join me." Wyatt held up his beer and they shared a toast.

"What made you join the force?"

"I followed my father's footsteps."

"Is he also on the force?"

"Was on the force. He was Chief of Police before he was murdered during a robbery. Truth is, I joined because I wanted to catch the scumbag who did it."

Tavares would've said that he also joined the force to prove that he was better as a cop than he had been on the night of the murder. But all of that was meaningless now.

"Did you catch the guy?"

Wyatt nodded. He hadn't, and probably never would.

The waitress slid the bill on the table face down, as the restaurant was set to close. Velvet reached for it, but Wyatt stopped her by putting his hand over hers. He closed his hand just as she did and they gripped each other tightly. It was a moment he desperately didn't want to let go of, but had little choice. The light behind the bar had been dimmed; it was time to leave.

"Please, allow me." Wyatt took the bill and left enough cash on the table for dinner and a tip. "I don't want this night to end."

Velvet beamed. "I know just the place for us."

THE HOUSE WAS QUIET and he was fast asleep when he suddenly awoke to a noise. It wasn't the crack of a shotgun, or the booming sound of thunder. It was an argument. What time was it? He was groggy, and his half night's sleep had already ruined his normally tidy hair. He leaned in the direction of the voices and strained to hear what they were saying, but couldn't make it out. Then the argument intensified. He sat up and looked around in the darkness. Who was it? Fear enveloped him when he realized only one of those voices was familiar.

He jumped out of bed and moved to the door. He opened it slightly, careful to keep its squeaky objections to a minimum. He wasn't sure what was happening, but felt a strong sense of danger. He carefully opened the door and the voices grew louder. They were at the end of the hall near the staircase, but he couldn't focus on their words because his mind was racing through possibilities and each began with securing a weapon.

He tiptoed into the bedroom across the hall and gently slid open the top dresser drawer. He reached under a mess of extra-large t-shirts until he felt the cold security of the Colt 45. He was just seventeen years old but his father had made sure he knew how to use it. He pushed open the revolver to make sure it was loaded. It was. Holding the gun in front of him, he treaded into the hallway and hugged the wall as he moved closer towards the staircase. Panic was setting in. He was just steps away from the end of the hall and could now see his father's back, over by the banister. He moved closer and kept looking, and as he peeked out further, his father's entire body came into view. The panic intensified. His father's arms were raised in the air.

An intruder. And he was armed.

But so was Wyatt.

Wyatt gripped the gun tightly with both hands and aimed it in front of him. He kept taking deep breaths, but they did him no good. He was too scared. He looked down, shut his eyes, and took in as much air as possible. He decided to go for it. He jumped out from behind the wall and onto the landing a few feet from his father. The gunman was at the base of the steps. Wyatt looked him over in an instant; jeans, sneakers, a baseball cap, mustache, and one hell of an evil smile. Their eyes met just as his father told him to go back to his room. But all that registered for Wyatt was the fear in his dad's voice, and that's when his brain gave the instruction. Wyatt pulled the trigger.

Nothing.

He looked at the gun with wide, fearful eyes as the intruder started to laugh. What had gone wrong? Yes, he was a teenager, but Wyatt and his dad had gone target practicing at least several times. Frank had taught him how to use the gun. But in the heat of the moment, Wyatt had forgotten the key instruction. He had neglected to pull back the hammer before shooting.

Wyatt's thumb hit the hammer just as the shot rang out and Frank slumped to the floor. He jumped to assist his helpless father and then looked up at the killer, he was now staring down the barrel of a sawed-off shotgun.

"Your turn, kid." It was a deep, gravelly voice that would forever be embedded in Wyatt's mind.

His hands were shaking as his life flashed before him. There was no way he could pull back the hammer and get a shot off before the killer would shoot him. He eased his grip on the gun and lowered it slightly in defeat, ready to take the bullet and join his father. Wyatt locked eyes with the killer, and the man was laughing. That's when the intruder slowly lowered the rifle and took a few steps back without taking his eyes off Wyatt.

A second later, he was gone.

CHAPTER FORTY-FOUR

Wednesday

WYATT SHOT UP AND sucked in air. He tried to gain his bearings, but the room was black and it took him a moment to realize where he was. After drawing a few deep breaths, he groaned and held the hair off his forehead as he searched for the clock on the nightstand.

"What's wrong?" Velvet stirred, her face hidden behind her hair.

"Nothing. Go back to sleep."

"Did you have a bad dream?" She reached over and rubbed her hand on his chest.

Yes! Intruder. Gun. Shots. Torso. Dead.

And wait, Nick?

"I think I just subconsciously thought it was time to get up."

Velvet rolled over with her back to Wyatt. "Good, we have more time. I'm going back to sleep. Unless you want to do it again?"

"Go back to sleep," Wyatt said, as he stole a glance at the bedside clock which flashed 2:52 in bright red. Since they had planned for an early start, Wyatt had set the alarm for 5:00 a.m. But he couldn't go back to sleep. Instead, Wyatt placed his feet on the floor and sat on the bed, his entire body chilled from what he had seen in his subconscious. It was the same nightmare, but with a troubling twist. Tonight, the nightmare had included something new, something different.

Something he'd never seen before.

"CAN'T THIS WAIT TILL a decent hour? I can get us there a lot quicker." The darkness had faded but the sun had yet to rise.

"No, it can't," Wyatt said. "Come on, you can rest when we're done." He wrapped his arms around Velvet's shoulders. "I'll even help you fall back asleep."

They stood by the curb at Canyon Junction, anxiously waiting for Marshall Owens to pull up.

Velvet exhaled frustration. "Are you sure I can't just drive us to the trailhead? It'll save, like, an hour."

Wyatt was tempted to agree because she was right, it would save them time. And at this point in the investigation, and given everything he'd learned about Nick, there was a part of him that felt like he was just going through the motions. Like his conscience wouldn't let him leave him town without feeling like he'd done everything possible. But, the detective in him wouldn't allow him to cut corners. If he was going to do this, he would do it the right way, by reconstructing the trip the way Nick had taken it.

Wyatt and Velvet grabbed their packs off the ground behind them, as the shuttle had just turned the corner and was slowly making its left turn onto Zion's scenic drive. They cringed at the shriek of the tires as the shuttle pulled to a stop just a few feet from where Velvet was standing. She turned to Wyatt with a last ditch plea. "Seriously, I can have us at the trail in less than five minutes. Guaranteed."

Wyatt stepped forward without even looking at her and waited by the door, like a commuter about to board the New York City subway. As it opened, Wyatt turned his head but not enough to meet Velvet's gaze.

"I want to retrace Nick's steps, and that includes riding the shuttle just like he did, so I can get a good idea of the timing."

"He's gone, Wyatt. Just face it, he skipped town. Can't we go back to bed? We can come here any time of day."

Wyatt boarded the bus with a disconsolate Velvet trailing behind. He said good morning to Marshall Owens and took a seat in the middle of the bus. The ride was quick and quiet. Only a few early-rising tourists had boarded the shuttle, and most of them got off at the earlier landmarks. As they reached the Weeping Rock Trailhead, Wyatt and Velvet exited and Wyatt noted that it was a couple of minutes after six, almost an hour before the 911 call.

Velvet extended her arms and yawned. "You owe me for this."

"Consider last night your recompense."

Velvet tugged at her straps to make sure her pack was tightly fastened. "I was thinking it's the other way around, slim." She nudged him as she walked past and started up the trail. "You owe *me* for last night, too. Let's go."

"Can I pay you when we get back to your place?"

She turned and smiled. "It's the least you can do."

Wyatt strapped on his pack and, after affixing the multitude of belts around his chest and stomach, he was set. A bomb could go off and no matter how far it threw him, the pack would still be attached. They made the swithchbacked ascent for about eight hundred feet before they reached the spot above which the rangers had found Nick's backpack. Velvet stopped just short of the area, took off her pack, and placed it down on the trail. Wyatt followed, and took out his file before setting down his pack.

He consulted his watch; it was 6:30, almost a half-hour before the 911 call had been made. He turned to Velvet.

"If Nick made it up here around the same time we did, what did he do for a half hour before calling the police?"

She thought about it for a moment. "I don't know. Maybe he used the restroom first at the trailhead. Or maybe he hiked slower than we did. And don't forget, there's reference to a mountain lion on the call. He might have hiked farther up the trail and encountered the animal before turning around."

Wyatt sighed. "Who knows?"

"Exactly. I told you, you're not going to figure it out just by retracing his steps, because there are too many variables to consider.

You should've let me drive. We could've been out of here by now and back in ..." She winked at him.

"Pulling out all the stops? You really want to keep me in Utah, don't you?"

"Whatever it takes."

"Right here on the trail?"

"Finish your business and we'll see."

Wyatt stepped to the edge and looked down at the spot where they had discovered Nick's backpack.

"What a nasty fall," Wyatt said. "A long rock slide shaped like a banana that leads into a black hole. I've never seen anything like it."

And that's when the realization hit him; there was no way *anyone* could survive such a fall. And even if they did, they couldn't be rescued.

"Neither have I," Velvet replied. "What the hell are you doing?"

Wyatt knelt to examine the terrain and was now on his stomach with his head hanging slightly over the edge of the trail. He had taken the pictures of Nick's hat and backpack out of the file and placed them on the ground next to him, held in place by a couple of rocks. "I'm trying to see if there's any blood on the rock, or anything else that may have fallen down there."

"We did an exhaustive search and didn't see any. Forget blood. And *we* were here immediately after the incident. If we missed any, the monsoons would have washed it away by now."

"You have any evidence bags with you?"

"In my pack." She went to grab one. "What do you got?"

"Give me a tissue or something. Do you have a tweezers?"

She handed Wyatt a tissue and he lifted a cigarette butt that was lodged inside some grass. When Wyatt stood, Velvet opened a plastic sandwich bag and Wyatt delicately dropped it inside. She sealed the bag and held it up as if she were doing a thorough examination.

"So do you know who did it now?" Wyatt asked.

"Are you mocking me for examining a butt?"

Wyatt forced himself up push-up style. "That's not the butt I expected you to examine. But still, it may be useful for its DNA, that is, if we can find a suspect."

"Does your friend smoke?"

"He used to, but I'm not sure if he still does."

"Do you think the cigarette may explain the time difference?"

"Nick doesn't hike and smoke." He reached into his pack and pulled out a granola bar. "Have you ever seen a mountain lion in the wilderness?"

"A couple of times."

"Ever see one capture its prey, or feed?"

"Thankfully no. Why?"

"I don't know much about cougars, but if you do, I thought maybe we could hike up the trail and see if we can find any signs that there may have been one in the area recently."

Velvet lifted her pack off the ground. "We can try. I mean, you might see some scat or old deer bones, but if you don't see anything, it doesn't mean it wasn't there."

"Is it worth taking the time?"

"Honestly? No."

Wyatt affixed his pack and glanced at his watch: it was five to seven, just a few minutes before the 911 call. He looked down at the switchbacks they had climbed. "Maybe you're right. Truth is, with everything I know, I'm not sure I believe he encountered a mountain lion."

"Good, then let's go find us a spot up ahead and make this early morning jaunt a little more memorable." She started walking but then turned around, sensing that Wyatt wasn't moving. And she was right.

Something had caught Wyatt's attention near the base of the trail. "I just realized the one thing we haven't seen until now."

"What's that?"

He stared straight ahead. "Another hiker."

CHAPTER FORTY-FIVE

HE PRESSED LIGHTLY ON the middle slat of the blinds covering the kitchen window and peered out into the backyard. Just seconds ago, he'd heard the cranking of an engine, followed by the earth's crumbling under the wheels of the mammoth vehicle. But what he was about to do was so dangerous that he needed to be sure to take all precautions. He had to be certain that Ethan and Clay were gone.

Satisfied, Bennie walked down the hallway and stopped just short of Nick's room. If he was ever inclined to check his blood pressure, now wasn't the time; he could feel the rapid and rhythmic pounding in his chest. Bennie took a deep breath and tapped his waist for the reassuring sensation that could only be provided by a Glock.

When he opened the door, he immediately locked eyes with Nick. No one else was in the house, but a neurotic impulse made him look behind anyway. There was too much at stake. Bennie felt his hand tremble and his brain made him speak before his voice was ready. The result: a long and pathetic throaty sound, which he cleared with a few burly coughs before trying again.

"Tell me, how can we prove I'm not one of the killers?"

WYATT AND VELVET WERE back on the shuttle, and Wyatt was thankful for some peace and quiet. Velvet had complained virtually the entire way in, and then, after leaving the trail without sex, had started again. Wyatt leaned his head back and rubbed his eyes. It was early in the morning, he was sleep-deprived, and Velvet was right: visiting the scene hadn't really proved fruitful. Wyatt was reasonably certain Nick wasn't stuck up there. Perhaps it was time to return to Phoenix. He had tried everything he could think of but could find no evidence of foul play.

Wyatt spent the rest of the ride in quiet contemplation. If he was going to return home, he needed to be absolutely certain that he'd taken this as far as he could. He replayed the 911 call in his mind, fake as it now seemed. They did find a backpack, but no phone or car. Nick's cell had been used again outside the park. The best explanation was that Nick had indeed taken his own car and disappeared, well before the FBI had cast its net. The life insurance policy actually gave Wyatt some comfort. At least Nick had the decency to make sure Ina was taken care of.

What else was left?

And that's when it him.

The hat.

The rangers had recovered the hat and while Amado had a plausible theory, Wyatt was still bothered by Marshall Owens' observation. Owens remembered *someone* wearing that hat, but when he pulled up to Canyon Junction, the man got on at the *back* of the shuttle. Why would Nick do that if he was planning to disappear? Wouldn't he go out of his way to be recognized, since that would only strengthen the evidence that he had been on the trail? Moving to the back only made sense if it was someone else trying to disguise himself as Nick. The hat might stick out, but if Marshall Owens got a good look at his face, he could later confirm that it was someone else, once he got a look at Nick's photo.

Sitting there on the shuttle, Wyatt realized there may be another way of determining who was up there. The answer would come through DNA testing. The sweat under the brim would provide the sample. What Wyatt needed, though, was a sample of Nick's DNA to see if they match.

No match would mean it wasn't Nick that was up there.

And as he rode through the park's majestic canyons, Wyatt realized that he may very well be in possession of plenty of Nick's DNA. It was all in a box in the trunk of his car.

Nick's camping gear.

Wyatt was about to call Amado but Amado beat him to it. He tried to get in a few words but Amado had something more important to tell him. Wyatt listened for almost a minute before hanging up and turning to Velvet.

"We need to go to Coal Pits Wash. Immediately."

CHAPTER FORTY-SIX

"SLOW DOWN," VELVET BEGGED, as they flew through Springdale.

"I can't, people are waiting."

"You want the turnoff for Anasazi Estates. There's a parking lot for hikers using the Chinle trail, which will take you to Coal Pits Wash."

"How far of a hike is it?"

"About a mile, maybe a little more. But there's nowhere else to park."

"Screw it. Amado said they're waiting in the wash just off the highway. He said there'll be a sign for it."

"Yeah, but where are you going to park?"

"On the shoulder."

"You can't do that," Velvet said. "We'll get a ticket." She made a face. "Can you please keep your eyes on the road? You drive like we're in midtown Manhattan."

They drove in silence until they came upon a sign for Coal Pits Wash. Wyatt pulled the car onto the shoulder and slightly off the road to provide more space on his side. Then he cut the engine and they opened their doors simultaneously.

"You're definitely getting a ticket. That is, if they don't tow your car altogether."

Wyatt laughed. "I've been here three days and I don't think I've seen a single police car, I'll take my chances." He reached for his pack in the backseat and made a beeline for the trail.

"I don't support this," she said, but he had already dropped down into the wash.

COAL PITS WASH WAS a lengthy drainage pattern that snaked its way through miles of open desert. In addition to the solitude of terrain that falls mostly outside park boundaries, hikers investing their time were rewarded with colorful close-ups of picturesque cliffs, and entry into a petrified forest. There wasn't a paved trail; the best way to navigate was the dry wash itself. Although today, the wash was muddy, having yet to recover from nature's most recent monsoonal assault.

Wyatt started up the wash where he saw a man and a woman sitting on a large boulder several hundred feet up the trail. As soon as he caught sight of them, he began to sprint. It was more like a light jog, given the slippery conditions.

"Are you the ones who called the Park Service?" he asked when he reached them.

Both hikers stood. "We did," the man said. He was six feet tall with a small build and a mustache. A large brimmed hat obscured much of his face. "We started out here a little while ago when we found this."

The man held a cell phone in his hand.

Wyatt set his pack on the boulder and started to reach in for a baggie when he realized it was pointless. *Their* prints were all over it. He took the phone in his hand.

"Maybe it's nothing," the female hiker chimed in, "but we heard there were a couple of incidents recently and we figured we better just call it in. You never know."

"Of course," Wyatt said. "Thank you for doing that."

"Where exactly did you find it?" Velvet asked, slightly out of breath as she approached.

"Right over there." The man took a bunch of steps towards the road and pointed to a spot in the sandy wash with his foot. "It was lying in the mud face down. Doreen picked it up to see if it was still working and if we could figure out who the owner is. Either the battery died or it got waterlogged. You can tell from the display that it sat in rainwater."

Velvet set her pack next to Wyatt's, unzipped the main compartment, and pulled out a camera. Then she stepped back and snapped off a series of pictures as Wyatt and the hikers backed away.

"Say, you guys need us anymore?" the man asked. "We're anxious to get moving, been waiting almost an hour."

"Go ahead," Wyatt said. "We appreciate it. Most people probably would have kept walking."

As the hikers set off, Wyatt tried turning on the phone but nothing happened. Next, he removed the battery. It was wet. He lifted his shirt out of his pants, dried the battery and its cubicle, and then put it back in and snapped the compartment closed. He tried turning it on again, but the phone was dead.

"Looks like it's been through a flash flood," Velvet remarked.

"It has." Wyatt paused. "It's Nick's phone."

"You've seen it before?"

"No, but I just know. It has to be. Makes sense. The triangulation. The last call registered not far from the park, and look at where we are. It fits."

Velvet looked up the trail. The hikers were still in sight. "Nice of them to call it in, but damn if they messed it up by handling it."

"Chances are that any prints were washed out by the storms anyway. Last night's alone was torrential, so it probably spent the night in a pool."

"But we still have to identify it."

"I'll take it to Amado, see if one of his boys can pull out the SIM card and call it in. Then we'll find out who it belongs to."

Wyatt put the phone away and glanced up the trail. The hikers were now out of sight. When he turned back to Velvet, she was wearing a devilish grin. She flicked her eyebrows.

"What, here?" Wyatt looked around again before meeting her kinky gaze.

"We can find a private place off the beaten path." She tilted her head like a schoolgirl.

"Yeah, maybe if we slide under the rocks and join the snakes." Wyatt stood and threw his pack on, his body language providing his final answer.

"Where's your sense of adventure?"

But Wyatt didn't hear her. He was focused on something else.

"Oh shit!" he yelped, and started running back towards the road.

"THE SHELLS."

"What are you talking about?'"

"The shells in those gravesites aren't from your gun," Nick said.

"That's right. But how does that help me?"

"Simple. You go to the authorities and cut a deal. You hand them Clay, Ethan, and Ethan's father, in exchange for immunity from prosecution. And you can prove your story using the shells in those gravesites, since they can trace them back to Ethan and Clay."

Bennie's face was like a rock. "What makes you think they'll believe me?"

"Because you'll give them everything: names, times, locations, and shooters. And when they dig up the bodies, it will confirm your story. Heck, you've even got the ID cards in the drawer here and you're not the one who owns this house."

Bennie didn't answer, spending the next few moments in stone-faced contemplation. Nick had a point, something Bennie had never thought of.

"Trust me, it'll work. When they find out what's been going on, they're going to want the principals, not a tag along."

"It's not bad, but I don't think I can do it. I'm too scared."

"I'm telling you, they'll cut you a deal for your testimony and, if you have any fear of retaliation, they can place you in the witness protection program. You'll get a brand new life!"

"But these guys are evil and relentless and, even if I get a new life, I'm not willing to spend the rest of it looking over my shoulder. You don't know what they're capable of."

"You're already looking over your shoulder," Nick said.

Bennie sighed deeply. "I don't know, man. I'm worried about what they've been saying, that they can prove I was involved because of the money. Maybe they're right."

"They're wrong! You gotta tell the cops exactly what you told me, and they're not going to care that you accepted some money. Remember, you *were* providing them with a service. Before all this, you were legitimately locating cars for them. And besides, you will be giving them God knows how many dead bodies and a detailed description of who killed them. They'll be able to close out a whole bunch of open cases and come away with the real killers. Everyone wins."

"But what if they don't? I don't want to go to jail."

"Trust me, you're not going to jail. Pick up that phone, call the cops, and tell them everything you've told me and they'll cut you a deal. You told me yourself that you weren't sure how long either of us will be around. Now's your chance to do something about it."

"I know, but—"

Nick cut him off. "You're in a bind here friend, and you need to make a decision. Save both of us now, or we die. Maybe I go before you, but you know what will happen eventually. At least if you come clean now, I'll be here to support your story."

Bennie couldn't maintain eye contact. "I need to think it over." He stood.

"Wait, where are you going? There's no time for that!"

But Bennie had already turned his back and stepped out. And as he was about to close the door, Nick said, "Please, they're going to kill my wife."

Bennie turned back. "What are you talking about?"

"They're going to Phoenix tomorrow to kidnap my wife. They're gonna bring her here and kill us both."

"Where'd you get that from? I didn't hear that."

"Ethan and Clay told me yesterday. They're going tomorrow. They're gonna kill us." Nick paused for a breath. "And our unborn child."

CHAPTER FORTY-SEVEN

RED LIGHTS FLASHED AGAINST the slickrock as Wyatt ran towards the road, with a vindicated Velvet yelling "I told you so" behind him.

"Wait a minute, what's going on?" Wyatt asked, as he approached the rental.

"I'm writing you a ticket, that's what's going on."

"I'm here, Officer. Please, put that away." Wyatt made his way around the front end of the car to meet the officer standing behind it.

"Sorry, I've got to write you up. There are plenty of places to park around these parts, but we don't allow hikers to leave cars wherever they please."

The officer completed the ticket and ripped it smoothly from his pad, as if he'd been giving them out all day. He held out the document and waited until Wyatt reluctantly took it.

"It's not what you think. I'm not a hiker, I'm a cop."

"I don't know, and I don't care. I figured you were a hiker because I've been sitting here for a few minutes running your plates. Then I got out and took a look down the wash, and I seen you and that pretty lady with your backpacks and figured you for hikers. Plain and simple."

Wyatt cringed and held onto his hat as several cars whizzed by. Then he pulled out his badge and held it up for the officer.

"Phoenix?" He looked back at Wyatt, eyes squinting in the sun. "If you're not hiking, what are you doing here?"

"Investigating a missing person."

"It's true, Officer," Velvet said, as she reached the road. "I'm a park ranger and we're out here following up on a lead."

"So what should I do about it?"

"How about tear up the ticket?" Velvet said. "We're working with Jess Amado and he's the one who sent us here. I'm sure he can vouch for us."

The officer nodded as he walked back and forth, kicking at the ground. "I know Amado. How come nobody notified the Springdale PD?"

Velvet shrugged. "I don't know, maybe 'cause there's only two or three of you," she said it jokingly, but he didn't seem to find it funny. "And we didn't expect to be out here very long."

"You two aren't working on that body that washed up in the park a few weeks back, are you?"

Wyatt looked at Velvet, but she wasn't looking at him. *Dead bodies, missing hikers. What the hell is going on out here?*

"Not that one, no," Velvet replied. "We're actually looking for Nicholas Perrone. He was last seen in the park on Monday."

Wyatt placed his backpack on the trunk and retrieved one of the posters Velvet had given him. But first, he put out his hand and introduced himself.

"William Sloan," the officer said, and shook Wyatt's hand.

Wyatt passed Sloan the picture. "That's Nick. He's a buddy of mine. I came out here to look for him."

"No shit."

A burst of hope hit Wyatt as he watched Sloan examine the flier, his face wrinkled in thought. "Do you think you might have seen him?"

Sloan didn't answer right away.

And then: "I saw this fellow just the other day."

Wyatt and Velvet locked eyes, and then Wyatt asked, "When, where?"

"I'm not sure ..." Sloan examined the photo again. "Actually, I think it was him. I'm not a hundred percent sure because of the face."

"What do you mean?" Wyatt asked.

"His face was all beaten and bruised. I even asked what happened, but he said he was in some sort of a bar fight. It was just the other day, in Rockville or Virgin. I'm not exactly sure."

"He wasn't alone?"

"There were four of them, three guys plus your friend. They were driving, I think, a Honda truck. Your friend was in the backseat behind the driver. I noticed his face was messed up when I peeked inside the vehicle. Wait a second." Sloan picked up his ticket pad and leafed through a few pages. "Here it is. Tuesday afternoon."

"You get the driver's name and address?"

"Sure did. He lives in St. George."

"Can I get a copy of that?"

Sloan shook his head. "It's my only copy. But you're working with Amado, right?" He didn't wait for Wyatt to answer. "I'll let you take down the information."

Wyatt took the pad from Sloan, wrote down the information, and then handed it back.

Sloan stood over his back. "If you call the department, I'm sure they can get you a copy. But right now, this is all I got and I haven't turned it in yet."

"Anything else you can remember about the car, or the guys Nick was with? Do you have any idea where they were going?"

"I remember thinking it was odd. They were four guys, one's face looks like it was kicked in, and the other three weren't very clean cut. They were speeding through town. I asked them where they were going and I think they said they were returning to St. George. I took their information, ran the plates and stuff, and the paperwork checked out. So I wrote them a ticket and sent them on their way."

"Is there anything else you can think of?" Velvet asked.

"That's about it. Sorry."

"You've been very helpful." Wyatt reached into his pocket and pulled out the ticket Sloan had written him. "And about this ticket ..."

"Have Amado call the department to work it out. You know the routine, right?"

WYATT TAPPED HIS CHEST to make sure his Kevlar vest was properly secured. It was only the fourth time he had done that since arriving in St. George. Next, he made sure his gun was loaded and that he had enough ammunition in reserve, in case things got out of hand. Butterflies twirled through his stomach. In his wildest imagination, even from the moment he learned of Nick's disappearance, Wyatt never thought he would have to do anything like this. He leaned back against his car, took a deep breath, and gripped the cold handle of his pistol.

"Are you Orr?" A lanky, baby-faced man with well-cropped hair stepped out of an Oldsmobile parked directly behind Wyatt. He was wearing a gray suit with a bulging button-down shirt and blue tie.

"That's me," Wyatt said as the man approached.

"David Behunin." He put out his hand and Wyatt shook it. "St. George Police Department. Good to meet you."

"Likewise."

Behunin handed Wyatt a radio. "It's set to the frequency we'll use in case something happens. I've got a pair of uni's on their way, best I could do on short notice. One of them will stay out front, the other will come in with us. Amado said we're looking for a missing hiker?"

Wyatt filled him in on the circumstances and showed him Nick's picture. Behunin scrutinized it until he was comfortable he'd committed Nick's likeness to memory. And then the two of them stood there awkwardly, occasionally glancing at their watches and waiting for backup.

"Nice town you got here," Wyatt said, trying to ease his tension.

Behunin shook his head. "It isn't too bad." He looked around but didn't see any sign of his reinforcements. Then he turned back to Wyatt. "Amado told me you're from Arizona. Phoenix or Tucson?"

"Phoenix."

Then, a police car appeared and Behunin directed them to park behind his. Wyatt and Behunin sauntered over as the officers got out and Behunin introduced Wyatt to two more of St. George's finest. The men confirmed frequencies, checked their radios, and discussed the plan of action before heading for their destination a few blocks away.

It was go time.

CLAY LOOKED OUTSIDE BOTH windows to make sure there was no one around. As usual, there were no patrons in the bar. He flipped the "OPEN" sign around and made his way through the backroom and out the door. The area behind The Shack was filled with dirt and weed, and several rusted cars that had been parked there for years. But today, there were two trucks parked next to the cars, one belonged to Ethan, the other to his father.

Ethan motioned for Clay to join him.

"Get in and quick," Ethan's father said. "I need to get back to the park as soon as possible."

Ethan jumped in front, Clay in back.

"What was so important that I had to drop everything?" Ethan asked.

Without looking at Ethan, his father said, "What's the matter with you?"

Ethan's head slammed into the door and bobbled its way back. Ethan reached for his gun but stopped when he realized his father was the one who had struck him. He frowned. "What the hell was that for?"

"For being an idiot and not listening to me."

"What are you talking about?"

Ethan's father punched the dashboard. "They know about us. I mean, you guys. They know about you."

Clay sprang forward between the two front seats. "They know who we are?"

Ethan's father looked at Clay with disgust before turning back to his son. "You stupid shits. You couldn't execute something as simple as driving that asshole to the field? You didn't tell me you got a speeding ticket the other day."

"I didn't think it was important," Ethan said.

"The Springdale pig that pulled you over identified our guy. He saw him in *your* car and the guy looked like he had been beaten to a pulp."

"So what?"

"Are you a moron? The cop is onto us. He knows Nick didn't just disappear. We need to do something about this."

WHAT WAS MODERN IN midcentury had since fallen into disrepair, and the apartment complex reminded Wyatt of a building from a bad "B" movie, minus the large palm tree that fronts virtually every apartment community in Los Angeles. The words "Horizon Apartments" were painted in black on the light colored stucco façade, just above the entrance. But something didn't feel right. Wyatt looked around and wondered: if Nick had been kidnapped and beaten, would his captors have taken him to an apartment complex? Probably not. There were too many people around. Too many potential witnesses.

Wyatt pulled the paper from his pocket and double-checked the address Sloan had given him. He glanced at the street number painted above the entrance; this was definitely it. And maybe it was too much for Wyatt to expect that they would just bust into the place and find Nick. Wouldn't that be too easy? But at the very least, he knew Nick was a passenger in someone else's car, and the driver of that car lived in this building. One way or another, this would have to lead them to Nick.

They entered the building. There were no gates, locks, intercoms or even bars on the windows. This was St. George, Utah, not New York City. Wyatt stopped to glance at the mailboxes and saw that they didn't contain names, only apartment numbers. Sloan had given him the number, but Wyatt had hoped to see confirmation that the driver of the car did in fact reside here. They ascended a rock staircase just past the mailboxes to the second floor of the two-story structure. Below was a pleasant, open-aired atrium with well-groomed bushes and what looked to be a well-maintained swimming pool. The calming sounds of running water came from somewhere on the lower level. At the top of the staircase, Wyatt found the sign providing directions based on apartment numbers. He motioned to his left and Behunin and the backup followed him to unit number 222. There was a window to the left of the front door, and the blinds were drawn. Wyatt looked at the pool area once again, to make sure that no one was there. Hopefully, things wouldn't get out of hand.

With a clear coast, Behunin motioned for Wyatt to step aside. Wyatt realized this was not an ego thing; Wyatt was a civilian and, as such, had no authority in Utah. They drew their guns and positioned themselves to the right of the door. Behunin made eye contact with each of the officers who shook their heads to confirm they were ready.

"Police! Open up!" Behunin pounded on the door.

Nothing.

Wyatt readjusted his grip on the gun as Behunin pounded on the door again. This time, they heard something. A squeal.

A crying baby.

"One second." A lady's voice from inside the apartment. The door opened as far as the chain would allow, and a woman holding an infant peered out. "What's going on?" she asked.

"St. George Police," Behunin responded.

"What's this all about?" she said from behind the door. "And how do I know you're really police?"

Behunin released his right hand, and retrieved his badge from his back pocket. He flipped it up and held it partially through the opening while she examined it. "Ma'am, we're looking for a man named Steven Colter and we understand that he resides at this address."

She furrowed her brow through the door crack. "I'm sorry, Officer, but no one by that name lives here. I am the only occupant, me and my one-year-old."

Wyatt loosened the grip on his gun.

"What's your name, ma'am?" Behunin asked.

"Am I in some kind of trouble? I don't understand. I told you that no one named … whatever that name was, lives here. And I'm not comfortable getting into details about myself with a couple of strangers. Police or not."

"Ma'am, it won't take me long to find out your name and come back with a search warrant. We have strong reason to believe that a Steven Colter is involved in the disappearance of a missing person. At the very least, we believe this individual has knowledge about the subject's disappearance, and this was the address Mr. Colter recently furnished our department. We need to take a look."

The lady closed the door momentarily while she unhooked the latch. She opened it, but stood in the doorway, holding her infant on her side and guarding the entryway.

"I've never heard of a Steven Colter, and I've lived in this apartment for three and a half years. I don't know what else to tell you."

Wyatt stepped forward.

"Ma'am, I'm Wyatt Orr. I'm a homicide detective back in Phoenix, but I'm here in Utah because my best friend was camping in Zion this week and seems to have disappeared. Our investigation into his whereabouts has taken us to your residence, and I apologize for the inconvenience. Would you have any objection to us taking a look, just for our own confirmation that my friend isn't somewhere in this apartment?"

"With all due respect, Officer, I told you already that we are the only ones here. I don't see any reason, or basis for that matter, for you searching my home." The baby started crying, and the lady shook him in her arms until he calmed.

Behunin stepped back in front of Wyatt. "Ma'am, we need to see the apartment. Now, you can either let us in to take a quick look, or we can come back with a warrant and trash the place. What'll it be?"

She stared Behunin down before finally stepping aside. "Go ahead and look around but don't trash the place. It's already enough of a mess."

Behunin and Wyatt entered the apartment. The young lady went to a small table near the door, grabbed her purse, and pulled out her driver's license. She showed it to Behunin who stayed with her while Wyatt and the uni quickly combed the apartment.

Seconds later: "It's clear," the uni announced, as he appeared from the bedroom.

Wyatt took out Nick's picture and showed it to the young lady. "This is the man we're looking for. Ever seen him?"

She looked at the picture, pursed her lips, and shook her head.

"I apologize for the inconvenience, but we appreciate your cooperation," Behunin said.

She quietly held the door for them until they left. Then she slammed it shut.

Wyatt, Behunin, and the uni left and went back the way they came.

"Fuck!" Wyatt yelled a little too loud as he descended the steps.

Now what?

CHAPTER FORTY-EIGHT

"THERE'S NOTHING TO WORRY about," Ethan assured his father.

"The pig who pulled you over gave this cop from Phoenix your driver's license information. They're out there looking for you as we speak."

"Let them knock themselves out, it's fake."

"I know the address is fake, but is the damn thing traceable? It's a real driver's license."

"Completely untraceable. Remember the license Beano got me in Vegas? Because he worked for the DMV, it was legit. So when we moved here, I swapped it out for a Utah license, and all I needed was Beano's license and proof of a Utah residence. I went into St. George and found some complex with a bunch of vacancies. I took down the address and opened accounts with the phone and power companies. Then, I went to the post office and filled out one of those moving cards so when they sent my new utility bills, they were diverted to our house. I removed the yellow mailing label, took the bills to the Motor Vehicle Bureau, and got my Utah license with my fake name and new address. Easy, and best of all, untraceable."

"But now there's an APB out for you," his father said.

"Not for me, for Steven Colter. But he doesn't exist. You think I would use my real name? Let those assholes run their little goose chase. What's the harm? A little foreplay without the, you know, culmination."

Ethan and Clay laughed, but his father did not.

"I don't care about the ID, I knew it was fake. What I don't like is that they know Nick was alive as late as Tuesday, and they know he'd been beaten. What's more, one of them has actually seen *all* you guys."

Clay leaned forward. "Why don't we just take Nick out to the Graveyard today? Put this whole thing to rest and move on."

"It's too risky. The cops are looking for Ethan, and presumably you and Bennie too. And they're gonna be stopping all kinds of people on the roads. I think we stick to the plan and take care of business right away. You guys leave for Phoenix tonight, or tomorrow morning at the latest. Grab the girl and come back. It's not a bad time to get out of town for a few days anyway. Meanwhile, I'll figure out what to do with that Springdale cop. You remember his name?"

"Sloan," Ethan said.

"Let me think about that. In the meantime, get rid of the car you were driving."

"I was going to ship it with Nick's and the others."

Ethan's father shook his head. "Don't. It's too risky. Just dump it. The information is all over the state by now."

"OK," Ethan said, humbled.

"That leaves us with one remaining problem. The friend. He's still poking around, and now that he knows Nick didn't die in that canyon, or stage a disappearance, I don't see him letting up."

"So what do you want to do?" Ethan asked.

"Take him out."

WYATT DROPPED HIS BACKPACK on the floor and settled into a squeaky office chair behind a desk that had seen better days. He shuffled aside a bunch of papers to make room for his file and almost knocked over a Styrofoam cup of cold coffee. He tossed the cup in a trash bin under the desk, adjusted the chair, and got to work. When the apartment lead came up empty, it was as if Wyatt's entire world suddenly shut down. Police work was like solving a puzzle that didn't come with pieces. You first had to find the pieces, and then put them together. And Wyatt had found a huge piece earlier that day, solid proof that Nick hadn't staged his own disappearance. But the trail had grown cold almost as quickly. Finding himself in St. George with no other leads, Wyatt decided to stop by Amado's office, just a few minutes away. Amado wasn't around, and after fifteen minutes of trying to talk his way in, a young deputy, one of Amado's assistants, recognized Wyatt and brought him back to an office bay.

Wyatt leaned forward and put his hands in his face. He was at a dead-end. Until this morning, all signs pointed to Nick pulling a walkaway. As much as he disapproved, Wyatt was ready to accept it and return to Phoenix. And then everything changed with the discovery of Nick's phone and the cop who had pulled them over. Nick was in trouble, and Wyatt knew that the chances of finding him alive were decreasing by the minute.

His guilt returned. Not just for abandoning Nick, but also for the misjudgments he had made during the investigation. Nick was unhappy in his marriage and had fooled around with someone in the campground. But everyone has to live his life and make his own choices. Who was Wyatt to judge, especially when Nick hadn't had the opportunity to explain himself? The two had once been best friends, and Wyatt had already suffered enough loss in his life. He had no room for another.

But where would he turn next? Wyatt decided to do what any prudent detective does when he's fresh out of leads.

Re-examine the file.

Wyatt laid out all the pictures and witness interviews, and opened an area map he had purchased at a gas station. Then he took out a map of the park and placed it next to the area map. Next, on the area map, Wyatt plotted all the significant places, including the location of Nick's hat and backpack, the 911 call, the call from Ina, the campground, Coal Pits Wash, the apartment complex in St. George, and the location where Sloan had seen Nick. He scrutinized the plotted points at length, but if there was a common thread among them, he wasn't seeing it.

The key questions were: who was Nick with? They certainly weren't friends, because Nick would've mentioned that he had friends in the area when they were planning the trip. Could they have been people Nick met out here? Perhaps. But, if so, where were they going when Sloan pulled them over? And why was Nick's face all beaten? Wyatt quickly dismissed them as friends and settled on the more likely scenario, that the men were strangers. But what were they doing? Had they beaten Nick or had he gotten in trouble first? Probably the former, since, if they were trying to help him, they would have asked Sloan for assistance when he pulled them over.

There were plenty more questions.

Who placed the 911 call? And what was Nick doing in a truck outside the park, when his pack was in a slot canyon? And who was this lady Nick met at the campground? Was she somehow involved? Just hours ago, it seemed like Wyatt had all the answers; Nick was a walkaway. But now, he had nothing but questions.

A wave of panic and despair fell upon him and he decided to take a break. He walked to the front of the room and asked one of the assistant deputies where he could get a drink. Following directions, Wyatt entered the dark cafeteria and made his way to the far right corner and the glare of a big Coke bottle displayed on the machine. He took out his wallet, surveyed the choices. Seconds later, he pulled out a dollar and slid the bill into the slot.

The machine spit it out like it was bad milk.

When it didn't work a second time, Wyatt tried smoothing the corners, but the machine apparently knew better. He put the defective dollar back into his wallet and scanned through his bills for another single, which he found near the back. Wyatt pulled out the crisper bill and with it, a small piece of paper popped out and glided to the floor. Wyatt bent to retrieve it and that's when he realized there was still something he hadn't looked into.

Another piece to the puzzle.

CLAY SIGHED, AS HE opened the door and stepped out of the truck. "I gotta get back to the bar."

"What the hell's your problem?" asked Ethan's father.

Clay leaned back in. "Nothing."

"You got something to say?"

Clay processed, working up the nerve. "I think you're making a big mistake."

"How do you say?"

"Why are we killing more people? And two cops? If we kill Sloan, everyone will know something's up. And if we also kill the friend? I thought our objective was to quietly remove the vulnerable, and do nothing that could draw attention to us."

"You're right, that *was* our objective. But we can't do that anymore. We're beyond that because you guys fucked it up! Ethan got a speeding ticket and the cop who tagged you knows what you look like. By now, they probably also know that Ethan's not who he said he was. We don't live in a big city, so I see no alternative but to remove the cop, the one guy that can blow this whole thing wide open."

"I agree with you, dad," Ethan interjected. "What about the friend, though? Are we making things worse by doing him too?"

"I don't think so, because once we off Sloan, everyone will know something's up anyway. Sloan's the only one who can identify you guys. Once he's gone, killing the friend is icing on the cake, just to give us the peace of mind that no one's hot on our trail. The county won't do much after that, and I'm on top of things at the park. Once we've taken care of business, we're gonna lay low for a while."

"And you're sure you don't want to kill Nick now?" Clay asked.

"I have bigger plans for him."

CHAPTER FORTY-NINE

WYATT GATHERED HIS FILE and left through the backdoor. It was easier than navigating the maze back to the reception area. He was scampering towards his car when he caught sight of Amado walking his way.

"Thanks for the call this morning," Wyatt said. "I appreciate you keeping me in the loop and letting me do my thing out here."

"It made the most sense. You were closest, to the park and the victim," Amado said, unenthusiastically. "No point in us driving an hour there and back each time something comes up."

An awkward moment of silence passed between the two before Wyatt broke it. "I take it you already heard about the sting this morning?"

"Actually, I did not." Amado looked away for a split second.

"The guy doesn't live there. It's a dead-end."

"Shit happens, Detective." Amado walked past Wyatt towards the door.

"Wait a second. That it? That's all you have to say?"

Amado turned around. "What else do you want from me?"

"I just thought you cared a little more."

Amado took two steps towards Wyatt and looked him in the eyes. "Of course I care about your friend, and I hope to God he's alive. But as far as this investigation goes, all I can do from this point forward is wish you luck."

"What the hell does that mean? I thought we were working together?"

"We were, and you've done a nice job. You proved Nick was kidnapped."

"So you're pulling out because you're upset you were wrong?"

"Not at all," Amado said firmly. "I've been taken off the case."

"Why?"

"Because kidnapping is a federal crime and that's the FBI's jurisdiction. So while it was a pleasure working with you, I'm afraid that if you want to continue, you'll have to do so in conjunction with Agent Nielsen. Now he's the one running the show."

"WHY ARE YOU SO worried?" Nick said. "I'm giving you a way out of this."

"You don't know these guys," Bennie said. "You have no idea what they're capable of."

"Fine. But I don't see how it matters."

"Let me tell you about this enterprise, OK? A couple of weeks ago, we kidnapped, I mean they kidnapped, a hiker who had just come off Angel's Landing. They drove him out of the park, pushed him off a huge cliff and into the river. And you know what happened?"

Nick didn't answer.

"The river dragged the body and it literally came to rest at the base of Angel's Landing. The sheriff just closed his investigation earlier this week and ruled it an accidental death."

"I think I heard about it," Nick said.

"And about six months ago, Ethan followed a middle-aged couple up one of the trails. He hiked behind them and watched as the husband went ahead, leaving the wife behind. When the opportunity arose, Ethan pushed her off the cliff, turned around, and hiked out. The sheriff investigates and the next thing we know, the husband is on trial for her murder. And you know what? They found him guilty."

"Then why did you guys beat the shit out of me in a bar of all places? Why didn't you just push me off a cliff?"

"That's just it. Opportunity, it presented itself. Clay owns the place, they'd had their eye on you, and once they knew you were headed there, they moved fast. And, even with you, they made it appear as though your disappearance was park-related."

Nick shifted as much as he could. "I don't understand your point."

"The point is that they are pure evil. They're not like normal criminals. They don't commit the same crimes over and over, so they're difficult to catch. They switch it up, and whatever they do turns to gold. I feel like that guy in the movie *Thief*, like someone who got involved with the mafia and has no way out. I could go to the feds and they could move me to some small town on the other side of the country, but I'll always be looking over my shoulder wondering when I'll take a bullet in the head while grabbing the newspaper in my front yard. I don't want to be that guy."

"I don't think you have to."

"I've weighed the options and the way I see it, if I contact the authorities and turn myself in, there's a fifty percent chance, if I'm lucky, that they'll believe and protect me. But there's a hundred percent chance that Ethan and his dad will hunt me down and kill me. I don't like those odds."

A KNOT PRESSED IN Wyatt's stomach as he reached for the door. Wyatt's only Utah ally had been removed from the case and now Nielsen was running the show. And Nielsen's words rang clearly in Wyatt's head: "If it were my investigation, you'd have no part of it." Things were about to change, and, as far as Wyatt was concerned, for the worst. Nielsen wouldn't want him anywhere near the investigation. But Wyatt had done everything he could and was following the last lead he had, the note he had found at Nick's campsite. He'd worry about Nielsen later.

There were no alarms or entrance bells on the door, but it didn't need one. Wyatt applied some force and the door finally gave, and it sounded as if he had actually broken or chipped away at the wooden molding. The door squeaked of un-oiled hinges, and while the sign on the window announced open for business, you could barely tell by looking inside. Wyatt made his way to the bar, placed his file on the counter, and took a seat on a stool.

"What can I get you?" the bartender said, with a look of surprise that someone had actually chosen to patronize his establishment.

Wyatt played a quick game of "should I or shouldn't I?" before deciding he should. "Heineken."

The bartender turned to grab one from the cooler on the other side of the bar. Wyatt thanked him, and then took a look around the place. *Had Nick been here? Hell, why would anyone come here?* Wyatt had only stopped in because he had to and, it didn't matter how good the beer was, after less than thirty seconds, he already knew he never wanted to return.

Turning back to the bar, Wyatt nudged the folder open just enough to slide out Nick's picture, as the bartender returned and placed the beer before him. Wyatt reached for his wallet, placed three singles on the counter, and told him to keep the change. His insides smiled at the prospect of alcohol, spurred on by the cool steam gyrating from the bottle. Wyatt pulled a prolonged swig, not just because he was thirsty, but also because he wanted to address his business, finish his beer quickly, and get the hell out of there. The alcohol satisfied his thirst but did nothing to appease his nerves.

"Have you seen this man?"

Wyatt placed Nick's photo on the bar.

CLAY EXAMINED THE PHOTO while trying to keep a straight face. "Sorry, never seen him."

"He didn't come in here at all in the last week?"

"Nope. Never seen the man." Clay put the photo down.

"You're sure of it?"

"I think I'd remember that city boy if he came in here because we don't get too many people to begin with. Look around, this ain't exactly Cheers." There were three elderly park workers at the far end of the bar. They barely looked alive.

Wyatt slid Nick's photo down the countertop. "Have any of you seen him in the area?"

The look on their faces told Wyatt he was interrupting an important conversation.

"I'm sorry to bother you," he said. "I'm a detective from Phoenix and I'm out here searching for my buddy who's been missing for several days. He was camping in the park."

They looked at the photo, then looked at each other and shook their heads in unison. Wyatt grabbed the picture and returned it to his folder.

"I hope you don't mind me asking."

"Not at all," Clay replied, doing his best to keep a straight face. He pointed at Wyatt's beer. "You good?"

"I'll take another," he said.

"No problem." Clay threw another Heineken in front of Wyatt. "I gotta step out back for a moment." He walked down the bar to the others. "You all good over here?" They nodded and Clay made his way towards the back room. "I won't be but a minute. Holler if you need something."

Clay walked through the dusty room and out back such that Wyatt couldn't see from where he was sitting. He peeked through the window just to make sure.

And then he made the call.

CHAPTER FIFTY

INA SAT AT HER kitchen table staring at the cordless phone on the counter. In Tucson, she'd managed to pass the time busying herself with the event. But now she was home, by herself, and all she could think about was Nick. Hours had passed since she'd spoken with Wyatt and she was eager for another update. Throughout the morning, she had thought of calling but decided to let him do his thing. He would call at his next opportunity. Of course, Ina feared that Wyatt might procrastinate if the lead he was following was a dead-end, knowing the news would only further distress her. But she could live with that right now because deep down she knew that if the news was bad, she wasn't ready to hear it.

Passing time was a serious challenge. After returning from Tucson, Ina had started going through Nick's office. But then this morning, Wyatt had called with the news that Nick had been seen, alive, a couple of days ago. She suddenly had renewed hope, and he told her she no longer had to look through Nick's stuff. With nothing else to do, she sat at the kitchen table, took a deep breath, and began flipping through the *Arizona Republic*. And it was all much of the same: robberies, murder, a house fire, war in the Middle East. She made her way through the different sections, checking the weather, and even reading the editorials, all the things to which she'd never given a moment's notice. But there, on the last page, was a single word, a headline, which sent the water gushing from her eyes as if the dam had been broken.

Obituaries.

CLAY RE-ENTERED THE BAR just as Wyatt finished his beer. Without a word, he pulled another Heineken from the cooler, deftly removed the cap, and placed it on the counter next to Wyatt's file.

"On the house," Clay said, removing the empty bottle. "You look like you can use it."

Wyatt sat back and ran his hands over his forehead and into his hair. He had gained no useful information from his visit, and was, once again, at a dead-end. Another beer couldn't hurt. He held up the bottle and thanked the bartender.

"No problem, dude. I'm Clay by the way." He leaned against the back counter. "You getting anywhere with this? Finding your friend?"

"A little here and there, I guess."

"That doesn't sound promising."

"That's how these things go." Wyatt gulped a mouthful. "It's up and down."

"What kind of work you do in Arizona?"

"I investigate homicides."

"This doesn't sound like a homicide."

"Right now, it's just a missing person's case. I don't usually do this kind of stuff, but the guy who's missing is my friend."

"I don't know how you do it," Clay grinned. "But I admire you. I just sell beer and listen to people bitch about their lives. Ain't much pressure in that."

Wyatt forced a hint of a smile. "That doesn't sound too bad right about now."

One of the other patrons motioned for another beer and Clay went to service the request. Wyatt finished his and pulled the bottle back a second time to savor every last droplet. He had already decided there would not be a fourth, at least not until later in the evening.

Wyatt plopped the bottle back on the counter and waved to Clay. "You sure I can't pay for this?"

Clay walked over and shrugged him off. "Don't worry about it."

"I appreciate it." Wyatt grabbed his folder and turned to walk out.

"Good luck finding your friend."

CHAPTER FIFTY-ONE

WYATT THREW THE CAR in reverse, pulled back, and drove slowly along the gravelly road by the dump trucks and backhoes. All he'd gotten out of his visit was something he'd been struggling to avoid for several years. Alcohol. At the very least, it had eased his inhibitions some and with nowhere else to go, Wyatt decided to visit Velvet. He reached for the phone to call her but his hand never made it.

The rear passenger window shattered into pieces.

Wyatt jolted the steering wheel and ducked as he heard the pop of gunfire. He was under siege. There were several "pings" from the passenger side. At least the gas tank was on the driver's side. Up ahead, the road had a slight incline, which led directly onto Route 9. Grasping the wheel for dear life, Wyatt pushed the gas pedal to the floor and the tires kicked up pebbles and dust, as the car went airborne and jackknifed onto the highway.

A string of bullets rang off the exterior near the trunk.

The vehicle was out of control as Wyatt had entered the highway at a perpendicular angle. He flew across the double yellow line heading straight for a mountain of lava-coated boulders on the other side of the road. He furiously twisted the steering wheel to the right, and shuddered, as another hail of gunfire came his way. Some of the bullets ricocheted off the boulders, while one cut some metal on the front passenger side.

Wyatt managed to steer the car back towards the lane divider just as an SUV came flying around the bend. They were seconds away from a head on collision. The driver slammed on his breaks, spun out of control, and slammed the back driver's side of Wyatt's car. The impact forced Wyatt against the back of the seat but, luckily, his seat belt kept him from flying across the car. Ironically, the SUV driver had done Wyatt a favor, as the impact helped straighten out his car. Wyatt forced the gas to the floor, as the back windshield blew out. He managed to safely navigate the curve, and as he flew on out, he stole a glance in the rearview but was too far away to see anything. The ambush had originated from the backhoes, but he couldn't ascertain who was behind it. Trembling, Wyatt decided to return to the hotel and regroup.

"WHAT THE HELL WAS that?" Bennie rushed to the window, twisted the rod, opened the blinds, and peered out.

"Sounded like gunshots," Nick said, as he tried to lift himself and the chair. "And it sounded pretty close. Maybe you should back away from the window."

Bennie ignored him and tried to pinpoint the source, but all he could see was dust over by The Shack.

"And could you help pull me out of the way?" Nick asked.

"It's coming from up near the road; I don't think we're in harm's way." The roadway was northeast of Ethan's house, up the hill.

Bennie flinched as the next round of shots rang out. Then he took two steps behind the window and tried looking out at an angle.

"I believe it as much as you do," Nick said. "Please move me to the middle of the house."

And then the sharp sound of ambush quickly gave way to an ear-piercing squeal immediately preceding the impact. Bennie couldn't see the shooter, or the shooter's location, but he was able to see the collision and the driver's escape from the scene.

"What the hell is going on?" Nick asked.

"I don't know," Bennie mumbled, still looking out the window. But he didn't really believe that. The gunfire almost certainly originated from Clay's bar.

CLAY'S PATRONS, ALL THREE of them, darted into the street, rushing to the aid of the SUV's driver. The car had spun off the road and come to rest on the north side of the highway, by the lava boulders. Luckily, the driver sustained little more than some trauma, a few bruises, and a story fit for Hollywood, which he would surely embellish in years to come. Clay followed slowly but ventured no farther than outside the door. He had heard the crash from inside and hoped they had gotten their man. But he couldn't tell since the road was above the bar.

Clay stood under the awning and looked to his right as Ethan climbed out of the backhoe with his shotgun. Clay held out his hands in a silent inquiry and Ethan shook his head.

The cop had escaped.

Ethan scrambled around the backhoe with primordial swiftness, got into his truck, and sped away. Clay went back inside. He had done his part, comping the cop a beer to keep him there long enough for Ethan to position himself. But it didn't matter. They had squandered a perfect opportunity and he had just lost his only customers for the day. Shootings and accidents were never good for business.

CHAPTER FIFTY-TWO

"GOOD EVENING, OFFICER."

The man knocked on the passenger side window and Sloan depressed the button to roll it down.

"How are you tonight?" Sloan said.

"Just fine," said Ethan's father. "I understand you're familiar with the missing hiker investigation."

Sloan was sitting in his vehicle parked in a dirt lot in Springdale, across the street from Blondie's Diner.

"I heard you got a look at our hiker during a traffic stop this week. I'm told that he was in pretty bad shape, but that you could identify the other passengers if you saw them."

Sloan shook his head. "Probably. I gave the information to one of your rangers. She was with some detective from Arizona. Did anything happen with that?"

"I'm afraid it was a dead end." He paused to look around. "In fact, that's why I'm here. Have you met my son, Ethan? He's a mechanic."

"I don't think so. At least the name doesn't ring a bell."

"After the police came up empty this morning, I figured I'd check with him. His garage is just outside Hurricane and he knows a lot of people there. And when I mentioned the driver's name, Steven Colter, he froze."

"He knows the guy?"

"Unfortunately. He says Colter's into some pretty bad stuff. Drugs and guns. They call him 'Coltergeist.' Ethan says he has a couple of disciples, guys he usually wreaks havoc with."

"Then maybe you should take him to see Sheriff Amado."

"We just might do that. But first we wanted to talk to you and make sure it's the same guy. My son's afraid to go to the sheriff unless we're right about this. He says this Colter is dangerous."

Sloan made a face. "OK. You want to bring him by so we can chat?"

Ethan's father crouched and placed his arms along the window. "Would you mind coming with me, or at least following me into Virgin to talk to him? He doesn't want anyone to see you two talking. He's pretty scared of these guys."

"What's he scared about? They aren't from around here, right?"

"Yes, but they're known to hang out in these parts. I mean, *you* saw them in this area, didn't you?"

"True."

Ethan's father shook his head and put his hands out. "So what do you say?"

Sloan took a moment to think it over.

"A man's life is at stake here," he prodded. "We need to find these guys. *And fast.*"

"You're right," Sloan relented. "Jump in. We'll go together."

SWEAT MATERIALIZED FROM PORES Wyatt didn't know existed. He was sitting in what was left of his rental, having finally reached the hotel parking lot. A wave of despair swept over him, a feeling that he was totally in over his head. Wyatt snapped his shirt outward to remove whatever shards of glass may have reached his body. He also checked for blood, but he was clean.

He scanned the area as he exited the vehicle, and examined every inch of the surrounding shrubbery. No snipers were waiting. Wyatt was certain no one had followed him; he'd left the scene doing eighty without slowing until reaching the hotel. And his eyes had been in constant motion; there wasn't a single car in his rearview.

Who had tried to kill him?

The incident was clearly related to Nick's disappearance, but Wyatt was fresh out of leads. Could it be related to his visit to The Shack? The bartender did step out. Where had he gone? Wyatt also retraced his own steps and reviewed the last half-hour in his mind. When the bartender returned, he was friendlier and gave Wyatt a free beer. Could he have been stalling, keeping Wyatt in the place to give someone else time to set up an ambush?

Wyatt decided it was better to go inside and analyze the situation than loiter in the parking lot like a sitting duck. He got out and quickly circled the car to survey the damage. The rental company wouldn't be happy. A couple of windows had been blown out and there was glass all over the backseat. There were multiple bullet holes in the front, side, and trunk. He was lucky the tires hadn't been shot out.

Wyatt grabbed his daypack, and shards of glass rained to the floor when he lifted it off the seat. He shook it to remove the more stubborn and clingy pieces, and then unlatched the trunk. As it slowly creaked open, Wyatt saw the box with Nick's camping gear and, given the beating the car had just taken, decided to leave nothing inside. After ensuring his hotel room was safely locked, Wyatt placed the box in the corner, took out his phone, and sat on the edge of the bed. Yes, the bartender's short break was suspicious, but had there even been enough time to set up an ambush?

Doubtful.

Unless someone knew beforehand that Wyatt was headed there. And there was only one person that knew where Wyatt was going.

Amado.

"I'm an idiot," Wyatt said. "Sure you can help with the investigation, just keep me updated on everything." He recalled their initial conversation.

Wyatt stood, as rage boiled in his veins. "And now that he's lost control, and can no longer monitor my activities, he tries to … this is bullshit!" Wyatt threw the phone to the corner of the room and it landed in the box with Nick's gear. "What are you up to Amado? Was it you who just tried to take my head off? Did you follow me from your office and just sit there waiting until I came out?"

The more Wyatt thought about it, the more it made sense. Amado had been curt with him in the parking lot. And while Amado's office had checked a couple of leads, it never seemed like they were really trying to find Nick. In fact, Wyatt was doing the work but Amado was on top of it all because Wyatt shared what he had learned.

"Now it makes sense," Wyatt said. "The FBI takes over. We already know Nick didn't run away or stage his own disappearance. He was kidnapped. And as long as Amado is in control, how far can I get without him knowing? I'm reporting *everything*. But now that the FBI has the case, he can't monitor my activities, and he knows that if I keep pressing, I'm going to find out what happened. So … "

Wyatt fisted his hands, as the urge to punch something was overpowering. He kneeled beside the box to grab his phone, rolling Nick's sleeping bag out of the way. He was staring at Nick's gear packed neatly in the box when it hit him. Wyatt rubbed the stuff sack and flipped the phone open as he said decisively.

"It's not Amado."

"WE'RE ON OUR WAY," Ethan's father spoke into his cell as he and Sloan left Springdale. After pressing a side button several times to lower the volume, he listened for a moment and then continued, "I'm in the car with a Police Officer and we're coming to meet you. You're going to tell him everything you know! Don't make this difficult, OK?" He listened another moment and said, "I promise it will all be done with the strictest of confidence."

He listened again, this time for almost a minute. "Now son, I know these guys are dangerous, but no one will know about our meeting. Don't forget a man's life is at stake. Sit tight; we'll be there in ten minutes."

They rode the rest of the sinuous highway in silence. Sloan lowered the blocker above his windshield but it didn't help much. The late afternoon sun was still fighting for its place in the western sky.

"Where are we meeting him?" Sloan asked, as they passed a welcome sign for the town of Virgin. "Other than a bar or two, there aren't many places around here where we can talk."

"You'll see. The turnoff is coming up."

They rode in silence for a few more miles until Ethan's father pointed above the dashboard to his left. "There, turn onto that dirt road."

"Where does this lead?"

"Nowhere specific, just some great hiking. But more importantly, a place we can talk where my son feels safe."

Sloan slowed and turned to Ethan's father. "How far do we have to go? These roads are pretty rocky and I don't like being back here with this car, especially so close to nightfall. Can't you just call and have him meet us in town?"

"Trust me, he won't do it. Not in plain view of others. We're almost there."

"Shit," Sloan said. "This better be good."

"Not to worry, Officer. We'll take care of business as quickly as possible."

Sloan pulled up to the silver Durango that was parked in the middle of an open field. After cutting the engine, he and Ethan's father stepped out of the car. The sun had just settled behind the canyons and the impending doom of darkness was in the air.

Ethan stepped out of Nick's truck and waited until Sloan approached.

"What can you tell me about Steven Colter?" Sloan asked, avoiding pleasantries.

Ethan met Sloan's gaze, and that's when Sloan's eyes grew wide. He swallowed hard, as it appeared his heart had received the message from his brain.

Ethan was Colter.

Sloan reached for his gun, but it was too late. Ethan's father pulled the hammer and poked Sloan in the side. "Don't even try." Ethan's father swiftly removed Sloan's gun from its holster.

"Come on, let's go." Ethan pulled Sloan by the arm towards the pit that had been blocked from Sloan's view by Nick's truck. It was the hole they had dug for Nick.

"What the hell are you guys doing? I'm a police officer."

"That knows too much," Ethan cut him off.

"Quickly," Ethan's father said. "We don't have time for theatrics."

Sloan protested, which prompted Ethan's father to strike him upside the head with the butt of his gun, knocking him out cold. Father and son dragged the only eyewitness to their latest crime and dumped him in the grave.

"You think we need to shoot him, too?" Ethan asked.

But it was too late.

His father had already pumped two rounds into the fallen officer.

CHAPTER FIFTY-THREE

WYATT QUIETLY STEPPED AROUND the back of the trailer and peeked inside a window. Dark. He started to turn the corner but stopped short of the front. He had to be careful; it was in plain view of the campground entrance booth, which was currently manned by a ranger who didn't look very busy. Wyatt waited for what seemed like an eternity until a car approached the booth. And when the ranger turned her attention to the camper, Wyatt swiftly turned the corner, jumped up the three steps, and gave a light, cursory knock on the door.

"Stan?" Wyatt looked through the oxidized screen, hoping the host wasn't around. After five seconds with no answer, Wyatt scanned the area and pulled open the latch, officially crossing the line between enforcer and transgressor.

The front door opened into the living room and, across from the entrance, a swiveling leather recliner sat bolted to the carpeted floor. To the left was the living room/dining room/kitchen. To the right was a raised hallway, which contained a bathroom and bedroom. Wyatt turned on his Maglite and closed the door. To his immediate left, a sofa ran along the front wall. Above it was a large window allowing a sweeping view of the campground, entrance booth, and Visitor Center. Wyatt reached for the string and pulled the drapes closed. Next to the sofa, in the far corner of the trailer, was a wooden table and chairs littered with old mail and papers. Wyatt leafed through them with hesitation; he wasn't sure what he was looking for. The one thing of which he was now certain was that Stan was involved in Nick's disappearance.

He was determined to find out how.

But nothing on the table proved helpful and so he began going through cabinets. Most of them contained food; Stan appeared to be prepared for Armageddon. Wyatt moved some around before deciding it was a waste of time. Would Stan hide anything behind it? Probably not. He tugged his shirt back and forth, "Man, it's hot in here." He made his way over to the recliner, and began opening cabinets that were filled with hard-covered books on religion, history, corporate America, and investing in the stock market. Exasperated, Wyatt took a seat. *What am I doing*? He leaned back, closed his eyes, and rubbed his temples; there was no place left to search. He could check the bedroom, but what would he find?

Wyatt swung the recliner, and the chair moved slightly but then stopped abruptly with a shriek. Something was obstructing it. He tried to push it further, but the chair wouldn't budge. He shined his light behind it and onto a large box on the floor. Applying some force, Wyatt swiveled the chair back in the other direction to open as much space as possible before reaching for the box. He managed to extricate it and felt its contents shift as he placed it on the floor in front of him. Then, he aimed the tiny bulb inside the carton and blew the frustration right out of his mouth. It was a stack of old magazines.

Time. Newsweek. Business Week. Forbes. Fortune 500. U.S News and World Report. Playboy. Hustler.

Wyatt grabbed a bunch with one hand and set them down. He shone the light on the next stack but found nothing of interest. He placed those on the floor as well. At the top now was a periodical opened to an article entitled, "Company Sues Family for Breaching Fiduciary Duty in Collecting More than Three Billion Dollars." Wyatt flipped to the cover; it was an old edition of *Forbes*. He skimmed the article, which involved allegations that the Rigas family had committed fraud on investors of Adelphia Communications, in collecting money from loans they covered by inflating capital expenses and hiding debt.

Wyatt dug further and found more stories of accounting scandals involving companies such as AOL/Time Warner, Arthur Anderson, Bristol

Meyers, Haliburton, Enron, Kmart, Reliant Energy, Xerox, WorldCom and others. Wyatt removed them all and placed them neatly on the floor. Now he could see the bottom of the box, where there were some loose documents and envelopes. He opened the first, a letter Stan had received from WorldCom. It began with "Dear Shareholder," a boilerplate apology from the company for Stan's investment losses. And there were a number of other, similar letters.

Stan had been a victim of corporate America.

Wyatt returned them to their place at the bottom, then grabbed a stack of magazines from the floor and dumped them in the box. He reached for the next stack when an envelope fell from amongst them, and he opened the typewritten letter. Bumps appeared throughout his skin and the hair on the back of his neck immediately rose. Something in the document gave him pause. It was two words that stood prominently near the top.

"Nicholas Perrone."

"WHERE THE HELL HAVE you been?" Bennie asked, as Ethan entered the kitchen through the back door.

"Cleaning my own mess, OK?" Ethan paused. "Besides, what do you care? What's with the attitude?"

"I think I have a right to know what's going on."

Ethan got in Bennie's face. "You have a right to know whatever we decide to share with you."

"Knock it off fellas." Clay stepped between them and turned to Bennie. "What the hell's with you?"

Bennie pointed in Clay's face. "Do you know where Ethan was just now?"

Clay met Ethan's gaze and then looked at Bennie. "The Executive Graveyard. Let's just say the town has one less policeman."

"Sloan? You killed a cop?"

"We had no choice." Ethan grabbed a beer and tossed one to Clay. "He identified us and it was only a matter of time. This town is small.

Chances are, he would've seen us again soon. So we nipped it in the bud."

"I can't believe this," Bennie said.

"Don't get your panties in a bunch. It was our only chink and we're back in the clear. Now we can show our faces again."

"But you don't really need to because you're headed to Phoenix tomorrow." Bennie turned to Clay. "You know that? Of course you do. You're going with him!"

"Look," Ethan said. "I'm sorry we didn't tell you, but it doesn't concern you."

"So, it's true. You're going to kidnap Nick's wife and kill her too. I thought you said 'no women and children'?"

"Just leave this to us," Ethan said.

Bennie stepped closer. "That's not an answer, Ethan."

"We did say that, Bennie, to make you feel more comfortable. Meaning, *you* won't be involved in killing women and children. But, this isn't the first time we've killed a woman. Remember we framed that guy by pushing his wife off the canyon?" Ethan pointed towards the hallway. "That man in the other room ruined our lives. Mine. My dad's. This isn't just another job, it's personal. It's revenge."

Bennie exhaled a hurricane. "You know what? I don't even want to know. I'm glad you didn't tell me. I think it's better you keep me out of this. All of it!"

Bennie started walking towards the door, but Ethan stepped in front of him. "Don't do anything you'll regret."

Bennie stepped back towards the middle of the kitchen where he took a position against one of the counters. "Fuck you, OK? Both of you."

Ethan let out a defusing smile. "Where's your appreciation? I saved your ass today."

"You didn't *save* our lives; you're the one that endangered us in the first place."

Ethan stared at Bennie but this time, Bennie maintained the ominous contact for as long as Ethan held it.

"I'd watch my back if I were you," Ethan said. "It would be a shame to see you make the same mistake Lyle made."

Bennie chuckled. "There it is again, the Lyle card. Is that the best you got? Drop the act. I already know what you're capable of. I've seen it with my own two eyes."

Ethan pulled a handgun from the small of his back and took a few steps towards Bennie.

"That's enough, both of you." Clay stepped in, but this time it was for naught. Bennie pushed past him and put his finger in Ethan's face.

"Shoot me, Ethan. Come on, let it rip." A tense few seconds passed while Bennie watched Ethan fiddle with the gun. "I didn't think so. You like to scare, but you're not going to kill me. You need me because you're running out of help. You can't kill em' all."

"Ethan, man, put the gun away," Clay pleaded.

Ethan slipped the gun back in his pants and stuck his finger in Bennie's face. "You better watch your back, 'cause no one else around here is."

CHAPTER FIFTY-FOUR

STAN AND NICK KNOW each other.

Stan had worked for Nick and Wyatt was holding proof of it in his hands. Nick had unknowingly set up camp right under the nose of a disgruntled employee. He held up the light and started to read through the letter.

But then he ran out of time.

The gravel outside the trailer crunched and grated at a slow, steady pace. Wyatt paused to listen, and that's when he heard a door close.

Footsteps.

Stan.

Wyatt placed the flashlight in the box so that Stan wouldn't see it as he approached the trailer. And it's amazing how something as easy as stuffing a letter into an envelope can be virtually impossible when you're harried. Wyatt fumbled; he couldn't get it to fit. The corner creased and it wouldn't stuff completely, but he didn't have time to fix it. He threw the envelope in the box, scooped the magazines off the floor and tossed them in as well. A few of them missed their mark and Wyatt rushed to get them in the box, as he heard more footsteps.

Sweat poured from everywhere, as Wyatt felt like he had stepped out of a swimming pool and put his clothes on without drying. He lifted the box and was about to shove it behind the chair when he saw the glare inside the box.

The Maglite.

Wyatt worked his hand to the bottom corner and took hold of the light, clicking it off before removing it. He would have to keep it off so as not to be noticed. The sound of Stan's distinctive walk grew louder, such that Wyatt realized there must be an open window somewhere in the trailer. It sounded like it might be in the bedroom. Wyatt hastily closed the box flaps, although one of them was stuck behind the magazines. No time to worry. He leaned over to put the box back.

But it didn't fit.

Wyatt was literally trying to fit a square into a triangle. He knew it could fit since the space was larger than the box. Stan had done it and Wyatt could too, if he had time. But he didn't. He could feel the magazines sliding as he wedged the box behind the chair as best he could. Feeling for his Glock, Wyatt stumbled as he climbed the steps and felt his way along the wall until he reached Stan's bedroom. He nudged the door open and immediately saw a faint light in the distance through a window. It was from the campground Entrance booth, too far away to help him see what he was doing. Wyatt tried to get his bearings in the dark, as the footsteps became more pronounced, until he heard them coming up the steps.

He's coming inside.

Wyatt's brain fired all kinds of missiles. Should he try and hide and wait him out? Should he escape out the window? Or should he draw his weapon and order Stan to lead him to Nick?

But what if Stan denies involvement? Or what if he refuses to cooperate, or even says that Nick's already dead? What would Wyatt do then, shoot him? What good is Stan dead? He had to, somehow, lead Wyatt to Nick. It's the only way.

"Ouch," Wyatt smacked his knee into the base of the king-size bed. He crouched and flicked on his Maglite momentarily to get a quick view of the room's layout. In front of him, at the far end of the trailer, was what looked like a decent-sized closet. Wyatt stepped around the bed, over to the closet, and flashed the light inside. But there was no room; it was full of Stan's clothes and luggage. That's when Stan entered the trailer and Wyatt came to a realization.

There was no place to hide.

"WHERE ARE YOU GOING?" Clay sprinted out the kitchen door behind Ethan.

"To see Velvet. It's been a while."

"I thought we're leaving for Phoenix."

Ethan held out Nick's key chain and pressed a button. The Durango chirped, unlocked, and the lights went on inside. Ethan opened the front door and turned to Clay. "We *are* leaving for Phoenix. In the morning."

"I know that." Clay made a face. "But I thought we were going to leave at first light and do you really want to be out late the night before? We're gonna have a long day of driving."

Ethan placed his arm on the inside of the car door. "I don't know about first light but we'll leave sometime in the morning. The original plan was to leave while it was still dark, but that was to avoid detection by Sloan. Since my dad and I took care of him, we can leave a little later, OK? Nothing to worry about."

"I don't know about *that*." Clay glanced towards the house, and then lowered his voice. "I'm concerned about Bennie turning on us. I think it might be time to 'dump the stock' as your father says. It feels like the market's crashed."

"I've been thinking the same thing, but Bennie's right. If we get rid of him, we'll be out of commission. Who's going to locate for us?"

"Didn't we decide that after this we're going to take a break anyway? I'm afraid he might go to the cops, and this may be our last chance to protect ourselves."

"We'll see. In the meantime, just keep a close eye and don't leave him alone with Nick." Ethan jumped in the car and reached for the handle to close the door.

"You sure it's a good idea to drive this around tonight?"

"Are you kidding? The paperwork's perfect. Besides, could there be a better time? Now there's an APB out on *my* truck, and no one's looking for his anymore. Before long, it'll be on its way to the coast."

STAN FLICKED THE LIGHT switch on the wall and the room instantly brightened. He set his keys on the kitchen counter and glanced at the answering machine in the corner. The light wasn't blinking. He started walking towards the bathroom when he noticed something out of order, an envelope on the floor just behind the recliner. He bent to pick it up and immediately saw the letter sticking out. It was folded and creased along the edges. The logo was all too familiar; he didn't need to read it again. It would only awaken demons and incite the interminable rage he'd felt since that horrible day.

But then Stan remembered their hostage and recalled the mantra he had used to get him through rough times. "Good things come to those who wait." Stan had been patient and sweet revenge had indeed come his way. And the feeling was gratifying. He folded the envelope in half and stuffed it in his pocket. Then he looked behind the recliner and discovered a bunch of magazines on the floor. The box wasn't where he'd left it.

He entered the kitchen and examined everything, like a homeowner returning after a robbery. Stan didn't notice anything missing or out of place. But then he saw that the drapes were closed and he always kept them open so he could see out into the campground.

There had definitely been an intruder.

A nervous chill swept through him. *It hasn't been dark for long and the drapes are closed.* He knew that, during the day, you couldn't see into the trailer unless you pressed your face up to the window. He had tested this when he first moved to the park, since he would often walk around in his underwear. But, at night, the contrast of light inside and darkness outside would allow anyone to see in. Whoever had broken in couldn't have done so long ago.

And could still be inside.

He glanced around but already knew that if the intruder was still there, he could only be in the bathroom or bedroom. Stan's gun was in the bedroom. He had another firearm in his truck, but decided that if the intruder was inside, he wouldn't step out and give him the chance to escape. Stan was certain the intruder was Wyatt, since Wyatt was the only one left actually looking for them. This could be the best, and perhaps last, opportunity to get rid of him. Stan looked around for a weapon. The fire extinguisher on the wall was a good choice, but not nearly as good as a butcher knife. He grabbed the knife from a kitchen drawer and fisted it downward, stab ready. He climbed the steps slowly and made his way into the hallway. Then, he arched the knife over his head and pushed the door open with his other hand. No one was in the shower. Stan switched sides and did the same thing across the hall; the bathroom was also empty.

Using his sleeve, Stan wiped sweat from his brow and took slow and calculated steps towards the bedroom. Holding the knife in front of him, he flicked on the light switch and jumped back, landing in a defensive posture. The knife stabbed through the air and almost fell out of his hands. He checked the closet, but no one was there. Stan even lifted the mattress and looked beneath.

Nothing.

Relief and frustration mixed in his head and, using a hand towel next to the faucet, he wiped the sweat off his face. Then he put the knife down, opened his nightstand drawer, and pulled out his pistol. He checked the chamber, confirmed it was loaded, and stuffed it in his waist.

Now he was ready to go to war.

CHAPTER FIFTY-FIVE

IT WAS DARK AND musty with a stench second only to a decomposing body, but it was the only place Wyatt could hide in a pinch. He was breathing hard and struggling to do so quietly. Sweat poured from his body like water escaping a canyon, but there was little he could do other than sit tight. When Stan entered the trailer, Wyatt found himself in Stan's diminutive bedroom. He was slithering carefully along the walls when he discovered a trap door in the floor. The small, carpet-covered square wasn't much larger than a foot by a foot, but it was all Wyatt had to work with. He lifted the door, stuck his feet inside and squeezed through, carefully lowering himself into a basket full of clothes.

Dirty laundry.

How long had it been since Stan had done a wash? If only Wyatt had caught him at the *beginning* of a laundry cycle.

The ceiling crunched with footsteps, and it wasn't easy resisting the urge to heave, cough, or express some reaction to the hideous odor. But he couldn't, because any sound could blow his cover and ruin his chances of finding Nick. Wyatt clicked on the Maglite and looked around. He was in an underside rollout storage compartment near the landing gear pull pins.

The ceiling crunch stopped directly above him. Wyatt froze and desperately tried to hold in his breath, which proved to be a welcome break from the odorous air. Then he felt something grab at his waist and he flinched and writhed in distress. A snake? Squirrel? He swatted several times, tossing some of Stan's clothes in the process. The thought of a snakebite sent shudders through his body until he realized the culprit: his cell phone. It was set to vibrate. Relieved, Wyatt tapped the handgun on his waist for reassurance before taking cover under more of Stan's clothes.

STAN MADE HIS WAY through the bedroom and towards the door when he thought he heard something. He took a few steps back and listened.

Nothing.

Stan was sure he heard something. Where did it come from? That's when his eyes fell on the door to his makeshift laundry chute. *Could anyone fit through that*? He didn't think so, but it was the only part of the trailer he had yet to search. Kneeling on the floor, Stan paused, clicked the hammer on his gun, opened the door and stuck his head inside.

I need to do a wash, Stan thought, as he took a whiff. The lower compartment was dark but the bedroom provided some light. Stan put his head and hand holding the gun through the opening and looked around, but didn't see anything. Suddenly, a sound startled him and he hit his head against the wall. He pulled himself back inside the bedroom and allowed the door to slam shut. He clutched the gun as he rolled along the floor until sighing from relief when the phone rang a second time. Stan clutched at his chest: *one day, that's going to be the end of me*. He grabbed the phone from his nightstand. "Yeah?"

He listened for a moment. "Fine. Let me get a couple of things together and I'll be on my way."

THE FOOTSTEPS HAD STOPPED directly above Wyatt and he realized that if Stan opened the chute and saw him, he'd be an easy target. Frowning from the odor, Wyatt grabbed a clump of Stan's laundry and cautiously slithered along the floor and into the corner. He settled there and waited, his heart beating like it was in the *Indy 500*. The tangy air was virtually unbreathable and the pitch-black compartment felt like an isolation cell in Alcatraz. But Wyatt could see no way out so he placed the gun by his side, covered himself in Stan's clothes, and kept his eyes locked on the ceiling.

Seconds later, the hatch opened and a modest amount of light materialized. Wyatt lay still as a corpse, banking on the fact that there wasn't enough light for Stan to see him in the corner. But Wyatt knew that if he was wrong, it was over. He clutched his gun just in case.

He watched as Stan peered into the compartment, waving his gun in each direction. It wasn't easy for Wyatt to resist the urge to pull the trigger. Not knowing if Stan could see him made it the most chilling seconds he had endured since his father had been killed. But then, Stan had been startled by an unexpected sound. The trap door banged shut and Wyatt heard Stan answer the phone. Despite his best efforts, Wyatt couldn't make out the muffled conversation. And then, moments later, Wyatt heard the trailer door close, footsteps, and then another sound.

An engine. Stan's truck.

He was leaving.

CHAPTER FIFTY-SIX

IT WAS PITCH BLACK.

Wyatt reached for the Maglite but it must've slid away when he'd watched Stan peer into the compartment. Wyatt was operating with a heightened sense of urgency since Stan was on the run. He wasn't certain Nick was alive, but if he was, Wyatt figured his only hope of finding him was to follow Stan.

But how? Stan was already in his car and Wyatt was stuck in the musty compartment. The one thing he hadn't considered when he slid through the trap door was how in the hell he would ever get out.

Wyatt felt along the floor for his flashlight. Large beads of sweat rained down his face until, seconds later, he located the light. He picked it up and clicked it on in almost one motion, and a small beam filled the compartment. Then he flashed it around to find the quickest way out, and set his sights on the rectangular door at the front end of the trailer. He crawled towards it, trampling over some of the clothes he had just discarded. As he reached the door, he set the light on the steel "S" shaped levers holding the door closed. There were three of them: two at each end and one in the middle. Before touching the levers, Wyatt pushed the door to see if it would open. It didn't.

Sweat dripped onto his hand as he anxiously twisted the two end levers, turning each "S" on its side, such that the top and bottom were even with the doorframe. Then, he tried the middle one but it was locked, a nail halfway down the lever held it tightly in place. There had to be another way out. He flashed the light around the compartment and saw another rectangular door at the far right end of the compartment, the exit of which would let him out behind the trailer. He scrambled over and tried opening it, but the same thing happened. The middle lever was nailed tight. This time though, Wyatt thought, if there's a door on this side, then there must also be one on the opposite side.

He did an about face and darted across the middle of the compartment, knocking over Stan's basket. After aiming it at the levers, Wyatt held the Maglite in his mouth and easily twisted the two end levers onto their sides. He took a deep breath and flexed his hands, like a thief before turning the knob after he's cracked a safe code. He removed the flashlight and blew air out of his lungs so hard that he felt it bounce off the wall and right back in his face. It felt good. He leaned forward and cranked the middle knob and just as it turned past the doorframe, Wyatt and the door flew outward and slammed to the ground. The impact, however, was muffled by a section of artificial turf Stan had placed along the front landing of the trailer. With time of the essence, Wyatt immediately sprung up when he caught sight of something that forced him to a sliding halt.

Stan.

INA NEARLY JUMPED WHEN the phone rang. "Wyatt, my God, I've been waiting to hear from you all day."

"It's Wanda."

She couldn't hide her disappointment. "Sorry, it's just that I've been waiting by the phone all afternoon."

"Still nothing on Nick?"

Ina settled into a kitchen chair. "Now they think he was abducted because he was seen, alive, a couple of days ago." She didn't want to get into a long story of how a cop saw Nick during a pullover. Mostly because she didn't want to answer the same question everyone had: How did a cop see Nick and not do anything about it?

"How are things over there?" Ina said. "I'd rather discuss that because if I keep thinking about Nick ... the mind can only go through so many possibilities."

"Everything's running smoothly; the hotel staff is really on the ball. The bankers arrived and some of them are really hot."

Ina tried to laugh but it was hard given the circumstances.

"I know, I know. You don't have to worry. Besides, I've heard some of their conversations and it's all numbers and money. I'm worried about you."

"I'm OK, all things considered." She rubbed her tummy. "I've been having more contractions but I'm holding up."

"Any chance of you coming back before the weekend's over?"

"Wyatt instructed me to stay in Phoenix where he can reach me. So, until he tells me otherwise, I'll be sitting right here. Waiting."

CHAPTER FIFTY-SEVEN

WYATT FIXED HIS EYES on Stan and tried to stay low as he slowly crept towards the road. Stan was at the campground entrance booth talking to one of the rangers. Wyatt's opportunity hadn't been lost after all. He carefully slid between the front of the trailer and the old truck Stan used to transport it, before sneaking away from the campsite using the truck as his cover. When he was satisfied Stan couldn't see him, Wyatt switched gears like a car speeding up to pass another on the freeway. He sprinted towards the Visitor Center—where he'd parked his car—with one eye planted on the back of Stan's truck, and when he saw the brake lights dim, Wyatt shifted into a higher gear.

Stan was leaving.

Wyatt dashed through the campground as the sky lit up momentarily. A short burst of rain had subsided, although flashes of lightning could still be seen in the distance. Clouds were fleeing the area in rapid succession, as if they were late for an appointment up north.

It wasn't difficult to locate the rental, and he jumped inside so fast that he bumped his head against the doorway. Tossing his flashlight on the passenger seat, Wyatt started the car and floored it in reverse. Thankfully, the Visitor Center was closed, its lot was nearly vacant. Wyatt smacked the gas and drove through the lot as if he was navigating his way through the Autobahn. After several left turns, he came to the park's entrance and zipped by the booth, its ranger occupant long gone for the evening. He pressed on the gas in pure supplication, as he knew he was asking the rental for more than was reasonable under the circumstances. But even though he'd spotted Stan at the entrance booth, Stan had gotten a pretty good start and Wyatt had no choice. He had to catch up.

Stan was heading west on Route 9, which would take him straight through Springdale. Traffic was light as Wyatt sped through the city's main strip, and he caught sight of Stan stuck behind a slow-moving tourist. Wyatt accelerated. The tourist turned left and Stan took off; seconds later, Stan had rounded a bend and was no longer in Wyatt's view. Wyatt sped up and as he made his way through the northern part of Springdale, an old Toyota Camry turned onto the highway right in front of him, forcing Wyatt to slam on the brakes. He swore, and swerved to look around it. The Camry was exceeding the limit by a few miles, but nowhere near fast enough to make up the ground Wyatt needed.

Wyatt followed the Camry for a short distance and then pounded on the gas as he swerved into the left lane. He began an attempt to pass the Camry, until he saw another vehicle coming at him from the other direction. He slipped back in behind the slow-moving vehicle, as they reached an apple orchard on the outskirts of Springdale. The road ahead was dark and windy and Stan was no longer in sight. Wyatt's immediate impulse was to blast the horn and he actually put his hand on it, but then decided to hold back. The driver wasn't driving poorly, just not fast enough for Wyatt to catch up to Stan.

His next impulse was to flash the brights and force the Camry to speed up. But he didn't. Instead, Wyatt engaged in extreme tailgating and swerved wildly into the left lane to pass, just as they turned a corner. His eyes grew wide as a delivery truck plowed towards him at a high rate of speed. Another near miss. Wyatt slowed the rental and slid back in behind the Camry, just in the nick of time. They rounded several more curves until the road straightened with enough room for Wyatt to pass. And that's just what he did, pushing the beaten rental to the max. Despite its serious wounds, he passed the Camry with ease and, when he made it back in the right lane, he didn't slow. In fact, he stayed at maximum speed for another five miles or so, even with the road containing more than just the occasional curve or bend. And he did that until the road finally straightened for what seemed like at least a few miles.

But there was a problem.

No one else was on the road.

STAN DROVE PAST THE Shack, descended the pulley bridge and crossed the river, following the dirt road as it snaked west. Several minutes later, he reached the end: the well-secluded house he had purchased with Ethan several years ago. It was also the place they would temporarily house and sometimes torture captives before delivering them to their final resting place.

He parked in the back and a smile creased his face; the excitement was too intense to suppress. It was time for retribution. The moment had been elusive. But tonight, Stan's life would come full circle. He had dreamt of this for years, playing it out in his mind time and again, as if he were an attorney about to give an opening statement. The only thing missing from those dreams was a definitive picture of the person on the receiving end. But fate had orchestrated a meeting with Nick Perrone and, while Perrone wasn't his first choice, he would do.

As Stan stepped out of his truck, he swelled with pride. He had made it. Persevered. The Lord had thrown him many obstacles and he had managed to survive each. And while he and Ethan and the guys would continue their business in the future, his quest for the ultimate revenge would culminate this weekend, when they disposed of Perrone and his wife. If Stan were to die the next day, he would accept his fate with a smile. For he had passed his tests. He had persisted in the face of evil and done his part to rid the world of its malevolence. This weekend would be the climax, Stan's imprint on this world that no one could ever take away.

He couldn't wait.

WYATT SLOWED TO THE point where his speed was commensurate with his mood. Stan was his only lead and now he was gone. Vanished. And Stan had mentioned that he had the weekend off. Who knew when Stan would return?

What next?

Wyatt approached a drive-out, a scenic overlook on the left side of the highway, where he parked horizontally across several spots. He grabbed his binoculars and stepped out of the car, his face flush with defeat. He walked around, onto a sidewalk, and up to a low block wall overlooking whatever scenery actually existed in the darkness.

A flash of light caught the corner of his eye as a car whizzed by, but seconds later, darkness returned. Wyatt squinted through the binoculars, hoping that he would see Stan and where he had turned off the highway. But it didn't take long to confirm what his heart and mind already knew.

Stan was gone.

He'd lost him.

CHAPTER FIFTY-EIGHT

"WHO ARE YOU?" NICK said.

Stan flashed a wide, toothy grin, so yellow that no amount of toothpaste could improve it. "I was hoping you'd at least show me some gratitude, but you don't even remember who I am?"

Nick regarded him for a moment. "Gratitude? For what?"

"I saved your life. Have you forgotten already? I'm the one who drove up the other day when you were about to become a statistic."

Nick was amazed that he should somehow show gratitude for being brought back to the house, tied up, and held there awaiting Ina's arrival for a full family massacre. Then he realized something.

"Don't you work for the park?"

"At least some of your memory's coming back. Where's the rest of it?"

"What are you talking about?"

Stan locked eyes with Nick's. "I used to work for you. At Great American."

NAUSEA ANNOUNCED ITS PRESENCE in Wyatt's gut as he scanned the dark expanse. He knew he was responsible for Nick's disappearance. If he had only gone camping with Nick, none of this would've happened; they'd both be home safely in Phoenix. As guilty as he felt, Wyatt knew that while he had made great progress, there was little else he could do. Stan was gone for the weekend and if Nick was still alive—a big if— would he last until Monday?

Probably not.

And neither would I, Wyatt thought. There simply wasn't enough room in his conscience for another tragedy. A coldness enveloped his body and he responded by dialing Tavares. It was all he could do to avoid a breakdown. He started shaking when her machine answered, and so he left an urgent request for a callback.

Wyatt hung up and decided to face reality. It was over. He'd done everything he could but had unfortunately come up short. And it wasn't for naught. There was still a viable suspect at large, but Wyatt realized that it was time to turn this matter over to the FBI. He wasn't going to hang around Utah for a weekend with nothing to do. Sure, he had connected with Velvet, but that was when he was reasonably certain Nick was a walkaway. Now that he knew Nick had been kidnapped, he couldn't, in good conscience, spend a lustful weekend with Velvet while waiting for his suspect to return.

And so, Wyatt decided to return to Phoenix.

He would do so first thing in the morning.

Wyatt took in a final gaze, praying that Stan would miraculously materialize and he'd be back in the hunt. And when it didn't happen, Wyatt jumped back in the rental and started the car. Tonight would be his last in Utah and if he couldn't reach Tavares for some consolation, at least he had a backup.

Velvet.

"YOU NEVER WORKED FOR me," Nick said, trying his best to hide the fear radiating throughout his body. "Before this week, I'd never met you in my life."

"Actually, you're right. We never met before this week. But we should've."

"What are you talking about?"

"I used to work for your company until I was fired, accused of a crime I didn't commit."

A shiver coursed through Nick as the picture began taking shape. As terrorizing as it was to be a random victim of violence, this was worse. Standing before him was the most depraved monster of all, a person whose very existence had been consumed with a single motive: revenge.

"How did you know who I was?" Nick asked.

"I worked in accounting and reported to that miserable bastard, Ellis Campbell. I had nothing to do with upper level management, but I knew who you were. Shortly after we took you from the bar, your wife called the park's office looking for you and the rangers sent over a phone message. They brought it to me and, as soon as I saw your name, I knew."

Nick pulled his arms and feet but to no avail.

"I guess you can thank your wife," Stan said. "If she hadn't placed that call ..." He lit a cigarette and blew smoke rings in the air. "Women really know how to mess up our lives, don't they?"

Nick didn't answer.

"Are you a religious man, Nicholas? Because I am. I read the Old Testament all the time. It was part of my upbringing. I come from a dysfunctional Catholic family, but sometimes dysfunction brings you closer to the truth. The Bible's my code, and believe me I follow it. Word for word."

"So what's all this then? I'm no Bible expert but I'm pretty sure it says thou shalt not kill."

"You're right. But the Bible's a pretty big book and when it says that, it just means arbitrarily, without justification. But this is justified."

Nick kept pulling at his restraints.

Stan flicked ash to the carpeted floor. "Ellis and I used to work closely together. I liked Great American. It was a good time in my life. I was married, and Phoenix is a great place to live. Until one day upper management approached me about money being diverted from the accounts. It seemed someone had been overpaying the company's liabilities, and when the vendors sent their refunds, they were diverted to an offshore account. Guess whose name was on that account?"

"So you're the famous Stanford Briscoe," Nick said. He could still visualize Stan's name on interoffice memorandums.

"That's me. But that offshore account wasn't mine. If it was, you think I'd be working at a campground in the middle of nowhere? But when I pled my case, none of you would listen."

"I remember, but over a million dollars had been taken and we decided not to prosecute."

"You should've, instead of dismissing me on the spot. Maybe the truth would've come out."

Nick felt the onset of something pressing on his chest. "What's the truth?"

"Ellis took the money. He admitted it to me. But the worst part? I lost my job, I was blackballed in the industry, and my wife left me. And in my mid-fifties, I was too old to be hired again. But Ellis? The bastard got promoted to Vice President."

Nick shook his head.

"I read it on your website. What a bunch of cowards you guys are."

"If you thought we should've prosecuted, why didn't you go to the authorities?"

"Ellis, I have to give the bastard credit. He put everything in my name, except access to the money. So when I confronted him, he laid everything out for me and said he would push them to prosecute *me.*"

Stan held the cigarette in his mouth and flexed one of his hands into a fist. "I decided it wasn't worth the risk. I couldn't understand why it was happening to me, but I'm a religious man and I figured it must be a punishment for something I did. Lord knows I've made my share of mistakes." His voice tailed off. "Ellis Campbell ruined my life."

"Then he's the one who should be sitting in this chair. Not me."

"I'll grant you that. Truth is, I came here because the bastard went on the last company retreat and I was hoping he'd be on the next one. But that never happened. Hell, we all want to date the prom queen, but sometimes you have to settle for the next best option."

"How is that justice?"

"The way I see it, all you greedy corporate assholes should be destroyed. You are Amelek."

WYATT MADE HIS WAY back to town, fighting gnawing feelings of despair. He craved a drink and some affection, and was in desperate need of a long, soapy shower, all of which Velvet could provide. He drove along the highway, using his brights to illuminate the meandering road, until he entered the town of Rockville. Wyatt turned right at Bridge Road and drove past two short blocks of clapboard homes, which seemed to evaporate in the darkness as he crossed a rusted bridge. He passed a quarter mile of empty farmland and made a right at Grafton, the entrance to a ghost town the locals were trying to revive. Velvet's place was several doors down on the left side, a one-story home painted off-white with brown trim.

Wyatt pulled up to the front, which was partially blocked by a lawn full of overgrown weeds. Velvet had an upside-down 'U' shaped driveway in which there were two vehicles. Wyatt recognized her red Jetta, but swallowed hard when he saw the other.

A silver Durango.

Nick's?

Wyatt fixed his eyes on the Utah plate and realized it was just another disappointment. Nick had a common car, in a popular color. This wasn't the first silver Durango Wyatt had seen in the area, but none belonged to Nick. Agent Nielsen was right: if the car was stolen, it was long gone by now. The FBI had been searching for it in several different states, and there was no way he would find it now in the same area Nick had disappeared.

Wyatt turned his attention to the more immediate issue.

Velvet had company.

He strained to get a look through the window and managed to see her sitting at the dining room table with a man. Disappointed and disheveled, Wyatt decided to return to his hotel. Could he really have expected any better? Velvet had a life here without him, and they had shared less than twenty-four hours together. He hung a uey and made his way back through town. After crossing the bridge, Wyatt checked the clock on the dash. It was eight thirty. There was one phone call he'd put off and still wasn't ready to make. But he couldn't escape the responsibility any longer. He had to tell Ina that he had made an important decision.

He would check out tonight and return to Phoenix.

CHAPTER FIFTY-NINE

"AMELEK. IT'S A BIBLICAL term. A nation that snuck up on Israel to destroy them."

"I don't know what you're talking about."

"That's because you're a sinner. Did you tell your wife what you were doing with that piece of eye candy in the site next to yours? Adultery is a serious transgression."

Nick had no answer. While not religious, Nick had confessed his shortcomings during his captivity and avowed that he would change if given the opportunity. But it wouldn't do him any good to share that with Stan.

"And you're a saint?"

"Just doing my part to rid the world of evil."

"In other words, you're playing God," Nick challenged.

"Just helping him."

Nick was speechless.

"See, when you read the Bible, there are references to nations like the Egyptians, Palestinians, and Arabs, all of whom exist today. But there's no actual nation called Amelek because they never really existed. The term represents an ideology, someone whose sole purpose is to enhance his own life by destroying others.

"And that's you, all you corporate animals. With your egos and greed, taking millions for yourselves while purging the savings and retirement set aside by the hard-working people that keep your companies operating."

"That is so twisted. Without us, people like you would be nobodies. Those of us who run companies give people like you a chance to earn a decent living."

"Is that how you justify it when you're on your yacht? Or driving your Lamborghini?"

"I don't need to justify anything. Corporations make the world a better place. They allow us to be innovative, to invent products that change lives. Just look at some of the advances we've made in medicine, electronics. Computers are our lives and now we can take them anywhere. And the GPS helps us get there. Music too. Everything. Without big companies, none of that would be possible."

"Like that CEO in Iowa? Peregrine Financial? He's the one that embezzled millions by falsifying bank statements. He used scanners, laser printers, and Photoshop to forge bank statements and steal from customers. Your innovative products at use."

"You can cite an example here and there but that doesn't mean everyone's greedy."

Stan made a face. "It's rampant. Look at the Walmarts and Targets of the world pricing the mom and pop stores out of business. You think that's a good thing? Ticketmaster charging ridiculous "handling" fees because they can get away with it? I can go on and on but what's the point? None of this helps anybody."

"Nothing is perfect. It would be great to have more mom and pop stores, but not at higher costs. If someone provides a cheaper good or service, isn't that a benefit?"

"Not when it runs people out of business. Not when it ruins peoples lives." Stan said. "Your point would be valid if people actually cared about each other. But it's every man for himself, and having these big companies have only fostered a greater sense of greed among those running them. You guys at Great American are no different."

Nick's natural response would've been that his company wasn't like that, but he knew it wasn't true. He was talking to one of their victims. Still, none of this made sense.

"So, because you lost your job with us, you decided to start killing people?"

Stan appeared to consider the question.

"After my termination, I lost everything. I was living in my trailer, which was all I had after my wife left me. My savings and retirement had already been cleaned out by my investments in Enron, WorldCom, Halliburton and other companies that screwed their shareholders. No one would hire a man my age.

"I decided to come out here to get away from everything. I stayed for a few weeks and got to know some of the rangers. They were having problems keeping campground hosts and they offered me the job. They said they would cover my expenses, which are minimal, and give me a stipend. It isn't much, but it was the best I could find."

Nick listened as Stan began to share the anatomy of his misdeeds.

"Several months after I got here, I met this couple in the campground. He was an executive at Motorola, and she, who knows where. But they were happy and well off, and that made me mad. It reminded me of my wife and me before the whole Great American thing. A couple of days later, I hiked to Angel's Landing and there was the husband, sitting on the top, at the edge, on the phone. But he wasn't just talking, he was screaming at his secretary, or a co-worker. There was something about it that enraged me. Like why should this punk have all that, when mine was taken away? I got so made that, when a small window of opportunity arose, I couldn't resist. I pushed him off the side. The next few days were tense because they started investigating, but when they declared it an accident—"

"A scheme was born," Nick cut in.

"Not really," Stan laughed. "But it was a revelation. I discovered that the park was the perfect cover. I didn't have to linger here the rest of my life like it's some kind of environmental convalescent home. I realized maybe I could do my own part to clean up society. And then, *you* fell into our lap."

Nick sneered. "You're just a murderous bastard."

"Exodus 21:24. I'm afraid you're wrong."

"Exodus what?"

"One of the more famous passages in the Old Testament. An eye for an eye. You ruined my life and now I'm going to ruin yours. By this time tomorrow, you'll reunite with your wife. You're going to watch her die and feel what it's like to lose a family."

"What about the prohibition against taking revenge on your fellow man?" Nick was trying to recall anything from the Bible.

Stan lit a cigarette. "Ah, yes, Leviticus 19:18. Thou shall not take revenge, and thou shall not bear a grudge against the members of your people." Stan blew a smoke ring and then raised his voice. "You shall love your fellow as yourself. For I am God."

Despite the onset of significant pain, Nick couldn't stop pulling and trying to free his hands and legs. The rope felt like it was starting to give a little, but not enough. If only he could reach the knife in his pocket.

"Not bad," Stan continued. "But see, I've reconciled this seeming contradiction. The way I see it, you aren't 'my people.' You're one of those cold, high society executives. Lowlifes who cash in every day working fewer hours but making more money, while hard working people like me do all the work. You're *not* my people, Nicholas Perrone, and the Bible does *not* instruct me to refrain from vengeance against you. To the contrary, it's my duty."

Nick's face was burning up, veins popping out of his forehead. "Kill me if you want, but leave my wife alone. She's carrying our baby."

"Save it. I lost my family. My wife said she never wanted to see me again."

"Did you kill her too?"

"I fucking should have! I didn't because of my boy."

"Ethan?"

"No, Ethan's mom's was my first wife and she's already dead."

"Then how did you get Ethan involved? He told me this was just about money."

"It is for the others, but part of what I lost in the market was the money I had earmarked for Ethan's college tuition. My life's not the only one ruined by you corporate bastards. Think Ethan wanted to be some mechanic out in the middle of nowhere? We're really just trying to recoup our losses."

"But you care more about exacting revenge because you lost your wife and kid when you were fired. Is that what you want me to believe?"

"Doesn't matter to me. We're not here to discuss my ex-bitch, let's talk about yours."

Nick thrusted his body and shook the chair. "Do anything you want to me, but leave her out of this. Please?"

"You know what? I'm disappointed in you. We've been talking all this time and not once did you show any remorse, or even apologize." Stan raised his eyebrows and pursed his lips. "An apology would've gone a long way."

Nick started to speak, but Stan raised his hand. Then he threw the cigarette to the carpet and stepped on it.

WYATT KICKED THE SIDE of the bed.

He had just told a devastated Ina that he was returning to Phoenix. Trying to comfort her, Wyatt said he would come by the house, but that was of little consolation. A myriad of emotions mixed through his mind; his seeds of doubt had sprouted into a garden of failure and insecurity. Wyatt felt responsible for Nick's disappearance, but was he doing the right thing by packing up and leaving? Then again, what was there left to do? He had reached a most unusual climax in what could very well be a homicide investigation: waiting for a suspect to return from vacation. But what if Stan's weekend plans involved Nick? What if Nick was still alive but would be disposed of sometime in the next few days? Wyatt had been right there with Stan in his sights and in a matter of seconds, lost him. He couldn't help but wonder if, somewhere in that expanse of darkness, when he lost Stan, had he also lost Nick?

Wyatt sat on the edge of the bed second-guessing how he had handled his pursuit of Stan. Overcome with despair, his head was in his hands. Wyatt had failed to save the life of someone close to him.

Again.

Like a starting pitcher late in the game, he knew it was time to hand the ball back to the manager. He pulled out his wallet, removed Nielsen's card, and dialed his cell. Nielsen's voicemail answered after four rings, Wyatt told the machine everything he'd learned, and when he clapped the phone shut, he actually felt better. Like he'd gotten a load off his chest. He sniffed the air around him and was reminded of how badly he needed to bathe. And a few minutes later, he stepped under the water to wash off the failure that had been Stan's trailer.

Standing there, Wyatt wondered how Nielsen would respond to his voicemail. He closed his eyes, soaped his face, lifted it into the water and began replaying his meeting with Nielsen. The man had been curt, rough. Did he not care about Nick, or was he just another asshole Fed with a jurisdictional stick up his ass? Wyatt recalled Nielsen's presentation of a list of Durango's they had looked at in the area. Each was a dead-end. And the rest of the meeting was little more than a synopsis of car theft 101. How Utah wasn't a place for a sophisticated theft ring, and that the chances of finding Nick's car were bleak. Nielsen had also covered VIN swapping, shipping cars overseas, and how an expert thief could make a stolen car look perfectly legal.

Unless.

Wyatt let the soap bar drop from his hands. He closed the water and sprinted out of the shower, grabbing a towel from the rack above the toilet. After just half a shower, he stormed out of the bathroom and tried to dry himself while fishing through his bag for clean clothes. He dressed in record time and ran his hand along the bottom of the bag until he found what he needed, pulling out his extra handgun and several boxes of ammunition. He loaded the gun and stuffed it in his pack along with his department issue, which was still loaded. Then he grabbed his wallet and keys and sprinted out of the room and through the parking lot to his car. If they were to open his chest at the moment, his heart would jump out and bounce around wildly like a superball.

Wyatt stomped on the gas almost as soon as he turned the ignition, and headed for the highway. There was no time to waste. While it really wasn't his fault, he had blown his best opportunity to break the case open when he'd lost Stan on the highway. He couldn't afford another setback.

Please be there. Please be there.

He made a sharp left onto Bridge Road and braced himself as he flew over the old bridge again. Then he slowed and cut the headlights as he neared Grafton Road. Instead of turning onto Velvet's street, Wyatt made a u-turn and parked the car in the dirt alongside the road, facing the bridge. He grabbed his binoculars, flashlight, a gun and ammo, and moved purposefully down the road with his gun drawn. He crossed the first entrance to the driveway not far from where Velvet's car was parked. He tried to steal a glance inside the house but couldn't see anything, so he moved cautiously to the second driveway entrance and knelt behind a bush in the corner. Then, he raised the binoculars to his eyes and focused on the windows but couldn't see anyone. To his relief, both cars were still outside. *What the hell were they doing in there*?

Satisfied they wouldn't see him, Wyatt tiptoed behind the Durango and got on his knees. As he reached for the flashlight, he scanned the area. It was pitch black. Wyatt extended himself until he was lying on the ground under the rear bumper. He clicked on the flashlight and nearly stopped breathing. There it was, shining in the small circular beam of Wyatt's Maglite.

The scratch Nick had shown him when he was washing his car.

CHAPTER SIXTY

"WHERE ARE YOU GOING?" The door slammed shut behind Clay, as he raced out to the front of the house.

"What do you care?" Bennie answered, without looking back. "I just came outside for a smoke. What did you think I was doing?"

Clay touched the gun in his waist to make sure it was still there. "I thought you were going for a cigarette, and I was hoping to join you."

Bennie removed a new pack from his pocket, undid the wrapping, and tossed it to the ground. Then he tapped the bottom several times until a cigarette stepped forward. And then a second, which he handed to Clay.

"Are you really going to do this?" The words were muffled since Bennie was holding the lighter inside his cupped hand.

Clay leaned in for assistance and they both welcomed nicotine into their lungs. "We're doing it."

A slight evening breeze was blowing through and Clay pushed some loose strands of hair behind his ear.

"You guys promised, no women and children. I remember it clearly, we were at the graveyard."

"We never promised you anything."

Bennie looked at Clay's waist and put his hands up. "You really are Ethan's disciple. If you want to shoot me, go ahead."

"I'm not shooting you, OK? We're just talkin' here."

"Then why do you keep touching the butt of your gun? Afraid I'm going to turn on you?"

"Chill, man." Clay patted the air. "We need you. You're an important part of this operation."

"You guys lied to me from the moment you made me a criminal."

Clay laughed. "Don't get all pious on me, dude. It's not like you were a law-abiding citizen until we came along. Besides, there's a criminal inside everyone. Don't blame us for makin' you rich."

Bennie tried to suppress a sad smile, but he knew what he was dealing with. He had gotten involved with hardened criminals who had broken through every moral fiber society implanted. Three guys who refused to conform to the ways of the world, choosing instead to have everyone else conform to their every whim. He should have known that all bets were off when they killed Sloan, because that was when the dominos began falling. They would kill a local police officer, they would kill a Phoenix detective, and the reality was now setting in. They would kill anyone else who got in their way.

Including him.

WYATT RETURNED TO HIS car and backed up until he was behind the intersection of Bridge and Grafton. He wanted to be out of sight, yet facing the road to the highway, since that was the likely escape route for whoever was driving Nick's car. He cut the engine, not sure what to do next. He was in virtually the same situation in which he'd been earlier in the evening. Identifying a lead was only half the battle. The real difficulty was seeing it through. And, just as he had done with Stan, Wyatt decided that anything short of following the Durango could result in Nick's demise. He was right back where he had been with Stan, but at least he had obtained something he'd given up on just a short time ago.

Hope.

If Nick's car was still around, Wyatt could only pray the same was true of Nick. He turned the key just enough to get the juice needed to open the window and fill his lungs with some fresh canyon air. The sounds of the river's flow were soothing. Wyatt despised stakeouts, especially by himself. At least with a partner, there were doughnuts on the dashboard, someone to talk to. But here he was, alone in a rental in the middle of a ghost town. A thick set of clouds covered a banana-shaped moon, and darkness permeated, save for whatever scant illumination emanated from the few homes lining Grafton Road.

The worst thing about solo stakeouts was the time Wyatt spent with nothing but his thoughts. As much as he tried focusing on Nick, he couldn't suppress a new thought: was Velvet also involved? Last night had been his most passionate in years, with a beautiful, sexy girl who was completely low maintenance. She had spent several years living and working in a remote part of Southern Utah, not exactly a meat market of available men. So, her expectations couldn't be too high.

Perfect for me, Wyatt thought.

Was last night just an act? Had she been ordered to stay on top of him and monitor his every move? If so, she had done a good job of it.

Literally.

Every one of their conversations raced through Wyatt's mind as he tried to determine if she had been playing him. But it wasn't a question he could answer. Maybe the opposite was true. What if Velvet's life was in danger? What if whoever had taken Nick had learned of Velvet's involvement with Wyatt and was there to exact retribution? The possibility sickened him, but as he thought about it more, he realized this probably wasn't the case. He had driven by an hour ago and caught a glimpse of them sitting and talking in the dining room. That wasn't the scene you'd expect if she was in danger. And so Wyatt decided to leave it be, as he needed to focus on his ultimate goal: bringing Nick back to Ina.

As time passed, his mind became a battlefield. How could he have allowed himself to get involved with Velvet when he was there to find his friend? Was he that much better than Nick, who was messing around with another woman while out here camping? The thought made him shudder. Frank's image popped into his head, because no matter where he was or what he was doing, Wyatt's greatest failure always seemed to materialize. Maybe a stakeout tonight *was* a good thing, because he was afraid to go to sleep. The nightmares he'd been having were too painful.

Wyatt glanced at his watch; it was almost ten o'clock, Phoenix was an hour behind. It wasn't too late to call. He flipped open his phone, dialed, and waited patiently through the first couple of rings. When Tavares' voicemail answered, his frustration rose to a boil about to escape.

"What the fuck is going on, Joan? I've called you, four or five times in the last couple of days? I don't understand why you're avoiding me at the time I need you most. This is truly unprofessional and I deserve more than ..."

A beep.

"I'm here," Tavares said softly.

Her words lingered momentarily, rendering Wyatt speechless. He'd been comfortable delivering a scathing message, but didn't think he could do it to a live audience.

"Why are you avoiding me?"

She didn't answer right away.

"I apologize."

"Do you treat all your patients like this or am I just special?"

"Wyatt, please, I said I'm sorry."

"You weren't going to call me back, were you?"

"I already told you I can't see you anymore, but I've arranged for someone else to help you. He's very good."

"Cut the bullshit and tell me what's going on!"

"You can't call me anymore."

"You're terminating our relationship without the decency to tell me why? You don't have the courtesy to return my calls. I have to hound you, and call you at home late at night, just to get you on the fucking phone? So what is it? You have feelings for me?"

She almost laughed. "Don't be ridiculous."

"I've seen the way you look at me."

"You have no idea what you're talking about."

"Are you going to tell me that you don't have a gleam in your eye every time I'm in your office?"

"Grow up, Wyatt. We're not in grade school."

"Is it because I stopped treatment for two years?"

"Of course not. Patients come and go, and I'm always here when they need. That's the way it is in my business. For whatever reason, you felt like you didn't need me for a while and that's fine."

"Then why aren't you there for me now, when I really do need you? I'm in Utah and …"

"What are you doing in Utah?"

"I was supposed to be camping with my buddy, but we had an argument. I got mad and bailed and so he went by himself. But now he's missing." He paused. "I came here to find him."

"I'm sorry about your predicament. But this is something you'll need to take up with Dr. Jennings."

"I'm not gonna leave you alone until you tell me why you're doing this."

"Please don't make this harder for me, OK?" she said in a soft, sad voice. "I have a conflict."

"If you have feelings for me, just tell me and we can work it out. But you can't just discard a patient like this, certainly not during a crisis."

The airways went silent.

"I'm not gonna stop hounding you until you answer me."

A moment went by and then Tavares started crying.

"I loved Frank."

A grenade exploded in Wyatt's stomach.

"I treated your father while he was on the force," Tavares continued. "And when he became chief of police, we fell in love. We planned to marry."

"I don't believe you. He *never* mentioned you."

"Before he died, we were trying to figure out how to tell you. Frank was worried that you'd reject me. And him, for being disloyal to your mom."

"He didn't owe her anything. She abandoned us." Wyatt tried fighting his own tears. "So that's why you look at me that way."

"I can't help it, you're the splitting image of your father and I miss him so much." She paused. "You were almost my stepson."

"When were you going to tell me?" He gave her a chance to answer but she didn't. "Oh, that's right, you weren't. You were going to refer me to someone else."

"You don't understand."

"Sure I do. A lot more than you think. In fact, things are starting to make sense. Your constant questions about what happened the night my dad was killed? You didn't do that to help me, you wanted to know what happened to him. Do you have any idea what you put me through?"

Her sobbing intensified. "He loved you so much. You meant everything to him."

"But you blame me for his death."

Wyatt felt the knife twist in his gut. How many of those close to him felt the same way?

Tavares didn't try to respond.

"I didn't kill him, Joan. I tried to save him."

"I know you tried."

"Then why do you blame me?"

"You're not the only one in therapy, OK? But you blame yourself, remember?"

"And you were supposed to help me get over it. Instead, you felt the exact same way and made me relive it again and again to serve your own needs. And now you want to dump me onto some schmuck in Scottsdale."

"I really did try to help you."

"I realize now that the only person you tried to help was yourself."

"That's bullshit and you know it!" She lowered her voice an octave. "I tried helping you many times."

"What are you talking about? I've tried to move on and live a normal life, but ..."

"That's what your dreams are, Wyatt."

"I don't understand."

"Your heart doesn't want to let go, but your mind is telling you to move on. That's why you weren't seeing Frank's face. Remember when you first came to me? You were reliving the incident through nightmares that ended with Frank staring at you."

"Yeah?"

"That was your subconscious talking. The staring? That's your own fear that *Frank* blames you for what happened. That's why, in your dreams, *his* eyes are fixed on you."

"I'm not the one who broke in that night, or pulled the trigger."

"You didn't kill him. And I think deep down, you know that. See, that's why, after time passed, the dream changed and you weren't seeing Frank's face. Your conscience couldn't let go of the incident, but your mind, your rational faculty, is covering his face because it recognizes your need to get past it. That's the only way to live a healthy existence. Don't you see?"

A tear rolled down Wyatt's cheek. "I haven't slept well here."

"Because of the nightmares?"

"I'm seeing the face again, only this time, it's not my dad. It's Nick."

"Interesting. The same exact dream?"

"All the way through the shooting. And when I get to the face, it's Nick's eyes staring at me."

She seemed to consider this for a moment. "It makes perfect sense. You're experiencing the same feelings of failure that you did with Frank. In your heart, you feel responsible for your friend's disappearance, so much so that your conscience has kicked in and convinced you that he, too, blames you for what happened. That's why, in your dreams, he's staring at you."

He glanced down the street. Nick's car was still parked there.

"You meant everything to Frank, and I know that if he saw you today, he'd be filled with nothing but pride."

"I doubt that. I can't keep a job, can't hold a relationship, can barely stay sober. My life's been one failure after another."

"That's for another time and place. And shrink," she added. "But I do owe you an apology. After Frank was murdered, I was devastated. I took months off work and sulked around the house, taking as many antidepressants as my body would accept. These kinds of tragedies are difficult to forget, but the passage of time helps you put them in the rearview, so to speak. I thought I had done that, until you walked into my office. I guess you're not the only one that's had difficulty moving on."

"I'm not going to start over with a new therapist. Maybe this is my reality and I need to accept it. I just wish these dreams would stop."

"They will, eventually. The human psyche can only deal with so much. But I think there's something you can do to relieve it. It seems clear to me that these two major events in your life are intertwined, your father's murder and your friend's disappearance. At least that's the way your psyche has catalogued it. And because of that, you've convinced yourself that you're a failure. But there's a practical solution.

"What's that?"

"Prove that you're wrong. Prove it to yourself."

"How do I do that?"

"Find your friend."

CHAPTER SIXTY-ONE

IT WAS LATE, BUT Nick was wide-awake, reviewing the day's dialogue. Working on Bennie had been mentally draining. It was like trying to beat a Stanley Cup goaltender: no matter what he threw at him, Bennie wouldn't concede. For the first time in Nick's life, an air of failure permeated. Nick was a closer. Million-dollar deals were a dime a dozen for the man who was on pace to run Great American by his mid-thirties.

Nick had prepared for today the same way he prepared for all his negotiations. He had gathered information, found a weakness, developed an approach, and wished for some luck. The first break Nick caught was when Bennie was charged with watching him. As soon as he realized that, Nick prepared to close the deal and save himself. He had already planted the seed the day before, and given Bennie something to think about. The hope: Bennie would have a sleepless night and return the next day a weaker man. Then, Nick would come on stronger and more persuasive, and close this thing before nightfall. And he had no qualms about saving Bennie too, if that's what Bennie wanted. It would all be part of the pitch. The pieces had fallen into place, and Nick had the entire day to persuade him. It was as if everything in his life had come full circle, all of which had led him to the biggest stage of all.

A negotiation for his life.

But he failed.

It was the first deal Nick couldn't close, and it would come at a huge price: the lives of him and his family. Suddenly, his heart ached for Ina and their child, and all he could think about was how thankful he was that she was safe in Tucson.

Nick knew that today's failure had nothing to do with his skills. Rather, it was because the negotiation had a most unusual component: the person he was dealing with was also, in a sense, negotiating for his own life. But Bennie had the upper hand, was gun-shy, and there was little Nick could do to make him feel comfortable. It wasn't much of a consolation, but Nick had scored *some* points with Bennie, evidenced by the constant food and drink Bennie had fed him throughout the day. Bennie had been generous with Nick's provisions and had even given Nick a significant break from the wrist restraints. One wrist at a time. As a result, Nick felt slightly energized.

And while Stan had revealed his twisted plan for retribution, Nick also realized that Bennie had secretly done something else to help him. He hadn't tied the rope nearly as tight as before. Of course, Nick didn't show it while Stan was in the room, but as he replayed the day's occurrences, Nick focused on trying to pull his wrists free. And that's when something interesting happened.

The knots began to give.

MORE THAN AN HOUR had passed since his conversation with Tavares. The moon had finally tossed its cover and now stood prominently in the star-filled sky. Wyatt felt strangely at peace. Maybe the ties Tavares had cut would benefit them both. The pain of her revelation had been strangely balanced with a peculiar sense of clarity. At least the past made more sense, even if his future was still cloudy.

The sounds of the river were interrupted by the slamming of a car door, jolting Wyatt from his thoughts. He reached for the binoculars, but by the time he had them in place, Nick's Durango was on the move, its headlights coming right at him. He tossed the binoculars on the seat and slid down to avoid being seen. And his car's positioning was perfect, as the man in the Durango could only see the driver's side, if at all. All of the bullet holes were on the passenger side. The Durango made a sharp left onto Bridge Road as Wyatt sat upright again, his eyes fixed on the taillights. He waited until it crossed the bridge, to start up the rental. Then he inched forward in the sand, staying on the side of the road until the Durango reached the intersection with Route 9. And as he watched the Durango turn left onto the highway, Wyatt flicked on his headlights and stepped on the gas.

Adrenaline coursed through his body; the tail was on again. And with it came a sense of relief, for, as the Durango had passed, Wyatt had positioned himself for a look inside. And while he couldn't see as much as he would've liked, he was at least able to tell there was only one person inside. And that answered one of his lingering questions.

Velvet wasn't in the car.

Wyatt followed the Durango at a safe distance. He needed to stay close enough not to lose him, but far enough away so as not to be made. Every thirty seconds, the Durango would vanish in the meandering road, only to reappear seconds later. Earlier in the evening, Wyatt had followed Stan on this very road, but had lost him to the darkness. Like a running back, Stan had received a few blocks from some slow-moving tourists, but now it was the middle of the night and the streets were completely empty.

Wyatt was determined not to lose his mark this time.

But then it happened.

Wyatt came around a bend and the Durango was gone.

"Damn it!" he yelled. He slowed the rental, his eyes scanning every direction.

That's when he picked up the red taillights heading south just below the highway. Wyatt cut his lights and pulled off Route 9 and onto a sandy road, perched above the river and valley below. He halted the car, grabbed his binoculars, and watched as the Durango cleared a narrow pulley bridge and followed the road past several homes before veering to the left. A large oak momentarily obstructed his view, but the Durango came back into focus seconds later. He watched the driver pull in behind a two-story, stand-alone house resting on a plateau overlooking the river. It was the last house in the small community and probably a good half-mile from the closest neighbor.

A perfect place to hide someone.

Before pressing on, Wyatt scanned the area. An air of familiarity hit him hard as he noticed the abandoned dump trucks, backhoes, and rusted pickup trucks. He was right by The Shack, the exact spot from which someone had tried to kill him. The memory was traumatic, but the revelation oddly comforting; he had to be on the right track.

Wyatt proceeded slowly down the hill, crossed the bridge, and followed the road to the house. Just before the entrance to a large dirt driveway, Wyatt cut to the left where another dirt road descended into a wash. He parked just above it, cut the engine, and readied for battle. Both guns were fully loaded and he filled his pockets with reserve ammunition.

Wyatt stepped out and holstered his backup piece. He took a deep breath and stood there for a moment, as if waiting for someone's command to ambush the opponent. And while he didn't have a plan, the good ones prevailed on instinct and Wyatt was a good cop. He opened the back door, reached into his backpack, and retrieved his night vision goggles.

Then he set off into the night.

"WHERE THE HELL HAVE you been?" Clay looked at his watch. "It's almost midnight."

"What's the big deal?" Ethan walked through the kitchen.

Clay smirked. "You've been getting it on all this time?"

"Hardly. Where's Bennie?" Ethan grabbed a beer from the refrigerator. "Want one?"

Clay didn't respond and Ethan didn't expect him to. It was like asking a hyena if it wanted some of your gazelle. He handed Clay a bottle.

"He went to sleep a while ago."

"Any problems tonight?"

"Not really." Clay paused for a swig. "So, if you weren't screwing, what the hell were you doing?"

"We broke up." Ethan didn't make eye contact.

"Really? Why?"

"I don't know, she met some other guy. She was very tightlipped about it. No biggie. She was just a good fuck, is all."

"And you didn't do her one last time?"

"It didn't go down like that."

"What happened?"

"We just talked. It was really kind of boring."

"Did you cap her in the end?" He seemed serious.

"No. Not yet, at least."

A knowing smile gripped Clay's face. "You're too sweet on her."

"You're probably right. Besides, maybe she'll change her mind. We agreed to speak again after you and I get back from Phoenix. Where's my Dad?"

"Let's go, already." Stan summoned them to the dining room as if on cue. "I've been waiting for you to get back so we can finalize the plan and I can get some sleep."

Ethan and Clay entered the dining room and joined him at a wooden table greatly in need of retirement. "What's the big deal?" Ethan asked. "We go, grab the girl, and bring her back."

"It's not that simple, but hopefully that fast. You guys ought to get to sleep because I want you out of here before sun-up."

"Why so early?" Clay said, yawning.

"You need to be out of the city before they realize that damn cop is missing. Once they do, it's going to get real tight around here, and I don't want any more surprises. That also means drive safely. Stay within the damn speed limit."

"Don't worry."

"I want her here by tomorrow night. You know how important this is to me."

"It's just as important to me, Dad. You know that."

Stan pulled a wallet out of his pocket and slid it along the table to Ethan. "You'll need this."

Ethan furrowed his brow as he took it in his hand.

"Sloan's shield. Knock on her door and tell her you're with the Springdale Police. Tell her you're investigating her husband's disappearance and you need to talk to her. This'll be your ticket into the house."

Ethan examined the shield and then looked up at Stan. "You don't think she'll be suspicious of cops coming all the way from Utah?"

"It happens all the time in law enforcement."

"I'm just concerned she may not open the door because our presence will come as a complete surprise."

Stan pulled out a small notepad, wrote something on the top sheet, then tore it off and passed it to his son.

"Wyatt Orr?" Ethan read.

"That's the detective you *tried* to shoot today. When you ring the bell, throw out his name. Tell her you're working with him and the FBI, that you have reason to believe that her husband may have met with foul play. Once she opens the door—"

"What about me?" Clay asked. "What if she asks to see my badge?"

Stan pointed his head towards one of the bedrooms. "Take one of the shields Lyle got for us before we killed him. I don't remember if it's real or not, but it looks good enough."

Clay nodded.

"And guys, one more thing," Stan said, as he eyed both of them. He waited until he had their undivided attention.

"Don't mess this up."

CHAPTER SIXTY-TWO

AS WYATT MADE HIS way up the incline, he felt a pop of adrenaline pump through his veins. So much so that he forgot about the terrain he was now traversing. He was almost at the top of the hill when he heard a sharp clatter, the unmistakable sound of a desert predator.

A rattlesnake.

The tolling bell of death for those who weren't careful.

Having grown up in Arizona, Wyatt was familiar with diamondback rattlers. He knew that the rule of the thumb was to stop, find the snake, and then wait until it passes or walk around it. He stopped sharply on his heels and looked everywhere for the blendy creature. Most often, the rattle was merely a warning, as the snake had no intention to strike, but Wyatt knew that if he got too close, he'd be in dire need of medical assistance.

The hard part was locating it in the dead of night. He didn't want to use his flashlight because that could announce his presence. But then, Wyatt remembered he had night vision goggles and put them on. He quickly scanned the area and found the slithery creature less than a foot to his right. It was curled in a defensive position ready to strike. Wyatt took a moment to re-compose himself, before taking a few steps back and around it on the left. Snake encounters were harrowing, no matter how much experience you had.

Wyatt trudged his way to the crest as the house came into view. There was no fence, gate, or enclosure. Only the circular dirt driveway, the inside of which contained grass, and some large oak and juniper trees, marked the front of the home. As Wyatt reached eye level with it, he entered a defensive posture and sauntered slowly towards the house with his gun aimed straight ahead. Then he stopped momentarily behind the bark of a large oak to survey the place. There were lights on in several rooms. He hunkered down and darted across the yard until he reached the front on the western side. The first thing he needed to know was who and what he was up against. Staying low, he moved along the wall until he reached a window, and when he tried to peek in, he couldn't see anything because the room was dark and the blinds were closed.

He pressed on, west to east, and stopped just before the front door. It was solid wood and painted red, with a peephole. They could see out but he couldn't see in. He carefully stepped up and over a paved landing, before dropping back to the dirt and grass on the other side. Moving further along the wall, Wyatt stopped on one knee just before he reached the next bedroom window, and took a moment to catch his breath. Here's where he had to be careful, the light was on and the blinds were partially open. He couldn't be caught looking in.

Wyatt removed the goggles, quietly pulled in a deep breath, and lifted his face just enough to see inside. The hair rose on his arms and everything stopped, even the crickets seemed to pause in mid-song.

It was Nick.

He was alive.

Wyatt pulled back from the window. Right there, he felt like calling Ina but managed to suppress his elation because he knew finding Nick was just half the battle. Rescuing him was the real challenge, and he had no idea what he was up against.

He took another look around, and, when he was comfortable that he hadn't been spotted, peered through the window again. Nick was tied to a chair, his eyes closed. Wyatt tapped the window lightly to gain Nick's attention, but there was no response. Then he tried again, tapping it twice, slightly louder than the last. Nick opened his eyes and his face sprang to life. Wyatt watched warmly as a tear ran down Nick's cheek. Using both hands, including the one holding the gun, Wyatt motioned for Nick to stay calm, as Wyatt still needed to formulate a plan. Then he mouthed the words "How many are there?" But Nick shook his head in response.

Wyatt pointed to his head and put his hands out, but Nick mouthed something he couldn't interpret. So he decided to flash two fingers at Nick, but Nick shook his head. Wyatt held up three fingers and, again, Nick shook his head. Then, Wyatt folded his thumb inside the palm of his hand and held it up for Nick but, as Nick saw it, his eyes bulged and he turned to face the door. Wyatt jumped down just as someone entered Nick's room. He could hear talking but couldn't make out what was said. He wanted to jump up and shoot through the window, but he knew it was too risky. Nick would be in the line of fire, and Wyatt still didn't know exactly how many abductors there were. Even if he hit this target, one of the others could easily kill his best friend. He waited several minutes until he finally heard the door shut. Then he lifted his face and when he was certain Nick was alone, put up his four fingers again. Nick was already staring at the window and when he saw Wyatt's fingers, he nodded and confirmed Wyatt's suspicions.

Wyatt was easily outnumbered.

Four to one.

"WHAT'S HE DOING UP?" Ethan said to Clay, referring to Bennie.

It was almost five in the morning, and Ethan and Clay were preparing to leave for Phoenix. They were having a bite in the kitchen before hitting the road.

"He's probably just taking his middle of the night whizskey," Clay said.

A few minutes later, Bennie entered the kitchen, opened the refrigerator, pulled out a carton of orange juice, and poured himself a cup.

"What are *you* doing up so early?" Ethan said.

"Having some juice," Bennie said. "What are *you* doing up?"

Ethan sighed and it sent a message: he was annoyed. Bennie finished his juice, tossed the cup into the garbage, and left the kitchen. When Ethan was satisfied Bennie was out of earshot, he turned to Clay. "I get the feeling he's up to something."

"Oh come on, I think he went back to sleep."

"He's got a gun with him doesn't he?"

"In his room. Why?"

"Because we're about to leave him alone with my dad."

"You think he'll try something?"

"I don't know, but if he was going to, wouldn't today be the day to do it? When you and I aren't around?"

"Good ol' boy Bennie? What do you think he would do?"

"How about shoot my dad, free Nick, and cut a deal with the cops by ratting us out? He could tell them everything to save his ass while condemning ours."

"You really think he's capable of that?"

"Let's put it this way," Ethan said. "I'm not sure our association with him will last much longer. He's not a team player, so I expect he'll do anything to save his ass."

"Should we take him to Phoenix?"

"No, he'd only cause us problems. I'm not quite sure what to do, but whatever it is, we need to act fast."

Clay looked at his watch. It was a couple of minutes to five. "When are we leaving?"

"Ten minutes."

"That doesn't give us a lot of time," Clay said. "Should we take him out back?"

Ethan looked at Clay like he was an idiot and decided not to entertain the proposal. It wasn't worth explaining the risks of waking the neighbors with early morning gunshots, not to mention the logistics of disposing of a body when they were about to hit the road.

"We can tie him to a chair and get rid of him when we return," Clay suggested.

"Now that's a thought," Ethan conceded. At least Clay was starting to think more practically. "I'm not quite sure we're there yet. Once we do that, there's no turning back. We'll be cutting ties with our locator, and that could put us out of business altogether. Are we ready for that?"

"We should probably discuss it with your dad first."

Ethan held back laughter. His friend was an idiot indeed. He pondered for a moment before blowing by Clay and leaving the kitchen.

"Where are you going?" Clay followed.

Ethan pulled a handgun from the small of his back. "To protect my dad."

He walked briskly through the dining room and into the hallway, and began calling for Stan.

"Shit. What the hell are you doing? I thought we said ..."

Ethan pushed Bennie's door open and found him sitting on the bed leaning against the wall. Bennie stiffened and then straightened himself when he caught sight of Ethan's gun. Ethan took a moment to size up his associate, and then moved a few steps closer, raised the gun, and pointed it between Bennie's eyes.

"What the hell's going on?" said Bennie.

"Where's your gun?"

Bennie's eyes were blinking rapidly. "Under my pillow." He made a move towards it.

"Stay right there." Ethan turned to Clay. "Grab it."

Clay approached the bed and tossed two pillows to the floor until Bennie's 9mm appeared. He seized the gun and held it out for Ethan.

"Just hold onto it," Ethan instructed, and then turned to Bennie. "How many others you got?"

"What's this all about?" Bennie asked.

"Just tell me how many others you have."

"None, you've disarmed me. Now, would you mind telling me what's going on? I thought you were going to Phoenix. You planning to kill me first?"

"Just making sure you don't cause any mischief while we're away."

Bennie moved to the edge of the bed and planted his feet on the ground. "What kind of crap is that? I'm on your side."

Bennie locked eyes with Ethan but when Ethan didn't answer, Bennie stood.

"Fine then, I'm out of here." He brushed past Ethan, almost knocking shoulders with him.

"Where are you going?" Ethan asked.

Bennie grabbed a half-empty pack of Marlboros and a Harley Davidson lighter from his dresser. "Outside for a smoke."

Ethan turned to Clay. "Go keep an eye on him until he comes back in."

CHAPTER SIXTY-THREE

THE FIRST SHOT WAS dead on and Bennie spun halfway around before falling to the floor. Clay, who was standing just a couple of feet between Bennie and the house, froze. At first, Clay was incredulous, wondering how Ethan could shoot Bennie like that when they had just decided not to. He turned around to ask Ethan what he was doing but the front door was closed. And that's when he knew he was in trouble.

Clay turned to the western side of the yard and squinted in the darkness. There was a slight movement behind an oak tree in the corner, and Clay took a few steps forward as he reached for his gun.

But it was too late.

Two quick shots from behind the tree, one of which ripped right through Clay's heart.

WYATT HAD SAT BEHIND the tree and watched the house for hours. An entire evening in the desert. Crickets whistled, coyotes howled, and hunted animals shrieked, as all gave way to the natural order. He knew he wasn't alone. There were snakes, lizards, owls, mountain lions, bobcats, jackrabbits, and at the moment, they all had something in common with him.

All were predators in the night, waiting for their prey to emerge.

And just before the first light of dawn, Wyatt's emerged.

Wyatt set himself as he heard the front door open. Two guys entered the yard and when he had a clear and comfortable shot, Wyatt didn't hesitate. The first target went down immediately, and it didn't take long for the second to look his way. It took Wyatt two shots to get the second kidnapper, but the guy went down like a domino. Wyatt wished he had a silencer, but such was life. The cat was certainly out of the bag now, but it didn't matter because he had just cut his enemies in half. And as Wyatt stood for his next move, he couldn't help but mutter:

"Now these are better odds."

ETHAN AND STAN LOOKED at each other.

"What the hell was that?" Ethan asked.

"Go check on Clay and Bennie," Stan said. "I got Nick."

Ethan pulled out his gun and headed for the front door. He opened it slightly and peeked out, but the walls of the U-shaped landing only allowed him to see straight ahead. There was nothing in his line of vision. He took a few steps forward and that's when he caught sight of his fallen comrades, just to his right. Neither was moving.

"Clay, Bennie, you OK?"

In his gut, Ethan knew they weren't. He thought of running to Clay to see if he could help, but he knew there was nothing he could do. Fear and anger mixed in his brain. Where was the shooter? Ethan didn't know the location but was certain he knew the man's identity. He had escaped a barrage of gunfire yesterday, but it wouldn't happen again. Ethan would be sure of it.

He grasped the gun in both hands and took another step towards the edge of the landing. It was still too dark to see anything and just by viewing his fallen partners, he couldn't fashion a guess as to where the shots had come from.

But he didn't need to.

A bullet whizzed by his head and took a piece off the wooden siding just below the roof. The shooter was in the corner of the front yard, to his right. Ethan jumped back, hugged the brick wall on the landing, and waited a few seconds before firing off several shots in the vicinity. They were literally shots in the dark aimed at keeping his adversary in place. He had little hope of hitting a completely hidden target. Two shots came back his way, but Ethan had already taken cover inside the landing.

"You all right?" Stan called from the hallway. He was crouched and clutching a handgun with both hands.

"I'm fine," Ethan yelled, his voice shaky. "But Clay and Bennie are down."

"Can you make the shooter? Where is he?"

"The corner of the yard, by the oak." He paused for a breath. "How about I keep him occupied while you go out through the kitchen and surprise him from the back?"

"I don't think that will work because I can't get behind him there. It's still dark and he probably has a better chance of seeing me than I do him."

"Then what do you want to do?"

"Keep him occupied, and don't let him move to the front of the house. Keep shooting in his vicinity so that he stays in the corner. I'll grab Nick and get him in the car. Then you'll join us and we'll try to run him over on our way out of here."

"Forget Nick! We're under fire. Go put a bullet through Nick's head and come back here and help me." Ethan turned back and fired off a shot.

"No, we can do this. Trust me."

"He'll have a clear shot at us as we're driving out."

"Yeah, but he won't pull the trigger," Stan responded. "Not when he sees his friend in the car with us."

CHAPTER SIXTY-FOUR

"WHAT ARE YOU DOING?" Nick asked, as Stan breathlessly cut the rope and freed his left wrist. "And where's everyone else?"

Nick had heard gunshots and wondered, hoped, they were from Wyatt and had hit their marks.

"Shut up. Now's not the time."

Stan made his way to the other side of the chair and cut the rope off Nick's right wrist. Just like the first piece, the rope fell to the floor. Nick flexed his wrists and hands while Stan frantically looked around for fresh cord. Two more cracks of gunfire rang out, forcing Stan to accelerate. When he didn't find fresh rope, Stan grabbed the cut rope off the floor and held up the pieces, assessing whether they were long enough to use again.

"What can we do to end this now?" Nick asked, as he realized that Stan was about to re-tie his hands. "What will it take to cut a deal? Say the word, and I can have my friend cease fire in an instant."

"The only resolution ends with you and your wife in a grave. It's not negotiable."

"You'll never pull it off. I heard the other two guys outside just before the gunshots. They're dead, aren't they?" Stan didn't answer. "See, you've already lost half your team and you're not going to beat my boy out there."

"Your friend's as good as dead. You're coming with us."

"You failed already once, didn't you?"

"What are you talking about?"

"The gunshots we heard yesterday. That was you guys trying to kill him, wasn't it?"

Stan grabbed Nick's wrists and tied them together as tight as he could. Then he cut the ropes off Nick's legs, pulled him up, and put the gun to his head.

"I'm telling you," Nick said, "You're not going to kill him."

"Then we'll have to just settle for you." He poked the back of Nick's head with the gun. "Now, we're going out the back and into the car, and if you try *anything*, I guarantee I'll pop you and leave your rotting carcass right here in this house. Understood?"

A crack followed a pop as Nick and Stan crossed the hallway and reached the front door.

"Cover me," Stan called to his son. "I'm taking him out back."

Ethan peeked out from behind the wall on the landing and fired off two shots to his right.

"Just give me two minutes and then haul ass out the back," Stan yelled.

"As soon as I hear the car start."

Stan pushed Nick past the front doorway and into the kitchen. Just before they reached the backdoor, Stan ordered Nick to stop. He switched the gun over to his left hand and wrapped his right arm around Nick's neck.

"You're going into the backseat and you're going to do so quietly." He pulled at Nick's neck as he escorted him out to the car. "See, you and me, we're not the same. I don't have anything left to live for. You guys took everything from me. All I've had is the dream that my day would come, and it has. I'm not going down without a fight. If you make so much as a sound as we're getting in that truck, you get a hole in your head."

CHAPTER SIXTY-FIVE

THE DAWN OF A new day was announcing its presence along the horizon. Wyatt held his ground behind the tree as a surprising calmness enveloped him. He felt strangely comfortable in combat. Two of Nick's abductors were down, he was engaged with a third, and he didn't feel an ounce of fear. Only sheer determination.

For the first time in his life, Wyatt Orr was locked in.

Several bullets came from the landing, but they were way off the mark and he knew why. He had seen nothing but a hand wildly pulling the trigger. The shooter wasn't really trying to hit him. He hadn't taken a look to see where he was shooting.

Cover fire.

They were up to something.

Wyatt quickly reloaded and decided to make a move. He slipped out from behind the tree and fired his own cover as he sprinted to the side of the house. Then he heard an engine revving up in the back. Pointing his gun upwards with both hands, Wyatt slowly made his way along the wall. He waited a moment and then stuck his head around the corner, just as the back door swung open and a man sprinted out.

That's when Wyatt jumped out and pulled the trigger.

"GET IN!" STAN YELLED through the open passenger window.

Ethan darted out the back door and staggered as a bullet whizzed by him. He slammed into the side of the car, the momentum too strong to curtail in time for a clean entry. The gun in his left hand made a "pang" sound, and scratched the paint on the outside of the car, as another shot came at him and missed. With his right hand, he ripped open the door and jumped inside, as Stan pounced on the gas and made a sharp turn in the far corner of the yard. Dust twirled in the air behind them, as Ethan grasped the inside handle for dear life. He was practically leaning out of the truck, struggling just to close the door.

"Slow the car! I'm not completely in yet."

Stan straightened the truck and let up for a second while Ethan slammed the door shut. Then, he hit the gas and they were racing towards the other end of the yard. From there, the dirt road veered left around the side of the house and then up the hill to the highway, which was where they were heading. But there was an obstruction near the side of the house.

Wyatt.

And he had his gun aimed right at their windshield.

WYATT LOCKED EYES WITH the owner of that fetid trailer in which he'd been stuck longer than anyone should ever be. He saw the smirk on Stan's face as the truck picked up and barreled straight for him. Wyatt took up a Weaver Stance, his feet separated, with both hands on his gun aimed straight ahead. He was about to pull the trigger when he caught a glimpse inside the vehicle.

Nick was in the backseat.

Wyatt lowered the gun and dove out of the way. Once the truck passed, Wyatt popped up, but immediately dove to the other side to avoid the hail of gunfire coming from Ethan who was hanging out the passenger window. He rolled on the ground until the gunfire ended and the truck had gained some distance. Then he jumped to his feet and began running through the cloud of dust that was slowly beginning to settle. He dashed through the brush and down the sandy hill to the rental, jumped in, fired it up, and sped off in what seemed like a single motion. The car slid, as the tires spit out dirt and rocks before catching its bearings and taking off. As he sped past the other houses, Wyatt located Stan's truck; it had already crossed the pulley bridge and was about to enter the highway.

Wyatt floored the rental and flew across the bridge as Stan made a right onto Route 9. It was the same direction Wyatt had taken to escape yesterday's barrage. While he wasn't a local, Wyatt knew there was a dead-end about fifteen miles up the road, and it was the kind of place that couldn't tolerate a high-speed chase. It was the very place that Nick's abductors had so cowardly hid behind, and used as their own personal killing ground.

Zion National Park.

CHAPTER SIXTY-SIX

THE SUN WAS STILL asleep, but the streets of Rockville and Springdale filled with muted early-morning light. Early risers, however, were being treated to a chase of NASCAR proportions.

"Steady the car for me and slow down a little," Ethan said, as he checked to make sure his gun was fully loaded.

"Just wait until we turn the corner up ahead," Stan responded.

They rounded the bend and Stan tapped the brakes as they entered the residential part of Rockville. Ethan waited until Wyatt got closer, leaned out the front window, and sent a storm of bullets at Wyatt. He started off aiming high but then slowly aimed lower. A kill would be ideal, but if need be, he'd settle for blowing out a tire.

Wyatt swerved to the left, across the yellow lines and into the other lane. Fortunately, they owned the road at such an early hour, and Ethan was a terrible shot. Ironically, that made Wyatt all the more tense, as he wondered what to do when the guy was shooting. Maybe he shouldn't swerve at all, lest he veer *into* the line of errant fire. There was no right answer. Ultimately, he did what made the most sense and swerved away from the direction in which Ethan aimed the barrel.

After surviving the round, Wyatt slid back in behind Stan's truck. But it didn't last long, as Ethan hung out the window again and shot off another set. With the gun aimed at the windshield, Wyatt reacted quickly and swerved to the left again, but not before several shots hit the front of the car, knocking out the passenger side headlights. Including yesterday's ambush, Ethan had now hit three sides of the car; a few to the driver side would even everything out. The road began to curve again when Wyatt slammed on his brakes and fearfully yelled out an expletive.

A Mack truck had just turned the corner and was heading straight for him.

THEY REACHED THE APPLE orchard on the outskirts of Springdale just a few miles outside the Park. None of the stores were open at this hour and the streets were deserted, save for a couple of early-morning power walkers. Nick was relieved when he saw that Wyatt had avoided a collision and was back in line safely behind them.

For now.

Nick had been checking on him frequently, and it seemed like every time he turned around, Wyatt was trying to avoid erratic gunfire. Wyatt couldn't return the fire and that made it all the more difficult to watch. Nick wanted to do something, anything, to prevent Ethan from shooting at his friend. But what could he do? His hands were tied.

Literally.

Nick thought about throwing his arms around Ethan's neck to try and suffocate him. But even if he caught Ethan by surprise, Nick was still at a major disadvantage. Unlike Nick, Ethan had use of both of his hands, and they were currently wrapped around a gun.

I've got to do something.

The ride had been unsettling. Not that Nick was expecting comfort, sitting in the backseat of a pick-up with his hands tied. But they hadn't belted him in—they didn't have time—and the roads were bumpy and windy. Nick was tumbling all over the seat and he'd been forced to prop his elbows against the door just to steady himself. And that prevented him from doing anything to help Wyatt, or even himself.

Nick stole a glance at the front as Ethan settled back in his seat and said something to Stan about reloading. Stores flashed by on both sides of the road, as they sped through town. A man who had started crossing the street jumped back at the last second, as the speeding pickup almost blindsided him. The man could be heard in the distance stepping back into the street and cussing at them, until he realized that there was another speeding vehicle bearing down on him. He dove to the side of the road just in the nick of time.

As they passed through the heart of Springdale, Ethan prepared for another barrage and Nick knew he couldn't wait much longer. Sooner or later, one of Ethan's shots would puncture a tire, strike the windshield, or even hit Wyatt himself, and that would likely mean the end of their lives. He had to act now.

And that's when he remembered.

The knife.

It was in his pocket.

While the road had straightened some since they entered town, Nick was still having trouble keeping steady. He decided to try gaining stability by pressing both legs against the back of the front seat. It wasn't the safest position in the event of impact, but that wasn't something with which he could concern himself right now. If they crashed, chances were Nick would die anyway, by impact or bullet. He twisted his midsection, swung both arms to his right, grabbed the inside of his pocket with the fingers of his left hand, and pulled to stretch it as far as he could. He grimaced as he stuffed the fingers from his right hand inside the pocket. Nick was pushing the rope's limits and while it was actually giving some, it was also burning his wrists.

Nick used his fingers to claw deeper into the pocket and pull the cloth forward. Seconds later, he felt the plastic of the knife on the edge of his fingers, as the cloth of his pocket bunched up in his palm. He clawed further, finally grasping the knife and pulling it out. Then he crouched deeper so that his captors couldn't see what he was doing. Nick pulled the knife open, extended both hands out as far as he could, and, twisting it with his right hand, lowered the blade under the rope.

"Keep this thing steady so I can get the shot." Ethan shoved the last few bullets into the magazine.

"Damn it, bury the son of a bitch! How many times have you missed already?"

"Not now, Dad. Steady, OK? I'll nail him once and for all."

THEY FLEW AROUND A corner and entered the park at over a hundred miles an hour. There were two entrance booths, side by side. Stan let off the gas and chose the booth to the left, hoping Wyatt would try to make up ground by taking the booth on the right. That would give Ethan a clear side shot, one even his fuck-up son couldn't screw up. But Wyatt didn't bite, choosing to stay directly behind them.

NICK FELT HIS HEART beating too fast for his body. He was cutting as hard as he could and the threads were definitely separating, but not quickly enough. Perspiration dove from his face, and his entire body was soaked in sweat. He continued cutting furiously, when he heard the magazine snap back into Ethan's gun. Time was of the essence, as the law of averages wasn't on Wyatt's side. Even a terrible shooter like Ethan would hit his mark eventually, especially when the target was right behind him. Out of the corner of his eye, Nick saw Ethan make a move for the window. He needed to act quickly.

The problem: there was plenty of rope left to cut.

CHAPTER SIXTY-SEVEN

THERE ARE TIMES WHEN you have just a split second to make a life or death decision. For Nicholas Perrone, this was one of those moments. Sure, he and Wyatt were in separate vehicles, one behind the other, but it still felt like they were miles away from each other. Despite everything they'd been through recently, at that moment, there wasn't a question in Nick's mind. Wyatt was his best friend. They were in this together. Wyatt had risked his life to save Nick, and now it was time to return the favor.

Ethan lowered the window and it felt like they were entering the eye of a ferocious tornado. As Ethan scrambled to stick his head and gun out, Nick had barely a second to decide: continue with the rope or try and stop Ethan? Nick dropped the knife, lunged over the seat, and threw his arms out as far as he could, as if trying to wrangle a stray calf. And they fit perfectly over Ethan's head. Ethan's gun fell out the window and bounced to the side like a football, as Nick swiftly slid his bound arms to Ethan's throat and pulled them back against the seat.

Nick focused all his weight on his upper body. He was gritting his teeth so hard they could've fallen out. But it was working. Nick had Ethan pinned to the seat and Ethan's feet were flailing, repeatedly smacking the front dashboard. Ethan desperately grabbed at Nick's arms but had trouble digging his nails into the flesh. The attack had been perfectly executed; Ethan never saw it coming. Nick's hold of his throat was airtight and Ethan's face was turning blue.

"GET THE FUCK OFF him!" Stan yelled.

"You wanna see what it's like to lose everything?" Nick pulled even harder.

Stan tried swerving the car to shake Ethan free, but it didn't work. Next, Stan made a cursory reach for Nick's arm but couldn't extend far enough. He had to do something. But what? His son was dying right in front of him, and he was trying to handle a pickup at more than a hundred miles an hour. And a new problem was rapidly approaching: they were coming up on a sharp turn.

Canyon Junction was just around the bend.

He had an idea.

Stan slammed on the brakes, slowing the truck just enough so that they wouldn't topple over when he made the turn. Then he took the right turn in the road as sharp as he could, hoping to throw Nick off balance. If he could force Nick to let up for a second, it would be all Ethan would need to get some traction and fight him off. The maneuver, however, was unsuccessful, as Nick slid slightly towards the passenger side window but managed to keep his stranglehold. Ethan was seconds from death.

So, Stan cut sharply to the left at Canyon Junction and onto Zion Canyon Scenic Drive. It wasn't where he had planned on going, since the road dead-ended at the entrance to the Narrows. But Stan had no choice. His son was running out of time.

THE SECOND MANEUVER WORKED.

Nick had been thrown back and forth, causing his grip to loosen. The truck plowed over a series of orange dividers, rods that were nailed to the ground to separate traffic on the narrow road. With the small window of opportunity, Ethan stuck his hands under Nick's arms and pushed them forward, allowing him to take in some much-needed oxygen. Nick fought to regain his grip, as Ethan pushed out as hard as he could. But Nick was closing in on him again, as he had a decided advantage. The seat between them gave Nick leverage. It wasn't long before Nick was back at Ethan's jugular, this time taking Ethan's hands with him. Ethan tried to bite Nick on the arm, but Nick's hold was too strong. And that's when he began to panic. There wasn't much more he could take and he was running out of options.

Then Ethan noticed something he could use.

The rope.

He repositioned his hands, placing one on each side of Nick's wrists, and began pushing them apart with everything he had. His face was blood red, but so were Nick's wrists; he was quickly inflicting Nick with severe rope burns. Both yelled in pain and might, as Stan picked up speed. They passed the Zion Lodge with the truck straddling both lanes.

FOR STAN, IT WAS an impossible situation, trying to drive at a high speed, keeping his eyes on the road, evading Wyatt, and helping his son avoid strangulation. Something had to give. And quick.

And then something *did* give.

The threads. Nick's wrists. Ethan's throat.

The rope snapped.

AS THE ROPE BROKE apart, Nick fell back in agony grabbing his wrists. Blood oozed from his skin in places, while others were discolored with blood trapped underneath. He could hear Ethan gasping, taking in air like water in the desert. Nick was certain that as soon as Ethan regained his breath, he would grab a gun, turn around and shoot. He had to do something fast before Ethan regained his composure.

So he reached for the knife.

But it was gone.

"YOU OK?" STAN YELLED to Ethan, who was hunched in the front gasping for air.

"I think so," Ethan coughed, swallowing as much as his lungs would allow. "I'm gonna kill that son of a bitch."

"Here." Stan passed a handgun across the front seat. "It's fully loaded."

Ethan grabbed the gun with one hand, while massaging his throat with the other. "We're headed for a dead-end, Dad. What are we going to do?"

"There's a turnaround ahead by the Temple of Sinewava. Shoot him and I'll get us turned around. In a few minutes, we'll be heading out of the park with a dead passenger in the back."

NICK DESPERATELY SCANNED THE floorboard, but there was no sign of the knife. His memory told him he had dropped it on the passenger side, so he dove to the floor, stuck his hand under the seat, and felt around. He pushed aside a bottle of water and some coins, and then felt his hand accidentally push the knife further away. At the same time, Nick heard Stan pass Ethan a gun.

Nick's head smacked against the seat, as he extended his hand as far as he could. This time, he wrapped his hand around the knife and pulled it out from under the seat.

Nick opened the knife just as Ethan swung around with the gun. But before Ethan could get off a shot, Nick shot up and stabbed him in the arm.

Ethan grabbed his arm; the gun fell to the backseat floor.

Nick went for the gun, but Ethan caught hold of his arm and shoulder and the two became entangled like hockey players in a brawl.

"Kill the son of a bitch!" Stan yelled.

STAN SAW THAT ETHAN and Nick were entangled. And Nick had the advantage, since the gun was resting not far from his left foot. Ethan was desperately holding onto Nick, but it was a struggle. Nick's strength was moving them closer towards the middle of the truck, and Stan had to do something.

Fast.

Stan watched as Nick's sheer strength brought him and Ethan closer to Stan's side of the vehicle. As they came within range, Stan pulled back and landed a hard right to Nick's face. Ethan let go of Nick just as his father landed the punch, and the blow sent Nick back against the seat. Ethan was about to jump into the back to grab the gun, but there was a new problem. Stan's punch had come with a price.

He'd lost control of the vehicle.

The pickup swerved off the road on the left, just past the Weeping Rock shuttle stop. They began barreling down a dirt-filled plateau with large boulders and acrobatic cottonwoods, their barks half-eaten by the park's beaver population. A hit at the base to any of them and they would tip over and land on the truck causing instant death. They sped through the maze of trees and boulders and Stan struggled to avoid taking one head-on. But even if he were successful, it wouldn't matter because they were about to hit something else.

They were heading straight for the Virgin River.

CHAPTER SIXTY-EIGHT

ALL WYATT COULD DO was watch in horror. He broke to a stop on the road as the pickup swerved out of control towards the river. His initial thought was that they were dead. They'd either strike a boulder—of which there were plenty—or hit one of those trees that had been chewed at the base. If they were lucky enough to avoid either, a raging river awaited their entry. Wyatt watched helplessly as they managed to dodge the first few impediments. But would it make a difference? Eventually they would strike something, and he had seen Nick rolling around in the backseat having just taken a punch in the face. Nick's heroics had likely saved Wyatt's life, and all Wyatt could do was watch. And hope.

Wyatt's heart swelled over what his best friend had done, at what they had done for each other. All he wanted now was to apologize for deserting Nick, and for the conclusions he'd drawn about him during the investigation. He decided to place himself in the best possible position to help Nick upon impact. He grabbed his guns, slammed the door shut, and began sprinting through the weeds across the plateau. Then he approached a ten-foot high boulder halfway between the road and the river and he took up position behind it.

It was like settling in to watch a plane fall out of the sky, and right now, that plane was carrying his best friend.

THE PICKUP PLOWED THROUGH the dusty, rocky terrain and Stan managed to somehow evade tree after tree, and the occasional boulder, as if he were playing a high-speed video game. But the obstacles started coming faster and in greater abundance as they moved closer to the river. Stan weaved sharply to the left to avoid a tree, and then to the right to avoid a boulder.

But he missed.

The truck's right side struck the boulder and Stan slammed on the brake, praying the pickup wouldn't spin out of control or topple over. The vehicle bounced off the boulder and slowed as it edged off the plateau, finally coming to rest on a rock-filled embankment just twenty yards above the river.

"Come on Ethan, let's get out of here. Now!" He threw the driver's side door open.

Ethan curled up in the front seat; it was the best he could do to absorb the impact. He looked disoriented, grimaced in pain, and held his right shoulder.

"Come on, son." Stan reached over and nudged him to life. "We gotta get outta here."

Ethan slowly sat up and pulled the handle, but nothing happened.

"The door's jammed," Ethan said.

"Mine's open."

Ethan slid across the front seat as Stan jumped out of the truck. "What about him?"

They looked at Nick lying on the floor of the backseat. He appeared unconscious.

"Damn it." Stan looked around quickly before his reality set in. "We need to get the hell out of here before the authorities arrive."

"But I need my gun. It fell in the back when we were ..."

"Can you see it?"

Ethan leaned over the back and examined the floor around Nick.

"Hurry," Stan pressed.

"Either it went under the seat or he's on top of it."

Stan reached inside the truck and pulled his son by the shirt. "Forget the gun. Just go. Run." He felt for the gun in his own pocket and sighed in relief that it was still there. Ethan had missed too many opportunities; he wasn't about to give Ethan his last gun.

"We need to split up. You go that way." Stan pointed towards Angel's Landing. "I'll head in the opposite direction. We meet at your shop as soon as possible."

"OK, but Dad?" Ethan said as they locked eyes. "Be careful."

CHAPTER SIXTY-NINE

WYATT'S IMMEDIATE IMPULSE WAS to take them out. He stepped out from behind his cover, crouched one leg on the ground, and took aim. But then he changed his mind. The cowards had gone in separate directions and were quickly gaining distance; the chances of a hit were decreasing with each step. His concern was whether Nick had survived the impact. If Nick needed medical attention, time was of the essence and he couldn't afford to waste any of it by engaging in a gunfight.

He decided to let them go. The police would hunt them for the rest of their lives; he had come to Utah for one reason: find Nick and bring him back.

Alive.

Wyatt sprinted to the truck, holstered his weapon, and opened the door on the driver's side as Nick was pulling himself off the floor.

"You OK, buddy?" Wyatt asked.

Nick groaned. "I've been better." He rubbed his forehead.

"You look like hell."

"That's pretty much where I've been all week. What took you so long?"

"I'll explain later." Wyatt extended a hand. "Let's get you home."

Nick raised a brow. "You killed them?"

"The cowards took off running."

"Then it's not over," Nick said decisively.

Nick made a move towards the door, but Wyatt put up his hand. "Sorry buddy, you're not going anywhere but home. Ina's worried sick about you."

"Which way did they go?" Nick slid along the seat to the door, but Wyatt blocked his progress.

"You're not doing this."

Nick locked eyes with him. "I have to."

"Let's go home, man. You're safe now."

"The driver, Stan? Used to work for Great American."

"I know."

"But we fired him. And this week, when he figured out who I was, he wanted complete revenge. Those guys were planning to go to Phoenix this morning to kidnap Ina and bring her here so they could kill us both."

Wyatt stared at him for a moment. How close they had been to an enormous disaster. He recoiled. "I think we should leave this to the authorities."

"They have my driver's license. They know where I live." Nick pushed his way ahead and made Wyatt step aside so he could get out of the truck. "If I don't end this now, I'll never stop looking over my shoulder. I can't live like that. You got an extra gun for me?"

Wyatt removed the gun from his holster, checked it, and handed it to Nick. He quickly showed him how to fire it. "You sure you want to do this?"

"Good," Nick said, ignoring Wyatt's question. "Now, where did they go?"

Wyatt pointed northeast. "Stan went that way." Then he pointed back the way they had come. "The other one went that way."

"I got Stan. You take Ethan, the other one. I'm not even sure he has a gun. One fell out the window, and I knocked the other out of his hand."

"I don't agree with this. We can still call the sheriff and go back to Phoenix."

"Not until I settle the score. I consider it part of my job."

"Then you better get a nice bonus."

WYATT INCHED CLOSER TO the water to survey the landscape. It didn't take long for him to see Ethan staggering downriver. Although he had gotten a good head start, Ethan hadn't made much progress due to the difficult terrain. He was attempting to traverse jumbles of rocks, boulders, and scattered tree limbs along the riverbank, and it was a tough go. Wyatt looked downriver and noticed that it narrowed to a point where there was no room to walk on either side. Ethan would soon have to make a decision: continue by trudging through the water, or seek higher ground.

Wyatt's money was on the latter.

During the chase, Wyatt had noticed a trail running along the plateau above the water. The narrow footpath ran north/south, the same way in which Ethan was now traveling. He looked back at Nick but he had already taken off after Stan like a man on a mission.

Wyatt cringed at the thought of having to explain to Ina that he had rescued her husband, only to allow him to carelessly chase his captor in this unforgiving terrain. Ina had sent him here to find Nick and bring him home, and, while it hadn't been easy, not once did he imagine that the "bringing him home" part would be the greatest challenge. Wyatt realized he had to take out Ethan and fast. If for no other reason than to help Nick with Stan.

He looked downriver and wondered where Ethan would be able to climb onto higher ground. Then he remembered that there was a footbridge over the water back at the Grotto Picnic Area, about a mile or so behind him.

"Let's get this over with," Wyatt said, with a sigh.

And then he took off.

FOR A RIVER, THE shortest distance between two points is not a straight line; it's the point of least resistance. As the Virgin River exited the Narrows, it snaked its way around the large, solitary canyon wall called the Big Bend. Stan rounded it without once looking behind him.

He, too, was trying to make progress alongside the river, but the terrain was quickly changing.

Stan reached the Temple of Sinewava, which marked the end of the Zion Canyon Scenic Drive. It was also known at the Gateway to the Narrows, the point at which the canyons constricted into seventeen miles of slots filled only by the raging river. And suddenly, there was no longer a riverbank. Stan stumbled in the knee-high water. It was cold and slippery and he was running on rocks at the bottom without any traction from his shoes. He struggled to keep his balance, but the rocks were slippery and his arms flailed.

A gale force hit him as he entered the shady Narrows. With little sunshine, especially at such an early hour, the air inside the slot was much cooler. It was downright frigid during the winter. The Narrows only saw sun for a short time every day, and that was normally close to midday, when the sun was directly above it.

On his right was a small, sandy beach. It was the entrance used by tourists who took the shuttle to the end of the scenic drive, and walked the one-mile trail to the river. From there, the brave would persist; the smart would take pictures and turn around. Stan stole a glance at the entrance and cut sharply to the right. But his feet came out from under him and he broke the fall with his right hand. His destination: a black bucket on the sandy beach filled with walking sticks to aid those tourists hiking in the river. Panting heavily, Stan took a moment to suck in some air and, for the first time, check to see if someone was chasing him.

He didn't see anyone.

Stan knew, though, that this didn't mean much, since his view from the gateway didn't stretch far. He couldn't rest. He dashed over to the bucket. Wet sand flew from his shoes with each step. There were six or seven sticks in the bucket, each different shapes and sizes. He picked the longest and thickest he could find, as he knew he'd need it to navigate the river.

He might also need it as a weapon.

CHAPTER SEVENTY

BIRDS SANG, DEER ROAMED, and bugs buzzed, as if it was a normal morning in the canyon. Wyatt steered the rental off the road near the Grotto shuttle stop. The drive back had been so fast that he doubted Ethan was anywhere near the footbridge. He'd tried, along the way, to look for Ethan along the river, but the road was set too far back for him to see anything.

Wyatt did his best to stay as quiet as possible. He opened his door, stepped out behind the car, and looked around, deciding to leave the door open. He spotted a boulder at least fifteen feet high, and about fifty feet from the bridge. He grabbed his gun, tiptoed across the weeds, settled in behind it looking out at the river. But the plateau was too high to see anyone walking below. He could not see Ethan, but, more importantly, Ethan probably couldn't see Wyatt.

Wyatt waited and listened closely, praying for silence from the canyon's morning orchestra. But after a few minutes, none of it mattered, because his ears provided confirmation that he had arrived before Ethan.

He could hear gravelly footsteps nearing the bridge.

ETHAN CLIMBED FROM THE river and onto the plateau, and looked around. When he saw no one there, he crouched momentarily with his hands on his legs, gasping for air. Water spritzed everywhere, as he stepped onto the footbridge and looked out at the river and where he had just come from. The coast looked clear. He wondered what Nick and his friend had done after he and his father bolted. The good news was that he hadn't heard any gunfire.

Ethan placed his arms on the rail and leaned out, wondering what to do next. He thought of taking the shuttle back but quickly dismissed it. Nick's friend had probably called for backup and even if he hadn't, someone in town had probably heard his gunfire and called the police. Once they learned that he and his dad were on the loose, they would undoubtedly be watching the park's shuttles. Ethan rubbed hard at his neck; it burned like hell. He didn't need a mirror to know that it was horribly red, as he had, just moments ago, narrowly escaped death by violent asphyxiation. But it wasn't the physical pain that haunted him, it was the emotional. He had let his father down. Too many mistakes, too many misfires, and because of that, they were fighting for their lives. He couldn't let his father down again.

But first he needed a break. His heart was pounding, and breathing had become a struggle. He tried to recapture his normal breath, but realized he needed to sit. There was a stone bench near the base of the footbridge and it had a good view up the river, the perfect spot to recharge. Ethan moved off the rail and tottered a little sideways, like an alcoholic leaving the bar after a night of heavy drinking. As he reached the bench, he took a deep breath and was about to sit when something stopped him cold in his tracks.

Someone called his name.

Ethan turned around and locked eyes with Nick's friend.

The cop.

He had a gun.

It was aimed at Ethan's head.

NICK'S FACE WAS BADLY bruised, his wrists were burned, and blood oozed from scrapes on his face and arms. His ankles and back felt sorer than ever, and, as he made his way along the river, he felt aches in parts of his body he never imagined could feel like that. But it didn't hamper his progress, as adrenaline fueled him up the riverbank. Stan had achieved a considerable lead, but after spending most of the week bound to a chair, Nick was invigorated by freedom and his own chance for revenge.

When he started out, Nick had Stan in his sights, but he lost him briefly when Stan made his way around the Big Bend. Nick sprinted along the same route and as he passed the Bend, he caught sight of Stan submerged in water. Nick couldn't help but chuckle as he watched Stan get up, take a few more steps, and then stumble again. This was going to be easier than he thought.

While he could see Stan at the entrance to the Narrows, he was still too far ahead for a shot. At this distance, Nick would need the purest of luck to gun him down. And besides, Nick was rapidly gaining ground and he hadn't seen Stan look behind him. If Stan didn't know he was being chased, a missed gunshot would only alert him to Nick's presence and fuel him to move faster. Not worth the risk.

As Stan entered the Narrows, Nick lost sight of him again. But Nick knew from his research that the Narrows were seventeen miles long and pretty much all river. There were numerous side canyons, but all indications were they were dead-ends, and Stan was too keen to box himself into a corner. So, Nick figured, this would simply be a race, and if Stan couldn't keep his balance before *entering* the Narrows, the rest would be a cinch.

Nick pushed forward, utilizing every inch of the riverbank until there was no more room alongside the water. He stepped into the river as he neared the Narrows' entrance, and then something unexpected happened.

He lost his footing on the slippery rocks.

"GOING SOMEWHERE?" WYATT HELD the gun firmly with both hands, as he emerged from behind the boulder and inched closer to Ethan.

Ethan stood and faced him.

"How many people did you kill out here?"

"I want a lawyer. I don't have to answer your questions."

"And I don't have to bring you in." Wyatt inched closer. "I don't even have jurisdiction here."

"What the hell are you talking about? You're a cop. You can't just shoot me."

Wyatt moved closer, now within forty feet. "You should have killed me when you had the chance. That was you yesterday in the backhoe, wasn't it?"

Ethan couldn't seem to get words out of his mouth.

"I thought so. You're a horrible shot. Hands where I can see them."

Ethan did nothing.

"Now!"

Ethan put his hands out. "Go ahead and cuff me. Take me in. I want a lawyer."

"Weapons. Hand them over."

"I don't have any. I'm unarmed."

"Bullshit! Where's your firearm?"

"I don't have any. I dropped one out the window, and the other on the floor of the truck." He paused. "Why don't you drop yours and take me on, mano a mano?"

Wyatt inched closer, keeping the gun aimed at Ethan's face. "This canyon is full of all kinds of animals, but none like you and your father. How many people have you killed?"

"I don't have to tell you shit."

"It's over, Ethan."

Ethan began retreating towards the footbridge. "You're fuckin' crazy, man. You can't do this; you're supposed to take me in. Cops don't do this."

"That's where you're wrong."

Ethan backed his way into the middle of the bridge and Wyatt followed. He was less than twenty-five feet away.

"What are you talking about?" Ethan asked.

"I'm not a cop anymore."

Wyatt pulled the trigger, but nothing happened.

The gun.

His backup.

Frank's gun.

He'd given his department issue to Nick.

And it was happening. Again.

Ethan flashed a smile like the one Wyatt had last seen on the face of his father's killer. Wyatt lowered the gun to see what had happened. Ethan didn't flinch. Recognizing the opportunity, he began sprinting across the wooden boards directly at Wyatt.

But Ethan's movement didn't register in Wyatt's mind, because all he could see was the assailant by the banister. Suddenly, he was back in his living room at the scene of the two most heinous crimes he had experienced: the one that took his father's life, and the one that tormented the rest of his. And here he was, years later and after all the target practice, looking down at that same gun that had failed him once again. That picture he had seen repeatedly in his subconscious, over the years, was playing out all over again right here in Utah. And Wyatt could almost see his own image, the face of a bewildered teenager, shocked at the failure of simple cause and effect. The pull of the trigger hadn't resulted in death to the bad guy. And then the crack, the quick rush of light like a small bolt of lightning emitted from the barrel. Not even a second passed before his father hit the ground. It was the shot that, for all intents and purposes, had killed him too.

Wyatt felt like a scuba diver who's just realized his regulator isn't working. Ethan was bearing down on him and, like the diver's instinct to jump to the shore, Wyatt almost threw the gun to the side to defend himself. But his father's face flashed in his mind, as he recalled Tavares' words.

Frank loved you more than anything.

Wyatt composed himself, and aimed the gun at the evil now just a few feet away. He calmly pulled back the hammer, then the trigger, a bullet flew out of the gun, and did what it had done every time Wyatt replayed the night he lost his father. Ethan took it square in the chest and fell backwards, staggering against the rail. Wyatt watched the killer's eyes change and relished their shock at the unlikely turn of events. And when Ethan took another step towards him, Wyatt didn't hesitate. He pulled back the hammer, fired off another, and watched Ethan fall backwards over the railing.

CHAPTER SEVENTY-ONE

RISING MORE THAN A thousand feet, the canyon walls had closed to just thirty feet apart, separated only by the now placid river. Most of the year, the water stayed a sparkling blue or green, but during monsoon season, it turned brown as a result of the silt it carried away during flash floods.

As Nick entered the mouth of the Narrows, Stan's repeatedly tilting body came into focus upriver. He wasn't running or even walking; he was lurching through the water, stabbing at it with a large stick. The early morning water was flowing with a peaceful serenity, making it difficult to imagine the power it possessed when whipped up by the rains.

Progress through the knee-deep water was slow. Stan wasn't falling nearly as much as he had been the last time Nick had seen him. *Lucky bastard*, Nick thought, until he saw the bucket of sticks on the shore at the Gateway. Nick rushed onto the sandy bench, kicking up water and sand everywhere. No deliberations, he grabbed the first stick he could get his hands on and swiftly headed back into the Narrows.

The stick worked wonders for his balance and Nick progressed up the canyon. Every so often, there was a short sandy beach on either side of the river, which gave him the opportunity gain some ground. But the respites were short and there was no way to avoid the continuous hacking through the tributary. Besides, the more time he spent in the water, the better Nick was becoming at its navigation. And before long, Nick found himself in a groove, artfully poking the stick between the slippery rocks.

The chase continued through the meandering Narrows and, after nearly two miles, Nick was bushed. The exhaustion, physical and mental, was starting to overcome the force of his adrenaline, and he needed a break. Chasing Stan was becoming an endurance test, and while Stan was considerably older, he was also in better shape. Stan hadn't been battered and bound to a chair for the better part of a week.

Nick put his hands on both kneecaps and sucked in air. He felt like sitting but there was nowhere to do it. It was just Nick, the river, and the canyon walls.

And Stan.

Somewhere.

Nick took a few more steps, but his chest was heaving uncontrollably. He staggered over to the wall on his right, and fixed the stick up against it. Then he placed his arm along the wall and put his head down inside it, as if he were praying. Conflicting thoughts clouded his mind. His emotions refused to let him leave until Stan was laid to rest. His mind, however, wanted to turn around and go home. There wasn't a pride issue. Proclaiming victory wouldn't be a problem, having survived almost a week in the throes of death.

Nick stayed there for a few minutes until his heartbeat came down to a more acceptable rate. He grabbed his stick and sloshed through the water until he saw a stream emptying into the river from the right.

A side canyon.

There was probably a nice dry place in there for him to sit, but with Stan nowhere in sight, he had to carefully check it first. He propped his stick against the wall and clutched the gun in both hands, like a cop about to bust into a perp's apartment. Then he inched his way closer to the junction. Blood made a mad dash through his body, sweat fell from his face, and his knuckles turned white from clutching the gun. He continued awkwardly along the wall, removing his right hand from the gun every couple of steps to steady himself against the wall. Specks of red sand filled his hand, as he dragged it against the sandstone.

Nick stopped just before the entrance to the side canyon. He counted to three, jumped around the corner, and immediately felt the pain in his wrists. The gun fell into the shallow stream, as Stan pulled back to take another whack with his hiking stick. Nick was holding his right wrist when he saw the stick coming towards his head. He ducked, and stuck out his left arm to deflect the blow. As Nick pushed the stick aside, Stan came charging at him and tackled him into the pebble-filled stream. Pushing down on Nick's chest, Stan landed a right to Nick's already-bruised face. Then, using both hands, he pulled Nick up by the shirt and connected another punch. He was about to strike again when Nick landed a kick to his crotch. Stan screamed and fell back, into the water.

The stream wasn't deep and was only filled with sand and small pebbles, making it easy for Nick to locate the gun. He turned and stumbled as he lunged for it at the same time Stan did. Both hit the water just inches from the firearm, but Stan slammed his elbow into Nick's back, pounced on the gun, and in a single motion, stood and aimed it at his foe. Nick quickly put his hands up and crawled backward in defeat.

"What are you going to do now Stan? It's all over."

"It's not over until I kill you."

Nick slowly inched backwards. "Clay and Bennie are dead, and Ethan's joined them by now. That leaves you, and you're not going to make it out alive."

"Perhaps. But neither will you. And I really don't care anymore. My life was destroyed long ago and, once I get rid of you, I can float away in this lovely river without a care in the world."

"Don't do it, Stan. It's not worth it."

"Enough." Stan put his hand up. "You don't get it, do you? Back there, you were the big-shot Vice President. But not here, pal. Out here, I'm the CEO and I'm about to fire your ass."

"I'm sorry for what happened, but you know I had nothing to do with your termination."

"You had everything to do with it!" Veins popped from Stan's forehead. "Just because you weren't the one who actually fired me? That means nothing. All you executives are responsible. You disgust me, with your fancy cars and mansions, trophy wives and stock options. It's guys like me who do all the work. We're the cogs that make the machine go and we're nothing but replaceable to you. Because it's all about the bottom line. Not the company's, but your own. We do the work, while you corporate assholes keep shitting on us. I'm taking a stand, even if it means my life."

"You killed innocent people." Nick tried to keep his voice calm.

Stan fixed his finger on the trigger. "Hey, if you guys don't play by the rules, why should I? Wake up to the real world, Nick. It's dog eat dog. We're no different than animals, except *we* have the ability to adjust the food chain. Don't you think a gazelle would love to sneak up on a lion and rip its head off? Heck, there are probably millions of sea lions out there thinking: if only we could do something about those damn sharks. Same thing here. Guys like you are at the top of the chain making it clear that guys like me will always be bottom feeders. I've just taken it upon myself to adjust the laws of nature."

Stan moved closer and continued, "Besides, no one's innocent in this world."

"That's enough!" A voice from the entrance to the canyon. "Drop the gun!"

Stan whipped around, but didn't have time to readjust his aim.

"Drop it or you're dead."

Stan let the gun fall from his hands.

"Who are you?" Nick asked.

"Special Agent Nielsen, FBI."

Nick sighed in relief and let his hands fall. "Thank God. Do you have any idea what this guy has done? And he's got accomplices, I can identify them."

"That's enough, Mr. Perrone. I know all about it."

"How do you know my name?"

"Because I'm in charge of the investigation into your where-abouts."

Stan reached behind his back.

"Hands." Nielsen yelled, before Stan could reach the gun in the small of his back.

Stan threw his hands in the air, looked at Nick, and then back at Nielsen. Nielsen's gun was still aimed at Stan. "What are you doing Marco? Put the gun down." He pointed at Nick. "Shoot him and let's get out of here. We can still make a lot of money together."

Nick's eyes practically jumped out of their sockets. He went for the gun in the water.

"Don't!" Nielsen said, now aiming at Nick.

Nick stopped, almost losing his balance on the slick pebbles.

"You screwed up, Stan," Nielsen said. "I trusted you and you let me down."

"Not at all."

"Why was that detective poking around?"

"Oh, come on," Stan said. "I can't stop some dumbass from asking questions. You know that."

Nielsen waved the gun at Stan and took a step closer to him. "That day when I came across you guys burying your friend in the field? I should've arrested you right there."

"But you didn't." Stan felt the tide turning. "Because the money was too damn ..."

"Fuck the money!"

"That's not what you said back then. In fact, if I remember correctly, we offered to cut you in and you were a pretty easy sell. All you had to do was keep us in the loop if anyone ever got close."

"You're a pompous ass. That's why this whole thing failed."

"Nothing's failed. All we need to do is shoot him and every base has been covered."

"You assured me everything would be clean," Nielsen said.

"It was," Stan defended. "I mean, it is. It still is."

"Then why wasn't he dead a long time ago?"

"What difference does it make? OK, you're right. I should have killed him right away. But we can fix that problem now and continue on. Business as usual."

"I don't think so. Everyone else is dead. You'd have a lot of explaining to do."

Stan's face turned. "Ethan's dead?"

"Two bullets from the other detective." Nielsen shrugged at Nick. "His friend. I saw it as I was driving in."

"Ethan's dead." Stan said.

"It's over."

Nielsen pulled the trigger and Stan fell backward into the stream. Nick shuddered at the gunshot but relished the finality of justice. Nielsen placed his gun in his shoulder holster, while Nick found a large boulder several steps behind him, took a seat, and placed his face in his hands. The ordeal was finally over.

CHAPTER SEVENTY-TWO

NIELSEN KICKED HIS DEAD cohort onto his back and took the gun from inside Stan's waistband.

"Mr. Perrone."

Nick looked up at the agent, and found himself staring at the barrel of Stan's gun.

"Sorry, but I'm afraid you heard too much."

"I didn't hear anything," Nick said.

Nielsen smiled meekly. "I know you didn't. But I can't take the risk that you did."

Nick stood and beseeched Nielsen with his hands. "Please, I won't say a word. I'll just … I'll be thrilled to get out of here alive and go back to my family."

"I'm sorry, my friend, but I have to clean up the mess."

"You're not going to get away with this."

"I'm afraid I will. See, I got to the canyon just a little too late. Stan had already shot you with *his* gun," Nielsen turned the firearm on its side to show Nick. "And when he turned to shoot me, I beat him to it. That will explain why he's got my slug inside him, and you're going to have his inside you. I've got a handkerchief in my pocket to clean off my prints, and everyone else is dead. See how it all works out?"

Nielsen straightened the gun again and his brain sent the message to pull the trigger. There was a loud pop, but Nielsen was a split second late. He collapsed face-first into the water.

He never saw his killer.

CHAPTER SEVENTY-THREE

"BENNIE! I THOUGHT YOU were dead."

"No, but I'm hurt pretty bad," Bennie said, holding his left shoulder where he had taken Wyatt's shot. He made his way over to Nielsen's body and kicked the gun out his hands. "I hate that asshole."

"We've got to get you outta here."

Bennie grimaced as he touched the wound. He stepped out of the stream and onto a bed of gravel just above it where he found a rock to sit on. "I've got to admit, that shot felt good."

"You're losing blood. We have to get you to a hospital."

Bennie made a hissing sound as he tried to move his shoulder. "I'm not going anywhere."

"You have to. You won't make it if you stay here."

"I can't do it. I can't make it back out." He took a pain-filled breath. "It was hard enough just to get up off the ground, follow you guys here."

"I can't thank you enough, you saved my life. Now let me help *you*."

Bennie started crying. "Honestly, I never wanted to kill anyone."

"I know," Nick said.

"I'm sorry, brother. I should have helped you when it was a whole lot easier. It's my fault. I shouldn't have let it come to this."

"Forget it now, it doesn't matter."

"I was just really scared of them, you know?" His voice choked. Tears flew. "I wasn't ready."

"You got a phone?" Nick asked. "We need to call for help. You're bleeding badly."

"You won't get a signal back here."

"Then come on, I'll carry you out. We'll go slow."

Bennie put his head in his hands. "How did my life come to this? When I was eleven, I stole some things from a convenience store in my neighborhood: a candy bar, a can of pop. And I got caught. My mom took it OK, but my dad? He thought getting caught wasn't enough. He wanted to teach me a lesson, so you know what he did?"

Bennie looked at Nick, who didn't say anything.

"He beat me to a pulp. I looked like you for a few days, maybe not as bad. But that day I swore I'd never forget what my mom told me after the cops dropped me off at the house. She said there's nothing so valuable, there's nothing that a person absolutely must have in this life that he has to steal it from someone else."

"She's wise," Nick said.

"She was," Bennie corrected him.

Bennie scraped the gun in the gravel and then met Nick's eyes. "I broke my promise," he said softly as he lifted the gun.

"It's over, Bennie." Nick took a step closer. "Now you get a fresh start."

"Yeah, in prison."

"You're not going to prison, OK? Why don't you give me the gun and let's get you some help."

Bennie shifted his body and grimaced as he brought the gun to his head. Then he stopped momentarily, and ran the back of his hand—with the gun—under his nose to wipe it. Tears rained down his face.

Nick moved closer. "Don't do this. Don't let them beat you."

"Back off!" Bennie snapped, and waved the gun wildly at Nick.

Nick put his hands up and stepped back, as Bennie replaced the gun to the side of his head. Nick saw the same resolve Bennie had shown earlier at the house, the one Nick couldn't seem to crack.

"You don't have to do this," Nick implored. "You've got your whole life ahead of you. You've got proof, remember?"

"Come on, man? Look at the big picture now. I'm the only one that survived this mess, and you know they're going to want a fall guy. They're going to stick it to someone, even if it isn't one of the main players. I could get the chair for what we've done."

"You won't get the chair. You told me yourself, you didn't kill anyone and you can prove it. *We* can prove it."

"That was just wishful thinking. There's no way anyone will buy it."

"But you have to try. You have to fight for your freedom. Look at me. I never gave up." Nick paused, and then lowered his voice. "I learned that lesson the hard way."

"It's too late."

Bennie pulled the trigger.

Nick winced and fisted his hands, watching the bullet pass through Bennie's head. In just a few minutes, the canyon had been transformed from magical and serene to a chaotic landscape of death. Three bodies littered the gorge and, as Nick turned to the entrance, he saw a fourth lying in the water.

"Wyatt!"

Nick ran to the canyon's entrance where Wyatt was lying in the shallow stream. His eyes were closed, he wasn't moving, and the water around him was red.

Nick knelt and grabbed Wyatt's wrist, searching desperately for a pulse. "Come on Wyatt." Nick clasped his wrist and after a few seconds, lightly smacked Wyatt's cheeks.

Nothing

"Damn it, Wyatt! Not you too." He tapped Wyatt's face. "Please."

And that's when the smile materialized.

Nick dropped his wrist in the water with a wide grin. "You asshole! Now's not the time for this."

Nick was about to shove him when Wyatt lifted his arms and said, "Easy man, I'm hit."

"Serious?"

Wyatt shook his head in the light stream and some dirt from under the gravel mixed in with the water. "The bullet went through his head and hit me, just as I turned the corner."

"Where did it hit you?"

"Smack in the chest."

"I don't see where." Nick was in a near panic.

Wyatt sat up and chuckled. "It's a good thing these vests really work." He looked around the canyon. "Did we get them all?"

"I think so," Nick said, as he put his arm around his best friend.

"Good. Now I can rest."

And Wyatt fell back into the water, pulling Nick with him.

CHAPTER SEVENTY-FOUR

"IT WAS THE CHIPMUNK."

Wyatt and Nick were driving the rental through the Nevada desert, and Nick was asking how Wyatt had solved the puzzle. There was a loud rattle from somewhere on the car's underside, but after an hour or two, they had gotten used to it.

Nick laughed. "I've gotta hear this."

"When you didn't answer her calls, Ina came to see me and let's just say gave me a little guilt. But she was right; I knew I had to come find you. So I did. During the investigation, I spoke with Stan and he gave me a box with your camping gear. It didn't hit me until later, but when I realized that everything was packed neatly in bags and stuff sacks, I knew something was wrong. Because ever since the chipmunk incident, my neurotic little buddy never left all the bags and stuff sacks in his tent. I realized that Stan must've had access to your car and *all* your belongings in order to have packed them that way."

Nick thought about telling Wyatt that this time, he *had* left everything in his tent. He decided not to. "The chipmunk, huh? My neuroses finally paid off."

"That was the first clue," Wyatt said. "And after that, I broke into Stan's trailer and found his termination letter. When I saw your name on the letterhead, I knew you were in deep shit."

"I'm glad you didn't give up."

"I couldn't. But honestly? Everyone thought you had staged your own disappearance, and there were times when I was starting to believe it. I kept replaying what you had said about your marriage when we were in your driveway last week."

"I should've kept my mouth shut."

"And then I heard that you hooked up with another camper."

"Not one of my finer moments."

"What the hell were you doing?"

Nick put up his hand. "I didn't sleep with her, OK?"

"From what I heard, you should've."

"The adolescent alcoholics across the way?" Their eyes met and they smiled. "Those kids wouldn't stop looking over and giggling. Yeah, she was hot and we fooled around, but when she wanted to go all the way, I couldn't do it. I couldn't stop thinking of Ina. Anyway, she left the next day, embarrassed, and I spent the rest of the week feeling bad for what little I'd actually done with her."

"That little nugget didn't help. And then we learned that you had taken out an insurance policy before you left."

"Ina's pregnant and I wanted to make sure that if anything happened to me, she and the baby would be taken care."

"Perfectly legitimate. But given everything else, the timing was suspicious."

Tumbleweed danced across the highway and Nick took a deep breath, enjoying the multi-colored landscape that, like an ocean, seemed endless. A quiet minute passed and Nick winced in pain when he tried to scratch one of the bruises on his face.

"I'm really sorry," Nick said.

"You? I'm the one that should apologize."

"No you're not. I never should have said what I did about the whole thing with your father. It's not my business."

"No, no, you were right. I need to move on. I guess I just wasn't ready to hear it. I feel terrible that I bailed on you. I'm such a shitty friend."

"Let's call it even, buddy," Nick said. "Besides, everything worked out in the end."

Wyatt gave Nick a questioning glance. "It did?"

"Absolutely. I learned a lot about myself. I'd been so caught up in success and my career that I took everything else in my life for granted. I never wanted a baby because I always thought it would be a huge inconvenience and interfere with my work. But sitting there? All I could think of was that, if they were going to kill me, at least Ina would have the baby she always wanted and you know what? It meant the world to me."

"She really cares for you, man."

"I lost my perspective. Everyone should spend a few days tied to a chair so they can realize and reassess what's really meaningful in their lives."

"Sounds like a new business idea," Wyatt joked.

"I lost focus on what really matters. I won't let that happen again. Not with Ina, not with the baby ..." Nick turned to Wyatt. "And not with you."

"Of course, buddy. I'm just glad we got you back alive."

"Enough about me. What about you? I feel terrible that you lost your job on my account. What are you gonna do now?"

They passed a sign announcing entry into the Las Vegas city limits.

"The job's not your fault. I screwed that up a long time ago. Wasn't a good fit."

"You know you're a great detective, right?"

"I think the break will be good for me. Besides, after I drop you off, I'm going back to Utah to help them sort everything out. They're going to re-open every missing persons case that was reported in the area since Stan moved out there."

"It's scary what those guys were able to accomplish."

"And we're just scratching the surface. They found the ID cards you described, but the rest of the house didn't land many clues. Amado told me this morning that they've been searching every dirt road for the field you described. The problem is that there's so many of them they haven't been able to find it."

"I don't remember where it was."

"They'll find it, eventually. Amado said they were bringing in bloodhounds from Salt Lake."

"I don't want to be there when they start digging."

"They've got their work cut out. That guy, Bennie, owned a chop shop and the sheriff told me they started going through his records and found what he was doing. They found an invoice for a Durango matching yours, and for a vehicle matching the one some guy named Henderson Taylor owned. He was killed a few weeks ago. They originally thought he fell off one of the rims, but now they're re-opening the case. And there's talk of overturning a jury verdict convicting a guy of pushing his wife off the canyon. It's crazy."

Replicas of some of the world's most famous monuments emanated from the strip, which appeared on their left. An endless sea of billboards advertised the appearances of washed-up entertainers, and, every half-mile or so, pictures of half naked ladies beckoned the weak to visit their houses of phony temptation. They exited the freeway.

"You need a pit stop?" Nick asked.

Wyatt shook his head.

"Are we low on gas?"

"Nope, we're good."

"Then why are we getting off here?" Nick paused a moment. "Are we exchanging the car for one without bullet holes?"

They passed a sign for the airport. "You've got a flight to catch, buddy."

"We're not driving back together?"

"You have to get back to comfort your wife ... and meet your new daughter."

The hair on Nick's arms and legs rose like the crowd at the end of a sold-out concert. His eyes welled, and he felt a warmth in his heart like nothing he'd felt before.

"Ina had the baby?"

Wyatt pulled out two large cigars, swiped one under his nose for effect, and handed the other to Nick.

"The stress of your disappearance was too much and she went into labor last night. Your daughter was born this morning." Wyatt tossed him a book of matches. "I'm told that mom and baby are doing fine, although I'm not so sure about the dad."

"The dad's never been better." Nick placed the cigar in his mouth and lit up.

They entered the airport and followed the signs to departures. Wyatt pulled to the curb, parked the car, popped the trunk, and they both stepped out.

"You're really not coming back with me?"

"After I drop you here, I'm gonna exchange the car."

"I'd love to see the look on their faces at the rental company."

"Can you imagine what the sign out sheet will look like for the next guy who rents this thing?" Wyatt said.

Nick laughed. "What are you gonna do after that?"

"Back to the park."

"Velvet?" Nick asked, as Wyatt lit his cigar off Nick's. "You don't think she was involved, do you?"

"*I* don't, but they sure are interrogating her pretty good. She doesn't need me, she needs a lawyer. A couple of days ago, she told me she had just broken up with someone, but I never imagined it would be Ethan. She was sleeping with both sides of the law at the same time."

"You gotta admit that's pretty freaky."

"I know," Wyatt said. "But these guys tried to kill me, more than once. And I keep thinking that if she was really involved, they would've been successful."

An airport security guard headed their way.

"Are you sure you won't come back with me? I'd love for you to be there when I meet my daughter. And I want her to meet her Godfather."

Wyatt took a long puff and then embraced his best friend. It was an extended man-hug, as they clapped each other's backs repeatedly. Then they separated.

"Thanks," Wyatt said. "That means a lot. But you and Ina need time alone right now. Besides, someone's got to drive your car back once the sheriff releases it. You *do* want it back, don't you?"

Nick slung a bag on his back, caught Wyatt's gaze and said, "No, I don't think so. It's got a scratch."

ACKNOWLEDGMENTS

THERE ARE A LOT of people who made this book possible and I will endeavor to name as many as I can. But, listed here or not, I hope they all know how much their contributions mean to me. To begin with, this book would not have been possible without the support, patience, and understanding of Naomi, Josh, Avi, and Joseph. They are the best! Thank you.

This book is a complete work of fiction and entirely the fruits of my wild imagination. To make it work, I had to "alter" some realities, one of which is the competence, dedication, and motivation of the National Park Service and Zion's rangers. I don't want anyone to get the wrong idea. Zion's rangers and employees are nothing but top notch. They epitomize professionalism, and make the park and the safety of its visitors their top priority. I've visited many national parks and one reason why Zion is my favorite is because of the way they run it. Many rangers and employees provided input for this book, and I appreciate each and every one of them.

I'd also like to thank Washington County Sheriff Deputy, Jake Adams, for taking the time to sit with me and explain how things work in Washington County. Richard Marshall shared with me his experience as the Watchman Campground Host. Jim Fitzsimmons and Joe Collier provided input on police procedure and shooting firearms. Lisa Strobel shared the ins and outs of an event planner. Jim Koch, of Little Dealer Little Prices, an RV dealership in Phoenix, allowed me to spend almost two hours in a fifth wheel trailer on their lot. It was there that I wrote the scenes that take place in Stan's trailer.

I also want to thank those individuals who took the time out of their busy schedules to review my work at its early stages and provide their input: Linda Mann, Michael Mann, Deborah Mann, Rachel Sassoon, and Jesse Fischbein. I'd also like to express gratitude to my editor, Carol Test. Carol persevered over several drafts of this book. She didn't just locate my errors, she helped tighten the story with her wonderful insight. Above all, though, I'm most appreciative of her continued encouragement and dedication to this project. Without it, who knows how this book would've come out! I also want to thank Joy Acree for her efforts and assistance in getting the manuscript ready for publication.

A special thank you goes to Marshall Gisser and New York Design Studio for designing an amazing jacket for the book. As always, his graphics and design work was superior.

The Shack, as described in this book, was a real bar that, as of my most recent trip to the park, appears to have closed down. While I gave it my own name, it was a real place and not the most comfortable to visit. I want to thank my close friend, Andy Chen, who accompanied me on my second visit to the bar when I wanted to get more details to include in the book. I don't know that I would've had the courage to return to that place alone, especially after I'd already conceived of this story!

If I missed anyone, I am truly sorry. Please know that I fully appreciate each and every contribution to this book. Any errors made therein are solely my own.

The maps at the beginning of this book are the property of "©OpenStreetMap contributors," and are available under the Open Database License as set forth in Openstreetmap.org.

Finally, I want to thank you the reader for taking the time to read this book. I hope I didn't disappoint you.

Made in the USA
San Bernardino, CA
21 September 2013